PRAISE FOR OLY

"Take a playboy Zeus with issues; a New-Age Hera; an idiot boy; another
who's half-bug, half-bat; an artist who walks backwards; and a woman who
lived inside a door for 2000 years… You'd think, with this melange,
no one but Eudora Welty could have made a moving and magical novel.
You'd be wrong. Leslie What has."
— HOWARD WALDROP

"If anybody can write about gods and goddesses, it's Leslie What. She's
had more close encounters with them than anybody else I know. In fact, I
suspect she's actually a goddess-in-hiding. Read on for a tantalizing and
tasty serving of divine madness."
— NINA KIRIKI HOFFMAN

"The Queen of Gonzo."
— GARDNER DOZOIS

"This novel is so much fun. From the woman in the door to bug bangs
(not the haircut) and beyond, the story is deeply imagined and wonderfully
realized. Yes, the book is a romp with the gods being the gods, but it is also
full of people you will come to care about like Penelope, and Possum who
is used to moody women, and Eddie who is destined for bigger things —
people who will linger in your mind long after you've turned the last page."
— RAY VUKCEVICH

WITHDRAWN
DODGEVILLE, WI 53533

OLYMPIC GAMES

BY

LESLIE WHAT

OLYMPIC GAMES

BY

LESLIE WHAT

TACHYON PUBLICATIONS
SAN FRANCISCO, CALIFORNIA

This is a work of fiction. All events portrayed in this book are fictitious, and any resemblance to real people or events is purely coincidental.

OLYMPIC GAMES

COPYRIGHT © 2004 BY LESLIE WHAT

COVER ILLUSTRATION BY MICHAEL DASHOW

TYPOGRAPHY DESIGN BY ANN MONN

All rights reserved, including the right to reproduce this book, or portions thereof, in any form.

TACHYON PUBLICATIONS
1459 18TH STREET
SAN FRANCISCO, CALIFORNIA 94107
(415) 285-5615

SERIES EDITOR: JACOB WEISMAN

ISBN: 1-892391-10-4

FIRST EDITION: AUGUST 2004

PRINTED IN THE UNITED STATES OF AMERICA
BY PHOENIX COLOR CORPORATION

0   9   8   7   6   5   4   3   2   1

DEDICATION

For my sisters,
Carolyn Du Clos and Stephanie Juarez,
goddesses both.

ACKNOWLEDGMENTS

I am forever grateful to my mentor Damon Knight, who suggested that I continue in the tradition of Thorne Smith and turn a short story into a novel. Thanks to Gardner Dozois for publishing "The Goddess is Alive and, Well, Living in New York City" in Asimov's. *Thanks and IOUs to Kate Wilhelm, James Patrick Kelly, Jacob Weisman, Teresa Nielsen Hayden, Linn Prentis, Jill Roberts, and Marty Halpern. Your insights helped me craft a better book. Thanks to Mitch Temple for help with menu planning and to Hank Dutchover for physical therapy.*

PROLOGUE

"We may gain strength from the mysteries of meditation. We may find joy from the Muses' song. We may be studied in the logic of man. Yet fate is stronger than them all and nothing can subdue her."
— EURIPIDES, 483 B.C.

The old man lived humbly in a land of excess, but this had not always been his way. When younger, he had fought in wars, gone through medical school, owned a house upstate (financed through the GI Bill). The old man had once been head of a family, managed a thriving medical practice, and was well respected by the greater community.

Now he slept in stairwells, beneath trees, or on subway benches. He spent his days cross-legged on the sidewalk with his back against a brick wall, begging for money and scraps of food. He washed in public restrooms, did his laundry twice a month. He cushioned his shoes with crushed flower petals to disguise the odors of the street and to continuously remind himself of the world's beauty.

His skin was dark as evening's shadow, his clothing ragged and dirty. He wore a wool plaid jacket gleaned from a garbage can, pockets bulging with smooth stones and paperback novels missing their covers. Few recognized him for what he was.

The old man was known as the Oracle, for he possessed the magic to see into the future. The power of this magic had nearly driven him mad and he was anxious to retire from the business. It had grown increasingly difficult for him to fade into the background, to act as an observer of life, rather than to be a full participant. The stress was getting to him. He had broken down recently and had been incarcerated after spray painting on a subway wall, "PROPHECY IS NOT FOR THE WEAK OF WILL!" To keep out of trouble, the Oracle was watching his step, in addition to everyone else's.

Being an oracle was no easy task, one reason why so few existed. Not many were up to the job and there were no training schools, no certification, no process for applying for work. An oracle was chosen by the Fates, who had always marched to a syncopated beat that was sometimes difficult to comprehend.

Little magic remained in the world these days, and but a few gods walked among mortals; the Oracle had seen only two since moving to the city. He speculated that the other gods had grown bored with immortality, perhaps found some way around it. He could sympathize with anyone looking to make a career change. A long life could indeed be tedious. The old man had wanted to retire since turning ninety, but he had only just learned of the whereabouts of his future replacement. The Oracle had known for some time that one called Eddie would take his place. Soon, he would journey to meet the young fellow who lived in the Catskills. Just in time, he thought with a yawn.

A schoolgirl hurried by and the Oracle shouted after her, "Watch out for that pile of ... " but it was too late. Not that the youngster would have listened. Most seekers only wanted to know their good fortune. Funny that the bad fortune had always been easier for him to predict. Ahh well. Perhaps it was better for man to tread in darkness. Better not to foresee a future if one could not change it.

Because he had lived on these streets for several years he recognized many passersby, yet only a handful ever glanced downward or took the time to notice or remember his face. He counted these few folks among his closest friends.

His dear friend, Alexander, the cook at the Parthenon Diner, was already on his break and pacing around the block as he did every morning.

"Hello there," said the Oracle. Though Alexander was a big man, he was not big enough to shoulder all his burdens.

Alexander smiled with only his lips, keeping the sad expression in his eyes that made him look older than thirty. One did not need the powers of an oracle to see this man's trouble.

"Will I see you at lunch?" Alexander asked, and the Oracle said, "No doubt."

Alexander nodded and continued on.

The Oracle foresaw a time of happiness in his friend's future. He allowed himself a slight smile. If only it were possible for every man to know only good fortune. But that was not the way of the world.

The handsome god, Zeus, who liked to disguise himself as a construction worker, came up from the subway staircase. Spotting the Oracle, he walked close. He was a vain god and it showed. He looked great for his age, amazing really, bronzed and fit as a chiseled sculpture. The god handed the Oracle a blue and white paper cup filled with sweetened coffee-flavored milk.

The Oracle remained cautiously respectful of the gods. One

need only look to their arrogance, their petty jealousies, and their foolishness, to wish they had seen fit to set a better example for man. Pity, for man surely could have used the help.

"Morning," said the Oracle.

"Morning," said the god.

Zeus was exuding magical charm; the Oracle could feel it from the way the spell made his skin prickle. Most people couldn't tell what hit them when the gods did their magic; not so the Oracle. Part of what made him an oracle was his ability to differentiate between the remarkable and the ordinary.

"Don't waste your spells on me," the Oracle said. He laughed. "I like everybody. You might as well save your power for someone more discerning."

The god tensed his brow. "What do you have for me today?" he asked. "Tell me something I don't know."

The Oracle closed his eyes and watched a daydream unfold—a young woman's tears; a sick child; a mountain top; the big Greek in desperate need of redemption; a goddess filled with rage; revenge; ominous clouds; the innocent known as Eddie—the images dissolved like grains of sugar stirred in hot coffee. He saw the handsome god clutching his chest, and sensed enough free-floating regret to fill Yankee Stadium. It all had something to do with a young woman. "Everything is about to happen," he said. "I'll tell you this: beware of scorned women."

"I've nothing to fear from women," said the god with a grin. "It's them that should beware of me." He snapped his fingers, as if to hurry time through his grasp, then tucked a hundred-dollar bill into the Oracle's front pocket and wished him a good day.

CHAPTER ONE

Long Ago, Far Away

Hera could practically smell the seduction on his breath; the way Zeus offered her a goblet of sweetened wine, how he plumped the feather pillows and tenderly slid them beneath her back. He rubbed her feet with clove-scented oil, then performed her favorite little trick: lighting the clouds on fire to leave warm, moist trails of smoke. Delightful. Oh, her husband was an expert at seduction when he wanted to be.

There was only one problem and it was a big one.

Zeus was not seducing her.

He strapped on his sandals and her suspicions increased. "Going somewhere?" she asked.

Zeus said, "Rest," his voice hypnotic and breathy.

Hera struggled to keep her eyes open as she gazed at the heavens. She stifled a yawn. "I'm not tired," she said.

Zeus brought the goblet to her lips. "Drink," he said.

The flavor of ripe cherries lingered on her tongue.

Her godly husband was up to no good, but there didn't seem to be a thing she could do about it.

"Rest," Zeus said again, and blew a breath warm as a blanket across her legs.

A sense of weariness beset her, and sipping wine only made things worse. She yawned. Her body grew numb from the lips down. She attempted to move her legs, but the effort proved too great. Come to think of it, she was feeling a bit sleepy.

"Rest," Zeus said. His voice seemed very far away.

Her lids grew heavy, her cheeks warm. "Perhaps, just for a moment," she said, closing her eyes.

When she awakened, some time later, Zeus was gone.

Typical.

Furious, she plucked a hawk from the air and sent it to the earth to spy on him. It soon returned to Olympus, with plenty of gossip about his whereabouts and actions.

Hera's fury raged. The clouds melted around her; in the distance, Vesuvius rumbled. How Zeus loved making her jealous. "What is this obsession with virgins?" she cried, setting out after him.

🐦

Penelope tried to calm her trembling hands to keep the other naiads from noticing her nervousness. She laced her fingers together, squeezing so tightly her hands stung and turned a fiery red. Her stomach ached, as if she had swallowed a lump of fool's gold for breakfast. All around her, naiads gossiped and laughed. They were sitting on the heavy tapestry covering the meadow floor. Penelope forced herself to smile because to do otherwise might arouse suspicion.

All ten sisters were there, along with four other families belonging to her clan. They formed a circle around festive silver platters, urns of flowers, and dishes filled with scented oils. Penelope sat between two other young naiads close to her age. She fumed at her queen for ordering her, on this eve of her fourteenth season, to sit with children. Had no one else noticed that she had become a young woman?

Every naiad there was clothed in finery: tunics trimmed with lace and gold thread, hair delicately oiled and tied with painted ribbons, sandals decorated with gemstones. So much beauty wasted on women forced to sit with women. Penelope had pulled her long hair up, off her back, and into the elegant knot favored by her mother. She was wearing a copper bracelet the color of her hair, matching ear cuffs, and a fine chain anklet crafted from water-soft links.

They ate their midday meal of chewy flat bread, chunks of fresh sheep's cheese, and soft green grapes with tart skins, all washed down with amber wine as thick as syrup. Penelope ate, despite not being the least bit hungry.

"Lovely feast!" a young one murmured.

Penelope smiled in agreement. She took a bite of bread, while chewing on her imagination. Any moment now, she would sneak away to rendezvous with the young man she had met at market.

The instant her mother pushed away her plate and yawned, Penelope ran from her place to stand beside her eldest sister, Helen.

At first Helen ignored her. Penelope knew that caution would work better than anguish, but sighed loudly in protest. She fiddled with hair that had uncurled from her knot and twisted the strand around her fingers, waiting for Helen to speak. Finally, she cleared her throat.

Helen flashed a sly look, but continued to pluck slowly at her grapes.

Unable to restrain herself any longer, Penelope placed her hand on Helen's shoulder and gave her a slight nudge. She cleared her throat again.

"I shall not be hurried," Helen said.

Penelope blushed, ashamed by her eagerness to begin her planned deception. "Sister," she begged in a whisper. "Do not fail me."

"When the time arrives I shall assist you in your plan," Helen said, quite firmly. She poured herself another goblet of wine. When she had finished drinking, Helen nodded that she was ready. "All right, Sister," she said. "Let us begin."

Penelope fought herself to keep from shouting for joy. Instead she pressed her bracelet and ear clips into Helen's greedy palm. The jewelry had been a gift from their father, Poseidon, and Helen had coveted the pieces for many years. Penelope had only seen their father once, so giving away his gift tugged at her heart. The copper sparkled with fire. It was beautiful, if not precious. Surely, Poseidon had expected its sheen would blind her to the fact that he was absent from her life.

Helen fastened the clips on her ears.

"They look lovely on you," Penelope told her sister. This was true.

Helen smiled. She was vain, though no more so than any of them. She stood and called upon the naiads to gather into a large circle. "A game!" she cried. "It is time to play a game."

Her mother eyed them both with suspicion.

Just in time, another of Penelope's sisters shouted, "Oh, yes! A game! A game!"

Two naiads from another clan began to twirl and laugh, their lightweight tunics shimmering in the sunlight.

"Penelope shall pick the game," said Helen. "Now, please, choose a favorite."

Penelope pretended to consider the choices. "I know! We shall hide," she said, "and let our sisters seek us out. One by one!"

"Yes!" shouted one of her sisters.

Helen lifted her hands toward Olympus, and pleaded with their river to sing for their amusement. The river obliged with a delicate melody, a trickling of waters the sound of a hundred harps.

"A water song. My gift to all the children!" cried Helen.

Penelope felt ashamed. She, along with the other young ones present, could not yet boast of magic. How her sister took joy in pointing out her deficit.

But that would change, she thought, and much sooner than

anyone could guess. Penelope pulled Helen into the center of the circle, tied a wool wrap around her eyes.

"Give us plenty of time," Penelope whispered, "before beginning your search. Otherwise, you will find me too quickly and ruin the fun."

"When you kiss him," Helen whispered, "you must make sure not to smudge the color on your lips, or Mother will suspect all when she sees you. I envy you just a little," she said. "That the first kiss shall ever remain the finest."

Penelope felt her cheeks grow warm, wondering how a kiss might taste. She spun Helen in circles, until a giggling Helen begged her to stop. Penelope smiled and turned to the others. "Go!" she said. "Scatter." When every sprite except her sister had disappeared in the woods, Penelope slipped away.

The moisture that had licked the meadow grass at dawn had baked in the sun and now turned to steam. A delicate wisp rose from the ground and tickled her ankles. The wind carried whisperings of her sisters' laughter and their squeals of disappointment. Penelope heard Helen shout as she found the spot where their mother had been hiding. She pictured her mother, head tipped back to laugh, round stomach filled with sweet wine and the first fruits from the harvest. A wave of guilt washed through her. She pushed away the feeling by conjuring up the image of the young man. Hiking up her skirts, Penelope tiptoed through the grass toward her river.

She stopped to rest by the gnarled trunk of a cherry tree. The rough bark had peeled away in uneven strips; their edges caught the skirts of her tunic as if trying to keep Penelope in one place. She heard the thin fabric tear. Her new linen tunic, already torn, though it was barely the first day of spring. Without magic she would be forced to use a needle and thread to mend the rip, no better than a mortal maid.

She cursed her queen—the giver of magic—under her breath. You cannot control me, she thought. I shall have magic when I want, not when you deign to bestow it. She reached up to pluck a cherry from a low branch and brought the ripe fruit to her mouth. The flesh was soft, so purple with juice that a drop leaked out, but stayed poised near the stem. She dipped a finger into the nectar and colored her cheeks and lips, added a slight blush to the rise of her bosom. The sweet scent warmed against her as the fragrance spread like temptation across her skin.

Beyond this meadow of knee-high grass their river drummed its water forward, beating steadily against the rocks in its path. Their wonderful river. She loved it so. It cleansed her, sheltered her, provided her with fish to eat and sweet water to drink. The young man had whispered in her ear, asking—no, begging—Penelope to meet him by her river. He had promised to help her find her magic.

She walked on. At midday, the air felt warm, thick and heavy with the dew rising into the sky. The wine and morning dances had made her head spin. Her stomach tightened, the same kind of hurt that came from eating too many cherries, yet she had eaten only the one that she had used on her lips. Then a ruffling noise from behind startled her; she turned to see if anyone had followed.

The bright sun stung her eyes. She watched as a shadow darkened the ground before her and grew larger. A white and gray mottled nighthawk was flying directly toward her. Its talons curved down, ready to strike. It opened its mouth and shrieked a high-pitched wail; Penelope dropped to her knees. The dark shape passed, but seeing a nighthawk during daylight was an omen of bad tidings.

Trembling, she sat up. She had stained her skirts green and brown, enough to deserve a thrashing. "May the gods show mercy," she said, wondering if she should return to her family before she stained her virtue as well.

Then she heard the strum of a lyre and a voice hollow as an echo. "My one, my only. When I open my eyes, they are blinded but to you."

He had written her a ballad. How wonderfully romantic. She rose to her feet and slowly pushed her way forward through the reeds to find him.

Her admirer sat facing her on a flat basalt rock at the water's edge. She ran to him, and the thrumming of the river current disappeared beneath the timbre of his voice. The world changed from a great expanse to a small shelter when she sat beside him. Warmth from the stone spread like a blush throughout her thighs and up into her belly. His voice was melodic as his lyre; his skin golden and smooth; his curls, soft and silky.

She was smitten. Perhaps he had enchanted her. If so, she did not care. Penelope sensed that the young man was a god. He would tell her his name when the time was right, when she would confide hers as well.

He stopped plucking the lyre strings and held the cherry wood body of his instrument close to his cheek. He caressed the neck and with his eyes closed, whispered to the wood, just loud enough for her to hear, "My new maiden awaits."

When he smiled Penelope felt her body grow weak.

He set the instrument on the grass beside his feet and snapped his fingers several times in succession. "Come closer," he said to her, "and whisper your name into my ear." He waved his hand in a graceful arc and she felt herself drawn into his embrace.

She saw no harm in telling him.

He fed her poppy seeds dipped in honey. "Penelope," he said, "you are mine."

"What about my magic?" she asked, gazing up into his eyes. "Show me how to find it!"

He glanced nervously toward the water. His chest heaved as he lifted her hand to his lips and kissed it softly, then turned her palm upward to lick her fingertips. "How sweet and dark you taste," he said, "of cherries and spring nights. Surely you are already one possessed of magic."

Penelope pitched against him. He caught her shoulders and held her tenderly in his arms to kiss her cheek, his lips moist, his breath hot. She let her hands rise to take hold of his arms and then dared to lower them until they reached beneath his shoulders to encircle his back.

The feeling in her heart was certainly a magical one, and Penelope was not surprised when, a moment later, the two began to rise from the ground in flight. They flew above the clouds until they came to a laurel leaf nest large enough to hold them. The bed was fragrant, with a moist woody scent. Penelope cried out from joy, feeling giddy as a drunkard.

He pressed his lips against hers and she opened her mouth to receive his tongue.

She could never trust the naiads again. Their warnings about men were wrong, so very wrong. Her mother had said that love was fleeting, but she had been lying, of this Penelope was certain. Love was eternal, powerful, solid as the earth. She whispered her love into his ear, unsure if he could hear her through his torrid breathing.

"I will love you always," she vowed. "You and only you."

"Me and only me," he answered. "I believe you, Penelope. I believe you will indeed love only me."

Naiads were so sickeningly sweet that sometimes Hera wanted to wring their necks and see if they bled honey. That would serve them right, the little twits. She was tramping through the meadow, disguised as a shepherdess out on a walk, when she came upon the tangle of water nymphs.

An adorable little thing no bigger than a toadstool grabbed Hera's hand and tried to get her to join in some stupid dance. Of course, the girl did not recognize her. Despite the fact that Hera's face was plastered onto every urn this side of Thebes, children never recognized her.

There wasn't time, or Hera would have asked the child some trivial question meant to test her loyalty. She loved to trick her subjects, catch them unprepared. Whenever they failed to please her, she was forced to teach them a lesson. Revenge wasn't the best thing about being queen of the gods, just one of the perks.

Zeus was nowhere to be seen; she doubted he was far away. The naiads were too tempting, and Zeus had never believed in resisting temptation. It wasn't one of the tenets of his religion.

"Penelope," someone shouted, sounding alarmed.

"Have you seen her?" another asked.

"Where has that girl gone to?" said a woman, obviously the mother.

Hera smiled. Penelope, she thought. The name had a nice ring to it. So that's who Zeus was after.

※

Zeus brought Penelope back to the warm grass, where he fed her ripe cherries, one at a time until she protested that she would burst. He held her in his arms and tenderly kissed the crown of her head. He fastened a silky golden chain with a teardrop charm around her neck. "I fashioned this," he said. "I think it perfect for you. Wear this ever after so I shall find you whenever I wish."

It was beautiful. Much finer than the trinket Poseidon had given her. She touched the teardrop and felt devoted to her lover. She loved her river, but not with the strength she felt for this young man. There were many kinds of love. She thanked the gods for allowing her to experience them all during her short life. "I adore you," she confessed. To her shame, he said nothing in return. Suddenly, she was afraid to inquire about his feelings toward her. In her mind she heard her mother's warnings.

But when he kissed her again her worries melted away.

At dusk the crickets began singing; Penelope heard the laughter of her friends trail away as they returned to the water for the night. She lay in the crook of his shoulder and felt more happiness than she had ever known was possible. In a few minutes she heard her mother calling her again, sounding frantic. Penelope bolted upright.

He tickled the underside of her chin, then ran his finger in a circle round her neck. "Where can I keep you, my pretty love?" he asked, "so that I may find you when I have time for you again?"

The question puzzled her. "Let me stay with you," she said, "for I can no longer go back to my home."

He smiled and shook his head. "I am sorry," he said, "but that is not to be." He snapped his fingers several times in a row. "It is better, my friend, that I find you."

She blinked to keep herself from crying. "Why do you say this?" she asked. "Swear you are my one and only true love."

"Surely," he said. "One and only." He hushed her with the touch of his finger to her lips when suddenly, a woman's voice screamed, "Zeus! Is that you, you rotting goat scrotum?"

His eyes glazed; sweat poured from his brow. He snapped his fingers together and trembled slightly as he kissed Penelope, then blew his sweet breath across her face.

Zeus. The one whom she and every other maiden had been warned to keep away from. She sighed, pushing her bosom forward, aching to press herself once more against him. No matter. They were all wrong; she loved him still as he loved her. She rubbed against him.

"Not now, but I'll be back," he said, "after I convince Hera that I've plucked no flower from the forest." With that, he stood her up and held her shoulders tight.

She closed her eyes and leaned forward to meet his kiss.

"Good-bye, my love," Zeus said.

Her eyelids stayed closed as if pressed down with a heavy weight. Her arms fell to her side, numb. She lost the urge to breathe and felt her toes rooting through the soft ground until they anchored her body to the spot. Her limbs grew thick and long.

She tried to speak, tried to call out to her river to save her, but had lost the skill needed to connect her thoughts to her mouth. Startled, Penelope noticed other things had changed as well. When she thought of herself, she could no longer remember what she looked like. Memory darkened, as if caught in the shadow of dusk.

Her body no longer existed. She remembered little of her sisters or mother. What they looked like, how they moved, even the sound of their voices. She could no longer picture the human form. Her soul felt hard and dense. The sounds of her river faded into the wind's sleepy breath. Soon it seemed that even her river had abandoned her.

She was alone. Her will sank slowly into the ground; her limbs thinned and sprouted branches; her toes dug roots deep into the dank earth.

He had changed her into a tree.

The wood felt rough and dry against her skin and she wept sappy tears, unable to relieve the itching. Before long, Penelope could not tell where her skin ended and where the wood began. She was surrounded by darkness, blind and cold. The warmth generated by the teardrop necklace around her neck dissipated like dew. No longer could she sense the difference between minutes and days. She existed in a state of unconsciousness, neither asleep nor quite awake.

Then, one day, the earth rumbled as if preparing to open. At first she thought she was sinking further into the earth, and she despaired, terrified that she had been ransomed like Persephone to Hades. But soon the quaking stopped. Penelope stayed awake. She listened and heard a voice.

Zeus.

He was back. So, he loved her still. Her hope was rekindled, but was soon replaced by bitterness. Another voice caught up to his. He had brought along Hera to flaunt his mistress before his wife and to flaunt his wife before his mistress.

Penelope sensed his strength and the warmth of his body as he leaned against her trunk. That unsettling feeling, that desire to give herself to him with utter abandon, returned. In spite of Zeus's trickery, she felt a longing for him. She listened to the rumble of his calming words.

"Hera, my love," he said. She felt the weight of him as he leaned against her trunk; she could almost smell the lemony aroma of his skin and smoky leathery scent of his clothes. "Hera," he said again. "You must know that I love only you and you alone."

Penelope was heartbroken.

And then, without a word whispered in confidence to Penelope, the two left her alone.

Her mother had been right, after all.

Time passed slowly. Buds formed, leaves sprouted, fruit grew heavy with juice, then rotted. Cycles repeated and she counted the seasons until she ran out of numbers. Her memories blurred, like thousands of raindrops falling into a pool.

Now and again, she awakened to feel Zeus sidle up to her trunk, often in the arms of another girl, each one as desperate as the next to capture his heart. His desire to show off his conquests angered her, and over the next few centuries, she began to plot revenge.

If Zeus chanced to walk through the forest, she would sever her branches from the trunk and strike him dead. She pictured him crushed and helpless beneath her, begging her for mercy. Yet her hatred switched to passion, then switched again back. He visited her often, reminding Penelope of all she had lost. She sank into a deep gloominess.

Winter left her feeling bereft: her limbs shriveled and without their thick coating of leaves. Harsh winds pierced her bark like daggers. Spring left her feeling alive, somewhat hopeful for the future. Summer brought a sense of womanhood as she swelled with new life.

Years passed like shallow breaths.

One summer day, as she stood bursting with ripe fruit, Zeus came to her. She felt the pinch as he plucked a cherry. He ate and spit the pit out at her trunk. "Here's looking at you," he said, and took another cherry. He sucked it lustily and spat the pit against her trunk. "I can't have you," he said, "but I can't just leave you be."

She had grown tired of his game. Though she could not will her limbs to break and crush him beneath their weight as she would have liked, her babies—the cherries—easily pulled up stems from their branches and dropped like a hailstorm upon his head.

He cried out in surprise and irritation.

She felt enormously satisfied, and rustled her branches in laughter.

He left, obviously angry, and did not dare to cross her path again.

As the years wore on, she cared less and less about earthly concerns. Another century passed, and then another. She changed entirely from a creature of water to a dryad, a creature of wood. Her heart no longer beat, but on rare occasions, she felt a pang of emotion emanating from the teardrop necklace. Zeus had captured her heart and replaced it with a trinket made from metal.

🌿

In time, a carpenter chopped down the magical tree. At the center of the trunk was a particularly dense piece of wood: eye wood, a bright reddish color, auspiciously gnarled.

It was the perfect wood for carving. The carpenter fashioned a round-topped door, quite knobby and discolored on the inside. He noticed a woman's face in the wood and worked her gently, sanding the wood smooth with a lighter touch than even Zeus had used. Around the outline of her face, he carved a wreath, routing out flowers and fruits that tied together in an oval. When the carpenter brushed away the sawdust with his fingers, he gasped at the quality of his work. The wood was smooth as silk, the carving fine as any master's. He polished the wood with a leather rag and Penelope regained her sight. He built a country estate for a rich gentleman, using the door as the centerpiece.

Late into the nineteenth century, the cottage caught fire. As the flames lapped against the door, Penelope drew her thoughts into a ring so tight she became impenetrable. The cottage burned, yet Penelope and the door survived.

She now knew she had magic: the power of making herself impenetrable. The talent might not have seemed like much to some, yet for one trapped inside a door, it had quite a profound effect. Once again she found reason to continue clinging onto life. No one would come close enough to harm her ever again.

Time continued to pass by without her needing to take part in it. One day, an American businessman, the father of a boy called Possum, bought the door at auction. He shipped it to his property in the foothills of the Catskill Mountains, in a sleepy little village named Williams Valley, which offered a temperate yet rainy climate. He was building a quaint summer cottage for his wife, who suffered from a mysterious ailment the doctors could not heal.

The businessman brought his wife and baby son to stay one summer in the cottage. They never left.

Penelope liked her new home, the scents, the sounds, the lovely voice—the stories and songs—of the businessman's wife, and the gurgling of the infant. She forced herself to practice mental skills that allowed her to focus her thoughts into something very real, with enough substance that her memories could be etched into the wood alongside the history written into the rings.

Many times, as she watched the boy grow, she felt the teardrop necklace glow and warm her like a hidden fire. Someday, Penelope hoped to walk beside the handsome young boy in the world of mortals.

CHAPTER TWO

H is legal name was Peter, but he had always been called Possum, and the name suited him just fine. Possums were solitary beasts, loyal and quiet. He imagined that he took after the animal in other ways as well. His eyes were set close to each other, colored a pure grass green without a hint of hazel. His form was slender and agile, his hair softly gray and skin very pale. He dressed in flannels and corduroys and jeans. Like the possum, he was a creature who knew enough to be timid around man.

He had lived on the family property in Williams Valley, in his family's one-room cabin with its magical door, for as long as he could remember. Now he lived alone; his mother had died almost a year ago.

From outside, the cabin appeared to be a square; in reality, it was asymmetrical. The back stretched along for thirty-two feet when measured from inside, while the front measured only twenty-seven feet. The side walls angled in and one measured ten feet less than the other. Measuring the perimeter from the outside yielded differing results each time.

"Shifting soils," his mother had once explained. Her reasoning had never made any sense, not that anything she had ever said to him made sense, but he had accepted her explanation at face value. It was easier that way.

The interior was surprisingly roomy, and felt even bigger now that his mother was gone. His bed was propped against the side wall opposite the "kitchen." The kitchen consisted of a washtub sink, a portable cabinet with an oak countertop that was marred from years of chopping, a rickety table, and two stools. A thick wooden door led to the alcove, a tiny room with access to the outside. Inside the alcove stood the wood-fired stove that was too hot for summer, yet too heavy to be moved from the house. In winter, Possum propped open the door and allowed the heat from the stove to warm the cabin. Along the cabin's back wall was a rock fireplace; in front of that, an over-stuffed reclining chair centered over a brown and yellow braided rug. But the heart of the tiny cabin was the beautiful carved cherry wood door. When he stared into the wood, he saw a woman's face.

An outhouse, the generator, a storage shed, and a solar shower stood out back, on the mountainside. The Calypso River flowed about two miles to the north. In winter, he hiked through the woods to nearby hot springs to bathe.

Possum expected that some day he might grow as crazy as his mother. He only hoped he noticed when that happened.

Of course, I could be crazy now, his rational self thought. *If so, I would not notice any changes.*

He did not really believe that. Having spent most of his life alone, he often subvocalized his thoughts. He used different voices in his head: a strong voice for advice, a boyish voice for self-deprecating humor, a calming voice when he was frightened. He knew that all the voices belonged to him. Possum hoped this was normal, not knowing how a *normal* person really thought about things.

When his mother had heard voices she had believed that they came from somewhere else, and when his mother had seen demons in the room beside her, no amount of reassurance from him could convince her that they did not exist. His mother would have been locked away if he had not been there to care for her.

Having *his* mother for his mother had been a grave responsibility, and one he had never taken lightly.

"Never turn your back on a door," his mother had taught him. "Walk backwards," she had said, "to keep the evil eye from seeing your weak spot."

She may have been crazy, but her fears were real. As a child, whenever Possum and his mother had come into town, the people had whispered loud enough for him to hear, "There's that crazy lady. Look at her. She don't know which way is front. Why don't they just go and take that kid away, put him in a home where someone could watch out for him."

The first time Possum heard the gossip and threats he understood the reason for walking backwards. There were strangers who wanted to take him away from his home over such small matters as which direction he faced or the imaginary things his mother saw or heard in her head. He learned not to speak of his home life while at school and to answer questions about his mother's well-being with lies.

At a very young age, Possum realized that his mother had foreseen many dangers that she might not otherwise have noticed had she faced forward.

There was only one way to protect yourself: to face the direction where you had already been. To do otherwise was folly.

When his mother had died, Possum had decided to change the future by trying to change as many things as he could about his life. His mother had taught him to eat just one food for each meal. For breakfast, they ate only a plateful of garden carrots; for lunch, several slices of dry toast. Dinner was commonly a dish of boiled eggs gathered from their hen house.

One night quite soon after his mother's death, Possum decided to try mixing different foods together.

Experiment, his wild side told himself, *and if the world collapses, so be it.*

He listened to himself, and combined textures, colors, and tastes: green onions fried in butter, scrambled eggs, smoked dry trout with shredded cheese melted over the top. Every part of him moaned with pleasure at the taste. It was, he had decided, not only the best thing he had ever eaten but also the most wonderful pleasure he had experienced in his life.

Other changes followed, though none so dramatic as his new diet. His fastidious self instructed him to take down the paper from the windows, and clean the glass enough to see through to the outside. His vain self told him to cut his hair, to shorten it from its shoulder-length tangle to a combed look just below his ears.

This morning, Possum sat at his small dining room table and snacked on breadsticks dipped in cinnamon and sugar. He moved aside an uncompleted drawing to make room for his coffee mug. The table jiggled. Coffee sloshed and spilled to the floor. The floor sloped downward, and a black trail traveled in a thin line toward the wall.

You've spilled some sugar, said his serious self. *Lick it up,* said his boyish self.

Do that and you'll get ink on your tongue!

He ignored the voices and blew the sugar to the floor. He hunkered down into the wood, chin dropping into his palm, and pressed his elbows into the table to keep it from rocking. He watched the coffee stream trickle downhill and pool in the crack above the trap door where he kept his savings in a locked metal box.

"You must always save something," his mother had once told him, "because no matter how terrible things seem now, they will always get worse." He added to his money collection whenever he could.

By the time Possum had turned ten, his mother had become so ill she had stopped doing the marketing and cooking. He remembered how they ate only cold food for almost a week, home-canned corn for breakfast, green beans for lunch, tuna for supper, until they ran out of those delicacies and had to turn to dandelion greens and soft potatoes.

His mother had grown worse, more feeble, less aware of the real world, until she spent her days lying on her bed, fretting, unable even to dress or walk outside. At some point she stopped eating, and she told Possum that he need no longer eat in order to survive.

His belly hurt too much to believe her, but something else troubled him as well. Possum was terrified of being taken away when the townspeople noticed that his mother had failed to make her monthly trip into town. He quickly taught himself the value of money, and took her place. He learned to shop, to cook, to pay the tax bills.

On one of his trips to town he had discovered the art gallery, one of the many shops along the boardwalk. He stared at a drawing and asked the owner, "How do you do this?"

The man gave him a box of colored pencils and some paper. "Show me what you can do with these, and I will give you more paper and pencils," the man said.

So Possum taught himself drawing. He drew everything in miniature. He drew hundreds of pictures with his mother as his muse and model, then found that he could draw anything he could imagine. He carried one of his miniature scenes to town, thinking he could trade it for more supplies.

The gallery owner smiled and said, "If you don't mind, I'd like to try and sell this."

That first sale earned Possum fifty dollars. The next sale earned him one hundred. The prices for his work continued to climb.

His mother eventually recovered enough to dress and feed herself, but things were never the same after that. At the age of fourteen Possum dropped out of school to care for their homestead. He had been a poor student, one who would rather doodle than take notes, and once he left, he wasn't missed.

Possum's inner voices faded into the background when he was immersed in drawing. His voices knew better than to advise him when no advice was needed. He worked best in miniatures and stood close to an easel holding a six-by-six-inch square of paper. In light pencil, he outlined a woodland scene with naiads dancing around a maypole. He tried to make the lady of the door queen of the naiads, though he was not doing a very good job of accurately drawing her face. Her features were just too elusive.

He yawned and forgetfully rubbed his eyes. A tear trickled down his cheek, a reaction to the smudged charcoal on his fingers. He wiped his face on the sleeve of his checkered flannel shirt and again hunched over, his head close enough to the paper to add detail to the tiny figures.

Possum looked up to stare into the face in the door. How he wished he could capture her beauty on paper. He had been drawing for over an hour, but had not managed to get the tilt of the eyelids right. He simply could not transfer the vague presence into an image real enough to stare back at him from his paper. It was frustrating. He switched from pencil to ink, but that did nothing.

He would need more money soon, and would sell one of his pictures to get it. The only decent thing on hand was a quaint pencil drawing of the boardwalk and tourist shops lining Water Street in town. It was uninspired, but cute, just the sort of thing to hang on the wall of a rich woman's custom bathroom. He would fashion a frame from twigs and baling twine because the gallery owner, Mr. Bringle, had told him "primitive sophistication" was "in." None of his drawings were larger than a piece of notebook paper, yet they sold for up to a thousand dollars each, of which he collected forty, sometimes fifty percent.

He was running low on food and supplies. Soon, on that inevitable day, he would pull his cap low and tilt the brim to the back. He would leave his cabin to walk backwards down the gravel road for two miles until he came to the highway. He would walk backwards another two miles toward town, refusing to accept a ride in the rare event one was offered. Once in town, he would make his way, still walking backwards, along the quaint street to Mr. Bringle's small gallery.

"Just the one?" the white-haired gallery owner, Mr. Bringle, would ask. "I could sell more, if you let me."

"Just the one," Possum would answer.

Mr. Bringle would protest meekly, but pay him an advance.

Possum would accept the money and walk backwards from the gallery. He would stock up on supplies from the grocer, sip a Coke with Eddie, the grocer's retarded son, have deep talks about life and things that mattered before heading for home.

He would walk backwards out of town. The locals had long ago given up trying to talk to him, but tourists might stare or point, shake their fingers, laugh. It bothered him that they thought him crazy. It would always bother him because he worried they were right.

He missed his mother. Nights especially, the loneliness was unbearable. He shuddered, and stood from his drawing to stretch. He rubbed his eyes without thinking and winced from the sting. He blinked hard and when his vision cleared, he saw the face in the door, what his mother had once called the "Evil Eye."

Though early, the day was already stifling and hot. He needed fresh air, and went to pull the heavy door open and stand in front of it. The outside world looked glorious from here. As he pressed his back against the wood, Possum distinctly heard the door groan.

❧

"No! No! No!" I hate it when he does this, Penelope thought. "Close the door! Don't leave me pressed against the wall!" She stared at the pocked yellow plaster barely an inch away from her face, counting the bumps, looking for faces or lines in the shadows, anything to replace the boredom of inactivity and visual deprivation. Her teardrop necklace hummed too dimly to provide enough light to see.

Darkness reminded her too much of that time when her captivity first began. She was furious, and without another thought as to what she was doing, Penelope began to plot revenge.

She felt herself swelling, unable to stand this deprivation, even for another second. "Stop," she screamed to her tormentor, "or you shall be very sorry." She imagined shooting splinters into his eyes or calling upon the forest to collapse upon his cabin.

Then something inside her tensed for harboring such evil against Possum. After all, he was an innocent young man unaware of her existence; to harm him would be childish and cruel. She did not wish to succumb to the temptation to do evil.

He had allowed a thin sliver of light to creep through the crack of the door. She calmed her thoughts, let herself feel warmed by that light. She remembered the phases of the moon and told herself that like those phases, all the terrible things on this earth must pass.

But then, the boy leaned harder into the door and the sliver disappeared. Penelope felt herself grow frantic. She cursed aloud, concentrating her mind until she was certain that her voice could be heard through the thickness of the wood. When nothing changed, she screamed again, fearing that if he did not let her go she would suffocate and die.

"You fool," she called out, angry and impatient. "Close this door at once!"

She waited, half expecting a reply. Indeed, the pressure lessened as he moved away, allowing her the chance for calm. She felt something soften, like timbers shifting. Perhaps it was her attitude changing. At that moment, Penelope wanted more than anything to speak to the boy. "Dear Possum," she called. "Talk to me!" Certainly, he was aware of her, for he always looked to her when he sketched at his table.

He stood there trembling.

"Boy," she called, making her thoughts hard and strong, focused like a single beam of light. "Close this door, please, for I must speak with you."

P ossum leaned against the door and heard a noise, a squeaking sound not much deeper than that of a mouse. Termites? Carpenter ants? A nest of bees in the wood? He scratched his head, wondering how long it would take insects to gnaw through such a magnificent door. There were few things he liked less than insects—especially the kind that devoured people's houses—social workers, perhaps, maybe judges.

He felt something move beneath his fingertips, a vibration as the house began to shake.

"What's going on?" his questioning self asked aloud. He stepped away from the threshold.

"Sit down and close that door," he heard a woman's voice whisper. Was he hearing things, just as his mother had done? His eyes burned and he felt suddenly trapped by the tiny room. Until this moment, he had always been certain that his voices came from within.

"What will I do?" his worried self asked with a glance toward the heavens.

"Mother," he called, wishing she were there. When Possum ran to his bed the door closed by itself. He lay over the covers and buried his face in his hands. His chest heaved and he wept until the coverlet was wet. At first he told himself in his gentle voice that he was crying for his mother, but before too long, even Possum knew that this was not entirely true, that he was weeping for himself because there was no one else left who could cry for him.

Penelope had not meant to make him cry. Now he could not hear her voice above his own tears. "Possum," she said, hardening her thoughts. "Possum, look here."

He lifted his head to look straight at her.

She could not tell whether he was seeing her or not. She had never really tried to talk to him before, and Penelope searched for the right thing to say. "Possum," she said. "Do not be afraid. I am your friend."

When he answered, "What do you want?" in a shaky, childish voice, she felt a cloudlike lightness fill her being.

"I am ready to come back into the world of the living," she blurted out, amazed that she had never thought to want this before now. "Please, say you will help."

❦

Okay," Possum said. "So I'm crazy, now." Funny, it didn't feel much different than before. He stared at the lady of the door. He had seen her face in the wood so many times, but now he saw her clearly enough that he could no longer pretend she was simply a product of an overactive imagination. She was more of a delusion, a hallucination—what a crazy mind saw, what a crazy man loved. He stood shakily, and walked toward the door to better examine her.

He reached out, touching the smooth wood on the rise of her cheek, then letting his hand drop. Trembling, he leaned in to kiss the wood, caress the grain of her hair, stroke the knots so polished they felt like marble. The wood beneath his fingertips buzzed, as though she were speaking to him.

I am crazy as a loon, said his cynical side.

If anyone were to see him bawling and hugging a door, they would surely take him away. He turned away, terrified that he had lost his mind along with everything else. "It's come to this," he cried.

❦

Her hold on him began to slip away and fear gnawed away at her that the illness that had taken the mother would now take the son. She could not let that happen to this young man, who had grown from a boy to a man before her eyes. As he fell to the ground and hugged his knees, Penelope felt something sticky push its way out from her core to the surface of the door: thick drops of resin oozing along the grain in the wood.

She had not wept in thousands of years and as she cried, the wood began to buckle from the moisture, as if it were also sobbing. She began to tremble, shivering either from cold or from fear. Her vision clouded and her trembling turned into a violent convulsion. The door rumbled and the floor quaked.

Penelope willed herself to speak to Possum, pulling her thoughts into something harder than an axe, something so hard, so sharp, that without warning, the wood cracked. Sparks flew as the wood split apart. With a thunderous sound, the door shattered into pieces, leaving Penelope of the Naiads sprawled upon the wooden floor at the entrance to the one-room cabin. She clutched her golden chain and teardrop charm and was filled with sadness as she remembered him who had given her this gift.

Her long red hair, now dulled to a dark mahogany, lay tangled around her neck and arms; her skirts were sheer as lacewings.

The boy staggered toward her. "Who are you?" Possum asked.

Her lips trembled and her mind felt weak, yet she willed herself to lift her chin to answer him. She did not know what to tell him. "I am your fairy godmother," she said at last, remembering one of the books his mother had read to her little boy.

She collapsed against the floorboards and lost track of the feeling in her fingers and toes. When she looked down, they were still there, the skin pale, unlined and hairless.

She had been a creature of wood for such a long time that her lower limbs had lost their fluidity.

She had forgotten how to make her will speak to her legs, how to ask them to carry her. She was helpless, an invalid, worse off than before. She feared she was about to fade away.

Penelope lifted her head to look into Possum's frightened eyes.

He stepped away, eyes wild, nostrils flaring. He swatted at a tear poised above his cheekbone.

"Help me, please," she begged, terrified that without his help she would sink into the wooden floor and disappear forever. He bit his lip, knelt and brought his hand forward to smooth the hair away from her mouth.

"Who are you?" he asked quietly, this boy she had watched since childhood.

She saw something familiar in his face, something in the tender way he scooped her in his arms to carry her to his bed. She looked into his eyes and saw an image mirrored of the love she had once felt for Zeus. This boy already loved her, and she had not even used a charm on him. She felt both pleased and ashamed by his devotion.

"Who are you?" he asked again. "Can it be? Are you ... the lady of the door!" He answered his own question and let his head rest upon her shoulder.

His hot breath burned against her skin as he sobbed. He lifted his head to look into her eyes and he nodded, as if to give her his vow of protection.

She met his glance and vowed to protect him as well. Since his mother died, he had needed someone else to care for.

He recovered his composure and looked at her with surprise, as if only now discovering her state of undress. "I'm terribly sorry. You must be cold," he said, shielding his eyes. He hurriedly covered her with the goose down comforter that had belonged to his mother, keeping his hand pressed against her shoulder long after he had let go of the comforter.

CHAPTER THREE

Hera had lived in New York City nearly four years without ever running into Zeus. Then, one day, while logged onto a computer bulletin board, she noticed her significant other among the riffraff. The roundtable discussion about the origins of modern fantasy was just threatening to turn academic when Zeus butted in, using the code name Old Greek.

A message had flashed across Hera's computer screen: "MGG (Married Greek God), tests negative, seeks goddess to revive fun and games," followed by a *900* telephone number. She had called immediately.

"It *is* you, you old Greek!" she said when he answered the phone.

They had arranged to meet at Zeus's favorite bar in the Village. The prospect of seeing him again had left Hera so excited she had barely slept a wink since.

Now that the day had finally arrived, Hera was too tired to think straight. What infuriated her most about the whole affair was worrying that Zeus did not pine for her as she did for him. If Zeus was trifling with her, Hera vowed to see his downfall, this time for eternity.

She stared into her bathroom mirror and considered what to wear. Her eyes were dark and round, her black hair braided into two thick strands that reached the floor. To highlight her dark skin, she decided on something silver. Despite feeling faint with nervousness, she wanted the appearance of strength.

First, Hera pictured a medieval knight until she envisioned him clearly, down to the lance nicks in the codpiece. From that vision, she fashioned a pantsuit made from chain mail that showed off her dark skin and lacy black underthings. This she modified with Velcro closures (in her opinion, one of the few worthwhile inventions of the twentieth century) that would permit her to undress without the assistance of slaves. She then looped her braids up around her shoulders. No point trying to look any better than that.

That little bit of magic left her fatigued.

An acquaintance had found her this apartment in Riverdale, a fashionable section of the Bronx that had always seemed to Hera like a place one would send one's mother-in-law to die. Beige rugs and plastic flowers in faux marble urns. Mirrors-in-the-hallways kind of decor. Doormen who could only afford to drink wine from bottles with twist-off caps. Nice enough, if boring.

She had not bothered to look for another apartment. Her most recent analyst had called her reluctance to change a symptom of depression, an "adjustment reaction to midlife." Disagreeing, she had zapped him into a broken parking meter, then set him out on the curb to rust. Yet now she wondered if the shrink had spoken truth, if she were in the throes of midlife crisis.

She thought about Zeus's code name and said, *"Kopros,"* Old Greek for shit. Okay, so maybe she was a little past her prime, so what? Older but wiser, as they said.

Good as she looked, the occasion called for a little makeup. She dabbed concentrate of cherry juice on her cheeks, lips, and neck. When warmed by her body, the concentrate released a delicate scent that made passersby close their eyes and swoon with love.

At least, that was the theory.

Satisfied, she turned to leave. Her armor clinked as she trudged down the hall.

She left the building and tramped to the street corner, where she pushed her way to the front of the line just as the bus arrived. Hera climbed up, charming the driver into forgetting she had not paid. Mortals were such rubes—not only were they easily charmed but they didn't even know it. When she stared at an old lady in one of the front rows the old lady hopped up and shuffled to the back. Hera took the seat for herself and mumbled a thank-you.

The bus rolled away.

"No stops," Hera called. She was pushing it.

"No stops," the driver repeated in a daze.

She closed her eyes to rest up from the spell of obedience.

They reached Tenth in seemingly no time and she exited. A dead leaf spiraled down from an oak tree. The serrated edge caught on her chain mail glove. Hera wondered if she might be overdressed. Then she noticed an old woman pushing a shopping cart filled with garbage. The way people ignored her, Hera would have thought the old woman invisible.

That gave Hera an idea. She turned herself into a bag lady. Beneath her threadbare beige cloth coat she fashioned a leopard skin G-string. When the time came, she would shed her coat and proceed with the seduction. She accessorized with animal hides, bones and teeth, and piled her hair above her head. Something everyone would notice, yet pretend not to see.

A familiar voice called out, "Yoo-hoo!" The Oracle had recognized her despite her disguise. He rose from a folding chair on his street corner and said, "Wait, dear goddess! Wait."

She slowed her pace and said impatiently, "You! Oh great. More dire predictions?" The old coot never said a damn thing worth hearing.

"Beware," he said, his eyes rolled upward, "the beast with sheer wings hidden by cape. He means no harm yet harm is what shall be."

"Beasts. Cape. Beware. Got it," said Hera. "The key word is 'beware.'" She gave him a twenty and hurried off before he could tell her any more.

🥀

The Village Value was dark and smoky. A singer with a Brooklyn accent bleated rockabilly music from the small raised stage. Hera's temples throbbed in syncopation with the drums. Dust motes, glowing like fairy shit in the spotlights' glare, wafted up from the dance floor, where several couples gyrated with abandon. She sat at a resin-coated table along the back wall, positioning her chair to face the door. The table was really just a wooden spool that had once held wire cable. In the modern world, things were seldom as they seemed.

The tall woman at the table beside her wore a foot-tall bleached-blonde wig and six-inch silver spiked heels. Hera suspected "she" was probably a "he." Her legs were much too perfect for a woman's.

At surrounding tables, young ladies spilled from their clothes, bubbling over their necklines like sugar-fed yeast in a glass. Civilization had truly died with the creation of America, and here was the proof. It wasn't like the old days, when only the young boys strutted around naked.

Dark oak planks decorated with life-sized posters of young women who sat in provocative poses and were scantily clad in black leather, covered the walls. Sneaking a glance toward the door, Hera noticed a perky blonde thing (who looked young enough to have been her great-great-great-to-the-hundredth-granddaughter) cozy over to a high stool at the bar.

"Howdy," said the girl to the bartender. Her voice was loud enough to carry throughout the room. She was wearing cowboy boots and a matching hat, a sequined Spandex croptop and white leather shorts. Her big brown eyes held an innocent, stupid look that made Hera picture her as the cow she would become, should Zeus pursue what he would surely consider a harmless flirtation.

A copper-haired waitress paused to light a candle in a holder fashioned from an empty Italian wine bottle, with years' worth of multicolored candle-wax drips clotting down the sides.

Hera fanned the flame until the waitress's eyebrows caught fire.

"Not again!" said the waitress, lowering her tray to Hera's table. She slapped at her eyebrows until she seemed certain they were no longer a danger.

"Did I lose much?" she asked.

Hera looked at the woman's face. Her eyebrows looked like a singed shag carpet. She tried not to laugh. "Not a bit," Hera answered.

With the waitress momentarily distracted, Hera pilfered a banana daiquiri from her tray to hide in her lap. She emptied the glass into her mouth, turning it upside down with one hand, tapping against the bottom with the other.

She stumbled from her stool and waved her empty glass around her head.

"Yo! Girl Ganymede," Hera cried to the waitress. "Come back!" Her voice sounded teeny as a mosquito fart and no one paid her any attention. If only she could hear herself think, Hera knew she could come up with a plan to win back Zeus's affection, but just then, the band began a deafening rendition of "Feelings." She took a step forward and winced, still smarting where her thighs were chafed raw from the metal leggings of her first costume. Suddenly Hera understood the value mortals placed on pantyhose.

It was all a bit too primal for her, too noisy, dark, and smelly. She felt a bit faint.

She found herself staring at the blonde sitting alone at the bar. She was helpless to alter what she sensed was about to happen between Zeus and that girl.

As if on cue, Zeus sauntered into the bar, his snug beige tee shirt bearing the legend "I'm so Virile I could Knock up a Rock."

"Start the party!" he yelled. "I'm here!"

He had dressed as a beefy version of himself with a six-thousand-year facelift. His biceps were tanned and his now golden hair flowed softly over his shoulders. His faded black jeans fit snugly enough that Hera could make out the bulge of well-defined thighs. Not bad for someone who had never believed in working out.

Some things never changed; it had been this way since the beginning of time. Zeus was born on the prowl—Hera had been given the role of trying to rein him in. One of her old analysts had made the mistake of calling Hera "co-dependent" and said she had "passive-aggressive tendencies." She had turned the fellow into a maple tree and planted him in a grove in Vermont.

"By Jove," said Hera, loud enough to irritate him.

Either Zeus did not notice her in the dim light, or else he purposefully ignored her, a sobering thought, considering the effort she had put into her disguise.

True to form, Zeus approached the blonde. He snapped his fingers, a nervous habit of his.

Hera leaned to the side, straining to hear their conversation.

"My name's Bo," she heard Zeus say. "What's your sign? No, let me guess."

He held the girl's small hand to examine the palm and stroked along the creases with his index finger. He fiddled with an opal ring on her left hand, as if to satisfy himself that she was single. He had some nerve, Hera thought. How dare he pick up a girl on the very same night he had arranged to meet his wife? Some things never changed.

Zeus licked his lips. "Do you believe in ... "

"Coincidence?" the girl finished. She giggled. "Only when all else fails, I guess. I'm Fawn," she said, her voice artificially high and breathy.

Zeus introduced himself. He snapped his fingers and the waitress approached, carrying a dark green bottle, the house Chardonnay. She gave Zeus the cork to sniff.

"Enchanting," he said, and palmed the cork, then fiddled with his hands long enough to bring forth a bouquet of daisies. "What I'd really like to be is an actor." He presented Fawn with the flowers.

"Oh wow! Is that right? Well, wouldn't everyone?" Fawn said, but she was obviously pleased by his efforts.

"It beats being a god, that's for sure."

"I know exactly what you mean. I used to be a secretary for a god," Fawn said, rolling her eyes. "Military man."

"Know the type," said Zeus.

Hera started to fume. It was past time to make Zeus jealous. She searched the crowd for an expendable man to parade around in front of him until Zeus exploded and turned the fellow into a stop sign. Someone like Jimmy Hoffa or that presidential candidate from several years back—John Anderson—who no one would miss if they were never heard from again. Not one man in the entire bar looked interesting enough to bother with and Hera sighed, fatigued with the mortal world. It had been thousands of years and Zeus was not yet tired of playing his games.

"Kopros," she said, "and by Jove."

Zeus grinned and poured two glasses of what was now sparkling wine. Hera heard the bubbling from her table. Typical. He had bought the cheapest white wine on the menu and turned it into champagne. The sneaky old Greek.

"To us," Zeus said. Fawn giggled.

Hera groaned and ran her tongue around the inside rim of her glass. She looked around the smoky room for help, but everyone seemed to be preoccupied living in their own personal dramas. A floozy wearing a tuxedo jacket and boxer shorts went from table to table, trying to talk the men into buying her a drink. Some clown in a clown suit, obviously in the throes of midlife crisis, cased the joint, looking for companionship. A young nurse sat alone at a booth, picking wax from the candle to remelt over the flame. No way could Hera compete with all of that.

Hera threw her glass to the floor to see who would care. No one did, but it was a cheap thrill, one that she would remember for at least another five minutes.

The waitress had made herself scarce, perhaps suspecting the goddess wasn't a big tipper. This was true, Hera thought. Tipping seemed a bit much to ask. In the old days, people had prayed for their chance to serve Hera. Those days were long gone. So she did what any self-respecting leftover goddess would do in such a situation: climbed atop the table and waved her short arms in circles around her pygmy head. No one seemed to notice that either.

She was kopros out of luck. One way to make a drink last through the night was to make herself smaller. Hera concentrated and rematerialized into a ladybug. Her small size made it possible to buzz Zeus's table and eavesdrop more efficiently.

That turned out to be a really stupid idea. At that size her blood alcohol hovered above ninety percent. When she came to, Hera found that not only was she looped, she was lodged inside a crevice in the tabletop with a dozen or so beetles waiting patiently for the chance to hump her. The fog slowly dissipated, and Hera perked up enough to zap her suitors into transit cops, then sent them outside to prowl the streets with the rest of New York's finest.

She zapped a tiny wristwatch onto her left front leg and stared as its second hand inched forward. With a start, Hera realized that she had been unconscious nearly fifteen minutes, during which time she had likely consummated a relationship with one or more shellac bugs. The caped beasts. By Jove, for once she should have listened to the Oracle and stayed out of trouble. Just Hera's luck to have been a minor fertility goddess in what seemed like a former life. All bets were off; she would probably get pregnant as a result of the unplanned tryst.

She sobered up quickly. The thought of a pregnancy at this stage of life left her feeling sick to her stomach, especially when she considered her offspring. Worse, there might be stretch marks. But there wasn't a thing to do about it, now. Deep down, it wasn't the beetles she was angry with, anyway.

Despite everything, Zeus would surely ask her to hop into the conjugal cloud without blinking an eye. To someone like him, fidelity was a four-letter word.

Well, he would have a surprise. Zeus may have been the king of the gods, but Hera was not so eager to trust someone who had dunked more hoops than Wilt Chamberlain. Even with a Trojan between them.

"Would you like a ride in my chariot?" she heard Zeus say to the vacuous blonde. He was utterly without shame.

Poor Fawn probably thought he was kidding and said, "Sure. Where to?"

"Slut," Hera shouted, but she was too small to be heard by anything larger than a cockroach. She flew from the crevice to the tabletop for a look around. By this time, Zeus and his date had vanished.

A drunk bumped against her table and Hera lost her footing and fell on her back. Above her, the ceiling had been painted with glow-in-the-dark stars, which trailed spider webs that were lit by stage-light and looked like dusty galaxies. Hera regained her composure and, when no one was looking, wobbled up close to the stage, turned herself into the drummer, then stuck the drummer's consciousness inside his drumsticks. She joined the band, letting the drumsticks play by themselves.

Percussion was the sound of modern angst. Too bad the lyre was out of fashion. Its music was calming, introspective. She never heard that kind of music anymore except those times she rode in elevators playing the melodic strains of *1000 Strings*.

A young girl, watching intently, caught Hera's attention with a wink. Hera realized that the girl was flirting with her, or at least with the rock star wannabe body she was temporarily using. It seemed a pathetic gesture, given the circumstances.

That reminded her of something. The last young man she'd

enchanted (and by young, she meant forty) had told Hera that when he was young (and by young, he had meant sixteen) every boy had wanted to be in a rock band and every girl had wanted to sleep with someone in a rock band. When Hera was young, and by that she meant in her first couple of centuries, every human either wanted to become a god, or else sleep with one. Seemed some things never changed.

One hour later, Zeus walked in, smiling sheepishly. He always came back, eventually. Maybe this time he would even stick around. Zeus sat at Hera's old table to watch the band; he tapped his foot and shrugged his shoulders in time to the music. He frowned, perhaps sensing this was where she had separated the nits from the boys. Hera couldn't bear to face him yet and zapped the spotlights to shine against his face to keep Zeus from seeing her. That was when she noticed the heart-shaped hickey Fawn had sucked on his neck.

Tacky, yes, but something in her snapped. From the corner of her eye she caught Zeus smiling. He tilted his head her way and she realized that he had seen through her disguise and was onto her. His hickey raised into purple letters that said, "Help me."

She felt her cheeks burn; the stage beneath smoked as her rage let loose. The air thickened with yellow steam. Hera's eyes began watering; she dropped the drumsticks and pulled away from the drummer. In a few moments, she had dissolved completely into vapor. She misted across the stage.

Behind her, the drummer's body slumped to the floor and the band stopped midsong to attend to him.

"Call 911!" shouted the pimply faced moron on bass guitar.

"Where am I?" asked the drummer when his consciousness transferred back inside his head.

Hera landed in an empty chair beside Zeus, with her back—as it were—to the band. She heard someone ask, "Is he all right?" answered by, "I'll take a look at him. Trust me, I'm a doctor." Hera waited a few minutes and then figured it was safe to transform. She turned herself into herself.

Zeus frowned, no doubt expecting someone younger. "Long time no see," he said. "How've you been?"

"Not too bad," Hera said. She hurriedly stuck a few king snakes through her hair to contrast with the color, and lowered the bodice of her chiton to nipple level. She gave her legs a tan, and polished the toenails with gold to match her sandals. "And you?" she asked. This seemed a pointless conversation, but she did not want things to get too pointed, yet. She opened her clutch and removed a pearl-shell compact to powder her nose.

Zeus started it. "Stay away from that girl, Hera," he said, shaking his finger in front of her face. "I want your word you won't turn her into some furry animal or another."

Hera drew on lipstick and smacked her lips together. She raised an eyebrow. "I really don't know what you mean," she said.

"Look, I've lost more dates to your petty jealousies than I care to remember. And for what? You know I love you more than I'll ever love her," Zeus said, lowering his glance. His lips quivered with humility; he was adept at pumping out the charm.

"Oh?" Hera said. She had heard him say this a time or two before. "Is that a fact?"

"Come on. I think about you all the time," he said. "You want to have a go at it again? Move in with me? I have an incredible pied-à-terre in the heart of the Village. Three hundred a month. Rent controlled."

"You'll tell your landlord that I'm your wife," Hera said, thinking that once she was on record, she could keep the apartment, in case things didn't work out.

He never gave anything without a concession. "I want you to swear you'll leave that girl alone," he said. "Promise me you won't turn my Fawn into a goat."

She grinned. "Why not, Zeus? The kid's already got a milky complexion." She sighed and stared past him to the door where a steady stream of underage gatecrashers kept the bouncer busy. "Don't worry. I won't turn that sweet thing into a goat." She crossed her fingers beneath the table—caring not a whit that this might be some vestige of the Christian tradition—after all, this was America, the great melting pot. Historical accuracy was not a requirement of citizenship.

"Well," Hera said, "now that that's all settled ... tell me, what do you really want with me?" She kept her voice steady, because she did not want him to see how much she cared about his answer.

He paused, as if uncertain. "What do you mean?" he asked. "It should be pretty clear by now how much I love you," he said, sounding almost sincere. "What's it been? Five? Six thousand years that we've been an item? Doesn't that mean anything to you?" He reached across the table to take her hand.

She yawned.

Without letting go, he floated his chair close beside her. He lifted her hand to his mouth, gently kissing each knuckle. "What about you, Hera?" Zeus said. "What do you want with me?"

She did not want to tell him, refusing to trust his solicitous behavior. She threw her hands up in the air like it was all a big joke and said, "You'll be hearing from my lawyers. I want more alimony than you gave Metis, your first wife," she said without meeting his glance.

Patting her hand, Zeus smiled. "I've been thinking more and more that I might settle down one of these days. Tell me the truth, now. Don't you ever feel old?"

"Old?" she said, keeping the jitters from her voice. "How would I know about old?" She leaned forward to kiss his cheek and he grabbed her shoulders and held her tight. He buried his face in her bosom.

Hera rubbed his back and said, "There, there." At that moment, Fawn stumbled into the room, looking lost. Hera felt a surge of power as adrenaline pumped through her.

"I can change the outside of me, but I'm old inside, and I can't change that," Zeus was saying. He nuzzled his cheek against her shoulder and gazed into her eyes. "Don't you ever wonder if maybe there's something more than all of this?"

"Poor baby," Hera said, cooing. She gestured around the room. "More than this?" She squinted at the soft, pale wisp of a girl, whose hair shone like spun sugar, but managed to keep her voice steady.

"Okay," Hera said. "I'll move in with you. When can you help me pack?"

Zeus tilted his head back, then laughed his deep roar. The wine bottle with its half-burnt candle began shaking and tipped over on its side. He let it smolder on the wood for a few seconds before snuffing out the flame.

"I knew you'd see things my way," he said.

When Zeus gazed into her eyes she met his glance, but what she pictured was Fawn. Magic flowed through her and she turned the girl into a bag of mini-marshmallows and transported the bag into her clutch. Hera felt her stomach knot. At first, she assumed it was guilt, but she quickly dismissed the discomfort as being nothing more than a slight case of morning sickness.

"So, Zeus," Hera said. "Do you have plans for later? I'll make dinner."

Zeus brightened. He patted her shoulder. "What a wife! She even cooks!" he said, and Hera heard his stomach growl. "What are we having?"

She felt tired of their game, but wasn't about to forfeit too easily. "Your favorite," Hera said. "My special recipe: ambrosia salad, the food of the gods, extra heavy on the marshmallows."

"Hera," he said, watching her warily. His eyes glittered and he hit the table lightly with his fist. "You promised you'd leave her alone!"

"Well, not exactly," she reminded him.

He groaned. "I hope you realize there'll be other girls."

She smiled sweetly and stood, prepared to leave. "But not tonight," she said.

He nodded, signaling defeat. "Okay. You win," he said, "Not tonight. I will admit I rather enjoyed making you jealous."

"Me!" she said. "Jealous over a tall blonde? Hah!" She would show him jealous. After they had made love, she would confess that she was pregnant. Zeus would puff himself up to play the part of the proud father. He would stay that way until the babies were born, when one look into their compound eyes would let him know they weren't his. She couldn't wait to see his face then.

Hah!

She would show him jealous all right. Oh, it might take a while to get over it, but eventually they would both get a good laugh out of this one. Maybe she would even dig out an old tradition and let him eat the babies. That should keep him happy, for a while.

He would leave her again. After all they had gone through there was no doubt in her mind that their pattern would continue. For now, at least, Zeus was hers and hers alone. Hera snuggled inside his strong embrace. They walked arm in arm toward the door.

CHAPTER FOUR

Possum woke before dawn. He folded up his sleeping mat and dressed in jeans and checkered flannel shirt before carrying out his socks and boots to the front porch. In the week since Penelope had appeared he had managed to neatly stack the chunks of cherry from her door beside the entrance. A burst of cold wind made him shudder. He had fashioned a temporary screen from a blanket, but today he would have to search the shed and see if he could find a better replacement. He picked up a postcard-sized block of cherry and tucked it in his shirt pocket. The wood was too beautiful to burn for fuel. Maybe he would practice his carving skills.

He stepped into his boots, not bothering with the laces. The morning light was still almost an hour away. Mindful of the quiet, he tiptoed off the porch and down the steps and headed out toward the shed. He did not want to wake Penelope.

He laughed at his "motherly" concern. Technically, from all she had told him, she was a hell of a lot older than he was, though one look at her smooth skin and dark eyes made him forget that. It was scary, hearing her tell about the past and all she had gone through. Not that any of that mattered now. However it happened, she was here with him. She might be an invalid, but he needed to be more careful not to treat her like a child.

At times he behaved like a fool. Yesterday, he had ignored her protestations that she did not need or want his help, and had carried her from her bed to the reclining chair for breakfast.

Penelope had stopped speaking with him, and the more he tried to apologize, the angrier she had grown. Her fury had pierced him like icy splinters. It had taken hours before he felt the warmth of her forgiveness. He would not make that same mistake again.

As he walked, he passed through the wet smell of pine needles and mud, and wondered, had it rained during the night? Odd that he could have slept through the sound of water trickling on the cabin's roof, which usually roused him from the deepest slumber. While his mother was still alive, he had slept always on the alert, wakening each time the floorboards creaked, because that might have meant she was running away. She had only managed this once, suffering no more than a bruised rib. After that one time, Possum had not been able to sleep through the night.

Now she was gone. His mother's death had lifted many burdens, but relief had quickly replaced those burdens, and the feeling of relief replaced by guilt. That had all changed, at least a little, the moment Penelope had fallen into his life. She needed him; there was no time to wallow in remorse.

Without a moon, the slate pathway was dark and strangely unfamiliar. He tripped over a stone that had become dislodged from its sandy bed.

Clumsy oaf, said his childish self, while his motherly self asked, *Are you okay?*

Long ago Possum had taught himself to see in the dark, to see shadows within shadows. Now when he gazed into the dark summer sky he saw Penelope's sweet face.

Maybe that was what they meant when they said love was blind. Because when all you see is the love in your heart, you forget what the world really looks like.

A bullfrog croaked from the pond, but stopped at the sound of Possum crushing an oak gall beneath his boot. He stood on the pathway and listened, hoping the bullfrog would begin its croaking again. As a child, he had held his breath and kept so very still, as if that was enough to keep his mother's demons from finding him.

A boy could learn to hide through silence. You waited in one place, croaking now and then, always hopeful the right person would hear your plaintive call and answer.

Whatever works, said his practical self.

The shed's foundation had continued to slowly sink and was foam-rubber soft and needed replacement. The door was ajar, but it was always ajar because of the sloped flooring. He stepped up to push past the door and let himself inside. The old shed was too much of a matchstick to chance lighting a lantern, so he relied upon the old generator, which crackled noisily when he flipped on the switch. Light flowed unevenly, flickering like a river tickled by wind.

He had been working in secret to repair an antique wheelchair that had been stored in the shed for as long as he could remember. The chair, he assumed, had once belonged to his grandfather. The seat back was tall and sculpted to conform to the proportions of the body. Sitting in the chair gave him a feeling of comfort, as if he were being cradled.

Despite a few surface blemishes, and layers of rust that needed to be scraped away, the chair had survived essentially intact. He had oiled the wheels and replaced two broken spokes, stripped away what was left of the tooled leather seat. He had sanded down the wood, restored the original walnut foot boards. The color was dark and lustrous, smooth as beetle wings.

It was finished. He tested the seat and found it comfortable. One corner of the cherry wood rectangle in his pocket poked his nipple, so he took it out and held it in his hand. The grain suggested movement and reminded him of ocean waves. It was an unusually beautiful piece of wood, smooth and light. Perhaps he would carve tiny wings to glue to the chair back.

The chair had turned out beautifully. Too bad he didn't know Penelope well enough to know if she liked being surprised. Soon he would find out. He carried the chair toward the cabin. It was light enough now that he could just make out the shadow of Williams Peak behind the cabin. The mountain was fifty miles away, but in the dim light, the perspective made it seem as if the mountain sprouted from the back of his cabin. He smiled. Which came first? If the mountain had grown up around his cabin that might help explain the building's odd shape.

He hoisted the chair up the stairs and onto the porch. He opened the door and left it just inside by the room. Penelope was strong of will and had exercised her arms until her muscles grew firm. She had learned to move herself about the cabin on a thick blanket, using her arms to propel herself forward. Her spirit amazed him. His insecure self worried that Penelope might resent his meddling gift.

On the other hand, said his motherly self, *this will bring her some sense of independence.*

Once she was more independent, would she leave him?

If it were possible to kick himself in the behind, his motherly self would have done so. It was really too late to take back the chair. Whether she liked it or not, he would have to face the consequences of honesty. His pride at his handiwork was about equal to his worry; he covered the chair with a thick wool blanket.

By now there was enough light to see the shadows of Penelope's face, the indentations of her eyes, the rise of her delicate lips and nose. He wanted to sit and watch her sleep, perhaps try to sketch her, but his modest self argued that this might invade her privacy. Before he knew it, he was arguing with himself about propriety.

Come on, said his practical self. *You've helped this woman use the toilet. Yet you think you shouldn't look at her face?*

In the end, he angled his recliner so that he had to crane his neck to see her. For the next hour or so he dozed and wakened, dozed and wakened, feeling cold, but too tired to get up for another blanket.

His muscles ached from his awkward position and his practical self did not hesitate to take advantage. *You haven't gotten any work done in days. What are you waiting for when inspiration sits only a few feet away? You are being a fool,* his practical self said, convincing him to angle his recliner toward her.

There was too little light to sketch her anyway; instead, he tried to memorize her features. But when he realized he was gawking, rather than regarding her with the impartial artist's eye he had worked so hard to develop, he blushed. So this was love. Forgetting everything, all the knowledge and certainty you had always taken for granted. Finding pleasure in the simplest of experiences. Surely, such a wondrous gift could not come to him without a price.

Finally, he could stand it no longer. He took out his pocketknife and started whittling away at the little block of cherry. The wood was weightless, smooth as skin, supple. He could have carved it with a fingernail. He closed his eyes and heard the sound of a raging river. The texture of the wood changed, grew warm like clay. His fingers moved on their own and the knife shaved off the thinnest layer of wood. Ridges and valleys formed beneath his fingers. The piece seemed to carve itself while he daydreamed about nymphs and wine and thunderclouds.

Through closed eyes he saw a ring of bright light and wondered if he might be having a seizure. But when he opened his eyes, he saw an intricate landscape carved into the wood, no line much thicker than an eyelash. In the foreground, rolling hills, flowers, majestic trees, swirling leaves and the circular patterns of wind. In the background, a river that seemed to move when he stared at it. And clouds with subtle shadows and an odd sense of movement.

Possum shuddered. It was one of the most beautiful pieces of work he had ever seen and that disturbed him. Although he held the knife that had shaped the block of wood, he doubted he was the real artist. Perhaps the Muses had used his hands to create their own picture. The carving was small, but it would command a high price. With regret, he decided to take it to the gallery owner, Mr. Bringle. He wrapped the block in several layers of newspaper and placed it near his pack. Then he sat back down and tried to draw Penelope on paper. "Why can't I draw you?" he asked. This wasn't like him. He changed to colored pencils, but stalled with the lead against the paper, and gave up. Instead, he drew a picture of the storefronts along Water Street at dusk. It turned out nice, nice enough to sell to Mr. Bringle, in addition to the carving.

In a while, she opened her eyes and stared blankly, not seeming to recognize him. Before long, a smile appeared as she came into the world of day.

His heart raced.

"Good morning," he said. "Did you sleep all right?"

She nodded.

She must think him a fool, a desperate and pathetic fool. If so, she was right. He had already established this much. He laughed. Love coursed through his veins, made his fingers tingle with every heartbeat.

He tried to talk, but the words came out in the bullfrog's croak. "I would like to sketch your face," he said. "What I mean is, I've been trying to draw you, but I can never seem to get the proportions right."

She yawned and elegantly stretched out her arms. She was wearing one of his mother's gowns. On Penelope, the fabric, thin from age, was a beautiful gossamer web. He resisted the urge to kiss her.

"You may draw me whenever you would like. I consider it a compliment," she said. "I'd like to see how you view me."

Her arms were pale as moonbeams, chiseled and strong as marble. "*Burrr!*" she said, smiling, not yet used to the chill summer mornings. She sat up and worked hard to transfer herself from the bed to the makeshift commode. She did not ask for his help.

"Excuse me," he said, a little embarrassed. He stepped out to the back porch and waited a few minutes before bringing back an armful of seasoned oak. He crumpled up a newspaper page and positioned a few splits of dry kindling over it, struck a match, added oak, and sat on the hearth to watch the firebrand.

"Thank you," Penelope said. She was sitting on the edge of the bed, brushing her hair.

How he loved her hair: its mahogany color, its sheen like rain running down a window, its woodsy scent.

"What is that?" she asked, angling her elbow toward the wool blanket he had used to cover the wheelchair. "What's under there? A present? For me?" She clapped her hands together.

His cheeks grew hot and he knew he was blushing. "Just something I've been working on," he said.

"Possum! What? May I see it?"

For one moment, he paused, wanting to ask for her promise not to be angry. It was too late to ask for that now and he knew it. Whatever her reaction, he steadied himself to accept that. He walked slowly toward the doorway and tapped his fingers as a drum roll on the wall. When he pulled off the blanket, it was as if he was unmasking a work of fine art.

She gasped, but as he wheeled the chair closer, her breathing turned to laughter.

"A wheeled chair!" she said, sounding delighted.

"Your coach, my lady," Possum said.

"This is exactly what I needed," she said.

Possum steadied the back while Penelope transferred herself to the chair. Her feet were caught up in the footrests, and he lifted up her heels and set them gently in their place.

"It is lovely," she said. She tested the wheels and mistakenly rolled over his toes.

"Ouch!" screamed his childish self.

"Please forgive me," she said. She reached for his hand.

Her skin was warm and very soft. "They have better ones in town," he said apologetically. "Electric chairs that move quickly and without effort, but they are heavy and big."

"This will do," she said. She brought his hand to her cheek. "This will do much better than you know."

Every part of him relaxed and he sighed a deeply felt sigh. His relief at having pleased her brought an embarrassing rush of tears. She touched his face, and when her fingers wiped away the moisture, his strength returned.

It had taken some getting used to, these new sensations, or rather lack of sensations. Below her hips, Penelope felt only a vague dullness or an occasional tingling through her limbs.

Odd that the wheeled chair was much more cooperative than her own body. The new chair gave her the ability to move like wind through heavy air. She felt as if she were sitting in the center of a rain cloud.

She could not exactly feel the wood beneath her bum, so she imagined that it was soft, and molded to her body like a pillow. She sat forward to explore the chair with her hands and he backed away, as he often did, when taking her leave. Possum needed to go to town for supplies but was afraid to let her out of his sight. He didn't believe her when she told him she liked being alone.

She smiled, wanting so to reassure him that there was no need to worry.

His shoulders and chin slumped as he sighed and began to relax. He groaned and looked as if he might again cry.

"What's wrong?" she asked.

His face reddened. "I was afraid you wouldn't like it," he said.

There were times when he seemed so very young. "How could I not love a gift you chose for me?" she asked. She gripped the wheels and urged them forward half a turn. She explored the room, soon feeling tenseness in her shoulders. This was hard work, she realized. She would need to regain even more strength in her muscles. "So this is how I will walk," she said with resignation. "Forever on, gliding like a fish."

He was watching her with a sad expression in his eyes. "Sorry about that. It would probably be easier in a better chair."

She tilted her head back to laugh. What he did not understand was that this chance to explore movement, however limited, opened a world of possibilities. "There can be no better chair," she said, and reached for his hand. "I am so happy," she said. "This is a wonderful gift. Thank you."

He smiled and approached her. She held his hand, wishing he could understand the depth of her gratitude and affection.

"When your arms get stronger you'll be able to push yourself away from this cabin. I'll build a ramp and also a walkway so you can get around outside by yourself. For now, I can carry you down the steps." He seemed so apologetic.

When Possum helped her bathe or dress, he was always careful to preserve her modesty. She appreciated his thoughtfulness and was charmed by his embarrassment at needing to care for her. Perhaps he feared she would become resentful, like his mother. "Thank you," she said, "for everything."

If she were completely honest with him, she would remind him that he had seen no more of her than she had seen of him on many, many occasions in the past. She had witnessed his first erections, seen him throw up on the floor, witnessed the first time he had pooped in his little potty-chair.

There was irony in everything, it seemed. There they were. The two of them. Acting like the insecure mothers of newborn babes. She shook her head and tried to wiggle her toes before remembering that her body no longer obeyed her.

"It is as if I am fashioned from rotting wood," said Penelope, tapping her legs. "I cannot move, yet my flesh is soft as water. I make no sense anymore."

Rather absently, he wrapped her hair around his fingers. "I can't wait to take you into town," he said. "Maybe when you're stronger. We'll go on horseback and you can see how the world has changed."

He sounded worried and she knew he was not ready to leave her alone.

She had the feeling he was hiding something from her, or maybe he was afraid she would disappear if seen by anyone else. She fingered her teardrop necklace, and for a moment wondered if that could be true.

She shook away the thought. "Sit beside me," she said. "Be my equal." She wheeled herself beside the recliner and patted the seat.

When he sat down, his leg brushed against hers. The warmth of his body seeped through his pants legs and through her thin garment and into her thighs. A small shock from the static electricity made her foot jump forward and fall off its pedestal.

"I can feel you!" she said, amazed. How was it she could feel him, yet not feel herself? This made no sense at all. Her heart sped up and she felt color rise to her bosom. She wanted him to touch her. He smelled of earth and sweat that made her scheme to bring his lips close to hers.

As if sensing her thoughts he leaned forward until he was close enough that his warm breath caressed her cheek.

For the first time, she saw him not through the eyes of a mother, but through the eyes of a young woman. The blessings of immortality became apparent: one could share the wisdom of experience with the passion of youth. She smiled, feeling alive in places she had thought were dead forever. "Come closer to me," she said, and he did not for one moment protest.

He pressed his hands against her, his fingers caressing the hollows of her neck and sliding back to hold her head aloft as he leaned forward to kiss her. His fine hair brushed against her forehead and her skin tingled as he nuzzled her cheek on his way to her mouth. His lips were warm and moist; he tasted sweeter than cherries, more intoxicating than wine.

"I can't believe you are real," he said, breathless and impatient. He stroked her neck with his fingertips and slid the sleeve of her gown away from her shoulder. "Oh please, please, be real."

She exhaled, an involuntary moan that came when she found she could encircle him, tightly grasping her arms around his back. "I'm real," she said.

He lifted her from the chair and into his lap and as they kissed he peeled away their clothing until he was pressing his bare chest against hers. She could not feel her legs, could only sense him caressing them. It was a delicious tickling, excitingly ethereal like remembered kisses.

She felt his breath hover in the shallow above her lips.

He smelled sweetly of skin, nothing more.

She opened her mouth and he parted her teeth with his tongue.

His tongue was warm, soft, precise.

He cupped her breast in one hand, and thrust the other between her thighs.

She did not think to push him away.

He pulled two of her fingers into his mouth, suckled and covered them with kisses.

Penelope laughed, feeling overwhelming joy from the knowledge that she was alive and in love. At last, after so many centuries of being trapped in a mundane existence, she was, at last, experiencing magic.

᠁

Possum readied himself for the trip to town. He unpacked his army surplus pants and the thick canvas shirt he would wear for his hike through the hills and into town. This time of year the blackberry thorns could practically cut through metal. He put on his cap and fiddled with the brim until it tilted backwards, just the way he liked it.

Penelope was still asleep.

He laced his boots and went out to the root cellar to bring in enough food to last Penelope a week although he hoped only to be gone for the day. For him, he packed a light lunch of several baked crackers lathered with enough butter to grip hard slices of cheddar. He filled his canteen with water, and wrapped two quarts of blueberry jam in newspapers. The jam and his lunch and a small box of home-cured lamb jerky went into the side pocket of his backpack. The strange little wood carving and the sweet pencil drawing of the shops on Water Street fit snugly into the center of the pack, wrapped inside two thick terry towels.

He heard Penelope stirring beneath the covers, and the creak of the bedsprings. She would soon be fully awake.

There was really nothing more to do but walk out the door.

On his own, he would not have used the stove all summer. He liked the brisk feeling of morning, and those few hours before the sun streamed in through the cabin windows and reflected the warmth of the outside. Penelope always ran cold, and relished the heat cast from the wood stove, so he lit a fire and started a kettle of water for her tea.

He sat on the reclining chair to watch her come into wakefulness. Reflexively, he picked up his sketchpad and began to draw her. He had wanted so to do her justice, but capturing her fragile beauty during these last few moments of sleep was more difficult than he could have imagined. His drawings of her were clumsy; the perspective and shading all wrong. No longer a master, he was content to fall back to apprenticeship.

The sun streamed in from the window to make her hair shine like a river. On his sketch, the contrast seemed too harsh and her hair looked thick as rope. He did his best, but could not mute the tones. It frightened him that he could not draw her. Why could he not commit to paper that vision he so clearly saw, even with his eyes closed? He flipped over the paper and began on a new sheet, to no avail. He wanted to touch her, reassure himself again that she was real and not some hallucination. *Have you ever had a hallucination?* asked his practical self. No, he thought, and chuckled softly.

Her lips pouted open and a few drops of spittle pooled in the corner of her mouth. She looked so young, so fragile. It was all he could do not to kiss her. Her chest heaved and shuddered; the neckline of her nightgown fell, exposing just enough of her breast to tease him into a state of excitement. Her skin was so delicate and fair, but that was all an illusion, for Penelope was as strong a woman as he could imagine. He knew enough of her past to know she *had* to be strong to survive all that she had gone through.

Her nostrils flared and she moaned and rubbed her eyes. She opened them before he could hide his drawing. "Hello," she said, smiling.

"Morning," Possum said. His voice choked and he cleared his throat. He looked away, embarrassed to have been caught staring at her.

"Let me see," she said, and he angled his sketchpad toward her. He longed to show her the cherry wood carving, to prove to her that he was a good artist, one she should admire, but he was afraid that she would know he hadn't really carved the wood.

When he got back his nerve to look at her reaction, he saw that she was frowning. When it did not matter, when the drawings were for strangers, they were always perfect. "I'm sorry," he said, ashamed by his incompetence. "Those are terrible likenesses. I'll destroy them right away."

"No! Don't! It's not what you think," she said. "The drawings are lovely. It just surprises me that I've grown so old. When last I saw my reflection I was no more than a young girl."

Old? She had no idea. "Trust me. You're not old."

"Well," she said. "I suppose it would be stranger yet if I had not changed at all." She pushed herself up with her elbows to a sitting position, and worked to bring her legs around until they dangled from the side of the bed. He had fashioned an overhead bar that she reached for and gripped with her left hand. Her chair was poised so that one corner of the seat touched the bed, and it was angled to give her enough room to maneuver. She hoisted herself up, and with a minimum of effort, transferred to the chair.

"I'm thankful you're not too young for me," he said.

She flashed him a playful look and he remembered that it was he who was too young for her. "It's me who ought to be thankful. Do you have very much time before you have to leave?" she asked.

"Do you want me to stay?" he said, quite seriously. "This can wait. I can go to town later, in another week or so."

She laughed. "If you wait too long it becomes impossible to move," she said.

He knew she was tired of his castoffs and even more so of his mother's ratty clothes. She had asked him to bring her new things to wear, in addition to fabric and other accouterments of sewing. She had asked him for lotions and scents and hair ribbons and sweets.

He wanted to bring her everything.

"I was thinking more of a simple dalliance before you go," she said. "We *do* need food, I'm afraid, and I dearly want you to bring me some supplies."

"I'm afraid that if we dally," Possum said, "I doubt very much that I'll have the fortitude to leave you."

"It was just a thought," she answered with an exaggerated sigh.

"Hold that thought," he told her. He stood and gathered up his pack. Ignoring all his misgivings, he walked close to kiss her cheek and bid her good-bye.

❧

Possum had given Penelope one of his mother's chamois jackets, which she buttoned over one of his lightweight plaid shirts. She wore the long skirt he had fashioned from an old pair of his denim pants. The thick wool socks were the hardest of all, and for those she needed to use the hooks Possum had made for her from hangers. She liked the skirt, which was constructed of such heavy fabric that she could almost feel its touch. He had cut apart the legs and sewn front and back seams. He had taken out the fastener, replaced it with something he called Velcro that he knew, from his experience in caring for his mother, was much easier to manage. Practical, but ugly. She could not wait to get her new wardrobe.

Possum did not vary his own clothes much, except to account for seasonal changes. He owned ten short-sleeved T-shirts, ten lightweight plaid flannel shirts. Ten pairs of Levi's jeans, ten pairs of wool socks and cotton ones, et cetera. She valued his predictability. With Possum, what she saw was what she got. There could be few secrets with someone like him, which also meant there could be few lies.

She wheeled her chair to the door and then onto the front porch. Each new day still seemed like such a miracle. The sky was streaked with red and orange clouds from a sun that seemed to offer no warmth whatsoever. Birds chirped and squirrels argued as they jumped from bough to bough. The squirrels were playful, practically squirrelly. They made her laugh. When she concentrated, she heard the rush of the Calypso River in the distance, beyond the trees. Possessing the freedom to experience such beauty should never be taken for granted.

She had so looked forward to being alone that it seemed odd how, the moment Possum disappeared from sight, she began to miss him. She thought she was in love with him, and that he loved her in return. Her joy was mitigated by a sense of shame, as if the very act of loving him were a betrayal. She fingered her necklace and tried to understand her complex feelings. They made no sense, but did anything?

Something held her back from loving him unconditionally. Was it fear? Mistrust? She thought of Zeus, and shuddered at the memory of his smiling face. She could not deny she still harbored feelings for the god who had been her first love.

She guided her chair over the uneven ramp and onto the gravel walkway Possum had covered with smooth boards. In only a few weeks of using the wheeled chair, her arms had grown muscular and strong. By now, she possessed enough strength to help Possum when he chopped wood. She used the small axe to split kindling. It felt great to wield the axe; she found the even rhythm relaxing. The fragrance of cedar and pine released as the wood split, awakening her senses. She remembered her sisters complaining about the work of making butter, and she laughed. *If they could only see me now.*

Using the outhouse was still a bit tricky, so she took her time, wanting to put off another visit for as long as possible.

A second walkway led her from the outhouse to the old shed. From the shed, a third walkway jutted out another twenty feet and ended at a square floor that Possum had covered with a canopy. Her outdoor porch, he called it. She wheeled herself to the floor and thrust her hands back into the sleeves of the chamois jacket. Her paralysis had left her with the ability to sense the sun's warmth without feeling its benefit.

She spent an hour just sitting here and gazing out at the land. She memorized the way the sky's brilliant blue faded to gray as it touched the tops of the trees. The trees started off black but, as her glance traveled downward, developed into a lush dark green and again turned black at the point where the earth met the trees. Beyond that was white, the river hiding from sight. As she brought her gaze forward a quilt of colors blossomed: delphiniums, lupines, poppies, and unknown meadow flowers, redbird, and tall grasses. When she angled her chair in the other direction, she saw the rise of Williams Peak and the play of the sun's shadow as it swept across the mountain.

Possum had been teaching her to draw; her charcoals and paper were stored in a canvas pocket hooked around her backrest. She took out a pencil and the sketchpad and did her best to transfer the beauty of what she saw onto the page. She wanted to draw a summer wind made visible as it traversed the sky: leaves spiraling down from the treetops to land upon the water. Her efforts were not pleasing. Perhaps she had learned this self-criticism from her teacher, alongside soaking up what she could of his skill.

She listened to the wind's gusts; hidden within it, she could almost imagine she was hearing her mother's voice.

Listen, it said.

Listen and remember.

What was she to remember? She thought about this for a while, though nothing came to mind. She picked up the drawing and sketched a few tentative lines.

In another couple of weeks, Possum had promised that the ground would be dry and hard and smooth. It would be possible to wheel her chair to the part of the meadow she could barely see from her outdoor porch. From there, he had said, if the day was clear, she might be able to *really* see the river, not just its color.

Listen and remember, said the wind.

Penelope stopped drawing and squinted in the direction of the river. She remembered some things from her past: the sheen of the water as the sun rose, how the heat warmed the surface of the rocks.

She remembered the smell of mud and dried grasses and the sounds of fish flopping against the nets. She remembered dipping her toes in water and the delicious cold that could turn so suddenly into icy pain. The memory proved so vivid that she pinched her leg, hard, to see if she were dreaming. She could not feel the bite of her fingers.

It had not really hit her before now: the extent of her infirmity. Perhaps she had been so taken with caring for Possum that she had not bothered to think about her own predicament. With Possum gone, would time again pass slowly? What else could she find to do besides consider the sadness of the present?

Would she *ever* feel her toes again? Or sense the position of her own legs without Possum there to touch them, and transfer the reality of his being to her? For the first time since her liberation, she wondered if she might have been better served remaining as the Lady of the Door.

She thought of her mother and her sisters and the freedoms she had once known. She had lost too much to give up hope now.

Her eyes burned, and soon tears formed and spilled down her cheeks. It shamed her to weep like a child, for she knew she should feel gratitude toward the gods for releasing her, finally, from the spell of the tree. She did not feel grateful; she felt alternately sad and furious. She wept until her tears turned cold. Then she stopped. Amazingly, and without her consent, her sorrow had lifted.

Above her, dark clouds had gathered as if to await her command. Shadows shrouded the outside porch, turning it into a cold and unfriendly place. "Be gone!" she cried; the clouds turned to mist before her eyes, the day again turned bright and warm.

The hairs on the back of her neck prickled; a shiver of excitement ran along the base of her spine. She gasped with astonishment, for she recognized what was happening. Her tears had called the clouds and then her command had dispersed them!

She managed to fill her hand with water by trapping moisture from the air, one drop at a time.

How long had she possessed this mysterious magic?

CHAPTER FIVE

Zeus kicked away the light summer covers and slipped from the bed where Hera slept. Her back was turned toward him; her nightie hiked up above the curve of her thighs. Her skin was olive-toned and usually very smooth, though during this pregnancy, her legs had grown large and avocado lumpy. He did not find her all that attractive.

Sunlight spilled through the sheers covering the small-paned windows. Zeus squinted, and then fumbled for the dark glasses he had set on the bedside stand the night before.

He hung the glasses lopsided over his nose and ears and tried to open his eyes, but the sting was too great. Despite several blinks, the burning did not lessen. Yesterday he'd had to ask his analyst to prescribe eye drops. After all, the mortal called himself a physician, and was supposed to know about such physical ailments.

Absently, Zeus reached for the bottle, then remembered with a twinge of aggravation that Hera had stowed all of his new medications away in the bathroom when she had "straightened things up" to make room for several blue plastic cases of baby wipes.

"Boils down to nothing more than sensitive eyes," his analyst had said. "You've probably seen too much and now your eyes are rebelling. The body begins to fight itself. Things like this happen to us all as we get older."

"Older," Zeus had said, accepting a plastic bag filled with sample eye drops, antacids, cortisone and hemorrhoid creams. "You must be thinking of someone else." A god did not *age* like wine left in a cask; he *blossomed* like a field of well-tended lilies.

"Got these free from the drug reps," his analyst had said about the samples. "But none of my patients ever needed them before. Mostly baby boomers. Guess things are changing, the graying of America and all."

"Thanks a lot," Zeus had said, then stiffed the fellow on his bill for spite. His analyst would most likely devote several sessions to talking about why payment was an important part of his treatment. The fellow had a lot of nerve charging a hundred and fifty dollars an hour. Good thing Zeus never paid any of it. He decided right then and there to cancel every one of his scheduled appointments. Whoever said that you got what you paid for was right.

He snapped his fingers, then snapped them again. He pulled on his bathrobe and tramped across the thick carpet to stand before the sink. The coolness of the silver faucet handles reminded him of a river. When the water warmed, Zeus splashed his hands and face, then tilted back his head to instill the eye drops.

The stinging stopped and he managed to blink and have a look around. Using magic he touched up his tan and reapplied hair to his head. He erased the wrinkle lines that had sneaked in overnight, saving a few around his eyes to make it look as if he were merry, and perhaps even kind.

A bothersome odor wafted up from the soap dish; Zeus looked down and realized Hera had thrown away his green deodorant soap, replaced it with something translucent and fruity smelling. His things were swept from the counter, crammed into one corner. She had taken all his wind-up toys from the drawers, replaced them with neatly stacked jars of cosmetics made from flowers and glass bottles filled with almond-scented oils. He looked through the cabinets until he spotted his favorite tin monkey. One of the cymbals was bent to the side. As if that were not bad enough, the key was missing.

That Hera. He started to scream out her name, but thought better of it, and drummed his fingertips on the tile-top counter, displeased about so many changes coming all at once. This was not what he had wanted when he agreed to give it another shot. She was trying to take over, just like she always did. It was as if he were being shoved aside, his wishes, his desires, all much less important than his wife's. Zeus grabbed the tin monkey and slipped it into his pocket. Pregnant or not, things had gone a little too far. He would not lose himself just to make things easier for her.

Clutching his eye drops and a roll of antacids, Zeus hurried from the bathroom and to the closet. There he agonized for several seconds over his choice of clothing for the day. Finally, he settled on his new linen suit with the pleated pants. He stuffed his floral tie into his pants pocket alongside the medications and tiptoed to the edge of the bed.

Hera had shifted positions to lie on her back. He looked at his wife, her eyelids still puffy from their argument the night before. They had argued over fatherhood, and the responsibilities that it entailed. Each had seen those responsibilities somewhat differently.

"I want something from you," she had said. "I want your promise to be more than the figurehead father that you've always been to your children. This is the new age," she said. "Men are active participants in raising their children."

To which he had answered, "I can't give you that, you know. I'm not like other fathers," but he had sensed that Hera was not being truthful, that the fatherhood issue was a ruse for whatever was *really* bothering her.

She had always wanted more from him than she had asked for, always expected him to know her mind without revealing its depths. Something was terribly wrong now and Hera was angry with him for not knowing. Damn if she'd make it easy on them both and fess up.

Zeus sometimes worried that what she really wanted was a different man, a better husband, a lesser god. He snapped his fingers together. Ridiculous, he thought. They didn't get any better than him.

Hera slept, covered from head to toe in a thin coating of one of her beauty creams that smelled and tasted of citrus and left her skin smooth and fragrant. She was quite passable when asleep, when at peace, or at least unable to be at odds with herself.

He reached out tentatively, thinking he would stroke the black hair that lay tangled on the pillow, but stopped himself midway, worried about waking her. There was something so humble, so vulnerable, about Hera when she slept. A tender feeling started in the pit of his stomach and spread through his chest, nagging at the very depths of his heart. He sighed and shook his head, then lowered himself to the mattress to tie his shoes.

They had gone to bed quite late the night before. Though it was nearing nine o'clock now, Zeus supposed Hera needed the extra rest, especially since (as she had confessed to him near the end of their argument) she was expecting multiple births. Her rosy lips pouted open and he watched her belly move beneath her thin nylon gown. She was hard and round like a basketball; her belly pushed out in spasms as their babies vied for a better position in utero.

Last night he had held his face close to her skin to listen for their heartbeats. Hera had assured him this would help him "bond" with the little brats. He had felt something sharp jab his cheek.

"An elbow," Hera had said, apologizing quickly.

Remembering the experience made him shudder.

Zeus sighed, and let Hera be, knowing now that she was sleeping for eight. He rose slowly and went to the kitchen to wet his dry throat. Porcelain bowls of fresh rose petals were set on the windowsill to dry, all a little too "femme" for his tastes. Tacked to the walls were two lists that Hera had written out, one of things for "Her" to accomplish, the other of things for "Him."

He could not help but notice that his to-do list was twice as long as hers.

1. Take Hera to Natural Childbirth class at the hospital.

2. Practice breathing exercises, at least twice.

3. Move the Nautilus out of the "nursery" to make room for the crib and changing table.

4. Have the maintenance man install metal screens to block the windows and keep the kids from flying out.

5. Take Hera to Bloomie's to purchase a layette.

6. Call Yellow Cab to ask if they can reserve minivan with eight built-in infant seats for the ride home.

7. Check with the White House about whether cloth vs. paper diapers pose the greatest threat to the environment.

8, 9, 10, 11 ... The list seemed without end.

Man, did he ever need a drink. Fuming, he saw that Hera had emptied out the last of his prized retsina, the very bottle he had swiped from some elderly peasants in the old country. She had stuffed an arrangement of dried straw flowers into the empty bottle. He snapped his fingers together, then dumped the flowers onto the counter and crushed them beneath a potholder. He brought the bottle to his nose, but could not smell any hint of the pungent wine, only the lemony metallic scent of dishwashing detergent, floral tape, and wire.

"Damn," he said, and felt his eyes stinging with rage. Without a trace of the old retsina, he would be unable to zap another bottle of the same. He struggled to remember the flavor; he had been drinking it for centuries and really should have been able to remember. Retsina was a common drink. Why did it seem so rare now that it was gone?

He tried to imagine how the flavors had been blended, the deep color and thick syrupy texture. He refilled the bottle by magic and poured himself a shot. Zeus brought the glass to his lips to take a swig, but the flavor was soapy, with a tinny aftertaste that made him retch.

He spat into the sink and cursed his wife. That enchanted bottle had traveled with him across time, country, and continent. What was she trying to prove by making his flat an "alcohol-free" home?

Last night she had called him selfish. "You don't pay enough attention to me. In fact you don't pay attention to anything," she had said. So this was her way of punishing him, the bitch.

He left the shot glass on the counter, then as an afterthought rinsed it and placed it in the dish drainer so she wouldn't carp about having to clean up after him. He tiptoed to the front door, where he opened his key ring and left his house and mailbox keys hanging on the hook beside the spares. She could have the rent-controlled apartment.

"Here's looking at you, kid," he said. Zeus blew her a kiss before walking out.

The one-way street was still crowded with cars, taxis, and buses, all headed south toward Wall Street. He waved to the Oracle, and tossed a bill his way, but didn't stop to chat. No time to hear the old man's blathering. He was making his escape, and the last thing he needed now was a distraction.

Cooking was so mindless a task that Alexander rather enjoyed it. The last thing he wanted to do was think. Cooking was an act of meditation, and it relaxed him. The grill was a needed constant in his life. A hamburger always cooked in eight minutes. Bacon—crisp—cooked in three. Eggs over easy cooked in half the time of toast. The grill could be depended upon, could be easily understood.

His work at the Parthenon Diner began at six in the morning and ended after three in the afternoon. His uniform was white pants and a short-sleeved white shirt, a cook's hat, black shoes. The mornings were frantic, but the crowds thinned by 10:00 A.M.; midmorning had become his favorite part of the day.

It was hot attending to the grill; his black hair was soggy and heavy with sweat that pulled his hat snug against his forehead. The screen door was open, but only a whiff of fresh air dribbled in from the outside. Alexander found the giggling sound of frying fat quite cheerful. He smiled, for the moment feeling perfectly content, and flipped the potatoes and seared the steak.

It was nearly 10:30. He faced the shiny wall behind the cooktop, wiped his brow with a napkin. He took a step to his left to peer out the pass-through window and survey the nearly empty restaurant. The waitress, Lilac, was clearing a spot at the counter for Father Constantine, who stopped by every now and then for coffee and a Danish. She walked back to the kitchen, smiled with full lips painted a garish shade of pink, said, "How's that breakfast special coming along, big guy?"

She was terribly flirtatious and he felt sorry that it was wasted on him. Lilac was much too young. Besides, it had barely been a year since his divorce. He wasn't ready.

"Almost," he said, "almost."

"Anything I can do to hurry things along?" she asked, leaning closer.

Alexander shook his head. "There's the Father," he said, nodding toward the flash of black. "Bet he'd like real cream for that coffee." Alexander opened the cooler, took a quart of cream from the shelf, poured some into a small ceramic pitcher.

"Honestly," Lilac said with a sigh. She grabbed the cream and wiped up the spill with a slender finger. "All the good men are queers." She blew him a kiss and left.

He shrugged, but saw no reason to correct her. Better she should think there was something wrong with him than with her. But oh, at times he was so lonely. He watched her work the tables through the pass-through window.

A man he had known from his days with the architectural firm walked in and called out his order: the breakfast special. He folded his newspaper and sat at the counter. He bent his head to peer into the pass-through window, smiled. He called into the kitchen, "Hey Alex! You read about the 'Simplicity' movement? In the *Times*? Seems the yuppies have started to feel guilty about being privileged. So they're giving up their jobs and trying to simplify their lives."

Alexander shook his head, pushed a plate of steak and potatoes through the window and rang the bell to signal Lilac that her order was waiting.

"So, Alex," said the man, "You're in that 'Simplicity' movement, right? What do you have to feel guilty about?"

"I'm not in any movement," said Alexander.

The man was a fool. It was hard to believe they had once shared the same office, during a time when Alexander had worn starched shirts and shiny shoes and thought he had all the answers.

"Too bad," said the man. "Better to suffer for a reason."

Alexander shrugged. He liked being able to scrape down the grill with his spatula, the way it came clean at the end of every day. He liked that every morning, when he started work, there was nothing left to remind him of the day before. The laundry was sent out, stains and accidents removed, sent back. His clothes began crisp and white, and once soiled, were no longer his responsibility. He liked facing the wall, how that limited his contact with the overly cheerful waitress and too-chatty customers, how he saw enough of his shadow on the wall to know that he was real.

Simplicity. There *was* something to it after all. A life full of complications could only bring unhappiness.

Take his neighbor, Mrs. Zeus. She had reconciled with her husband, gotten pregnant, and moved into his building several months ago, perhaps not entirely in that order. She wasn't happy, and neither was her husband.

He pictured Mrs. Zeus, her round belly, her swollen breasts, her full lips. When she laughed, the noise shook the halls. She was one of the most alive women he had ever met—seemingly unafraid of anything. It embarrassed him to feel attracted toward her. It wasn't rational, it wasn't even sexual. After all, she was another man's wife, and besides, not his type. Too brassy. Too vulgar. Too selfish. The anti-Alexander, he thought with a laugh. Still, there was something quite enchanting about her. The babies were due any day now, and her husband had all but said he didn't care. What a waste, Alexander thought, to have children one cared little about.

Father Constantine poked his head around the door and said, "Will we be seeing you at services?"

He always asked, and Alexander always smiled, raised his hands as if holding up a weight, and said, "No." The church was no longer a part of his life and the old man knew that.

Father Constantine said, "We'll be there next week," and Alexander said, "I'm glad to know that," and waved good-bye. He envied the priest for his ability to believe that there was a higher purpose.

After the lunch crowd had left and the kitchen was put pretty much back in order, Alexander took his break. He fried up thinly sliced strips of steak and even thinner slices of onions and when the onions were almost translucent, he added mushrooms and cut open a couple of hoagie rolls to brown in the juice. He took out a tray, silverware, two amber glasses filled with milk. He scooped out salads and piled the sandwiches thick with fixings, cut them into halves. Then he went out to the back to eat.

It stank like the day before garbage pickup, but he had learned, for the most part, to ignore the smell. One could get used to anything by ignoring it.

The Oracle was already waiting, as usual. He had set out the milk crates in a small circle, a symbol of the unbroken chain of life.

Alexander nodded his hello and waited for the Oracle to tell him where to sit.

The Oracle pointed to the crate nearest to the door, said, "Sit down. Set the food down next to you. What do we get today, anyway?" he asked.

Alexander said, "You tell me."

The Oracle smiled, but he cheated, looked at Alexander's tray before guessing, "Steak sandwiches?"

Alexander said, "Is there anything you don't know?" and the Oracle got a wistful look on his face and said, "I don't know how to pick the horses."

Alexander said, "Perhaps racing doesn't come under the heading of fate," and the Oracle shrugged.

They ate. Alexander started with his salad in order to save his sandwich for last. He would have done more for the old man, if the Oracle had allowed it. Given him a place to live, clean clothes, breakfast and dinner as well as lunch.

The Oracle said, "I'll be leaving soon. Big journey."

"Will you be back?" Alexander asked. He would miss him.

"Oh yeah. Sure. But don't worry, you'll be taking a journey, too. To the mountain. Sooner or later, that's where we all end up. An 'It is written' sort of thing." He sighed. "You can't fight the power of symbols. Ever read Joseph Campbell?" The Oracle took the last bite of his sandwich and finished his milk. He picked up the salad bowl, frowned, rooted through the lettuce as if searching for something lost, set the bowl back down and looked at Alexander's plate. "You gonna eat the rest?" he asked.

Alexander said, "Trade?" and swapped half his sandwich for a bowl of salad he would leave for the rats.

The Oracle looked thoughtful. "One morning you'll wake up and know it's time," he said. "You'll seek out destiny, and I'll see you there. We'll do lunch."

"I worry about you," said Alexander.

"That's the problem," said the Oracle. "Worrying about things you can't do nothing to change." He stood, stretched his arms. "That's what strangles us. Me, I'm gonna die and I know that. Already found me a replacement. Near the mountain. Young kid. Got nothing better to do than take my place. Them's the best kind of folk to hold the world together."

"I wish I could hold the world together," said Alexander. He was serious.

"That's why you're unfit," said the Oracle. Anyone wants the job's not qualified. Rules, you know. I didn't make them."

"Who did?" Alexander laughed bitterly.

"That's the question," said the Oracle. "You learn the answer, you pass Go. You collect your hundred dollars."

"Two hundred," said Alexander.

"The amount isn't what's important. If you're smart, you take whatever you can get and ask no questions."

"I have to ask questions," said Alexander. He picked up the empty dishes and the dirty silverware. "I have to try to find the answers, even if there are none."

"You'll get over it," said the Oracle, "or maybe not. Problem with you is you don't know when to quit. Problem with you," said the Oracle, "is that you're afraid to give up, afraid of what happens once you realize there's no hope."

"There has to be hope," Alexander said. "Rules." He helped the old man to stand. "Anything else I can bring you before you go?" he asked.

The Oracle scratched his head. He gave Alexander a thoughtful look before breaking into a toothy smile. "Since you're pestering me I will take a dollar or two, if you don't mind, but just in case I run into any beggars."

Alexander walked him around the alley to the street, handed him some bills from his wallet.

"Don't pay any attention to what I said before," said the Oracle.

"What did you say?"

"About there being a problem? You knew I was just kidding, right? There is no problem with you," the Oracle said. He waved good-bye and hobbled off down the street.

🜚

Zeus clutched his briefcase and felt like a boy on the first day of school. Snapping the fingers of his free hand, he hurried away from the apartment, toward a twenty-four-hour live sex parlor that served pretty good donuts and coffee. "Got a busy day ahead of me," he told the proprietor, and ordered two cherry jelly-filleds and one cinnamon cruller with a double Irish coffee to go.

He ate quickly, amused and repelled by the idea of the king of the gods resorting to fast food and a subway getaway. He was a shadow of himself; there had to be more than this. He could barely keep open his eyes against the brightness of the day.

A man wearing a dirty raincoat was sprawled across the closest bench, surrounded in a sea of brown bags and broken wine bottles. Zeus snapped his fingers, calming down enough to turn the man into a return-for-deposit soda can. He conjured up a small gale to clear the air, covered the bench in oak leaves, and sat down, exhausted.

Zeus caught it then, the scent of the forest, an innocent and clean scent that reminded him of young love, of first love unblemished by unreasonable expectation. Flashes of visions from a time when he was invincible rushed through him like flooding waters, and left him empty with longing. He inhaled deeply, then stood up on his toes, closed his eyes and strained to fortify himself with the power of his memories. He pictured a girl, a young girl, with powers of her own, though she had not yet come into them.

Ahh yes, he thought. No matter how much time had passed, how well he remembered the sweetness of that afternoon. How pure the love that belonged to him and him alone. Now, what was her name? Pinea? Or Pyrrhea? Or something that started with a "P"? Zeus opened his eyes and stood quietly on the platform to await the train heading north.

He caught the scent again and smiled. He wondered if it was the same maiden, or if another was calling him. A pang of guilt twisted around his stomach as he pictured Hera, still sleeping, but he quickly put all thoughts of her out of his mind. A god could not fulfill his potential with the needs of others weighing him down. He lifted up his head and concentrated with all his being to track the maiden's scent. Then he felt the warm glow emanating from the chain he had tied around her neck. How clever he had been to mark her with his trinket.

He found it again, the woodland scent, fruity, moist, and alive. He reached out his hand and felt a vibration pounding in the air beneath his skin that told him a woman was calling to him, a woman and a new life he desperately needed to find. The time for change had come. He emptied out his pockets: the artificial tears, the pills for heartburn, the tie and monkey toy. Aided by the tin key and mechanical workings, the monkey played its drum and cymbals.

"This isn't real," he called, and watched until the toy wound down. He finally understood that the feeling in his heart was more, much more, than simply something in the air.

CHAPTER SIX

When Hera opened her eyes, the sun had risen to the level of the highest pane of glass. Rainbows danced across the sheets and covers, breaking into vibrant drops of color that splashed over the carpeting and walls. Hera squinted at the light streaming through the window. The highest level of pain, she thought, knowing that any second now she would begin labor.

Every inch of her felt overripe, ready to burst. "Kopros!" she said in a growl.

Her breasts were huge, hard and warm, her cheeks puffy and red, her legs swollen and tender.

She rolled herself into a semiupright position and went over her story one more time. "I don't know how it happened," she would tell Zeus. "It was dark. I'd been drinking. He didn't say his name ... I thought it was you in disguise," she said. "You know, the way we used to do it in the old days."

If she couldn't successfully lie to her own husband, she didn't know who she could fool.

She belched and shook her head, disgusted with how her body had taken on a life of its own. Her tits had more red lines than an audited tax return. Her lower back pulsed with pain; she used both hands to press against her sacrum, which made only a small dent in the discomfort. The babies had dropped during the night and now pressed against her bladder. Kopros, she hated this part.

She took a long, slow breath, and tried to remember from her last pregnancy what came next after this.

Oh yeah, more pain. Great.

"Zeus," she called in a cajoling tone of voice, a little perturbed that he was taking his time in the bathroom when she had to pee. Her bladder felt like it was being compressed by a black hole. He'd better look out because the big bang was about to happen.

"What are you doing, hon?" she called. She checked the clock— nearly four in the afternoon.

When he didn't answer, she pushed one hand into the bed, held her belly for support, and shakily stood up. By Jove, this was gross. Another day, she told herself, before it would all be over.

"Are you there?" she asked.

A burning pain spread upward from her thighs. Deep breath,

she reminded herself. "Zeusy. I need to use the potty." She trudged away from the bed, feeling huge, barely able to lift her swollen feet off the carpet. Tiny sparks flared as her soles rubbed against the nylon fibers.

The only thing that still fit was a Day-Glo orange muumuu, and she slipped it over her shoulders, leaving her nightie on the floor. She pounded her fist on the closed door. "Let me in!"

She tore the handle off the door and pushed her way inside. The drawers were pulled open; bandages and hairbrushes lay strewn over the floor. Zeus had removed the medicines from the cabinet and piled them haphazardly on the counter. He had stuffed the toilet full of baby wipes despite the fact that the cases were clearly marked with warnings of "DO NOT FLUSH!" This sabotage forced Hera to pee, squatting in the bathtub. She'd never forgive him for this!

The old god had abandoned her. Some things never changed. She glared into the mirror so hard it shattered into a thousand pieces; she could not remember feeling so alone.

In a while there was a violent pounding at her front door. She noticed her reflection in the mirror, her hair sticking out like Medusa, her face wrinkled like a cauliflower. She was sweating hailstones. She screamed, a guttural, inhuman wail, and found it easy to ignore the pounding at the door, though it increased in tempo with each of her successive screams. At last she managed to call out, "What do you want? By Jove! Leave me alone!"

The pounding continued and a deep voice managed to penetrate through the walls. "Mrs. Zeus, it is me!"

The voice belonged to her six-foot-plus Greek neighbor, a quiet short-order cook named Alexander. The one she had been planning to lust after, once her sex drive returned. She had been quietly enchanting him when Zeus wasn't looking and, naturally, he was devoted to her.

"Is everything okay?" he asked.

"No, goddamm it, everything is not okay!" Hera yelled. She reached out her arm and swept the counter, pushing everything onto the floor in a clatter. A glass bottle, half-filled with a thick pink antacid, wept over her feet.

"Mrs. Zeus," he said in gentle warning.

She kicked a bottle out of her way and stormed from the bathroom, pulling pictures down from the wall as she struggled to reach the front door, not caring what she looked like. If Alexander turned to stone once he saw her—good riddance.

But Alexander, still dressed in a starched white apron stained by coffee, catsup, and grease, only scratched his forehead, shook his head, and took a step back.

"I guess you are ready to have your babies," he said. He rolled his white shirtsleeves up above his elbows. "Is Mr. Zeus at home?"

"No, dammit!" she screamed, and kicked a small hole in the plaster the size of a football. "He's not at home, that lying sack of sheep 'nads."

Alexander nodded. He removed his apron and folded it into quarters. His shirt was wrinkled from sweat, his pants worn from where he had rubbed his hands a bit too low on his apron. He smoothed back a lock of shiny black hair from his forehead. "So I will take you, now," he said.

"Normally, I'd accept your gracious invitation, but right now? I don't think so!" She lunged toward him until she managed to grip his dark neck in her talons. Her nails were painted blood red and she dug them into his tender flesh with vengeance.

"I don't want these fucking babies," she looked up into his face.

His cheeks reddened, his eyes bulged, but Alexander calmly patted her hands with his until she relaxed her grip. He pried her fingertips away.

"Yes, I know. You do not want the babies," he said, "but you must have them, anyway. What else is there to do?"

She burst into tears and looked around for something, anything, to throw at him.

He patted her back when she started to scream. "Where are your house keys?" he asked, calmly.

She answered in obscenities.

"Where is your purse?" he persisted, so matter-of-fact that she wanted to kick his balls up into his eyes. He brushed past her, ignoring it when she kicked another hole in the wall, and came back after a few minutes, carrying her purse, a robe, slippers, a comb and toothbrush.

"Where is your husband?" he said very softly. He set the slippers before her and helped Hera step into her robe. He said, "Mr. Zeus should be here, at such a time."

"You think I don't know that?" she screamed, and kicked over a table.

He shrugged. "So, is your coffee maker and stove turned off?" he asked.

"Leave me alone," she wailed, but let him lead her out the door and into an elevator with liver-brown carpeting that made her feel even more nauseated. Hera pressed the emergency button and let herself scream louder than the blast from the alarm. She screamed again and pulled down a strip of wallpaper. The highest level of pain, Hera thought, knowing she had yet to reach it.

CHAPTER SEVEN

Eddie didn't like it when new things happened. He liked it much better when everything stayed the same. On weekdays he got up at seven and took a long hot bath before going downstairs in his robe to eat his cereal. Next, he did the dishes, first his, and then his dad's. Then he cleaned up the kitchen real good until it was time to watch *Sesame Street.* He never told anyone how much he liked *Sesame Street* and Mr. Rogers, too; they would have told him he was too big to watch it. People always said stuff like that to him. But Mr. Rogers was a lot like his dad, and besides, Eddie did not believe you could be too big for anything.

He would have watched even more TV, except his dad always said that watching it would give him cancer, and he didn't want to get cancer because if he did then he'd be dead just like his mother and then his dad would have to live all alone until *he* was dead, and Eddie didn't think his dad would like that very much. So it was better not to watch any more TV, even though he wanted to. After all, Eddie was an adult now, and his dad said adults had to be responsible.

On Saturday morning he would wash all the clothes and wash his bath towel. He had always washed the clothes on Saturday mornings, except that one time, maybe six months ago, when his dad forgot to bring home the Tide, and made Eddie wait until Sunday afternoon. He wasn't supposed to wash clothes on Sunday afternoon, so it was very upsetting. Sunday was the Lord's Day, the day Eddie went to church and ate salads made with red Jell-O, sour cream, and canned grapes at his neighbor's house.

These days he made triple-sure his dad wouldn't forget to bring home the Tide. Every Monday, he checked inside the box to see if it had gotten low since the last time he had used some, and when it did get low, Eddie drew a note for his dad, placing a red check mark beside a hand-colored picture of the orange box.

Then he put that note up on the refrigerator with Scotch Tape and remembered to put the Scotch Tape back in the drawer by the potholders because putting things away was as important as using them in the first place. After his dad got home from work, Eddie would show him the note and remind him about the laundry at least three times every day until his dad remembered to bring home the

Tide. Then and only then would Eddie throw the note away and be able to relax.

Today was Wednesday. After *Sesame Street*, Eddie showered and shaved and got dressed. He wore his brown leather belt and tucked his short-sleeved shirt inside his pants. He wore his brown socks. His Converse sneakers were always black. He put his dirty underwear in the laundry hamper and brushed his teeth, and while he was still in the bathroom, picked up his towel from the floor and hung it over the rack to dry for tomorrow. He wiped his glasses clean on the hand towel.

He had three more days to go until Saturday morning.

It was almost time to go to work. Eddie liked to go to work exactly on time. He looked at his watch and waited for the big hand to touch the "9," then he locked the door and started down the street.

It took three hundred and twenty-four steps to get to work. Three hundred and fifty-two steps if he counted going to the back room where the punch clock was. Eddie took his card from the rack and waited for the big hand to be at the "12" and the click that meant it was now time to punch in. The clock always told him exactly what to do. He punched in and put his card back on the rack. Then he took his special white apron from the rack and tied it with a double knot around his back.

"Hello, son," said his dad, coming into the room. His dad had to go to work much earlier than Eddie, and stay much later, too.

"Hi, Dad," said Eddie. He always felt so happy to see his dad.

There was a calendar on the wall with pictures of different puppy dogs each month. His dad had given Eddie a red felt pen to mark off the day because that way, Eddie always knew what day it was. Today was Wednesday. Tomorrow would be Thursday. Tomorrow would be two days away from doing laundry.

One thing Eddie didn't like about his job was never knowing what day he might have to go out and do a delivery for a customer. His dad always said, "There's nothing to be done about that," so Eddie tried not to complain. He looked at the calendar again. "Dad," he said, "do you think I'll have to do any deliveries today?"

His dad chuckled and said, "No telling, Eddie. I'll have to let you know a little later."

Eddie had known he would say that.

"Tell me as soon as you know," he said, and his dad smiled and patted him on the back.

Another thing that bothered Eddie about his job was that he

never knew exactly what day his friend Possum would come into town to do his shopping. He only knew the day was coming soon because it was near the end of the month, and Possum always came before the new month came. Possum would buy groceries and ask Eddie to deliver them. Eddie would borrow a horse from Mr. Fletcher and ride to Possum's cabin. He never got lost. Eddie looked at the calendar and counted up the days.

There was only one week left before the next month would start. When it got close to the end of each month Eddie always asked his dad when Possum was coming and his dad always looked at the calendar, always scratched his forehead as he pulled his lips into an uneven smile and said, "Any day now, Eddie. Any day now." But that could mean a Monday or a Tuesday or a Wednesday or a Thursday or a Friday or a Saturday or even a Sunday, so what good was the answer?

Still, he had to ask. "When is Possum coming, Dad?" Eddie knew his dad didn't know the answer

"Any day now, Eddie," said his dad. When the old man smiled his eyes narrowed and gave him an almost serious look.

Eddie nodded solemnly. He worried that Possum might come on the wrong day, and make him deliver groceries on Saturday morning when he was supposed to do the laundry. "I wash the laundry on Saturday mornings," he reminded his dad.

"I know," his dad said. "Don't worry. Things always work out."

Eddie tried hard not to worry, but that was just about impossible when he had so many responsibilities.

He swept the stock room floor and cut up boxes for recycling. He moved the milks to the front of the cooler, then went to check the customer bathrooms to make sure they had enough toilet paper. He washed his hands after, even though he didn't use the toilet. One time, about a year ago, he had checked to see if there was toilet paper but not washed his hands. Waiting on the other side of the door was the crabby cash register lady, who said, "Did you wash your hands? I didn't hear the water running!" and made him feel stupid.

Since then, Eddie had figured it was simpler to make sure to turn on the sink so that anyone who was waiting on the other side of the door would hear the water running.

Sometimes you just had to do things that didn't make any sense and that's the way it was.

Possum left his cabin and walked a couple of miles toward the mountain. Past the edge of his property, he clambered down to the gravel road leading to the highway. He was trying something new: walking with his face forward, trying to ignore his heightened sense of anxiety. He rather liked seeing what was ahead of him. It made him somewhat dizzy, yet seemed to make the journey go a little faster. Which was good. Ever since Penelope had arrived, his inner voices had retreated. Without the voices, or Penelope at his side, he couldn't ignore the fact that he was utterly alone.

He couldn't wait to reach town and get rid of the strange little carving. It made his skin prickle; he could feel it moving beneath the layers of newspaper, feel the river rage and the clouds blow and the tall firs sway in the wind.

After walking less than a mile, he started to sweat and become short of breath. His chest burned and his heart thudded. He managed to calm himself only after turning to walk backwards. When he reached the boardwalk, he waved at the town locals who had already seen him coming long before he could see them. He heard their whispers. No one was intentionally mean; they just couldn't understand him. He walked backwards into the gallery and walked backwards past the counter until he found himself face to face with his benefactor.

Mr. Bringle was delighted, as always, to see Possum. He was a pale man, thin in face and chest, with a shock of straight white hair and a diamond stud in his left earlobe. He dressed all in white; even his belt buckle was carved pearl. His white mustache was waxed and shaped like a fern frond.

"Nice to see you again! What have you brought me today?" asked Mr. Bringle.

Possum hesitated for a moment before setting down his pack on the lush carpet. The carpeting was white, his pack gray with dust. To set it down was to contaminate purity with filth. He looked to Mr. Bringle for guidance.

"Go ahead!" said Mr. Bringle. "Live a little."

"Thank you," Possum said. He smiled at the joke. He unwrapped one of the jams and passed it forward. While Mr. Bringle exclaimed and *oohed* and appreciated the treat, Possum unwrapped the pencil drawing and waited modestly for Mr. Bringle to finish with his acclaim.

"Oh, isn't that delightful!" said Mr. Bringle. He sounded disappointed.

Possum hesitated. With another mouth to feed, he might need

more money. "There's something else," he said at last. "I'm not sure I want to sell it." He unwrapped the small carving, feeling sneaky and guilty, but also curious about its value.

Mr. Bringle set the Water Street drawing on his counter. He took out a magnifying glass to examine the other piece. "It's beautiful," he said. "Absolutely amazing! A kinetic carving! I've never seen anything quite like it! A new interpretation of *plein air.*"

"What's that?"

"A type of art, popular some time ago. Painting the outdoors, natural settings ... landscapes and the like. What you have here is the kinetic version. Quite an improvement. Utterly charming."

Possum nodded in agreement. Charming. The wood was charmed. Why was it still so difficult to believe in magic, given everything that had happened? He stared at the woodland scene, now replete with river waters that rushed forward at the blink of an eye. A dark cloud hovered menacingly in the background. The cloud moved forward, too, and as Possum watched he had a premonition that the carving was not his to sell. It belonged to Penelope.

"This could fetch a pretty penny," Mr. Bringle said. "I've a good feeling about this new style. I hope you'll do more like it"

Except that Possum could not sell it. "Never mind," Possum said. "I've changed my mind. It's not for sale. Sorry."

Mr. Bringle raised an eyebrow and looked as if he were about to say more. He opened his mouth, then closed it just as suddenly with a small *pop.* After a bit he said, "Fine. This will be fine," and took out three one hundred dollar bills. "Bring me more when you have it. Something with a bit more substance perhaps. Like that cherry wood piece. I understand your not wanting to sell the prototype. Make me another one like it when you can."

Possum thanked him and pocketed the money. Carefully, he wrapped the little carving in paper and cushioned it inside his pack. He turned and walked backwards out the door to complete his errands. Behind him, he felt something stir, and he knew a storm brewed in the small kinetic carving, and the winds bowed the trees forward enough that their branches scratched across his back.

◈

Penelope ate a cold lunch of chewy jerky and even chewier crackers, crisp green apples picked a little too early, and water flavored with a slice of dried lemon rind. Possum was forever apologizing for the plainness of the food he had on hand. He never believed her when she tried to reassure him that everything was wonderful. The tastes and textures of the simplest things, even an old potato from the cellar fried with an onion, was a heavenly delight when compared to the bland taste of wood pulp that had lingered in her mouth for thousands of years. Possum had promised to bring her something he called chocolate, something he promised was the embodiment of the taste of joy. She smacked her lips together in anticipation.

She used the outhouse again before returning to her favorite spot on the outside porch. If only she could have remembered the words or a bit of the music, Penelope would have sung a ballad or two, but her memories of those days frolicking in a meadow were too foggy. She wondered if Possum knew any songs.

The tent canopy shielded her from the sun, perhaps a little more than she would have preferred. When Possum returned she would ask him to open the porch to the summer air. She was always a little cold these days. If there were a choice, Penelope would have preferred too much heat to a bit of chill. It felt good when her skin flushed, or rivulets of sweat ran down her back. It reminded her that she was alive.

She looked out to the line of the horizon and the meadow. She wanted more than anything to travel there, to stand once again in the presence of a river. She wanted to call out to its naiads and learn if anyone like herself was still alive. She doubted this, for she felt no sense of the presence of other magical beings.

Her heart filled with anticipation for the time, not far away, when she could travel on her own to the meadow. A couple more weeks, Possum had said, and the ground would be dry enough to travel on. And perhaps by next year he would extend the trail to the meadow so that she could travel there year round.

She heard a whooshing sound not far above her. A white and gray mottled nighthawk came from nowhere and landed in the field beside her. It flapped its wings, then folded them up into its body. A feather floated to her and landed in her lap. The nighthawk looked at Penelope with one cold gray eye, the other covered by the flap of a sunken lid.

She gasped, amazed and a little afraid.

They stared at each other. Sunlight glittered off the nighthawk's eye. There was a brilliant flash that left a prickly heat upon her neck. She lost her vision and saw only blackness; her hands felt leaden. There was a sensation of sinking, then of being entombed, followed by vivid memories of terror of her years in silence.

The gods had found her out and were punishing her for claiming her own destiny. "No!" she screamed. "Go away!" She could not go through this again, being held prisoner for a thousand years. "Let me die," she pleaded.

The breeze picked up and stroked her cheek. *Don't give up*, said the voice of the wind.

By concentrating, she was able to wiggle her fingers. In a while, she could lift her arms and open her eyes. How glorious that there was a world still there to view!

Listen and remember, said the wind. *Beware. There is danger. He will come for you again.*

The winds gusted and surrounded her with a beautiful ballet of spiraling leaves. And just as suddenly as it had appeared, the nighthawk vanished inside that whirlwind.

She pulled a length of string from her shirt and used it to tie the feather into her hair. As she looked into the sky, the winds took on the form of clouds.

She felt overcome by emotion. Tears formed and spilled over her eyelids. The wind picked up and swept through the tent; the nighthawk feather hummed.

Listen, said the wind.

She tried to understand its message.

The wind blew hard against the shaft of the feather, riffling through the barbs with heavy thudding like a sleepy child's footsteps. The wind closed off sound, as if its hands pressed tight against her ears. She could hear nothing of the outside world, only the beating of her pulse caught inside a rush of wind. A breeze blew across her forehead and stung her eyes. Everything became blurred, like a world viewed from the underside of a waterfall.

She tried to call out, but the wind masked her voice so well that even she could not hear herself speaking.

Suddenly, there was thunder and the scent of wet grass and a gentle plopping as the first drops hit the canopy, followed by another, and another. Rain thudded like galloping horses. Clouds turned brown, like paper just beginning to catch fire. In a matter of minutes the sky had grown smoke black.

The river rose as small tributaries emptied into it; underground springs overflowed, flooding the meadow.

Penelope blinked away tears until her vision cleared. The once dry crevices in the ground had filled with water and the golden grasses had turned green at their edges, softening as new life flowed into the valley. The promise of a pathway disappeared beneath a mud flow. Penelope watched her freedom drown in the downpour, wondering if she would ever leave this place on her own.

🦋

Penelope wheeled herself up the ramp and inside. Despite the hard work of movement and the muggy warmth of the summer rain, she was shivering. She slipped off her wet things and hung them over a chair to dry. She pulled her down comforter from the bed and wrapped it tightly around her, with a longing gaze toward the hearth. An open fire could so quickly get out of hand; she dared not risk it, no matter how cold the cabin. Still, it would be nice. Would she ever be able to trust her own magic to save her? Maybe sometime later, she thought, but not yet.

How much magic of the Old World had managed to survive into the New? Very little, from the look of things. Possum had assured her that the gods lived no more, at least he'd never heard of them. If magic had survived, it had evolved into a disembodied spirit under the universe's control.

But now she knew differently. Zeus lived. Not only that, but she sensed he would find her.

She wheeled herself to the front window to gaze out in the direction Possum had gone. There was snow on the top of the mountain. Her teeth chattered. Was this what it felt like to be lonely?

Sad.

Bored.

Cold.

She decided to fire up the stove and make herself a cup of tea.

The chair barely fit through the doorway leading into the alcove. Wood and matches were stored in a box elevated on the seat of a chair. She checked the flue, and loaded a bit of crumpled paper and the wood into the stove's side door, and lit that with a match. Possum had thoughtfully left the kettle full of water on the griddle. She waited with her hands close to the stovepipe for the water to simmer.

A low shelf held her most commonly used supplies. She measured loose tea into a strainer, and used a mitt to hold the kettle as she carefully poured water into her cup. This part always scared her just a little, the worry over spilling and the likelihood of seriously burning herself.

Would that really be so terrible? Sometimes she doubted that.

Perhaps she would finally be able to feel something, anything, again, even if that *thing* was pain?

But there were no guarantees. Maybe it would be worse to hurt oneself without knowing it. Her uncertainty over the matter only made her cautious.

As the tea steeped to a dark brown color it released the fragrance of cinnamon and oranges into the air. These were sweet scents that should have been enough, she knew. It wasn't. She added too much sugar, according to Possum, and stirred the syrupy mixture with a spoon. Heat from the cup warmed her hands, the tea warmed her belly, and the sweet flavors warmed her spirit. For the moment she felt content.

Warmed at last, Penelope sat before the mirror to brush her hair. She stared at the image of her unlined face, and pinched her cheeks in a futile attempt to bring out some color. Possum had told her she was beautiful, as soft and fair as water. At the time the compliment had backfired, and left her feeling insubstantial and invisible.

Her necklace glowed like a sun-lit raindrop and brought her a pleasurable shudder. She had almost forgotten what it meant to be a naiad. Water was beautiful—clear, smooth—with powers to cleanse, to renew, to nourish life, or to destroy it. The comforter fell away from her shoulders and her hand dropped to her breast. She cupped it as Possum had done, then played with the nipple until it grew hard between her fingers. She lost track of the passage of time and of the room and of her wheelchair as she caressed her belly, then slowly let her hand drop to the downy hairs concealing the entrance to her womb. She brought her fingers to the cleft of her vulva. She closed her eyes. Her heart pounded. The memory of him thrusting inside of her left her breathless.

She remembered his face, lost in ecstasy. A grimace like pain that had meant something else entirely. His hands had touched her everywhere, gliding over her skin like a waterfall.

She licked her lips, imagining he was there to kiss them. The memory of his desire and his desperate need for her made her smile with excitement and delight. He could not have gone on living without possessing her. "I love you," he had whispered. "I love you."

She moaned. She loved him also, utterly, madly.

Her vagina shuddered with pleasant contractions.

But soon the image of his handsome face was replaced by the image of another just as desperate.

Zeus. Moaning. Thrusting. Whispering his devotion. Letting her know he could not have gone on living without possessing her.

She had loved him also, utterly, madly!

Her breath caught in her throat. She gasped. The room came slowly into focus. She saw her reflection: a woman naked as a baby, sprawled indelicately in her chair. Her body was flushed, her long hair wild and clinging to her skin.

She lifted her hand and stared at her own moist fingers. The revelation at how easy it was to mistake the pleasures of the body with those of love left her not only confused, but afraid.

Did she really love Possum? Or did she love the act of his body melting into hers?

She could no longer be sure of what she really felt. She wanted to cry, but did not want the clouds to gather and bear witness to her shame. She brought up her hand to finger the teardrop charm out of habit, but pulled back her fingers immediately, for the gold was hot to her touch. She could smell something burning—the chain would soon leave a scar on her skin. She was being branded, marked as property. "No!" she screamed. Despite the pain, she managed to pull the chain from her neck. Now and only now did she remember.

"Wear this ever after," Zeus had said to her. "And I shall ever be able to find you."

She laughed. How long it had taken her to recognize his promise as it really was: a warning!

So, he lived still. And he would come for her. Perhaps, she hoped, Zeus would not find her quite so easy a mark as before.

Zeus had never loved her. Somehow, this came as no surprise. But had she loved him? Sure, she had been filled with lust and infatuation and maybe rebellion. Was it possible that all she had loved was the idea of being in love?

Because now she understood love. Because of Possum.

She wheeled herself to the window and flung the teardrop necklace as far as she could. "There!" she said. Where the weeds devoured the necklace, a small flame burst up, then smoldered out, leaving a dark circle behind.

She squinted, anxious for Possum to return.

Penelope smiled, but still she worried. Was she really free of Zeus's spell?

CHAPTER EIGHT

Hera awoke, groggy, fingers numb. Her lips were stuck together as if they'd been glued shut. She felt empty, as if every vital fluid had drained out, leaving her a brittle shell. She found herself strapped to the bed with a cream-colored canvas restraint that squeezed her waist. Her head was propped up on two hard plastic-covered pillows at an angle that pinched her neck. Her mouth tasted dry and hairy, as if she had just chewed the fur from the front half of a rat. The room smelled of mouthwash, rubbing alcohol, and piss, unsuccessfully masked by some vaguely floral hospital perfume.

A fluorescent light glowed from somewhere behind her, casting a dim blue tint to what she could see of her skin. If she felt any pain, at least she was too drugged to recognize it. She could not feel her legs. For all she knew, they had amputated her body from the waist down.

Having just accepted the thought of a future without her lower half, she became aware of a dull pulse emanating from her belly and spreading down to her thighs. Someone was playing the bongos in her womb. Next her toes wiggled and her legs trembled. She felt hot, then cold. Apparently, despite her first impressions, she was still in one piece.

A thin cotton gown was slung over one shoulder, exposing both breasts. A drop of yellow fluid stood poised above one nipple. Colostrum, nature's signal that her milk would soon come in. A clear plastic tube led from a plastic bag into one arm; another tube, draining dark urine from below, lay across the bed beside one thigh.

Ahh, the joys of motherhood.

Then she noticed Alexander, sitting hunched over in a chair at the side of her bed. Hera had forgotten what it took to move her lips in order to talk to him. His eyes were closed and his dark lashes fluttered in sleep; she realized that communication at this stage was unlikely. Just as well. She drifted off to sleep.

When she awoke, the room was dark. She heard the whispering of nurses waft from the hallway into her room. Someone snored in the bed next to her, invisible behind a beige curtain suspended from the ceiling. Hera strained against her bonds, but was too weak to break them.

"Good morning, Mrs. Zeus," said Alexander.

"Is that really you? Can you untie me?" she whispered. She saw his shadow stir from the chair where he had been sitting. He really was a sweetheart for helping her out. Of course, she'd been casting charms of devotion since the day she met him, but even so.

He switched on an overhead lamp and when she looked into his dark eyes she sighed with utter relief to see him there with her. "Mrs. Zeus," he said. "You are awake at last."

"What happened to my babies?" Hera asked him.

Alexander said, "I'm so sorry."

Hera screamed, "What happened? Tell me!" and a nurse appeared and injected a yellow-tinged bolus into a bottle connected to the tube that led to Hera's arm. Drowsiness smothered her will to speak and she fought to keep her eyes open.

"You lost the babies," Hera heard Alexander whisper through the fog. "All but one. And that one, well, he is not the most beautiful of boys."

🦋

The next time Hera awakened, a child-sized nurse was sticking a thermometer under her armpit. Hera's breasts throbbed, overdue for a first milking. Her legs trembled and her teeth chattered. "What happened to my babies?" she asked.

The tiny nurse blanched. "Nobody told you?" She took a step away. "Do you mind waiting until I get my supervisor?" she asked, and turned away.

In a few minutes, the small nurse, led by a super-sized nurse in a sanitary-pad-white uniform. "May I help you?" asked the big nurse.

"Tell me what happened," asked Hera, trying to keep the tremble from her voice.

The big nurse stood at the foot of the bed and smoothed out a wrinkle from her starched skirt. "Your doctor should have explained," she said with a drawn out sigh. "You had a difficult delivery. They did everything they could, but seven of the babies just weren't strong enough to live. I'm sorry.

"Baby boy Zeus is in the neo-natal ward, and we think, with proper care, we think he's going to make it."

She could not believe what she was hearing. "I have to see him, now," Hera said in a whisper.

The big nurse placed her hand on Hera's shoulder. "Your doctor doesn't think that would be a good idea. They want to do some more tests on the baby," she said, fidgeting. "They're trying to determine the extent of his deformity. He's rather, um, unusual. There isn't even a name for what he's got, though right now, the pediatrician, Dr. Sanders, is thinking —Sanders's Syndrome."

Hera closed her eyes. Sanders's Syndrome? I don't think so. If this doctor thought that she or her offspring were no more than a textbook case, he had a thing or two to learn. Adrenaline pumped through her and she felt younger than she had in years. She was, after all, the goddess of fertility. Let them try to keep her from her offspring.

After the nurses left the room Hera dropped sixty pounds of flab and gave herself a full body tan and bleached hair. Magic was easy when you were this pumped up. She forced herself out of bed, threw on a tunic, grabbed her purse, and walked down the hall toward the nursery.

The walls of postpartum ward were flocked with little yellow ducky paper. Isn't this sweet, Hera thought as she approached the glass-walled room where the babies were displayed like packages of roast beef in a meat department.

Her heart pounded. Where was he, her monster baby? She scoured incubator after incubator, looking for her name on the card, until at last she saw where several nurses had gathered in a small anteroom off to one side.

A weasely little doctor held a small bundle at arm's length and thrust a stethoscope to its chest. The doctor had thin gray hair, gray eyebrows, and a bushy mustache; his lips were scrunched up and resembled a butthole. She knew somehow that the infant he held was her son.

The doctor set the bundle down and looked at the baby with an evil grin. He signaled for the nurse to take the baby and wrote something on the chart before turning to examine another infant.

Her son looked straight at her. His eyes were all iris, black, and framed by full dark lashes, and his tongue darted out, as if sniffing the air. When the nurse picked him up to hold against her shoulder for a burp, Hera saw he had a hunchback and scrawny brown wings that wrapped across his back like a cape. His tiny feet were shaped like hooves.

Despite his deformity, Hera was overcome with motherly love. Tears welled up in her eyes and she longed to hold the boy and sniff his hair. This had to be hormonal. He was gorgeous, so tiny, such a fighter. And he was hers, not theirs, to do with what she wanted. Let them have their own babies if they wanted to experiment.

The second the nurse was distracted by the telephone, Hera

waltzed into the nursery, feeling she had every right to be there. In the blink of an eye, she changed her son from a baby into a football. She picked up her little pigskin and held him under her arm, feeling momentarily disgusted. It was only an outer shell, she reminded herself. Inside, he was her son. She carried him in one arm into the hallway, but slowed when she noticed the weasely doctor watching her through the glass.

She read his nametag: Sanders.

He shook his head, obviously trying to place her as he gave her a look with his steely eyes.

She felt her resolve weaken and struggled to regain the upper hand. But giving birth had taken enough from her that now this mortal possessed more power than she. Queen of the gods or not, she felt trapped by the nature of the doctor-patient relationship. She must leave at once, before exhaustion overcame her and her magic faded.

The nursery was in an uproar as the staff discovered the missing Sanders's Syndrome baby.

Stay cool, she told herself. Don't attract attention. She began walking casually down the hall. When she turned the corner she transformed herself into a teenage waif and transformed her son into an electric guitar. She cradled the guitar in her arms and hurried toward the stairs.

She heard footsteps and shouting behind her.

Every muscle ached; each step sent a stabbing pain through her crotch because of the episiotomy. She bit her lip and pressed on, knowing she had return home before allowing herself to collapse. Her vision blurred as if she had soap in her eyes, but she kept going until she reached the outside. She shoved a nun out of her way to commandeer a taxi. It felt good to successfully challenge a competing system of belief, especially using violence.

"Home!" she screamed, giving him the address.

The driver left her at the front door of her apartment house. Her stitches pulled as she made her way up the steps, the guitar cradled in one arm. At the landing, the guitar grew soft and began to struggle. The boy was hungry and was nuzzling her breasts with his frets.

By now Hera was too exhausted to control him with magic. He returned to his infant form. God, he was ugly, but she loved him anyway. She patted his head and let him root at her chest. It was strange, nursing something with wings. If only she were the goddess of another religion she could proclaim him an angel and be done with it.

The boy's eyes closed, his mouth scrunched up to one side as he looked for sustenance. Her milk began to flow and her shirt grew moist. She felt herself change until she was herself again, a size sixteen dressed in the only thing that still fit: her horrid muumuu. She didn't dare go to her apartment—they probably had the address at the hospital. She paused at Alexander's place, and trying the door, found it open.

Rough terra cotta tile was laid diagonally on the hallway floor and the walls were covered with dark oak wainscoting. She carried her son into the living room and practically collapsed on an oversized plaid tweed couch. The squalling baby lay across her belly. He was warm, like a heating pad, which kept the pain of her afterbirth cramps from overwhelming her. His head smelled of Sweet William and summer days. She nuzzled her nose against the downy stubble.

She kissed his cheek and laughed as he opened his mouth. She pulled down the neckline to free a breast. The second she put him to her breast he began to suckle, and all the tension she had managed to damn up spilled over like a river flooding its bank. The feeling was intense enough that she wept, sobbed, moaned, and thrashed, until at last a sense of release took hold and Hera fell fast asleep.

It was nearly dark when Hera awakened; the baby was sleeping peacefully by her side. A teapot whistled in the kitchen.

"Alexander?" she called. "Is that you?"

"Yes," he said, and when she saw him standing in the doorway, she felt everything would turn out just like she hoped. He switched on the overhead light and dragged a leather chair beside her. With a nod he returned to the kitchen. He came back holding two porcelain cups. "Tea with honey and milk," he said.

"Thanks," she answered. How considerate.

"Mrs. Zeus," Alexander said, sitting down. He sipped his tea and she noticed he drank it black. "I had a feeling you would be here. I am glad that you feel so much better."

The sound of his voice made her want to hug him and she felt her face flush. She hated herself for feeling so emotional. "I must have given you quite a start," she said.

"No," he said. "I am happy you are safe. They are looking for you. They want to take your son back to the hospital."

"I can't stay here," she said. "That doctor will find me. We have to leave! Alexander, you must help me!" It was more than a request, though he couldn't have known that. Mortals never felt the magic.

"That doctor is not to be trusted, but are you ready to travel?" he said.

"I have to go. If he finds me, I can't fight him."

"I will accompany you. You will need help."

"That's right. I'll need help."

"Such a rough time you had. You screamed and cursed and made it all sound terrifying."

"My mouth," Hera said in a falsely coy voice. "You must think me quite common."

"Oh no," he said, smiling proudly. "What a woman says when she makes love and when she gives birth is not for the ears of mortal man."

Hera hid her grin behind her teacup. We'll see about that, she thought. When the stitches heal we'll see about that.

"But where will you go?" he asked.

She scraped her teeth over her lower lip and considered her options. "The baby needs a father," she said, already scheming of ways to make Zeus jealous. She wanted him back, sure, but it was more than that. After thousands of years, Hera was tired of raising the earth's children on her own. She wanted a partner in life as well as in love. Hadn't Zeus ever heard of Women's Liberation? Zeus wouldn't get away from the responsibilities of parenthood so easily this time, even if, technically, the kid wasn't his. She had been chasing Zeus since childhood and had grown weary of their game. Destiny was unfair, but there was nothing she could do about it.

When Alexander gave her a frightened glance, she hastily tried to reassure him that her intentions were honorable. "We've got to find my husband," she said.

He looked visibly relieved. He stood and shuffled back to the kitchen with the empty cups. "Whatever you say, Mrs. Zeus. Whatever you say."

CHAPTER NINE

They took the train north into Connecticut. Only a couple of days old, and Igor was already trying to crawl out of Hera's lap. His face was no longer quite so scrunched up as before, and his skin tone was quite dark, beyond Mediterranean. He had gained so much weight that Hera's back ached from holding him. The good news was: she felt so terrible *everywhere* now that she hardly noticed the pain from her incision.

Rapid growth and eating like a pig must have been traits the child had inherited from his father's side, like the soft wings, curling tongue, and hoofs. She hoped, for his sake, the kid had inherited her wit and intelligence.

Hera leaned over and complained to Alexander. "My tits are more shriveled than dried Kalamata figs."

He practically blushed. "Oh, Mrs. Zeus! Such things you say!"

She had always had a soft spot for tall swarthy men who were embarrassed to be caught next to a woman who could swear like a truck driver. "You like dried figs, Alex?" she asked.

He didn't seem to *get* what she was hinting at. At the moment, she could charm him into loyalty, but not love. He was too resistant, she too weak.

Just as well, she thought. At least my reputation is still safe. She was wearing a tan button-down smock that fit her like an apple pie crust. Beneath the smock her body was lumpy, soft, and sore.

But Alexander looked so fine. His white pants and shirt contrasted with his dark skin and hair. The look was hot neo-Greek. Six more weeks, she thought. Less, if she could swing it.

At the Stamford stop, Alexander picked up the suitcase and the baby bag and hurried them out. He announced that it was time to rent a car and drive the rest of the way. He was worried they would be followed. "We must cover our tracks," he said. "We can hide much easier in a car."

Hera was too mired in diapers to micromanage their journey, as was her druthers. She had no choice but to trust Alexander's judgment. She hated that.

Alexander was being tight-lipped about their destination. "We are going someplace safe," he said. "And from there we can organize a search for Igor's *gadabout* dad."

Igor dropped the suction on her nipple with a loud smack. He looked at Alexander. "Dadabout," said Igor.

Hera gasped. It was his first word, dammit. How special that his first word was about that two-timing low-life AWOL Zeus. Her anger dissolved the moment the baby gazed up and gave her a four-toothed smile and pawed her chin with his grubby little hand. She stroked the bony ridges at the base of his wings.

He really was kind of cute for an ugly kid.

They rented a nondescript, matte blue-gray, midsize sedan, something called a *Generica*, which featured a built-in car seat. The interior was covered from ceiling to floor with a blue-gray faux velour that was rough, as if made from recycled plastic soda bottles. As if that weren't horrid enough—the Generica was a talking car.

"Welcome," it said in a high pitched voice she instantly christened PeeWee. "Are your seatbelts fastened?"

Igor's little face turned red and wrinkled; he clenched his fists and his seams ripped as he filled his lungs with air and began to wail.

"Gadzooks!" Hera said. "Don't tell me he wants to nurse again!"

"Perhaps it is just growing pains," said Alexander,

She really didn't want to argue, but she'd raised more kids than Father Flanagan. As far as she knew, Alexander was a single guy. "It is not just growing pains," she said. "The kid is hungry."

Igor's stretch terry romper fell away from him. He stopped wailing.

"Okay," Hera said. "So maybe you were right."

Alexander nodded.

"Bless you," she said when he didn't laugh or try to rub it in.

She stared at Igor, filled with pride at how he was developing. The diapers still fit but now none of the baby clothes were big enough. "We're going to need to buy him something to wear," Hera said.

"Not yet," said Alexander. "Let's get far away before we stop. Maybe you can wrap him in one of my shirts."

"You'd do that?" Hera said. She wouldn't have, and Igor was her kid. But she was a goddess and always had to think about the greater good, and the greater good did not include impinging on her sense of fashion.

"You are exceeding the speed limit," warned PeeWee. The car giggled.

"Where are we going?" she asked

Alexander didn't answer. He drove through town then doubled back and wove through a residential zone and finally made his way onto the highway. He pulled onto off-ramps, then got back on immediately as if part of some well-thought-out plan. It was like a wild car chase, except that no other car was chasing them.

Or so she hoped.

Baby Igor was so defenseless. Come to think of it, at the moment so was she. This was exhausting, being dependent upon magic or Alexander to keep her safe. She yearned for the security of being dependent on Zeus. At least with him, she usually knew how far she could safely push before he'd desert her. Being abandoned wasn't that bad, as long as you saw it coming in advance.

"Acceleration while driving over speed bumps causes wear to your shocks and may invalidate your warranty," said the car.

Her stomach felt like an accordion being squeezed by a trash compactor into a harmonica. Hera had no idea at any time in which direction they were headed. The sun burned through Alexander's side of the car. Hera reeled, feeling dizzy and ill. The baby's squalling made her nervous. She closed her eyes, but that only made things worse. When she opened her eyes, the sun had moved to her side of the car.

Not a moment too soon, Igor's wailing turned to a lazy bleating. With a final shudder, the baby closed his eyes and fell fast asleep.

❧

The hours passed quickly. Alexander didn't have a clue as to what he was doing. For the second time in his life he had left everything behind him, this time to be with a married woman and her baby. He sensed the wily doctor would try to follow them to steal back the baby. Alexander knew only too well that a man could be followed only if he truly wanted to be found.

If the clock was correct, it was nearly three. He increased his speed, wanting to get far away before dark.

He did not understand his feelings for Hera. Despite her many flaws, she was bewitching. He felt affection—maybe love—toward her, that was true, but in a different way than a man loved a mother, a sister, a daughter, or even a wife. He had felt this sense of duty and responsibility toward her from the beginning. Who could understand it? He hardly knew her. Yet, in so many ways, he felt he knew her very well.

He turned left from Main onto a side street. He drove around the block three times before connecting back onto Main.

"Where are we going?" Hera asked.

He drove on without replying.

When she looked frightened, she looked very young. She talked tough, but she was vulnerable—that was obvious. He felt obligated to protect her and her baby from harm. Better that she did not know where he was heading, that they were about to revisit an abandoned life, a place he had not been in three years. He pulled into the drive-through line at Burger King.

When he reached the speaker he ordered four onion rings, four Whoppers, two coffees with no cream but lots of sugar, and two giant bags of fries. He would need to stop for groceries before too long, but this should be enough to hold them for a while.

The line was moving slowly enough that Alexander took a moment to turn and sneak a look at the boy. Igor was a homely brute, but there was something else (besides the hunchback and the feet and those wings) that seemed a bit off. Something else besides his astounding rate of growth. His proportions, Alexander decided at last. The too-long arms and thick fingers. The legs that seemed short, but only when compared to his long abdomen. Poor little guy. Life would not be easy for this one. Alexander vowed to do all that he could to help the boy.

Finally, Alexander reached the pickup window and paid for his order. He placed the sugars and the coffees in the drink holder on the dashboard. He lifted out one of the Whoppers and the top box of onion rings, and handed the steaming paper sack to Hera.

She smiled seductively as his hand touched hers. He pulled away feeling stung by her flirtation.

She frowned and pouted, but her attention was soon diverted by her first onion ring. He watched her lick her fingers.

When she saw him staring, she licked them again. She extended her tongue and sucked on her index finger.

He found her behavior somewhat embarrassing.

How many babies had the doctor said she'd lost? Six? Seven? She seemed not to remember any of them.

He was starving, but pulled out onto the street before unwrapping his food. He wanted to get out of town as quickly as he could.

"Use your turn signals for maximum safety," said the car.

Alexander shook his head. "We will stop in another hour to get gas. You can nurse the baby then, while I stock up on supplies."

"Where on earth are we going?" Hera asked.

He shrugged. "Even if I told you, you do not know it," he said.

They got back onto the highway and after driving a few miles, the car said, "I would be happy to slip into cruise control. It is really the most efficient way to drive!"

"This talking car is very annoying," Alexander said.

"Boy, I'll say. If he doesn't shut up soon I'll wring out Igor's diapers in the gas tank."

She was kidding, he knew, though with Hera one could never be sure. His stomach growled; it was past time to eat. He steered with his left hand and peeled back the paper on his Whopper with his right. He took a small bite and marveled at the medley of flavors and textures.

She was staring at him. "You are incredible," Hera said. "You didn't spill *one* drop! I got grease stains on my chest even before we starting eating."

"Just something that I picked up while I was in the service," he said.

"Navy?" she asked.

"The Foreign Legion," he said.

"Wow!" said Hera.

He didn't bother to confess that he was kidding.

Alexander looked in the rearview mirror. The baby was no longer baby-sized, but had become toddler-sized in a matter of minutes. "I cannot understand this," Alexander said. "The baby is huge!"

Hera smiled. "That's my boy!"

There were loud belching and puffing noises from the back seat as the baby passed some gas, and from the smell of it, something else.

Alexander wrinkled up his nose.

"Packs a powerful punch for a little fellow, don't he?" said Hera.

The windows rolled down automatically and the blast of warm wind picked up napkins and wrappers and blew them out the windows. "Toxic emissions can build up in enclosed spaces much faster than you'd think," the car informed them. "Oh, and littering is punishable by a three-hundred-dollar fine."

"That does it!" Hera shrieked. She gritted her teeth and furrowed her brow. She looked as serious as a farmer about to butcher his only cow. She tensed her shoulders, then suddenly relaxed, and the Generica let out a shriek. But after that, it was strangely silent.

By evening, Igor had learned enough words to make himself understood when he wanted Alexander to pull over so he could take a piss.

"Go potty now!" Igor said. "Now, now, now, now, now, now!"

Alexander immediately whipped over to the shoulder and got out to help the boy.

She watched as he showed her son how to pee on the side of the road without spraying himself. "What a guy!" she said. Hands-on. Not afraid to show his sensitive side. It had been ages since the last time she had been attracted to someone like him.

Seducing Alexander was sounding more and more like a good idea. Damn this episiotomy! She was using all her magic to charm Alexander and couldn't spare any for healing. She'd have to wait for what she wanted. How mundane.

The boys finished their business and got back into the car.

"Do it again," cried Igor.

"No!" said Hera. "Not now."

Igor sang a little tune, something she had never before heard. The words were "Do it again! No, not now!" He added a chorus of "Gotta go! Gotta go!" then sang through the entire piece. It was really quite charming.

"He has talent," said Alexander, sounding proud.

Hera smiled. "That's my boy," she said. So this was Alexander's weakness. He loved children. That was cheating, but whatever worked.

The kid's vocabulary increased; over the next half-hour, he learned the names of all the dinosaurs.

"Diplodocus," he said. "Apatosaurus and pterodactyl." His next song was titled "Tyrannosaurus Is the Dinosaur for Me." It sounded like a marching band song; the lyrics were simply a repetition of the title. The kid asked for, and received, the remnants of their Whoppers and onion rings. By the time Alexander stopped the car to refill the tank, Igor had outgrown his carseat.

When Hera tried to nurse him, he refused. She acted as if she didn't care, but it was far too early to wean the little brat. Her breasts were full of milk and harder than green tomatoes. It all seemed so pointless. Love. Marriage. Mating. Childbirth. The works. What was the point in going through any of it, once you knew that nothing would last forever?

She cried for twenty minutes until the sadness turned to anger. Men. They used her like Kleenex, then threw her away once they were finished. Even her own son.

"Is something the matter?" asked Alexander.

Hera put on a false smile. "Oh, nothing," she answered.

He looked worried, but said, "Okay."

She was feeling energized enough that she could have used magic to dry up her milk. Instead, she decided to repair the car's PeeWee voice. It would be a no-brainer, bending *a machine* to her will.

She drummed her fingers against her chin and tried to remember the right transformation spell. It wasn't a spell she had attempted all that often; too many things could go wrong when one was dealing with the mysterious forces of life. Form a man out of mud and he might turn into a rowdy golem who would think nothing of stomping on his creator.

It seemed safest to lower her expectations. She picked a speck of dried mud from the floor, held it between her fingers. She tried to imagine the very essence of a man, but was unable to see much or anything. Men! Who could understand them? Still, one didn't need to have a Ph.D. in psychology to be a mother—now wasn't she proof enough of that? She concentrated, and managed to breathe life into the speck, then blew that speck inside the radio to dwell. Hera laughed, and ignored Alexander's questioning glance. She liked the idea of controlling a man by playing with his knobs.

Hera wasn't speaking to him, and Alexander wondered what he had done to make her angry. It was often this way with women. They were moody, expected him to read their minds.

His head throbbed and his eyes had begun to burn. He rubbed them and let out an involuntary sigh. Embarrassed, he sneaked a glance toward Hera and saw her leaning into the dashboard. She was talking to the speaker. He heard her laugh and then heard the voice of the car laugh and then heard them both laugh raucously together. He was certainly the butt of their jokes.

They had come far enough north that some of the elm leaves were already starting to change. His turnoff was just up ahead and he signaled, slowed, eased off of the highway. The pavement ended after a couple of miles, and there was a rough gravel road that went on for another mile before degrading into a bumpy dirt road. He wasn't paying close enough attention, and caught the front wheel on Hera's side in a pothole.

"Watch it, buddy," said the car in a threatening voice.

"Sorry," said Alexander. "Is everyone all right?"

"Do it again!" screamed Igor with delight.

He drove a little farther, and almost missed the driveway, a dirt path whose entrance was obscured by brush.

"I'm tired," Igor said.

"Almost there," said Alexander.

"Where?" Hera asked, sounding annoyed. She whispered something to the dashboard, then sat back with a smug expression.

Grass had crept onto the driveway; Alexander drove slowly, unsure of the condition of the ground beneath. It was silly, and he knew it, but the car scared him. He parked, closed his eyes, and waited as long as he could before asking the car to open its doors and let him out.

⁂

It might have been a nice place once, but with the weathered wood, mossy roof, and overgrown landscape the place looked like an abandoned movie set. It had two stories and a steep pitched roof and a decrepit wraparound porch. One of the chains holding up the porch swing had fallen, leaving the bench angled like a slide.

All the charming New England inns they had passed and he had brought her *here*? "I should have guessed," Hera whispered to the car.

Igor was already out toddling through the lands—pointing at rocks and naming trees as if the first one to identify them—but she would be damned if she was going to get out of the car and get dust all over her sandals. These were her only gold pair. Let Alexander carry her like a gentleman, if he wanted her to come inside. She made him leave the keys in the ignition so she could talk to her precious pixie.

"What do you say we skip out and find us some excitement," PeeWee said, as if reading her thoughts. She was glad she had thought to grant him the power of extra-intuitiveness.

"You're too good to me," she said, though that wasn't true. Nobody could be too good to her. After all, she was a goddess. She deserved much more than she would ever get from these imbeciles.

"I should have hard-wired you to give me foot rubs," she said.

"Stick your toes up to my speaker and I'll turn on my fan and give you a blow job," said PeeWee in a most suggestive voice.

"I adore crude men," Hera said. She stroked what she imagined was his chin with her pinkie.

She watched Alexander rehook the swing's chain to the eaves. He tested the seat for strength, then sat and pushed himself back and forth, seeming completely immersed in thought.

Within a few more minutes, Igor ran up the stairs and jumped up and down. He was ready to explore the house.

Alexander fiddled with the lock. The door swung open, and the two disappeared.

Hera waited, feeling increasingly annoyed.

When at last it became clear no one was coming out to get her, she took off her sandals and stuck the ball of her foot against PeeWee's mouth. "Now!" she ordered.

"You go, girl," said PeeWee.

But she couldn't relax because she kept peering out the window to see if Alexander was coming to get her. PeeWee blew stale air with the odor of burning tires over her toes. "How's that?" he asked.

"Horrible," she told him. After a few minutes of putting up with this irritating tickling, she kicked him in the chops. She slipped on her sandals, got out of the car, and walked straight into the house.

Igor threw his arms around her legs the moment he saw her. "Mama," he said.

"Whatever, kid," she said, and pushed him away.

She walked forward into the parlor. Scattered like fallen blocks along the floral carpeting were yellowed papers and dusty dishes and the rattiest looking dolls she had ever seen. Alexander sat on a sheet-covered couch and stared off into space. He was holding something: a brass Latin cross.

A row of framed photographs sat like tombstones along the mantel; she walked closer to examine them. She blew the dust off the closest one and looked at a smiling red-cheeked little girl.

"Who's this?" she asked. The child had blonde ringlets and green eyes. Her expression reminded Hera of Alexander.

Alexander stood. He walked like a zombie to join her at the mantel. Gently, he took the photograph from her hands. His eyes were glassy. "Her name was Stasia," he said, his words catching in his throat as if he were fighting to push them back inside.

"Stasia?" said Hera.

"My daughter. This little girl was my daughter."

"What do you mean by 'was'?" Hera asked. "What happened to her, did she disappear?"

He brought the picture to his lips to kiss, then hid it beneath his hands above his heart.

She was about to make a joke about the pitfalls of falling for inanimate objects (she was thinking of how that kind of thing could lead to PeeWee blowing on your toes), when she came to the startling realization that the child was dead. So Alexander had lost his little girl, eh? Things were all starting to make sense. "I'm so sorry," she said with as much sincerity as she could muster. "I didn't know."

"How could you know?" he asked. "You do not know anything about me." He walked away and stood by the window.

She gasped, surprised to hear such anger in his voice. She tried to follow but stumbled over a pink quilt, leaned over to pick it up. Gray cotton batting poked through the fabric. A mouse had nibbled through the cover before deciding it didn't like the taste of the stuffing. Mortals and rodents had more in common than they wanted to acknowledge. Mortals stuck their fingers into every damn piece of chocolate in the box before deciding if it was good enough. More often than not, the chocolate was rejected, put back in the box for someone else who was not quite so picky, someone desperate for chocolate. Usually that desperate one was Hera. She let the quilt slide to the floor. Alexander turned away from her. He stared out the glass and she watched his reflection, watched him gaze into the distance as if he were looking back, to a time before sorrow.

Alexander shut the door behind him to keep Igor from following him inside his room. He wanted to be alone, for just a little while. He looked at the dusty guitar case and carefully unhinged the lid. The instrument was three-quarter sized, made for smaller hands than his. He kept himself from touching the strings, because any music he might make would be too sad, and gently set the guitar back in its case. There was an old suitcase under the bed; he pulled it out, undid the latches and popped open the lid. He turned his face until the odor of musty abandonment escaped into the room. In the satin pocket he found an old rosary. It had been a while since he'd held one in his hands. He fiddled with the beads, but the rosary slid through his grasp and dropped to the bed.

The bed sagged under his weight. He was too big and too tall for the mattress. The room had always been inadequate, an attic he had remodeled into a bedroom far too tiny to contain a marriage. He hadn't really noticed until it was too late. A man without clear vision was not much of an architect. No wonder his wife had left him.

He remembered the last time he had slept with her in this bed.

He remembered eating breakfast, scrambled eggs. A lifetime later, well after lunch, he remembered hearing the sheriff's knock at the front door, the frightened look on his wife's face when she came into the kitchen to get him. He remembered the plans he had been drawing for the expansion of the chapel, and how his arm had grazed the paper and smeared the ink when he stood up. He remembered being angry with his wife for having disturbed him.

He remembered how the sheriff cleared his throat and looked down, staring intently at the floral carpet as if he could find his next words hidden in the petals.

" ... an accident ... did all they could ... need you to identify the body."

Alexander had not believed him. He remembered looking to the spot in the carpet where the sheriff's gaze was fixed, as if the man's words could be found there. He had no idea how long he had stood there before he felt hands on his shoulders. The sheriff led him out the door and down the steps and into the green and white car.

He remembered the cold room and the coroner's tired face but could neither remember coming home again, nor his wife's exact words when she blamed him for their daughter's death. He could not remember who attended the funeral. The doctors had assured him that this memory loss was typical, a normal reaction to grief, and nothing to worry about. But Alexander had lost his child. Wasn't that enough? How could God demand he abandon his memories of her as well?

He remembered existing in the house through a period of time he could not measure. He remembered turning into a man who needed to sleepwalk through life, so great was his fear of being awakened.

He remembered his stubbornness, how he had refused to allow anyone to change things, any things, even unimportant things like picking up dirty laundry from the floor, or washing dishes from their last meal, as if his inaction could prevent the dream from ending.

He remembered discovering that he was utterly alone.

He remembered knowing when it was time to return to his world, but thinking that the only way to get back was to leave his home and drive as far away as he could manage.

And now that he was back, he could hardly remember anything of the past four years in New York, or even of the past few days.

He found his old shaving brush inside the satin pocket, and when he touched the handle, remembered when Stasia had frosted lather over her face and pretended to shave with a finger. She had licked that finger, only to gag and then spit the soap upon the floor and yell that he had not used whipping cream.

His hand trembled. He held the brush so tightly his fingers grew numb. How could he have left so many precious memories behind?

⁂

H era was getting tired of her secret car meetings with PeeWee, but he was really the only one she could talk to. The kid was just a kid and about as interesting as a hairball, and Alexander was adorable but so damned serious. The only solution was to make PeeWee a bit more versatile.

One day, she carried an empty blue baby wipes canister to the Generica and sat in the passenger seat for her morning PeeWee kaffeeklatsch. She had wanted to fashion something more appropriate, perhaps a golden chalice, but Igor had distracted her with a beach ball throw, causing the spell to misfire. Instead of a chalice she had created an ashtray. She hadn't had the energy to fix the spell. Wasn't it the thought that counts? Good thing, too.

"Mirror, mirror," Hera said.

"You are," said PeeWee. "I anticipate your every need."

They laughed.

"Now that that's settled, z'up?" asked PeeWee.

"How would you like a little freedom?" said Hera. "Get out a little more, see the world, do some traveling?"

"Sounds great," said PeeWee. "What do I do?"

"Give yourself to me," Hera said.

"Oh baby," said PeeWee. He giggled.

"I'm serious," Hera said. "Empty your mind of any thoughts of yourself and think only of me."

PeeWee quieted, and Hera sucked in a deep breath, pulling his consciousness from the car's electronic "brain." She exhaled his essence into the empty blue plastic canister, and the transformation was complete. Voila! A portable PeeWee. It would be nice, hanging around with him.

She brought him back to the house and opened the lid to show him around.

"You're in for a treat," she said.

"Oh, goodie," he said, and she knew he was utterly sincere.

"I'm going to paint my nails," she said.

"What color?"

"Shimmering green."

"I think that's a lovely color on you," PeeWee said.

She smiled, and put on the first coat.

"You missed one," PeeWee told her.

"What are you talking about?"

"Big toe. You missed it."

Sure enough, he was right, the irritating little golem. Why was it that those who knew everything felt compelled to rub it in?

She snapped closed his lid and heard him shriek. He wasn't especially fond of the dark, and screamed, "This 'Baby Powder Fresh' scent will be the death of me!"

"Tough luck," she said. Everyone was a victim of his circumstances. But after a while, she relented and popped open the lid to give him a breath of air. PeeWee was a bit too much the know-it-all, even for a trusted advisor. If he didn't lighten up, she might very well decide to recycle him.

They stayed for a couple of weeks, just long enough to let Hera recover her strength. Igor had been growing at an alarming rate and was bigger than most four-year-old boys. It was as if the child were rushing through life. We are all rushing through life, Alexander thought, though most of us never notice until too late.

Igor sat on the living room floor beside Hera's chair. Alexander sat on the couch, staring at Igor.

The boy was bare-chested because he didn't like the feel of fabric against his wings. He had dark eyes and obscenely long lashes and was oddly handsome. He started singing in his boisterous voice, "Itsy Bitsy Spider," and tried to get Hera's attention by climbing her leg with his fingers.

She was enthralled with the latest issue of *Cosmopolitan* and stayed his wrist. "I'm busy," she said. As always, the blue plastic box was open on her lap. PeeWee could be heard whistling "Dixie".

Igor's wings twitched and he looked sad. Finally, in desperation, he turned toward Alexander.

Alexander watched him sing the piece three times, smiling and applauding the end of each performance.

"Would you knock off that racket?" Hera said. "You're giving me a headache." She pointed to a picture in the magazine. "Do you think I'd look good with a nose ring?" she asked PeeWee.

"You'd practically sneeze sex," PeeWee said, and the two of them chuckled at the joke.

It seemed clear to Alexander that Hera's interest in the boy was limited—it troubled him, knowing this about her. In so many other ways, not that he could think of anything specific at the moment, Hera was a wonderful person. But there was something about her, something so enchanting he felt compelled to cleave to her side. How could she throw away her chance to be a parent? He wanted to give her the benefit of the doubt, to believe that she was a good woman going through a difficult time, perhaps suffering from postpartum depression.

The boy seemed quite fond of Alexander. Too fond.

"Will you make me a peanut butter and jelly sandwich?" he asked.

Hera looked up from her magazine. "Who, me?" she said.

"No," Igor said. "You put on too much peanut butter. 'Xander knows how to make it with enough jam."

Alexander nodded and got up to walk into the kitchen. He worried about what would happen once they found Igor's father, that there might be confusion about loyalties. There seemed no way to prevent that, unless he ignored the boy, and Alexander was unwilling to try that. Being able to nurture the child seemed like a second chance.

He poured the milk into a cup, made the sandwich and cut the bread into four triangles. He brought out Igor's lunch and set it on a TV tray. It felt good preparing food, one way a man could nurture another without words.

CHAPTER TEN

Zeus believed that the Fates had brought him to Williams Valley, and now that he was here, all he needed to do was wait for his destiny to be revealed. While he was waiting, why not take advantage of a town that was conspicuously drowning with rich supplicants in need of spiritual advisors?

Williams Valley provided a charming resort, a much-needed vacation from the stress of city living. He sat at his favorite table in front of the Water Street Cafe. Water Street was the happening spot in town, a one-way street with diagonal parking spaces. A wide boardwalk flanked the stores on one side. The boardwalk had been designed to accommodate a steady stream of foot traffic, and there was more than enough room for a row of small tables next to the Cafe. Zeus sipped the last of his latte, marveling at the deep flavor of the coffee and the lightness of the steamed milk. Modern civilization had been largely a mistake, with the notable exception of cappuccino machines. The froth of the gods.

He had not felt this excited and alive in years. He snapped his fingers, noticed he had resorted to his habitual behavior, and stopped because those sorts of habits made one appear timid. Fear had been the curse of man since the dawn of time. Something about this place reminded him of the good old days. The air was clean and the townspeople vapid enough to be respectful. The biggest grocery stocked a cheap retsina and a feta cheese made from the milk of local sheep.

In the two weeks he had been here Zeus had already managed to sleep with two young women, both the daughters of ex-hippies, who were ten times more promiscuous than their mothers had ever been, and also far less hairy. They dabbed French perfume on their pulse points instead of that *gadawful* patchouli scent favored by the previous generation. They preferred lacy brassieres and panties over long johns. Okay. So maybe progress had brought other improvements beyond froth.

He felt great. Better than great. He could not pinpoint exactly why, for nothing out of the ordinary had occurred. True, he had left his wife of some eight thousand years, but that wasn't exactly unprecedented. No, something else explained his good feeling, something magical in nature. Ahh, Fate. He sensed his life was about to change for the better, a prospect that made him giddy.

For now it was time for a stroll along the boardwalk. The storefront facades had been restored to a glory beyond that of the prewar years. The buildings were painted in pastels with contrasting trims that made them all look somehow edible. Beside the Cafe stood Craftsman Furnishings, which sold hardwood desks, chairs, tables, and chests, each painstakingly crafted from bird's-eye maple, or cherry wood, or black walnut. He filled his pockets with paper money, easier to manufacture than gold. How he lusted after anything one-of-a-kind!

He approached the Face and Bodywork Factory, the decidedly yuppie spa where his personal groomer, François, worked. The yokel business class was a fine mix of old timers and recent arrivals of the *Have-Modem, Will-Relocate* persuasion. He was glad the newbies had thought to bring all their city-living creature comforts with them. Treating himself to a mud wrap sounded like a good idea, and he pushed open the door.

"Mr. Z!" A tanned young blond wearing white shorts and a white jersey rushed over to clasp his hand in greeting. His grip was firm, but brief enough to avoid any suggestion of impropriety. "Nice to see you again! You're looking fabulous." The blond leaned close to whisper something, as if in confidence. "We have a special *today only* on our beeswax ear candle treatment," he said.

Zeus tried to look as if he were seriously considering the offer, though why in Hades would anyone want hot candle wax inside their ears? Or high colonics, for that matter. Some things were best not known. He felt stiff and was in the mood for a massage. He'd been working out to give himself more definition. He wanted to look the way his image looked when sculpted in marble, only with a bigger penis.

"Sounds great, Barney, but I think I'll go for 'The Mummy' if François has time to work me in." He winked and in the wink, watched the shudder of magic work through Barney. He was cheating, but only a little, using a charm spell to augment his natural charisma.

Whatever worked.

Barney was appropriately reverential. He went through the pretense of checking his book. "I am *so* sorry, Mr. Z, but François has the day off. The good news is, it looks like Richelieu is free in twenty minutes," he said. "May I show you to the saunas to relax until then?"

"Of course I'm disappointed, Barney, but I want you to know

how I appreciate all your extra work on my behalf."

Barney smiled broadly, and waved away the proffered ten dollar bill. "It's nothing," he said. "Really." He was on the effete side, which, in the Greek tradition, did not bother Zeus in the least. Live and let live, Zeus thought.

"Now, come on, let's get you in for a quick sweat, shall we?"

Zeus followed him into the hallway, feeling quite smug. Hera had always thought of his charisma as manipulation, but what did she know? It opened a lot of doors, got him free haircuts and shoeshines and political favors up the wazoo. I ought to form my own cult, Zeus decided.

Three middle-aged men shared the benches, a black real estate developer from Long Island, an Irish-American executive from Connecticut, and a nervous little man from D.C. They wore their towels tightly wrapped around their middles. Zeus had left his towel intentionally slack. As long as they were comparing themselves to each other, well, why not compare it all? Especially since no mortal could measure up to his standards.

The sauna walls were lined with fragrant cedar. Steam and moisture rising from the red-hot coals drew out an aromatic masculine scent with enough bite that Zeus could almost taste it. Men sweating with men brought out an erotically charged atmosphere that mortals were too anal to appreciate. What a shame. They'd do better to revel in their expressions of manliness instead of being afraid to be turned on by it.

The hot steam soon had them all feeling relaxed, vulnerable, and slightly faint. This was precisely the state of being that made male bonding possible, once they stopped worrying about the possibility of latent homosexuality. Before Zeus knew it, the group became fast friends, all but the nervous little man, who cowered in the corner and pretended to be twitching in his sleep.

The Irish-American confessed he was on a business retreat, and never wanted to return to work or his wife or two kids. His name was Elton Arthurs; he had realized since coming here that something was lacking in his life, something that had not been met by family or career. "I'd give anything to better understand why I'm here," he said. "Why we're all here. In a cosmic sense, I mean." Elton was a big man, maybe fifteen pounds overweight, silver-haired and clean-shaven. Good looking enough to get a woman without opening up his wallet.

Elton sat beside the black fellow named Don Reed. Don had a rat-tail mustache; Zeus soon understood why. The man twiddled incessantly with the hairs, every now and again pulling one out to stare at it as if he had no idea where it had come from. Zeus surmised from this gesture that Don was not entirely happy with his life. Don had come to Williams Valley to evaluate the resort potential of an abandoned hot springs.

"Anybody know where I can go for some guided meditation?" Don asked. It turned out this was something Don had read about in the *Utne Reader* and had been wanting to try for quite some time. "Something not *too* woo-woo. No naked men drumming in the woods or drugs or anything like that. Well, maybe a little. The drums, anyway. But something where I can explore my needs and my goals and not have to think about everyone else."

"I'd be up for that too," said Elton.

"I don't know about me," said the nervous little man.

Zeus had been one of the first opportunists in recorded history. He snapped his fingers, stalling for time, as ideas formed. Then inspiration hit him like lightning, and he knew what direction to go with his life. This was *exactly* the right type of cult for a god like him. Rich men. Men with intelligence, taste, and connections. Successful men, temporarily caught in the throes of midlife crisis. Men who could afford to be healed by the king of the gods instead of someone cheaper and less qualified Zeus would get back into the business by ruling a small local kingdom. Six months to let word of mouth get out, then on to world domination.

He would develop a cadre of worthy devotees, no pseudo-hippies in need of baths and razors, no stuck-in-adolescence divorced men trying to find themselves without spending any money, no men on disability beating on bongos because they had nowhere better to stick their fingers, no men who preferred sharing a joint over an extravagant cigar, no men who did not know the difference between wine and water glasses.

Real men. Men who were ready for change.

He let his hair show some gray around the temples, and added a couple of lines to his forehead to make it look like he spent a lot of time immersed in thought. He smiled, as if he had been caught doing something illicit. "Actually," Zeus said. "That's what I do. Usually, I mean. Except right now, when I'm on vacation. I *hate* to call myself a shaman," he said with false modesty, "though my students have often given me that title in respect."

"What do you do?" asked the nervous little man. "You're not going to make us drum or anything, right?"

"Drumming is fine," said Zeus, "but I have something a little more real. It's all about adapting to change. About embracing your base nature. Ever think about turning into an animal?"

"All the time," said Elton. He laughed. "Well, actually never."

"Let me give you a taste of it," said Zeus. "Close your eyes and keep them closed. Make a fist and think about being strong. Now say, 'Inatrockle Rosen Risen' and repeat that softly three times."

None of this was necessary to his plan, but he supposed ritual added drama. He cast a spell to ignite their inner-wolves. They would pay to grow fangs and a pelt; this was only a taste of what was possible. He watched the men sniff at the air as their heightened sense of smell evolved. Don began to howl, softly at first, swelling to a cry that echoed off the walls. The others, unable to resist, joined in.

The nervous little man bared his teeth and growled.

Zeus gave them a minute, then turned off the spell.

"Wow," said the nervous little man. "That was something else."

Elton said, "Did what I think just happen really happen."

Zeus nodded.

"Who are you?" Don the developer asked. "Didn't catch your name?"

"Zeus."

"I thought I recognized you," said Don with a whistle of appreciation.

The Oracle took his time traveling. After all, he thought of the trip as his last paid vacation. He loved this part of the country, the gnarled trees, the brilliant sunsets, the faint fragrance of marshlands and wild roses in the breeze. It had been many years since he had last passed through and he wondered if he should retire here? Try as he might, he could not look into the future and see himself. Which was probably a good thing.

The weather was too glorious for him to stay cooped up inside a boxcar, so he abandoned the train to the truly hard-core hobos and decided on the more scenic route. Mornings, he walked along the shoulder of the highway. When the sun rose above eleven o'clock he stopped for lunch at the first roadside diner. There was usually someone to buy him a meal in return for a hearing about future good fortune. Another pleasant reading and he found a ride for the next leg of his trip, sometimes even a nice place to stay the night.

Several days into his trip, the Oracle stopped for an early

breakfast: coffee and a cinnamon roll in an eatery called Homebaked. The cinnamon roll was delicious, one of the best he'd ever had. There was a rack of postcards by the door and he picked out the ones that best showed the changing leaves in fall, the quaintness of steepled churches. He thought about sending postcards to his friends in the city, but the Fates had probably already sent them this way, so there was no point. He bought several postcards just the same. Likely as not, he would see his friends soon enough. If the mood struck, he could hand them a card.

He recognized the weasely man with the crossed eyes. The man passed by the Oracle's corner daily, but had never given him a dime. If anyone deserved his future, it was this man. He was enough of a meddler that he might have made a formidable demigod in another age. "It's time," remarked the Oracle to the woman at the register, "to pay the piper."

"Oh," she said, pointing to the postcards. "Why don't you just take them." She wrapped up a cinnamon roll to go.

He thanked her and told her not to worry about her son.

"How did you know?" she asked, but he silenced her with a finger to his lip.

"It's just a phase," he said. "He'll snap out of it," and she nodded solemnly.

She wrapped up a second cinnamon roll and put it with the other in a white paper sack.

The man with the crossed eyes was eating the "Healthy Start-Up" breakfast of granola, plain yogurt, fresh fruit. The Oracle fought not to feel superior. His cinnamon roll had been buttery, spicy, and sticky sweet. How could anything be healthier than experiencing the joy of eating?

The cross-eyed man noticed the Oracle and gave him a temporary smile, as if trying to sort out where their paths might have crossed in the past.

"Hello again," said the Oracle.

The man nodded. "I don't believe I caught your name," he said.

The Oracle shrugged. "I believe your name is Sanders, right?"

Sanders said, "Yes. What did you say your name was?"

The Oracle said, "I didn't say. I used to do peer reviews for *The Journal*, but no more."

Sanders brightened. "Oh," he said. "For a moment I'd forgotten where I knew you from."

They chatted, and after a while the Oracle said, "Go on and finish up your food. Then we'd best be going, don't you think?"

Sanders said, somewhat surprised, "You're coming with me?"

"It's time. And you do have room in your car," said the Oracle. "I know you're ready for some company. Besides, we're headed for the same place. Only I know how to get there. How's the research coming along?"

"How do you know where I'm going?" asked Sanders.

"That's my job. I'm in the destiny biz," said the Oracle. "I know where you're going for the same reason I know where Hera has taken the baby. I have some other business to attend to and I'm headed that way; I know you want to go there with me. Even if you didn't want to go, you'd give me a ride because that's our destiny."

"I don't believe in destiny," said Sanders. "I've a bit more of a rationalist mind than you."

"It doesn't matter what you believe," said the Oracle. "Makes no difference at all. You have your part to play in our little drama and I have mine. So how are you gonna do it? Get the baby away from Hera?"

"I have a court order," said Sanders. "She's endangering her child's life."

"Well, we'd best be going then, don't you think?"

Sanders put down his spoon, leaving some yogurt and a few apple slices. He stared at the Oracle with a bemused look that suggested the doctor thought the old man was insane.

"You gonna eat that?" asked the Oracle. He reached for a spoon.

Every night for the next week, the men met in the sauna where they sweated and talked and worshipped Zeus. They now left their towels hanging outside on wooden knobs, a symbol of their newfound openness and kinship. They discussed personal and business problems with each other; Zeus acting as the therapist. At the end of every session, Zeus let them howl for thirty seconds, just enough to whet their appetites.

The men agreed that howling was their favorite part.

During an impromptu massage session on the bench, François outed Barney. Instead of allowing them to give in to their first inclination and despise the towel boy, Zeus taught the men how to be assertive about their own sexuality. "There's no need," he said, "to be threatened by a queer unless you question what you really want and are afraid to learn the answer."

Elton did not look all that convinced. "But it's unnatural," he said.

"So is wrinkle cream," said Zeus. "Get over it." Because he cast a spell of understanding, that was that. Reasoning with this one would have taken too long, but everyone else seemed to get it.

A stranger, upon hearing their discussions, might have said they sounded like a bunch of complaining women, something Zeus would have angrily disputed. It was good, he told them, to open up, but only when there was complete trust. To do so otherwise was folly. "To confess," he said, "before those who might hold your words against you saps your strength."

"True," said Don, a lapsed Catholic. He admitted to them all that his intentions were good, but that his failure was in follow-through.

"Good intentions," Zeus said, "are vastly overrated. There's no failure in making a few mistakes now and then. Experimentation! Exploration! The rocket ship would never have been invented had those men been afraid to take risks."

The nervous little man said, "I'd like to have bad intentions but I never get the chance."

"Then you've come to the right place," Zeus said. "Stick with me."

"My wife," said Elton, "she's so demanding. Ever since the kids came, she's grown worse. I can't even go out for a drink after work without her expecting a phone call saying where I am. I have no privacy."

"She treats you like a child, not a man," said Zeus. "Too many women mistakenly believe that everyone is in need of mothering. This kind of thinking accounts for much of the misery in the world." He told Elton to put himself first. "You are not being selfish—that's just what a society controlled by mothers will tell you to keep you from knowing true happiness, from enjoying the freedom you've earned and deserve. But it's not selfishness that leads you to care for yourself. If you are not for yourself, then tell me, who can you be for?" He'd stolen the last line from some medieval Hebrew philosopher, but they would never know that.

Their belief in his words was tangible. Zeus led the men from the sauna and into the dressing area. They carried their towels over their shoulders; no need to cover one's manhood unless he was ashamed of it. They walked straight and proud, and refused to be intimidated or embarrassed in front of Barney, who shamelessly checked them out.

"This is cool," said the nervous little man.

They formed a healing circle in the showers, with Zeus at the center. The warm water beat down upon them.

"I want you to think about what you really want, and when you're ready, I want you to speak your desire, whisper it aloud."

They closed their eyes and stood immersed in thoughts and the warm showers.

Zeus wanted so many things he found it difficult to speak the name of one. Until it hit him like a lightning bolt between the eyes. "Penelope," he said softly. His skin prickled. Penelope. Now that he had remembered her name he could not get the image of the lovely young nymph out of his mind. He wondered what she was up to now?

For the first time in years, Elton's psoriasis cleared up, and Don experienced sudden hair growth in his bald spot. Even the nervous little man stopped twitching, though he soon developed a new tic in his right eye. The men smiled like young lovers. They were in love, with themselves and with their brothers. They had, as they said in the trade, bonded.

Two weeks after their first meeting, Zeus called his first group hug under the stars, inviting Barney the towel boy, an honor that made him cry. They discussed plans for the future that provided Zeus a more permanent home and financial security. They talked about incorporating and forming a board of directors.

The next night, Don the developer said, "I just made an offer on the hot springs property. Nice lodge, built in the fifties, with a huge stone fireplace. A little rustic, but big enough to hold a group. And there's a fantastic view of the hills!"

Elton the executive beseeched Zeus to consider Don's idea. "We'll be silent partners," he promised. "We'll assume all risk and put up the money, but let you run the ship."

"Sounds promising," Zeus said, and paused long enough to build anticipation in his new devotees. "But get someone in to clean it first. And I'll need someone to manage and hire the staff."

"I propose we begin promoting the retreat immediately," said Elton the executive. He revealed that he had closed his personal and business accounts, cashed in his retirement and stock options, and was anxious to move the money around into something secured and hidden before his soon-to-be-ex-wife got wind of his plan.

Zeus shrugged. He instructed Barney to give out his phone number and said, "Call me up when things are all arranged." He mentioned to the nervous little man precisely which podium and table from Craftsman Furnishings would best suit his purposes. "And have a caterer call me right away," he said. "I'll want to go over the wine list."

"So, you mean, I can come too?" asked the nervous little man from his corner.

"Of course, brother," said Don the developer.

❦

This was sure to be the best month ever, thought Mr. Bringle. Business had been booming ever since Possum's last visit. He could barely contain his excitement. That boy was good as gold. Possum had already developed quite a following of collectors, both locally and from out of town, but that postcard-sized carving, the one he had decided against selling, was a museum-quality piece. Mr. Bringle felt annoyed with himself for not pushing harder to acquire it. If the boy were smart, he'd carve a dozen or more little blocks of wood. Mr. Bringle envisioned a one-man show of Possum's work. He would call it, "The Living Landscape. Kinetic Plein Air."

The rarity of Possum's work kept the unmet demand consistently strong and prices high. And this new piece was so unique. It would sell for a small fortune. He wanted Possum to do more, but not too many. Control access and you controlled prices. The only thing better for prices than rarity was when an artist died and collectors bought up all available works in a frenzy.

Mr. Bringle decided to close early. He had barely locked up when an exceedingly handsome gentleman of thirty-five, or maybe forty, certainly no more than fifty, walked up and asked him to reopen. The man said hello and shook his hand. He practically oozed charm and well-being with every gesture. Most likely a politician from downstate.

"I've been admiring the El Greco you have in the window."

"You have excellent taste in art," said Mr. Bringle. The El Greco was an oil called *Zafiro*. Pictured was a circle of men ascending toward heaven. The work had been painted in shades of blue with frantic flamelike strokes. It was one of El Greco's minor works, true, but a rare beauty nonetheless. Mr. Bringle had obtained it from a Kraut he suspected was a former Nazi. As the price had been right, and since he didn't *really* have any proof that the work had been illegally obtained—or that the man was a Nazi or even a Kraut, when it came right down to it—he had not allowed some vague moral uneasiness to get in the way of his business sense.

When a price could be affixed to something considered priceless, only a fool failed to take advantage of the opportunity. Mr. Bringle was many things, but he was not a fool.

"Would you like to arrange for a line of credit?" he asked, and the gentleman smiled and nodded yes.

"We have several other pieces that are remarkably affordable for the private collector," he said, steering the gentleman away from the window. "May I show you this very fine Daumier litho, quite reasonable for a nineteenth-century master." It was a trifle, really, a comic piece. He wouldn't have bought it for a third of the asking price, though people valued anything created by an artist whose name they had heard of.

"I can show you an original Miró, and a Picasso print—a Pablo, not a Paloma," said Mr. Bringle, trying to hide his disgust. "And several darling Dali lithos."

The gentleman was quite polite about the lithos, almost too polite, which tuned Mr. Bringle into the fact that he was much better educated as to art than most of his customers. The gentleman gushed about the beauty of several other gallery works, but shook his head sadly, apologizing that they weren't quite what he had in mind. He snapped his fingers, a nervous habit that Mr. Bringle pretended to ignore.

"I'm looking for local color. Something decorative, as well as artistic." He was so gracious about the whole thing that Mr. Bringle apologized for his selection. "I do have something," he said at last, and brought out Possum's Water Street drawing.

The gentleman staggered back, overcome with emotion. He sniffed the air and looked as if he might faint.

Mr. Bringle brought him a chilled bottle of water.

"I thought as much," said the gentleman. "She's here!" he said. "I can feel her presence in this drawing."

"Who?" said Mr. Bringle. "Who's here?"

"Never mind," said the gentleman. "This is charming. I'll take it. But I wish you had more by this same artist."

"I'll save you his next piece," said Mr. Bringle.

"Where does he live? Perhaps I could visit his studio."

Mr. Bringle smiled. This fellow was a live one.

"The artist is very reclusive and doesn't produce much work," he said. "But I represent him exclusively. I'll speak with him and ask if he might be interested in a commission."

"Yes," said the gentleman. "A commission. Something with the king of the gods at the top of the mountain. I could pose."

"Wouldn't that be charming?" said Mr. Bringle. This stranger was destined to become a most *special collector*, of that, he was certain. Rarely had he come across such taste and refinement in a customer. Mr. Bringle, a little embarrassed by his desire to impress the gentleman, mentioned that he had seen a piece, a wood carving by this promising young artist. "I'm not sure it's for sale, but let me talk with the artist."

The gentleman agreed to take a look at it. "I'd very much like to see this charming piece," he said. "If it's all that you say, I'm sure that I'd be interested."

He was awfully persuasive. And when the gentleman asked if he could rent the original El Greco and several other pieces from the catalogue for a weekend workshop he was holding at the old hot springs, Mr. Bringle found to his surprise that he could not refuse him, even though the idea of renting art might normally strike him as crass. He almost cried as he accepted the token dollar offered for the weekend rentals. It did not seem right to charge *anything* for granting so small a favor to this charming and wonderful person.

"Get me that carving," said the gentleman. "I'll make it worth your while."

"I'll have it for you soon," said Mr. Bringle. Perhaps he'd accompany the grocer's buck-toothed coke-bottle-glasses dim-witted boy to Possum's home and sneak into the studio. Art belonged to the public, not the artist. Possum owed him; after all, he'd been supporting Possum's work since he was a child, since before the boy was marketable.

The gentleman seemed pleased with his purchases and asked Mr. Bringle if he wanted to attend the upcoming workshop at the hot springs. Such was his gratitude for this invitation that Mr. Bringle took out his checkbook and wrote out check number 8792 for the five-thousand-dollar tuition without so much as flinching.

After all, when a price could be affixed to something so priceless. Opportunity rarely knocked, and when it did, well, foolish was the man who did not immediately leap up from the table and rush to answer the door.

It took Eddie four hundred and forty-two paces from the kitchen back to the store. He was tired, and went into the back room for his break. He worked five hours and got one fifteen-minute break each day. He moved a chair to face the time clock so he would keep track of all the minutes. While he was there, he checked the calendar again. It was getting awfully close to the end of the month.

After his break he went out to the register to ask his dad if there were any special chores, and his dad told him the tuna needed restocking.

The grocery carried two brands, and each brand came packed in both water and in oil. Which meant that Eddie needed to carry out four boxes of tuna each time he refilled the shelves. Sometimes, it didn't come out even—because people bought more of one kind than the other—so he had to hide extra cans behind the clams. His dad wanted all the cans on every shelf facing forward where customers could easily read the labels. Restocking took a really long time, and sometimes it made Eddie mad, the way people picked up cans and put them back without paying any attention to whether or not they were doing it the right way.

He was concentrating really hard and didn't pay attention when his dad called him to come back to the front of the store. But his dad yelled louder, and then Eddie paid attention.

There wasn't time to cut up the empty boxes; Eddie just left them on the floor and hurried toward the register. "Sorry, Dad," Eddie said as he walked up, and that was when he saw Possum.

"How you doing?" Possum asked. He was smiling.

Eddie wiped his hands against his jeans. Seeing Possum made him feel happy. "I was hoping you would come today," Eddie said. This wasn't exactly true, but his dad said you were allowed to lie if it made the other person feel good. "Are you going to need a delivery?"

Possum said, "That would be great."

Eddie looked to his dad, who nodded. He felt proud that Possum trusted him enough to let him help with the groceries *and* deliver them. Just then Eddie remembered. He stopped walking. "Oops," he said. "Forgot about the boxes." Without further explanation he ran to the aisle to finish restocking the tuna. He stowed the boxes in the back, in an out-of-the-way place where nobody else would notice them. All this rushing around made it hurt to breathe.

Possum paid for everything, and stuffed what he could fit into his backpack. Eddie would deliver the rest in the morning. Eddie hurried to the register to help put all the perishables in one box. He put that box in the cooler. He put the dry goods in another box that his dad had labeled with Possum's name and put that box in the cooler just to keep track of it. He had another hour to go before his shift ended.

"Any more deliveries for today?" he asked his dad.

CHAPTER ELEVEN

It was late in the afternoon before Mr. Bringle caught up to Eddie, the grocer's son. He held the boy by the shoulder while he chit-chatted on and on about nothing, as if he hadn't anything else on his mind. The boy wasn't really a boy, he just acted like one. Ironic that eternal youth had such a high cost. Mr. Bringle wanted to trick Eddie into letting him come along in the morning for Possum's grocery delivery. He needed that little carving for his special collector.

Eddie was all tooth, and his dirty glasses had frames taped at the sides. He was a little on the chubby side (his father had him on a continuous diet with no discernible effect) and dimwitted to boot, but hardworking and loyal. The kind of person who was born to be taken advantage of. Although Eddie was nearing thirty, he still seemed like a little kid, which was odd until you got used to it.

"So," said Mr. Bringle, "been busy over at the store?"

"Yes, Mr. Bringle," Eddie answered. He was trying to squirm his way out from Mr. Bringle's grasp, but was too polite to be efficient.

"How's your father doing these days?" asked Mr. Bringle, observing that the boy always had the look of an unmade bed. He restrained himself from tucking the hem of Eddie's shirt back into his pants.

"My father is doing fine, Mr. Bringle. Maybe I should go back and see him."

"Ahh, you see him plenty. It must mean a lot to him to have you there helping at the store. I'm sure your father is very proud." Mr. Bringle didn't believe this. If one needed to produce offspring, it seemed wasteful to produce those willing to work for less than the minimum wage.

But Eddie smiled and relaxed just a bit.

Mr. Bringle put his arm around Eddie to lead him to the Food Emporium with the promise of a thick chocolate malted. Eddie's father discouraged his son from eating sweets and other high calorie foods. One could best exploit another by understanding his weakness.

The Emporium was decorated to resemble a gingerbread house. Eddie sniffed the faux red licorice on the door and stuck out his tongue as if to taste the chocolate piping on the siding.

"Now, now," said Mr. Bringle. "Wait until we're seated."

The tiled entryway alternated with red and white squares, and glass bins filled with brightly colored candy lined the walls like pockets on a coat of many colors. The hostess sat them at a small round table painted to look like a swirled peppermint. The padding on the chairs was sewn from a pink and white striped fabric.

Très tacky, thought Mr. Bringle. Art for the masses.

But Eddie took in the aroma of the grill and the decor with wide-eyed wonder. The menus were silk-screened in four colors, with lavish descriptions of the food for those who did not believe what they were seeing.

"Rich chocolate ice cream with a lethal limit of butterfat," the menu proclaimed. "Real malt syrup topped with fresh whipped cream and sprinkles carved from chocolate bars specially imported from Switzerland."

Mr. Bringle ordered for them both and let Eddie read over the menu until their malts arrived.

Not until the boy had spooned off all the whipping cream and eaten most of the ice cream did a look of worry cross his face. "I have to go," he said, letting his gaze wander from the frosted glass to his benefactor. There were still a few bites left. He licked his lips and shifted in his seat, looking quite uncomfortable.

"What's the big hurry?" asked Mr. Bringle. He scooped a spoonful of ice cream and held it tantalizingly before his lips.

"I have to get up early," said Eddie, gaze transfixed on the spoon like a dog begging for a treat. "I've got a delivery in the morning and I have to make sure I get enough sleep."

"Relax," said Mr. Bringle genially. "Finish your malted. Maybe you'd like a hamburger, too. Or some French fries. Don't worry. I'd like to help you make that delivery."

"Oh no. I always go by myself."

"It's okay, Eddie. Sometimes people need a little extra help. And Possum wouldn't mind. He told me so himself. I tell you what! First thing in the morning, we'll load up my car and drive to the stables and take a couple of horses. That way, you won't even need to groom and feed your dad's horse when you've finished. You'd like that, wouldn't you? I'll take care of everything."

Eddie's innocent face could not hide how seriously he was taking this proposal. "French fries too?" he asked.

"Or onion rings, if you'd rather."

"French fries *and* onion rings," Eddie demanded.

"It's a deal," said Mr. Bringle, feeling so clever he could barely contain his smile.

W hen Mr. Bringle took Eddie out to eat, he let him eat all the things his dad said he shouldn't eat very much of because then he might get fat and get a heart attack and die just like his grandpa did.

Eddie didn't want to get fat and get a heart attack and die, but he sure did like eating all those things his dad said he shouldn't eat very much of. They were good, and besides, maybe it was okay to eat them just this once.

Then another odd thing happened and Eddie didn't know if it was good or bad. Mr. Bringle said that Possum had told him it was okay for Mr. Bringle to ride along for the delivery. Mr. Bringle had never come with him before, but Eddie's dad had never sat him down at the kitchen table, taken off his glasses, and pointed his finger at Eddie to tell him *not* to take Mr. Bringle along, so it was probably okay. He wondered if he should ask his dad, just to be sure, but he decided not to. If he asked, Eddie was going to have to tell his dad about all the things he ate that he shouldn't have.

And if he told his dad about eating all those things, well then, for sure he was going to get fat and get a heart attack. People never seemed to get fat and get heart attacks unless other people knew how much they ate and then talked about it behind their backs, at least that was how it seemed to work. So, if you were sneaky enough then you could eat whatever you wanted as long as nobody knew. The luck was in being sneaky.

So Eddie told Mr. Bringle it was okay for him to come, even though he didn't exactly know if that was true or not. But the good thing was, since they were going to ride horses from the stables, Eddie knew for sure he would get back in plenty of time for work.

There was really only one thing to worry about now, and that was whether Possum would tell Eddie to give Mr. Bringle some of his tip money. Eddie didn't want to do that. He didn't like Mr. Bringle, but there was more to it than that. Eddie liked to keep all the money for himself so he could buy things, sometimes even food that he wasn't supposed to eat. There was even a bigger reason not to share his tip money. Eddie didn't want to give Mr. Bringle any money because Possum always gave him a twenty dollar bill after the delivery and if Eddie had to give some of that twenty dollar bill away, he was going to have to figure out how to make change, and making change was just one too many new things to have to worry about on top of everything else.

It seemed to take Possum forever to get back home. He returned to find the river had meandered closer to his property and was blocking his way. How odd, he thought. It hadn't rained in several weeks!

This can't be true, his practical side announced. *Let's walk around the perimeter and find another way in.*

Possum tried this, but gave up after a half an hour of wandering through the brambles. His back and legs ached from the weight of the pack. He slipped out from the shoulder straps and set the heavy pack on a patch of dry grass. The day was hot, but dry enough that he wasn't even sweating. The grocer's son, Eddie, was supposed to ride over with the groceries and supplies by tomorrow.

Possum laughed. *Hope he brings an inflatable raft,* said his playful side. He sat beside the pack and leaned against it to think. The water in his canteen tasted old, but he sipped it anyway, and tried to understand how the river had encircled his property!

His paranoid self whispered, *It's that Penelope! She covets your home for her own! And here's the proof!*

No, said his trusting self. *She loves you as much as you love her.*

Possum blushed. He found it rather comforting that the voices had returned.

He stood and readjusted his pack. His hands were scratched and bleeding from the unexpected tussles with the blackberry bushes, but despite the pain, he pushed through reeds and stood on the sandy beach to watch the river pass by him. "Penelope!" he cried, not that calling out her name would do any good. She could never have heard his voice above the rushing of the water. But he wanted to let her know that he was coming home, just later than he'd promised.

To his left he spied a place where the river slowed, and made his way there to cross. He took off his pack to leave on this side of the bank, rather than negotiate the river carrying the added weight.

You can come back and get it, said his practical self.

I know, he thought. He hated leaving all his purchases behind, even temporarily. He wanted to show his gifts to Penelope. He pictured her smiling face as she watched him remove her presents one at a time. Pleasing her brought him such happiness. He rooted through the inside pockets and retrieved the soft cooler holding her chocolate bars and fresh-squeezed cider. It fit nicely in a small plastic bag from the grocery. If he could bring her nothing else, at least for the time being, he would give her these!

He stepped carefully into the water and felt his way before taking the next step. It frightened him to walk where he could not see.

Don't worry so much, said his comforting self.

That's easy for you to say, said his cynical self.

But suddenly, the level of the water dropped by nearly a foot. Then two feet. He almost fell, but caught his balance just in time. The water slowed to a trickle. He made his way across the slippery rocks along the riverbed. The moment he had reached the other side, the water changed from a trickle to a bubbling glass sheet. The water rushed forward, even higher than before.

He scrambled up the bank, terrified, and ran toward the road that would take him to the cabin.

⚜

They started before dawn. Mr. Bringle picked the gentle mare named Sniff for Eddie and a black gelding for himself. Because it had rained the day before, there wasn't much dust on the trail. A bit more mud than Mr. Bringle would have preferred, but despite that, they made pretty good time.

The boy, though an idiot, could navigate blind through the Amazon Basin. He was an idiot savant human compass—maybe that explained things—maybe he had a magnetic brain that let him get wherever he was going without understanding why.

Mr. Bringle wasn't sure what he would do once he got to Possum's cabin. It wasn't so much a question of thievery. Mr. Bringle was willing to pay Possum for his work, so long as he possessed all there was of it.

It was past nine when they arrived, and just on time. Mr. Bringle was getting a blister on his pinkie and felt a tad saddle sore. Good thing he'd brought moleskin. He saw a gold flash, perhaps a tiny fire in the tall weeds surrounding the cabin and decided to investigate. "Go on," he told Eddie. "I'll catch up to you."

Mr. Bringle halted the gelding and jumped down to the ground. He ran toward the fiery apparition, never taking his eyes off of the glint. Like so many things, the fire was illusory. Hooked around some brush was the loveliest piece of jewelry Mr. Bringle had ever seen. The chain was as fine as the skin of a baby and there was a tiny crystal teardrop with an actual flame inside it. Beautiful. Bringle put the necklace in his pocket, feeling warmed and joyful at his find. Then he went to greet Possum at the door and help Eddie unload.

Possum looked terrified to see him there, but he was polite

enough and invited them inside. His new redheaded girlfriend wasn't quite so nice, though she seemed to take to the dimwit, Eddie.

"If you'll excuse me, I'd like some fresh air," she said, and wheeled herself out to the porch.

Mr. Bringle didn't appreciate her condescending attitude.

Possum shrugged and stepped outside to help Eddie bring in the last of the groceries.

It was the opportunity Mr. Bringle had been waiting for. He spied Possum's backpack sitting against the wall and tugged at the strings until the mouth gaped open and something practically leapt out at him, like a small animal trapped in wadded newspaper. The kinetic carving. He stared at it greedily and exchanged it for a wad of fifty dollar bills. "I'm doing this for your own good," said Mr. Bringle, not that he ever believed anything he said.

The old resort was about an hour's drive from town on a twisting, narrow road. The unpaved road leading from the highway to the entrance needed a few truckloads of gravel to fill in the holes, and the rusty gate and fencing needed work. But beyond those few faults, the site was simply magnificent. Zeus stepped from his Jeep and surveyed his new home.

Seventy-five acres of pasture and rolling hillside and just enough ancient forest to be scenic. A fork of the Calypso River suitable for fishing ran along the back edge of the property. When he turned, he saw an uncluttered view of Williams Peak. He strolled along a pathway, fragrant and soft from a century's worth of crushed pine needles. About a quarter of a mile from the parking lot were the mineral springs—some enclosed in cedar huts, the rest outdoors with minimal improvements. They smelled a bit like old eggs, nothing that couldn't be masked by fragrant oils. Another trail led to a wood-fired sauna with a Plexiglas skylight that offered a view of the moon and the stars. Beyond the sauna was an outdoor pool kept naturally heated to a toasty temperature by geothermal energy. The trail continued off into the forest; Zeus turned back to have a look at the lodge.

It needed some cosmetic touches. But it would be passable after some sanding, maybe a dark stain over the cedar siding, a couple of coats of paint along the trim.

Wide cement steps led up to a partially enclosed veranda and large sunny deck. Zeus walked through the veranda to the entrance to the lodge. A pair of faded totem poles guarded the entrance. An atrium, with many hanging planters but no plants, led into the "Big Room." The Big Room had knotty pine walls and maple flooring and horrendous chunky furniture fashioned from logs. One staircase led up to the sleeping rooms, another to the basement.

On the wall opposite the entrance stood a massive stone fireplace with a rock hearth that stretched halfway across the room. Mounted to either side of the chimney were a matched set of grinning moose heads on wooden plaques. Behind the fireplace wall was a large dining room that overlooked the river. The rage and power of the river was intimidating, even from this distance.

Zeus peeked into the kitchen on the left, but what went into a kitchen did not interest him so much as what came out. He retraced his steps to check out the "Manager's Suite" through the heavy double doors on the east side of the Big Room. But they would all have to stop referring to it as the Manager's Suite. The manager could take the trailer that was parked out by the service entrance. Suites to the sweet, wasn't that what they said?

The suite was awfully plain, a large open living area and a large bedroom with a privacy hedge and a view overlooking the river at the back of the property. One of those oversized whirlpool tubs would go rather nicely in that bedroom corner, Zeus thought. He would have the designer redo the suite before starting in on the rest of the interior.

Mr. Bringle had agreed to act as a consultant and help choose the appropriate art. Zeus wanted overstated elegance with the look of no expense spared, which was easy enough to do when you didn't have to pay much for anything.

Zeus made his way back to the Big Room to sit on the hearth and gaze out the clerestory windows at his lands. The verdant hillsides were lush blue-green with spruce and pine, the sky clear and blue with edges of brilliant gold. The top of Williams Peak was shrouded in white clouds. He stared, dumbfounded, for several minutes. The magnificence of it all overwhelmed him. This place was incredible!

He decided to rename the resort "New Olympus" at once, then slowly reinstate himself as king of the gods. It shouldn't prove as difficult as that last time, when he'd had to fight enemies at every turn, even his own family. The glory days, but what a pain. Thank the gods competition was essentially out of the picture. A simple proclamation, or better yet, a declaration by his devotees, ought to do the trick.

Elton the businessman had managed to sign up twenty rich

"seekers" for the first weekend workshop. Don the developer had promised to bring in another fifteen. Zeus had convinced a few stragglers to give things a try, bringing the number of guests up to forty. He had hired Barney as the executive towel boy. Oddly enough, the nervous little man, the most insecure being Zeus had ever run into, was an expert on security and had already volunteered to oversee operations. Everything was going according to plan.

A truck rumbled up the driveway and parked in the lot by the service entrance. The new chef, Mr. Tom, had arrived. Zeus hurried out to greet him. "Welcome aboard," he said.

Mr. Tom stepped from the truck. He had the look of a man who was always thinking ahead: a slight frown of concentration, eyes lost in thought, the habit of cupping his chin in his hand like Rodin's *The Thinker*. He was carrying a crisp paper sack.

He looked around the site before answering Zeus. "Thank you," he said. "Nice to be here. Have you already eaten lunch?" He held up his paper bag. "Sandwiches," he said. "I think you'll approve of the *cornichons.*"

"I like your style," Zeus said.

There could be no religion without the right ambiance; everything about New Olympus had to help create the proper mood. The food was of critical concern. "How are you?" Zeus asked, making his tone drip with concern.

"I'm okay," said Mr. Tom, gazing ahead toward the lodge.

"Anything you need," Zeus said. "Anything at all. Just ask."

Mr. Tom nodded. "I appreciate that," he said.

They walked into the kitchen like best friends and sat at a small prep table to eat their sandwiches and go over the menu.

The bread was chewy and flavored with sweet onions and walnuts and smothered with thin slices of tomato and hickory-smoked turkey, a zesty whole cranberry sauce, garlic aïoli, and just the right amount of horseradish. "Delicious," said Zeus.

Mr. Tom shrugged with false modesty.

It made Zeus sad to think of just how often he had settled for less than the best. No more. He was king of the gods and it was long past time to act like it.

"What's for dinner on opening night, Mr. Tom?" Zeus asked. "Amaze me."

Mr. Tom suggested grain-fed prime rib, new potatoes, grilled summer squash, and a mixed salad with field greens. Raspberry sorbet and koulourakia—one of Zeus's favorite cookies—buttery but not too sweet, shaped like pretzels and coated in sesame seeds.

"Sounds wonderful," Zeus said. "The perfect start."

Mr. Tom smiled.

Steak and eggs, juice and coffee for Saturday breakfast. A simple lunch: cold retsina served with slabs of hard cheese, cold meats, chewy breads.

"I'll want something way spectacular for the Saturday night banquet," Zeus said.

"I've a splendid idea," said Mr. Tom. "We could roast a whole lamb over a barbecue pit. Spiced with garlic and wild rosemary and served with grilled vegetables."

Zeus clapped him on the back. "Perfect!" Zeus cried. "I'll arrange for the belly dancers. The food I'll leave to your capable hands!"

Mr. Tom nodded and stood to explore the kitchen. "I'll need a few things," he said.

"Don't even concern yourself about the budget," Zeus lied. He cast a spell of frugality and hoped it would take. Once the money started rolling in, it would be another story but until then, it was best to be cautious.

He was thrilled with how things were coming along. It had been years since he had called the shots. Zeus could hardly wait to reign again.

There was only one thing missing: he was going to want a queen. If worse came to worse, he'd go fetch that old hag Hera, but he preferred someone younger, someone a tad more pliable. What mortals called the "trophy wife." Preferably a virgin, or someone who would feel a sense of undying love for the first man who ravished her.

Someone he could make very happy without expending much effort. His thoughts strayed to the lovely red-haired naiad from his youth. It was no coincidence she was calling to him and he couldn't wait to find her. The Fates were kind at times, at least to him. He wasn't sure how the young lady would feel—he had turned her into a tree and left her alone with the termites. So, she'd broken the spell, the little firebrand.

Zeus snapped his fingers. He laughed. He was truly shameless. And damned proud of it.

CHAPTER TWELVE

The big Greek spent way too much time cozying up to her son, and once in a while, that made Hera feel guilty. Like right now. It wasn't that she didn't love the little bugger, of course she did. She loved *all* her children; didn't every mother? It was just that raising children was so labor-intensive. And when a goddess labored, she expected better results for her efforts than just seeing to a well-placed poop or a plate devoid of broccoli. Never before had she been expected to attend to these mundane details. Damn the demise of slavery and the extended family.

Alexander could convince Igor to do anything. He was better at cajoling/nagging than any mortal she had ever met. Ahh, to have *his* offspring. She fantasized Alexander as a delectable mate who not only didn't bite, but had less than six legs. Curse the Fates! Aphrodite had had all the luck, landing the choice role of goddess of love. Why was Hera chosen to be the loyal wife? After all these years, it was getting old. The one time she'd been unfaithful was with an invertebrate with a hard shell, and not where it counted.

Gadzooks, but she felt frustrated. She carried her blue box containing PeeWee and sat alone at the dining room table.

Alexander sat cross-legged on the wool floral carpet beside Igor. They were playing with that damned ugly bean bag toy that Igor called Horsie. The thing was evidently Alexander's from childhood, and so old that every few days it popped another stitch and lost all its beans. Alexander filled it up again like he would a gas tank and tried to repair the damage.

Igor stood and toppled a shelf filled with knickknacks. Alexander waited patiently while the child put everything back where it had been.

Hera perched one foot on the edge wooden table to paint a coat of polish on her nails. She peeked at Alexander and kept herself from visibly lusting. What a guy. First things first. She blew on her foot and wiggled her toes.

"I know what you're doing," said PeeWee.

"Shut up, blue boy," Hera said.

Only a few weeks old and Igor was learning how to tie his shoes. She'd heard that kids grew up too fast these days and now she had proof. Today he had refused to wear his pants with the elastic waist.

His jeans were too big and he had not quite mastered pulling up the zipper. Alexander had promised to go into town and get the boy a white button-down shirt just like his. Until then, Igor had agreed to continue wearing a too-small striped jersey.

Igor glanced at Hera now, a plaintive look in his eyes, and without asking, took off his shirt. He looked like any kid, at least any kid with a tuft of bad hair, hooves, and wings. Maybe Igor wasn't the ugliest child she'd ever borne, but he was close. Whatever did Alexander see in him? And more important, how could she get him to see that in her?

"Put your shirt on," Hera screamed. "Cover up those wings, will you?"

The boy crossed his arms and said, "No."

Looking at his wings reminded her of that horrid night at the bar. She shuddered—not that she remembered much about it.

Igor got to work putting together a 300-piece puzzle. He did the edges first, then began to fill in the background. She didn't understand how Igor could see *anything* on that wretched busy carpet. The puzzle pieces practically disappeared inside the flowers. It was nauseating to watch. She held her head high, worried that she was old enough now to need glasses.

"How long are we going to stay here?" she asked.

"Until you are completely well," he said. "Until the baby settles into a schedule."

"But I am better!" Hera pouted.

Alexander gave her a comforting pat on the back. "Soon," he said.

A cackle sounded from the blue box. "I know where Igor's father is!" said PeeWee. A part of him was still simpatico to the car's brain, probably in constant communication with every Generica this side of the Rocky Mountains. "My sources have informed me of a new religious cult of men who like to dress up as werewolves. Apparently, last Sunday, there was something about it on *60 Minutes*."

It turned out that a cult had been founded in some hick town called Williams Valley, about a three-hour drive to the north.

"You never know how long these things last," PeeWee said. "I suggest we get going."

"Dang!" Hera said. "Religion! Why's it always have to be religion?" Men! They were either porking virgins or founding new religions; never anything in between.

PeeWee said, "Aren't you glad you've got me? Neither man nor beast." He told her all the gossip about Zeus.

Zeus's new religion, called "Denihilism," preached empowerment—granted by the self as well as by society—for its followers. Promiscuity without paternity. Hot tubs and unlimited retsina. Cigars. Sports. The elevation to the divine of physical beauty. Transformations by moonlight. Only men could gain full membership, though women were allowed to serve in the auxiliary for a fee.

Denihilism reeked of Zeus and his old-world ideas. Whatever else she could say about the old Greek, he was predictable.

Predictable. She rather liked the sound of that. Being predictable meant Zeus was someone she could count on, a rather nice attribute for the ersatz father of her child, when she thought about it.

"I'm well enough to go now!" she cried.

Alexander nodded. He looked at her for a long time, as if considering. "Perhaps you are. But what about the baby?" he asked.

"Igor is not a baby! Just look at him!"

Upon hearing his name, the boy abandoned his puzzle. He stood and looked at Alexander with a goofy smile. He rushed toward him.

"Where's Mama?" Hera said, using baby talk. "Come to Mama!" she begged.

Igor stuck out his tongue at her. He threw his chubby arms around Alexander's neck and planted a wet kiss on his cheek.

"Well," said Hera. "That kid sure knows how to sizzle my oysters."

"You are right," said Alexander. "This is not good." He hugged the boy, then gently pushed him toward Hera, but Igor screamed, "No!" and ran back to work on the puzzle.

Alexander looked worried. "You are right," he said again. "It is time to go on. We'll leave here in the morning. Let me pack a few things," he said.

"You pack for the boy," Hera said. "I'll just bring my cosmetics. I need a new wardrobe anyway."

Alexander trudged upstairs and brought down a suitcase from the closet. He packed a few shirts and slacks and socks and folded boxers; a few extra things for Igor to wear until they had a chance to buy new clothes.

Perhaps he would take a few of Stasia's favorite toys to amuse the boy. He knocked on her door out of habit, expecting no reply. It just seemed wrong to burst in, until he had waited a respectful amount of time.

He set the suitcase on her bed, considered what to bring.

Sunlight filtered through the dirt-smeared window, bringing cobwebs and dust motes to life.

He picked out as many of her things as he thought a boy might ever want. A small guitar. A deck of playing cards. A set of drawing pencils. Three of her favorite *Oz* books. A picture encyclopedia. A favorite blanket and a favorite game: Monopoly. The bean bag terry cloth horse with blue button eyes that Stasia had liked to snuggle with because of the way it changed its shape to fit her mood.

The suitcase was too full, but he found he could not close the lid on the little horse. He took it out and held it tightly to his chest. What was left of the beans poured through a hole in the stitching. He smiled and brought the cloth to his lips and then rubbed it against his cheek as he had often seen her do.

Minutes passed before he was able to fold the horse into a square that fit into his pocket. He held the suitcase in one hand and the guitar case in the other. Eyes moist and burning, he steeled himself to go downstairs.

Eddie was in love and when a person was in love, they wanted to shout it from the hills. Only he couldn't tell anyone, ever, because the woman he loved was already someone's girlfriend: Possum's, and Possum was his best friend. You didn't try to steal your best friend's girlfriend; though he'd had no personal experience in this matter, he knew that from watching television.

But maybe it was okay just to think pretend thoughts about the pretty red-haired lady and how happy he would be if they were the only two people in Williams Valley and she was his girlfriend. He thought pretend thoughts for a while, but it didn't take long before his daydream made him sad. Because, if the pretty lady and Eddie were the only people in Williams Valley, then what about his dad? And what about Possum? It would never work out for Eddie and the pretty lady and that was that.

Are we there yet?" asked Igor from the back seat.

Hera said, "No, we're not there yet! Now shut up," as she had said to her children for thousands of years.

"We have a long way to go," Alexander said.

Hera turned and watched her son unfold his dark wings like a cape as he tried to find a comfortable position. The seat cushions weren't made to fit a boy with wings. She used a bit of magic to zap indentations into the upholstery, to give him more room. Nice eyes, she thought. Big, black, bright. When she stared into his eyes she could forget about his deformity. Igor was at that annoying stage of childhood where he could reach anything, wanted everything, and listened to nothing. He sat forward and stuck his head between the front seats to blow spit bubbles. "Can I look at PeeWee?" he asked, and grabbed for the blue plastic diaper wipes box.

PeeWee started whining. "Let me out!" he said.

Hera said, "Honey, leave your Uncle PeeWee alone," and opened the lid to let PeeWee have a breath of fresh air. She set the box just out of reach on the floor. PeeWee tuned the radio to a twenty-four-hour talk show station and somehow fixed the controls to prevent her from changing stations.

After a commercial for term life insurance, a woman named Cheri called in to ask for advice. "I don't know what to do," she said. "My husband wants to have an 'Open Marriage' and has had several affairs. He goes to his girlfriend's house on weekends, leaving me and the kids alone. Well, to make a long story short, there's a man at work that I'm very attracted to. He's so nice to me, pays me a lot of attention, doesn't have kids of his own but likes mine … ."

The talk show host, a woman who called herself a doctor and acted high and mighty like a god, said something along the lines of, "And you want to know if it is morally acceptable for you to forsake your vows and betray your children by taking a stranger into your bed."

"Wait a minute! How does having sex with strangers betray anything?" Hera demanded. "Just because you're married to someone doesn't mean they own you."

PeeWee answered her from his perch on the dashboard, "Because when you hold someone's heart in your hands you must keep your fingers gentle." His voice was accusatory.

Hera smiled. Her little pet was jealous, jealous of Alexander. She reached over to pat the big Greek's shoulder.

Cheri on the radio said, "Well, when you say it like that."

The doctor said, "And just how did you expect me to say it? How does it repair the world for you to act immorally? You cannot use the actions of others to justify evil."

Cheri began to cry.

"You tell them, Doc," said PeeWee.

Hera said, "That's it, you monkey-faced fool! I don't need any of you to tell me how to live." She hit the dashboard with her palm. "Turn off the damn radio or I'm tossing you out the window like a dirty diaper. I'd like to turn that doctor into a diaper pail," she muttered.

PeeWee made a strangling noise as if to protest, but obeyed her command.

Alexander said, "She's right, you know," and shook his head.

Hera wanted to punch him. Tell Zeus, she thought. Not me.

They drove on. Hera took out a map from the glove compartment and unfolded it. They had at least another couple of hours before getting to Williams Valley. The air inside the car felt heavy, hot and charged like an electrical storm. She opened her window and promptly inhaled a bug.

Igor broke the uncomfortable silence, "Are we there yet?" he said.

❦

Soon after getting into town, Sanders tried to get the Oracle to join him for a little R&R at the health club, but the Oracle swore he had better things to do than go all moony with a bunch of rich middle-aged men. So they said their so-longs and the Oracle thanked the squinty-eyed man for the lift into town.

The Oracle said, "Happy researching!"

Sanders smiled and said, "Thanks. Happy oracling!"

The Oracle didn't care much for Sanders, but he had to laugh at that one. The Oracle walked toward the store to meet the boy whose destiny was intertwined with his. Did the boy suspect anything about what was about to transpire? Old and wise as he was, the Oracle himself had only the barest inkling.

Eddie stood on the sidewalk watering a wooden flower box filled with orange and yellow nasturtiums. He wore a plaid shirt and baggy faded jeans. His hair was oily but combed into place.

"You can eat those, you know," said the Oracle. He didn't especially relish flowers, except in an emergency, but such things as this were important to know. The boy should be prepared, just in case.

"Eat the flowers?" Eddie said. He laughed.

"I said you *can* eat them," said the Oracle. "But you don't need to do everything in this world just because you can. Remember that."

Eddie thought that over and said, "Uh huh."

The Oracle said, "You're happy, aren't you, son?" and Eddie

nodded, but looked a little confused.

"Mostly," he said. "Mostly, I'm happy."

"Listen to me, son. You'll be happier yet," said the Oracle. "But first you must go on a journey. Don't be afraid of the unknown. Your dad will be so proud of you, and everyone in the world will seek your advice. You believe me, don't you, son?"

Eddie broke into a smile. "I believe you," he said.

"Promise me you'll do something," said the Oracle. "Stand up for yourself. When opportunity knocks, you've got to answer the door."

Eddie turned around and looked at the door leading to the store. "I don't see no one there," he said.

"Turn around," said the Oracle. "Look at me." There wasn't really any official ceremony for the changeover, never had been, though most people expected such a thing. The Oracle dug through his pockets and found a Mercury head dime. "Here," he said, and gave the coin to Eddie. "Now put that in your pocket and leave it there until after the journey. That's when you'll start to see the future."

"How could you see the future?" Eddie asked. He stared off in the distance and squinted.

"That's a hard one to explain," said the Oracle. There were big concepts, like destiny, fate, and duty that were difficult to condense into teachable sound bytes. And yet the boy deserved an explanation. The Oracle made a fist and rapped on the flower box. "Knock, knock," he said.

Eddie's eyes lit up and he asked with great expectation, "Who's there?"

"You are," said the Oracle.

CHAPTER THIRTEEN

Possum stared at Penelope's profile. He set his pencil down and she wondered what he saw in her, and if he'd see that forever.

"You're wasting my time," she said.

"What's wrong?" Possum asked.

"Shouldn't you be doing something productive?" she asked.

He wasn't even pretending to draw her.

"Like what?" he answered. "I've already chopped enough wood for the next two seasons. We have money and groceries. What's left to do?"

"I don't know," she said. "I just think you should do something." Put up a fence or sharpen the knives. Anything but watch her. She knew enough about being in love to be frightened. It wouldn't last. How could it? The gods were capricious and something would happen to muck things up, because that was the way of the world and all you could do was wait, and watch as your life fell apart.

He looked hurt. "Sorry," he said. "Didn't mean to bother you."

She forced herself to calm down. He could not know that something was troubling her, and she wasn't about to tell him. Possum had enough troubles of his own without being burdened by hers. And she had no proof that she was in danger, just a vague unsettling feeling that settled over her like fog. "Don't sketch me anymore, at least not now," she said. "Let's go outside, and you can help me with my painting." He was teaching her how to work with watercolors.

"Sure," he said. He shrugged. He was adorable when he shrugged—the way he cast his glance downward and curled his lips into a half-grin. He slid a pad of paper beneath his arm and stuffed a plastic cup with brushes in his shirt pocket. Then he waited for her signal before stepping behind to take her chair. He leaned down and nuzzled the top of her head. "Love you," he said.

She tilted her chin upward but was so overcome by emotion she could not speak.

He touched his lips to hers and said, "Let's work on perspective today." He wheeled her out the door and down the ramp and around to the new deck along the back wall.

It was a gorgeous afternoon, sunny and warm with just enough of a breeze to cool her yet not kick up dust to ruin her watercolors.

Possum brought over her easel and looked thoughtfully at the landscape she had started.

"You have trouble with illusions," he said. "And that's what perspective is—nothing more. It's just fooling the eye into thinking that your painting has dimension, and that some things are closer to the front."

"Trouble with illusion," she said. "I suppose that's true. I always think that what I see is what I get."

"You do, when you look at me," he said. "What you see is what you get." He grinned and again she was overcome with affection for him. She had never felt so secure.

But security was quickly replaced by the nagging memory that everything could be taken away in an instant.

"Do you ever have the feeling that things are too good to be true? That it's about to fall apart?"

"All the time," he said. Such a look of worry darkened his face that she wished she could take back her words.

🌿

Williams Valley was a dull little town, with charming well-kept areas for tourists and a trashy but cheap area where the locals lived. Hera decided it would be easier to hide amongst the locals.

Alexander found them a rental cabin three blocks from Water Street, at the end of a shady gravel road called Old Gravel Road. The landlady lived in a manufactured home next door with her two homely daughters.

The cabin consisted of three small bedrooms and the outside shingles painted in various shades of brown, as if the painter had run out of paint before completing the job. Inside, the rooms were paneled with bizarre combinations of knotty pine boards, faux oak wainscoting, and wood-toned Contact Paper. It either looked woodsy or like something made from dried flesh, depending on how Hera was feeling. The front door led directly into a cozy living room, with exposed beams and a wood stove in one corner. The whole place was haphazardly furnished in *period garage-sale* style.

Hera had detested "country living" since the old days. Williams Valley was even deader than Alexander's homestead. What was it mortals hoped to find when they moved to nowheresville to get away from it all?

Three days after moving in, she told Alexander, "I gotta get out. Can you watch *the brat*?"

"Could you pick up a few things?" Alexander asked. He made her a list, which she stuffed into her handbag beside PeeWee and his ever-present baby wipes box.

Hera walked out to the porch and held her nose at the stench of a neighbor's floral scented-dryer sheets. They didn't even smell like flowers. Civilization had taken things a little too far. She headed into "town."

It was a little hard to believe that Zeus had come to this sinkhole on his own. The Fates were somehow involved, but why here? Why a place where people washed out their underwear in the sink and left them out to dry on clotheslines where anyone could spy them?

Hera stood at the foot of Water Street and thumbed her nose at the culture. She whittled down her body to Tyra Banks trim, bleached her hair white and put it up in a ponytail like the one she'd seen on reruns of *I Dream of Jeannie*, the only show anyone could get around here without cable. She wasn't sure how she felt about the harem pants, though the metal bra felt great against her skin first thing in the morning, and the dangling coins added a nice touch. Truth be told, she possessed a stunning décolleté. She had recently given her tits a magical lift and now they were round and firm as cue balls. Her spike-heeled sandals were to die for, despite the difficulty of maneuvering over the dirt and gravel.

PeeWee screamed, "Are you there?" from his baby wipes box. He could be so annoying. Yesterday, he had given her pointers (something he had picked up on an AM radio call-in show with Martha Stewart) on baking irresistible brownies. As if Hera's situation weren't wretched enough, she had gone ahead and followed Martha's recipe. She'd made the frigging brownies to the best of her ability (it was her first time mixing by hand). But because they were almost out of food she'd had to be creative and substitute a few "suggested" ingredients. The brownies had ended up gooey as tar and tasting like chocolate lasagna. To make matters worse, PeeWee had gloated a bit too merrily at her failed effort.

"Hey, Hera," PeeWee said. "Time to let your genie out of the bottle. Let me out," he begged. "Have a heart."

He irritated her to no end and she was tired of it. Maybe it was time to find a new sidekick. "Oh, why not?" she said, and dragged out the baby wipes box and shook it up enough to make PeeWee dizzy. She opened the lid to tell him off, but snapped it tight before he could answer her. There was a time and place for everything, and PeeWee's time had ended. She wound rubber bands around the container to keep him from escaping, and dropped him into a garbage can by the entrance to the grocery store.

Grocery store, she mused. Was there something she was supposed to pick up? Whatever it was, she couldn't remember and decided to revive herself at a café where they served fried garbanzo balls wrapped in flatbread, something the waiter said was Mediterranean and called felafel. She ended her meal with the most amazing slice of Reine de Saba (Queen of Sheba), a rich chocolate cake with mocha buttercream frosting.

A large woman saw the cake and said loud enough to be heard, "I just look at food like that and I gain weight!"

Hera smiled. She took a big bite of cake and said, "So true!" The rich taste made her shudder. She stared at the large woman and magically sent six hundred and fifty calories her way. Look at it and gain weight? What did they think? The calories had to go somewhere—those were the laws of physics. Why not give them to somebody who was already fat? If they only knew that magic was the key to maintaining a svelte figure maybe they'd learn to shut up and stop trying to stay on a diet.

"Delicious," she said loud enough for the fat woman to hear. To drive home the point, she licked the plate.

Next she decided to treat herself to a bikini wax at the Face and Bodyworks Factory. A good-looking Frenchmen with a red fleur-de-lis tattooed on one muscular shoulder nodded at her, then frowned as he answered the phone. "No!" he cried with a pronounced accent. He seemed panic stricken. "Not today! *Zut alors!* We are understaffed! Barney, our towel boy, quit and took several of my best men with him! That is impossible for you to come in!" His chest was bare and he wore tight black leather pants and sandals made from tires.

He was giving her inappropriate ideas. "Got room for me, *garçon?*" she said. She took a provocative stance, her eyes lowered, her lips parted, her chest thrust slightly forward.

The Frenchman practically ignored her. He curled his lip and shook his head, no.

"That's what you think, Monsieur Elvis!" She growled, then zapped him with an incantation of submission that straightened out his lip, in addition to adjusting his attitude.

He apologized profusely for his rudeness. He admiringly looked her over. "Can you ever forgive me?" he said with a bow of his head.

The spell had left her so weak that Frenchie had to carry her to the back, where he gently set her down on the leather-covered massage table.

She allowed him to undress her. His fingers felt hot against her flesh. "The works," she said. Screw the Fates! She hadn't gotten laid in a month. Why should her husband be the only one permitted to play around? It was Hera's turn now. "I want you to do everything you know how to. Make me bark like a dog if you can do it."

Frenchie began by enrobing her in scented hot mud like she was his bonbon. Before the mud dried, he led her to the showers and helped her lather off. He loofahed her back and gave her a thoroughly professional breast massage with the soap on a rope. He worked his hands expertly down her body.

She felt squeaky clean and dirty all at the same time.

He brought her back to the massage table and toweled her dry with soft thick cloths. It had been a while since any man had complimented her on her creamy thighs or gazed upon her breasts, eyes ablaze with longing. The second time his hands grazed her crotch, Hera guided them toward her vulva. She moaned with pleasure at his touch.

"What's your name?" she whispered.

"François," he said, nearly as breathless as she.

"Ever been love slave to a goddess, François?" she said.

"No, Madame. That pleasure has not yet been mine."

"There's gotta be a first time for everything, don't you agree?"

François nodded. "Tell me what you would like for me to do," he said.

"Oh, don't worry," Hera said with a laugh. "I'm not at all shy. You'll never need to ask if it's as good for me as it is for you! Because if it isn't, I'll kill you."

From his wry smile she knew he thought she was kidding.

"Shall I wear a sheath?" he asked.

"Oh, I guess," she said. "Though I don't mind using a towel to mop up the wet spot as long as you're the one who does the laundry."

He blushed. "I meant to protect us from diseases, you know, *dis-EASE-es*."

"I'm probably immune," she said, "and you don't matter."

He smiled and brought his lips to hers and probed her mouth with his soft tongue. He tasted sweet, of meadow flowers. Most likely it was Juicy Fruit gum. He kissed her neck and licked her ears and tickled her nipples with his nose.

Alexander. Oh, sweetie, she thought, and imagined it was his big hand stroking her buttocks, his strong arm supporting her back, his gorgeous body snuggling beside hers. She imagined the big Greek trembling with desire, his breath hot against her neck, his more-than-a-mouthful manhood pressing against her.

"I love you," said her dream lover. " ... can't live without you ... must have you. Hera! Hera! Hera!"

Why was it that so often the best sex wasn't even real? It did not take too long before François had satisfied her. She pushed him off before he was ready, and said coldly, "I'm ready for my bikini wax, *s'il vous plaît.*"

🦋

Igor took Horsie and went outside in the yard to play in the sandbox behind the cabin. He spent some time clearing away damp leaves and garbage before smoothing the sand flat and making a road with plastic blocks. He brought out a box filled with his trucks and put Horsie in one of them to deliver sand to the barn. His clothes were too tight and his wings hurt from being crushed by his shirt. He did not wear shoes because he thought the shiny hard skin of his feet looked just like army boots. His feet never got cold, either, though sometimes he found it difficult to walk. They were sort of small, compared to the rest of him, but his mother told him not to worry because his father had small feet and that hadn't kept his father from getting a job as king of the gods.

The little girl from next door came out and stood at the side of the yard. She wiggled around and looked at him with bright eyes that made him feel funny. She had very long black hair and a pink dress. She ran toward him and sat on the edge of the sandbox.

"Can I play with you?" she asked.

"Sure," Igor said, as if he did this all the time. She was pretty and she smelled sweet, like milk. He sat with his legs curled beneath him, so that she could not see his feet.

He had seen her several times from his window, and ran to his room the moment she noticed him and waved. Now he didn't want to run away.

"I go to first grade," said the little girl. "Where do you go?"

"I'm home-schooled," Igor said, remembering what his mother had told him to say.

The little girl told a joke. "What has two legs and flies?"

"I don't know."

She laughed. "A dead guy."

At first, he didn't get it.

"My mom owns your house, you know," said the little girl.

"So?" Igor replied, but the little girl looked pleased with herself just the same.

They played with Igor's trucks for a while, but then the little girl started to pout and said that since she had played his game for a while it was time to play hers. "I want to play house," she said. "You be the daddy and I'll be the mommy."

"Okay," said Igor, though he didn't really want to.

They made a sand baby and then made sand food for all of them to eat: sand salad and sand pudding and sand cookies.

The little girl tried to serve the food in Igor's trucks, but everything fell apart. "That's okay," she said. "It all falls apart in your stomach, anyway."

They washed the "dishes" in the sand box.

The little girl yawned. "Time to go to bed," she said. She took off her shirt right there in front of him and lay down on the sand.

Her chest was flat, not at all like his mother's, but somehow different from his. He wanted to be close to her.

"Aren't you going to put on your pajamas?" she asked.

"I don't have any," he said.

"Then you'll have to pretend. Like me." She closed her eyes. "It's okay. I won't look till we turn out the lights."

He unbuttoned his shirt and stretched out beside her. He gave her a dry kiss on the cheek.

"Can I look now?" she asked.

"No!" Igor cried. "Not yet!" He gave her another kiss. And then another one.

"I'm cold," said the little girl. "Wish we had a blanket."

He was scared, but hoped against hope that she wouldn't make fun of him. Igor took off his shirt and unfurled his wings. He wrapped them around her.

The little girl smiled and put her arms around him. That was when she noticed that the blanket grew from his back. She sat up abruptly, stared at him and screamed. Then she ran away.

He didn't dare tell his mother because he worried she might hurt the little girl. Igor decided then that he would never again try to make friends. And he would never again take off his shirt in front of anybody.

Hera hobbled home and saw Alexander wave from the kitchen. From the appetizing aroma she knew he was frying up the last of their food: chopped garlic, onions, and thin slices of eggplant. After that, it was peanut butter and jelly sandwiches until someone caved in and did the shopping.

She let herself in and checked the counter to see if Alexander had left her some coffee. He had. Good boy. The perfect man. In so many ways.

"Did you buy groceries?" Alexander casually inquired.

"I forgot," Hera said. Buying her own food seemed beneath her. Being asked to buy it for others was an even lower blow.

"We are out of milk and cereal and almost everything else, too."

"Alexander, I just don't *do* groceries," she informed him. "That's a bit mundane, wouldn't you say?" Just *who* did he think she was? Williams Valley ghetto living or not, there were still a few levels below which she was not willing to stoop.

"I'll do it, but you will have to watch the boy," said Alexander. "For an hour or so."

"Oh, all right," she said, and gave him her most flirtatious smile. She suspected François would be over soon enough, and he could watch the boy.

❦

I want to try sculpting next," Penelope said. They were sitting at the table and she was bored. She had practically given up on watercolors. Her paintings never resembled anything she was trying to capture on paper, but weren't abstract enough to look purposeful.

"Don't be afraid to experiment," Possum said. "Failure is part of the process. That's what art is. You explore each piece and see what happens. It's never the same. That's why I love it."

He started her on red clay, promising to teach her to carve only after she had practiced shaping the clay with her fingers. He gave her a board and warned her not to make the sculpture too thick. "We'll have to sun-dry it," he said, "and that's not as stable."

The clay was cold and hard beneath her fingers. She loved its heft and the way it made her work to mold it to her whim.

He worked alongside her, sculpting puppies with large eyes and thick tails.

"We should get a puppy," she said, and he nodded, but looked unsure.

"You have to pay a lot of attention to puppies," he said. "I've never taken care of anything like that before. I don't know if I want the responsibility," he said.

"You take care of me," she said.

"Not really," he said, nearly stuttering. "I think you take care of me."

He was wrong. She did little for him. She could barely cook a meal without him setting out all the ingredients before her first.

She shaped a wide tree and used her thumbs to press a woman's shape in the center of the trunk.

"Nice," Possum said. He sounded very sincere.

She knew he was in awe of her, but couldn't understand why. She had done nothing to deserve his respect—she was an invalid and utterly dependent on him.

He set his puppy beside her tree. "Hope it doesn't christen it," he said, and laughed.

She could not bring herself to smile. Its teeth looked sharp enough to bite through the clay and its eyes were darker red than the rest of it. "Oh," she said, the feeling of unease once again taking root inside her. She looked away from his clay creature. "I didn't realize." It was no puppy he had created, but a wolf.

Alexander walked away from the cabin without confronting Hera. He was afraid that if he said anything his words would turn into weapons as they had so often in the past. The children's rhyme was wrong. Words could hurt as much as, or maybe more than, stones. He remembered telling his wife that it was all her fault, that if she'd been watching Stasia instead of letting her play at the neighbor's. He remembered how she had blamed him, and how easy it had been to accept the blame.

The sun was making its descent and had passed the treetops; the air was very warm, but not at all muggy the way it would have been if they were still in the city. Hera could be so self-centered. It hadn't bothered him before, perhaps because he thought she was going through some phase. She did not show Igor the affection her son craved and deserved. By all rights Alexander ought to despise her, yet he felt mysteriously drawn toward her, a conspiratorial attraction that made it difficult to meet Igor's glance without guilt. He no longer knew to whom he owed his loyalties.

He listened to the crunching of gravel beneath his shoes. The sound reminded him of foot soldiers marching in an army. If only he knew who he was fighting, or even where the battle was to be.

This morning he had disobeyed Hera's wishes by calling a specialist in Manhattan to ask about Igor's disease.

"Of course it's hard to say without a proper examination," the doctor had said. "But from the symptoms you've described, well, I would have to guess, Progeria."

Alexander had not understood the word, and had asked the doctor to repeat it for him.

Progeria.

Ironically, the word was from a Greek word meaning old age.

"What can we do?" Alexander had asked.

"Nothing," said the doctor. "It's not treatable. Poor prognosis. Of course, it's important to keep the kid comfortable, especially in the late stages."

And then the doctor had urged Alexander to bring Igor to his clinic for a thorough examination. "I'd like to run some tests. Perhaps enroll the child in a study."

And from the doctor's tone of voice, Alexander knew that he must do all he could to keep Igor from the clutches of anyone who wanted to study him. There was no cure for Igor. The doctor had confirmed this. There was only explanation, and all the explanations in the world could not help the boy.

The child grew older with each passing day. Alexander shuddered. Igor might become a teenager within weeks. How long could he survive? Another few months if he were lucky. Perhaps even less. Perhaps that would be luckier still.

The grocery was the first store on the boardwalk. They kept it very clean and bright, with a wonderful selection of fresh foods and wine and the heavenly scent of bread baking in the store's bakery. Sunshine and warmth poured through the large windows paneling the front wall. Shopping here was as pleasurable as anything he had done in the past few years.

He wanted to cook something nice for Igor, perhaps to compensate for those things he could never provide. He bought far too much, filling up his cart with more food than he could manage to carry home. Fresh feta and cucumbers and olives and Roma tomatoes and milk and even two types of bread. Flour and sugar and eggs and salt and pepper and fresh basil and oregano and rosemary. Sausages and hard salami and a plump chicken. Red grapefruit from Florida and sweet local carrots. Plums and apples. Roast beef sliced paper-thin and mustards and horseradish. Cold pressed olive and walnut oils. Red wine vinegar and garlic bulbs and sweet onions. An estate Merlot produced by a local vineyard; a cheap Italian red perfect for cooking.

He apologized to the grocer at the checkout stand. "I will need to make a couple of trips," he said.

The grocer was a kindly old man, who asked if Alexander wanted to arrange delivery to simplify things. "My son," he said, "Eddie's his name. Loves to help. He'll bring everything over in the afternoon."

"Thank you," said Alexander. "That is most kind." He paid for the order and wrote down his address. A slow-witted young man stopped sweeping and came over to ask, "Got any deliveries?"

The grocer nodded, and pointed to Alexander. "This is my son," he said.

Alexander shook the young man's hand. "Hello, Eddie," he said. "I appreciate your help."

Eddie said, "I can go right now," and Alexander protested, not yet wanting to return home. Some day he would have to face the weakness in him that made him want to run away every time his life became too difficult. "I'm not going home right away," he said.

"That's okay," said Eddie. "I can go out later. If nobody is home, I'll just wait."

Alexander gave him a five-dollar tip and said, "There's someone home. A woman and a child. You can leave the groceries with them." He left the store empty-handed.

A white Lincoln crawled along the street as if in search of a place to park. The driver slowed and a window rolled down.

Alexander looked inside the car and was overcome by a creepy feeling he couldn't explain. Suddenly, the car picked up speed. It zipped around the corner and made a U-turn on Calypso Street.

"Must be out-of-towners," he heard someone say. A tanned blond man in tennis white was standing on the sidewalk, passing out handbills to tourists. "Ooh!" he said, "You look like just the kind of man we want to reach out to." He gave a flier to Alexander, who immediately tossed it into the trashcan without as much as a cursory glance.

But the oddest thing happened next: Alexander heard a familiar voice cry out, "Help me!" from the garbage. Startled, he reached back toward the can and pulled out a plastic blue box. Inside the box was the invisible man, the one Hera called PeeWee.

"Thank the Goddess you've found me," said PeeWee. "But you

know the rules. I'm your slave now."

"I do not want a slave," Alexander said.

"Try it before you knock it, big boy!" said PeeWee in his high-pitched whine. "Now look, there's something I want you to see." He instructed Alexander to fish the handbill from the garbage can.

Alexander did as he was told. "Got it," he said.

"Good," said PeeWee. "Study it. I think you'll find an answer to one of life's many questions."

Alexander sat on a wooden bench to read.

The handbill advertised a series of weekend *Denihilism* retreats at a resort called New Olympus. "Accompany Zeus on a shamanic journey to reawaken your soul. As men, our sense of joy is often lost to our sense of responsibility. Recapture that lost self, and grow into a Man who is unafraid to be a full and equal partner with the Goddess and Mother Earth."

Zeus. Hera's ex. He had not expected to find him quite so easily.

"Through guided imagery, sacred sweats, drumming circles, new and ages-old rituals—all in the private and safe company of other men—we will celebrate each other and watch our spirits soar."

"Did I tell you or did I tell you?" PeeWee asked.

"You told me," said Alexander. "More than once. Now quiet, please. I need to think."

He sat back to read the notice in its entirety again. For reasons he did not understand, this notice of Denihilism filled him with tremendous longing. He folded up the handbill and stared out at the street. Off in the distance stood the solitary mountain, Williams Peak, independent yet strong. Alexander stuffed the handbill in his pocket to take home. Hera had implied that Zeus was a fake, yet the retreat sounded interesting. Authentic. He felt curious.

He had been taking care of others since the day his parents had brought him to America. One grew tired of the endless responsibilities of being a man. Of standing alone yet needing to lean on others. He felt trapped. What would it be like to join the circle of men? To run free in the forest, then skinny-dip in mineral springs? Forget, if only for a moment, about the past. Despair overwhelmed him, for he wanted more than anything to search for, and perhaps find, that joyful part of his soul he feared was forever lost to the world.

"There's a free lecture going on right now," said the man who was giving out the handbills. "No obligation."

"Sounds interesting," Alexander said.

"Over in the high school auditorium. Check it out." He pointed Alexander down the street. Tracking down Zeus had been Hera's goal, but only because Alexander had not known before now that it was his fate to meet with the god.

"Master," said PeeWee. "I hate to bother you, but can you find me some other vessel besides this plastic box? There's some sticky green *schmutz* on my side and I desperately need a bath."

"Fine," said Alexander. He found himself walking toward the high school. Absently, he took a handkerchief from his pocket, shook it out, and emptied PeeWee into that. He folded the cloth back into a square and replaced it in his pocket.

"That's just fine," said PeeWee, with a grateful sigh. "I like it better here already."

CHAPTER FOURTEEN

Because of his mother, Possum was used to moody women. Still, his feelings were hurt whenever Penelope yelled at him. Since the small carving had disappeared, it seemed she yelled at him more each day. It could have been a coincidence, but he also worried that she simply didn't like him anymore. He was afraid to ask. Because unless he learned for sure otherwise, he could blame it all on her emotions. And emotions could change like a river current, from gentle to raging.

The blackberries were ripe; he had gone out picking and now carried home two full buckets, enough to make jam. His mother had taught him how to can back in the days when she was well enough to put up fruits and vegetables each summer. Putting up jam was historical preservation, a way to store the sensation and taste of summer.

Together, he and his mother had washed and peeled and chopped and boiled and sweated out summer days. They had kept the stove stoked, even though it was blistering hot outside and in, sterilized jars in the old steamer and filled them with jam and some produce from the garden. His mother let him hold the tongs to fish out the processed jars of blue lake beans, corn, and squash. Those days canning with his mother were among his favorite memories.

His favorite though, was making jam. Just sugar and pectin and berries mashed flat and boiled in a special pot to syrupy sweetness. The aroma was heavenly, like beeswax and lilacs. When the last of the jam had been emptied into the last of the jars, and the pot was cool and the syrup hard as taffy, his mother allowed him to pull the confection from the sides of the pot and scrape the spoons to eat as much as he could get. The jam at the bottom of the pot was scorched, with the flavor of caramel.

It was silly, but he hoped making jam would cheer up Penelope. He set the buckets on the porch and knocked at the screen door. She hated when he barged in without knocking.

"Possum?" she asked.

"Who else would it be?" he answered, picking up his buckets and toeing open the door. He brought a bucket close and held it before her. "Berries," he said, immediately regretting his inane need to identify everything.

She smiled, briefly, but long enough that he could close his eyes and take his fill with the pleasure of having seen her happy. "May I have one?" she asked.

He set down the buckets and fed her a berry, then another, followed by another. They stained her lips dark. "Yummy," she said.

She noticed his purple fingers and stuck out her purple tongue.

He reached for her and bent to pull her into his embrace. The flavor of berries lingered on her lips. He urged his tongue into her mouth. "Yummy," he said.

She pulled him onto her lap. At first he tried to keep his weight from her, but before long, he let himself sink into her body. It felt good to let her hold him aloft. "I love you," he said.

She was about to answer when a gust of wind banged the screen door and she bolted upright and pushed him away. "What's that?" she screamed. When she frowned, her face darkened to red.

"It's the wind," he said. Why was she so jumpy? He knelt beside her and tried to catch her eye, but the tender moment had passed. Not wanting to let go, he prompted, "I love you."

If she heard him, she gave no answer. Instead she pulled away into herself, to a hiding place so dense and private he could not come near.

❦

Romance was exhausting. Hera took a nap and left François to watch the boy. When she awakened, she found the two of them sitting on the floor, playing a game of checkers. Worse, it looked like François was letting the kid win. Sycophantic suck-up. Was this the best she could do? Apparently so.

"What are you doing, boys?" she asked in her sweetest voice.

"You're awake." François smiled. He stood, accidentally kicking over the checkerboard.

"Hey!" Igor scowled. "Watch what you're doing." He picked up the pieces but didn't give Hera the time of day. Not that she ever paid attention to him, but he was her kid. He was supposed to respect his mother no matter what.

"Come here, cutie," she said, and François hurried over to attend to her needs.

"What about our game?" said Igor, pouting. He had grown at least two inches since morning.

François turned and took a step back. He looked confused. "We were almost through," he said with a shrug.

He wasn't a top-quality love slave but she wasn't up for finding another one. And he looked good, which might at least make Alexander jealous. "I told you to watch the kid, not play with him. Now, I said, 'Come here,' and I meant it!" Hera raised her voice enough to let him know she meant business.

"You always ruin all my fun," Igor said. He stomped his foot and ran off toward his room. He slammed the door and there was a loud thud as if he had thrown himself against the door to keep them from coming in to get him.

He was probably sucking his thumb and hugging his Horsie. "And you!" she screamed at François. "What about my needs?"

He looked contrite and bustled over to rub her feet.

Hera laughed. She could get whatever she wanted from any man with guile or magic. It was almost too easy.

Eddie finished up the sweeping, waved good-bye, and pushed the cart out the door. It was evening, the part of day his dad said was called twilight. Somewhere around four hundred paces, he lost track of his count. In a few more minutes, he reached the address where the big man had told him to deliver the groceries.

A mean lady answered the door. "Is Mr. Alexander here?" Eddie asked. "I have his groceries."

"He's gone out," she said. "But go ahead and bring in the food and I'll tell him you said hello."

Eddie peered past her to where an ugly dark kid sat reading in the corner. Beside him sat the handsome man who worked at the body salon. The ugly kid looked up and waved. Eddie waved back.

The handsome man said, "Hello there, Eddie. How are you?"

Eddie wondered how anyone as mean as that lady could manage to get two nice boyfriends.

He knew he shouldn't stare, but the ugly kid fascinated him. The boy was dark as twilight and if Eddie didn't know any better, he'd have thought he saw wings poking out from his shirt.

The mean lady said, "What are you staring at, goon?" when he tried to get a better look. She yelled at the ugly kid and told him to go to his room.

"See you later," said the ugly kid.

"Okay," said Eddie. He hoped that was true.

Eddie had been called a lot of names, but nobody had ever called him a goon. He wasn't even sure what it meant and that made him feel terrible, but he wasn't sure what he had done wrong. He was going to tell his dad about her, even though he already knew what his dad would say: "Sorry, Eddie. There will always be people saying mean things. Don't let it get to you." But Eddie would feel better for telling.

He brought in the groceries as fast as he could and left without saying good-bye.

Eddie walked home, curious about the ugly kid. He wished he'd had the chance to talk to him.

𝕊

The old coot had been nosy and annoying and self-righteous, but once they parted ways, Sanders began to miss the Oracle. It had been nice, in a way, having someone around to talk to.

Now he had to get to work and find the kid and his obnoxious mother. Williams Valley was a small enough place that the locals knew one another and would notice when someone new moved in. He learned that someone new had moved onto Old Gravel Road, someone the locals didn't approve of because of her lifestyle and that she took on airs. He learned she had a son with some strange deformity. Sanders was an adept enough spy to ascertain that indeed, the woman in question was Mrs. Zeus. But the baby was no longer a baby, and more than ever Sanders longed to study him and assume his care. He called the family practice group in town and learned that Mrs. Zeus had never brought in her son.

Clearly the boy needed medical attention. The child had never had immunizations; his health was imminently in danger. Sanders patted his pocket. It shouldn't be too difficult to persuade a judge to lengthen his seventy-two-hour hold and buy a little more time to run more tests.

The police station was a one-room brick building staffed by a big stupid-looking baldheaded man with a broken nose.

"Hello," Sanders said to the officer, who gave him a blank stare and took a minute or more to respond in kind. Sanders saw a picture on the wall of the policeman wearing a red satin robe over black satin shorts, boxing gloves, and a mouth guard.

"That you?" he asked.

"That's me," said the dimwit. The man had evidently taken one hit too many in the head.

Sanders explained his predicament.

"That's too bad," said the bruiser. "What do you want me to do about it?"

"I have a court order authorizing me to remove the child. I'd like you to come with me, for protection."

"Who you need protection from?" asked the bruiser. "I seen this lady—she's a teensy thing." But he agreed to accompany Sanders and make sure nothing got out of hand. "When do you want to go?" he asked.

"Right away," Sanders said.

"Go ahead and have a seat," said the big man. "It's going to take me a while to remember where I put my keys."

Hera looked through the bags of groceries. Damn that traitorous tawny-faced Greek. He hadn't been considerate enough to remember her M&M'S.

Suddenly, from out of nowhere, tires screeched to a halt and footsteps thudded on the walkway. There was a fierce pounding on the door, but before Hera had time to react, the door swung open and two men rushed inside, toppling furniture and floor lamps in their wake.

"Where is he?" cried the smaller of the two. "What have you done with him?" He rushed forward, knocking François to the floor. "They have him locked up," said the little man, "we haven't a moment to spare!" and the other grabbed Hera and held her hands behind her back before she had time to realize what was happening.

"What do you want?" she cried to her assailant.

The little cross-eyed fellow spoke. "Just stay calm, Mrs. Zeus, and nobody will get hurt. We have a court order to take your son in for treatment. It's for his own good. He'll die without intervention."

"He'll die *with* intervention, asshole," Hera pointed out.

François stood. The big cop barked an order for him to stand with his hands against the wall. He leaned over to speak to Hera. "You gonna behave?" he asked.

She nodded.

He left her and walked over to François to snap on handcuffs him. "We don't want any trouble," the big fellow said. "Where's the boy? We just want the boy."

Hera had a bad feeling about the whole thing.

Igor must have heard the commotion from his room. He skipped into the living room, wearing only his pajama bottoms. When he saw François, he screamed.

"That's him!" shouted the little man. "Look at the wings! The feet! Holy Mother of God. But he's huge. How can this be?"

She recognized his reedy voice. It was that evil weasel, Dr. Sanders. His smugness worried her until she realized Sanders could not harm her. Their doctor/patient relationship was over.

The big thug touched the butt of his gun to remind them all that he was armed. "Everyone stay calm," he said. He stood, and moved toward Igor.

The boy sank to the floor, terrified.

"Stay calm?" Hera screamed. "You burst into my house and try to kidnap my son and you tell me to stay calm?" Fury surged through her and made her body rigid. "Men!" She felt like a full water balloon ready to explode. "You think you can just take whatever you want any time you feel like it, without even asking or bothering to say please!" She whirled about, enraged. The big man stared but made no move toward his gun. Books tumbled from their shelves and cheap knickknacks flew off the mantel and shattered on the floor.

The evil doctor ran toward Hera and thrust an arm around her neck.

The little fool was trying to immobilize her. Who did he think he was? She'd show him a thing or two about immobilization. She socked him in the groin and when he doubled over, she thrust a high heel to the back of his knee.

"Shit," said Dr. Sanders in a pained falsetto. He moved away, but not quickly enough.

The bitch was back, in full command of her powers. "You can say that again," Hera cried. "Consider this as my post postpartum checkup." Magic flowed from her fingertips. François's handcuffs dissolved into sand. She pointed to Dr. Sanders, blew him a kiss, and turned him into a statue version of himself.

The other thug froze, startled by the transformation. "What do I do now?" he asked the statue. Obviously, he was not the brains of the operation.

"We don't want any trouble," Hera said. "Want a kiss?"

The big fellow blanched and ran out the door.

She let him go.

François's first action was to see about the boy. "Are you okay," he asked. "Did they hurt you?"

Igor's face was wet with tears. He said in a halting voice, "I'm okay."

"What about me?" Hera cried. "Aren't you going to ask about

me? How *I* am?"

"Come on, Hera," said François, sounding irritated. "He's only a kid. He's scared."

"But he's my kid and don't you forget that! Nobody gets to touch my son but me!" Hera screamed. "Not Dr. Sanders. Not Alexander. Not you. Only me!" With that she rushed over to push François away from her son. She smoothed Igor's hair and said, "There, there. Everything will be okay, now. We'll play checkers. You and me. We'll find Daddy and bring him home."

Both Igor and François looked a little lost.

"Make yourself useful," she told François. She pointed to the evil doctor's statue. "Now, be a dear and move that thing into the garden."

❧

The auditorium had filled with men desperate to escape from vacations that were no doubt planned by their pushy wives. Zeus tried not to let on that he was nervous, but it had been some time since he'd had followers, and he didn't want to mess up. He needed Denihilism as much as it needed him. What good could a god do without a populist movement?

He concentrated and breathed out a spell to induce astonishment and wonder. "Men," he said, "My ideas are not new and my message may be one you've heard before, but my words are as true today as they have been for thousands of years. If you give it all away, what do you have left for yourself? If you put everyone before you, how will you ever get around them? If not now, when?"

Applause from the sympathetic crowd filled him with newfound energy and Zeus cast another spell meant to engender loyalty. He prattled on about brotherhood and masculinity, but he could have been reading selections from the Minneapolis phone book for all that mattered. The audience was in his pocket. Men's cheers echoed off the walls. Zeus felt good. Someone, no doubt Barney the towel boy, threw flower petals at his feet. Could he possibly recapture the glory of Ancient Greece?

Elton had set up a registration table at the back of the room, and Zeus gleefully noted that a line was forming as men hurried to sign up for the weekend retreat. He had sweet-talked the men in the audience. Soon it would be time to get to work on the women.

❦

It was dark by the time Alexander returned. "What happened here?" he asked. The front door had broken off its hinges and stood propped against the siding. Alexander peered inside the house from the porch. A lamp and ladder-back chair lay overturned; newspapers and broken glass were strewn over the carpet.

Hera seemed oblivious to the evidence of pandemonium all around her. She sat beside Igor on the couch, listening to him read *The Wizard of Oz*.

Alexander smiled. Wasn't this what he had been hoping for all along? For Hera to take an interest in her own son? An inexplicable feeling of jealousy overcame him. Igor had grown another three inches in as many hours, Alexander thought. His hair was long and shiny, his skin smooth as smoky glass. His eyes were mesmerizing, large and dark. His wings poked through his shirt to form a dramatic cloak. He would be a striking man, should he live that long. He noticed Hera watching him with a satisfied smirk, and turned away from her stare.

"What in the world is happening?" Alexander asked.

"Just a little botched attempted kidnapping," said Hera with a dismissive wave of her hand. "Nothing to get excited about. Since *you* weren't here to protect us, we took care of things on our own. Go on," she said to Igor. "Finish the book."

Alexander paced the floor. An attempted kidnapping? "Will someone please tell me what's going on?"

It took several run-throughs before the story started to make sense, and even then, it didn't. Not really.

Why would a doctor be so selfish as to try and take a child away from his family? Didn't the doctor know that only a god possessed the power to command? Or had the doctor mistaken himself for a god?

Maybe that was the real problem, Alexander thought sadly. Maybe attitudes had changed so much from the time of creation that there was no longer any significant difference between man and his gods.

Our loss. Not the gods'. He fretted about the boy's safety, but something else troubled him, something he couldn't identify, some premonition of trouble ahead. He was not generally a superstitious man, which made it all more disturbing.

Igor closed his book. He looked at Alexander. "Can I play guitar?" he asked, and when Alexander nodded, Igor walked over to the closet where the instrument was stored, and removed it gently from its case. He plucked away at the strings, before long managing to find a crude melody and a refrain in a minor key that did not sound so terribly out of tune. "It's very beautiful," Igor said.

The boy would outgrow the small guitar before long, but no matter. Alexander smiled. "Keep it," he said. "I look forward to hearing you play."

Igor's expression looked pleased. "I might need lessons," he said. "Or, maybe you can teach me?"

"I don't play," Alexander said. His wife and their daughter had been the musical ones.

"Too bad Igor's father isn't around," Hera said. "I'll bet he could teach you. Zeus plays a mean lyre."

"Yeah," Igor said, his voice bitter. "I'll bet he could."

At the mention of Zeus, Alexander remembered the handbill from the grocery. He pulled the paper from his pocket, and smoothed out the wrinkles. "That reminds me," he said. "I found something you will be interested in." He handed the paper to Hera,

She read the handbill, looking amused. "Why, that scheming old Greek!" She drummed her fingers thoughtfully on her chin. "I think you are about to commune with nature, sweetie," she told Alexander. "I want you to sign up for a Denihilism retreat, be my spy."

"It sounds intriguing," he said, with a worried glance toward Igor. Was it safe to leave him?

Hera said, "Don't worry. We can handle things just fine. Go ahead. Have some fun! Think about it: Hot springs. Massage. No dishes for a weekend. You'll have a great time and come back and tell me all about it. Igor and I will hold down the ranch."

She had no trouble convincing him to go. Funny that he could not tell if he was making up his own mind or simply bending to her will.

Igor said, "Yeah. Go ahead. We'll do okay without you. I'm getting big enough to take care of Mom, you know."

Alexander stood still as a statue. I am not the child's father, he thought. He held his head high and resolved that he would do whatever was in the boy's best interest.

Hera gave her son a hug. "That's my boy," she said.

From the handkerchief in his pocket, PeeWee whispered, "It's hot in here. Why don't you let me out?"

"All right," said Alexander. He took out his handkerchief and opened it on the coffee table. "You're free to go," he said, and a rush of warm air swirled around his hand, then dissipated.

PeeWee was not only invisible, but finally, silent.

⚜

Thank the gods, PeeWee thought. It was a miracle. Alexander had released him from the spell. He was free—a free man. Well, not exactly.

It was weird, being him, being invisible while seeing everything in circle-vision. He was like a campfire spark: ephemeral, capable of causing destruction, aggravating as Hades. He tried to move and found that without a master, he could levitate his consciousness.

He practiced flying around the room, dizzying, but not altogether satisfying. It was all so aimless. He wondered if he were experiencing some sort of syndrome: Posttraumatic Slave Syndrome. Once released from bondage, did all slaves feel their lives lacked direction?

He floated through Hera's chest, trying to—at the very least—cause discomfort. But he couldn't even make her giggle. She didn't seem to notice him at all, which was not exactly a new way of relating to him, but still. He tried to pinch Alexander's ear. Still no response.

"Hello," he called, or at least thought he did. It was obvious that no one could hear him. He floated around some more and practiced going up and down like an elevator. After a while, even this got old.

If he was going to do any more than float, he'd need a body. He looked around the room. Damn. It seemed that all the others were already taken.

He floated out the door and into the yard, where there were likely to be more possibilities. He could not feel where his essence ended and the world began. He entered a tree, and though it pleased him to learn that he could make the branches shimmy, he didn't care much for the feeling of being rooted in the ground.

He pulled out of the tree and entered the consciousness of a gray squirrel. The two of them together were just, well, too squirrelly. PeeWee Squirrel chattered and jumped from limb to limb and threatened the neighbor's cat and picked at fleas and ate a least a dozen acorns and buried another forty beneath the compost pile. His heart was beating so fast he thought it might explode.

He pulled out, and looked around the garden for a more suitable host. And then he saw the statue. Aha, he said. A body with no essence. The perfect match. He entered the stone and felt it come to life around him. He focused all his energy on making it move. He wanted to get as far away from Hera as he could.

It took some doing, but he managed to move the legs in a

scissorslike gait. He walked very slowly, but it was probably better that way. He didn't want to attract attention. The work left him feeling very, very hot. He desperately needed water, and stopped to soak his feet in a puddle before continuing. What he needed was a bigger puddle, something deep enough to really cool off.

At some point he passed through the gate and had to make a decision about which way to go next. He decided to find Zeus. After hearing so much about him, PeeWee was curious about the old Greek. Besides, no matter how much a tyrant he proved to be, Zeus couldn't have been any worse than his ex-wife.

In only a few days, Igor outgrew most of his children's clothes. Since his new goal was to become a famous rock star, he used the opportunity to acquire clothing that was all black. It surprised him that his mother approved of his new look when she seemed to disapprove of everything else about him. One afternoon, when Hera wasn't looking, he sneaked outside behind the wood shack to smoke a cigarette. He found the little neighbor girl's older sister was already there, sitting on the edge of the sandbox.

"I heard all about you," she said. She had yellow/white hair and rings pierced through her lip, nose, and eyebrow. She wore a black leather skirt and torn fishnet stockings and a tank top that didn't quite cover her bra straps.

Igor was tall enough to reach her shoulders.

"Got a smoke?" she asked, but without waiting for his answer, she took away his cigarette and inhaled. She leaned close and blew the smoke back in his mouth.

And then she kissed him.

His tongue tasted the metal ring on hers. He pulled back, a little surprised, and maybe afraid.

"My sister told me. I want to see them," she said, and before he could answer, she said, "Let's fuck," and pulled off her shirt.

Her bra was see-through. She had very nice breasts.

He had only a vague idea of what she wanted from him, but that didn't matter. She knew enough for the both of them. She showed him where to touch her.

She ran her tongue along the veins in his wings; he shivered with delight. He resolved to never hide his wings again.

They did it twice before she said, "I have to go. Can you sneak out here later tonight?"

"Sure," he said, feeling happier than he could remember.

As she walked away he called after her. "Wait! I have a joke!"

"Okay," she said. "Go ahead."

"What has two legs and flies?" he asked, and though she laughed, she said nothing. He didn't bother telling her that the answer was Igor.

CHAPTER FIFTEEN

Zeus was happy to let Mr. Bringle supervise the restoration of the lodge to its original grandeur. Everything looked beautiful and clean, the pine paneling lustrous and aromatic, the camp furnishings culled from antique stores and specialty catalogues, the artwork extravagant and rare.

Mr. Bringle was a self-centered piece of work, but the man knew a good painting when he stole it, a trait that Zeus reluctantly admired. Bringle had suggested they hang the El Greco in a prominent place in the dining room and had scattered quaint etchings and name lithographs along the walls. The effect was lush and rich and cultured—exactly what Zeus wanted.

Bringle had rebuilt the stone fountain, which stood in the center of the circular driveway out front. Then, overnight, it seemed, a most charming moving statue had appeared in the water. Zeus found the piece absolutely fascinating—he would have to remember to thank Bringle for finding it—a lifelike male figure in contemporary dress but with a Byzantine feel. Horrible and beautiful at the same time. The sort of thing that made you glad you could stare at it and then move away. And it was kinetic, too. Mr. Bringle certainly had a way for finding art that moved. This one stayed in place while you were watching it, but imperceptibly, the statue traveled the circumference of the fountain, like the shadow of a sundial.

Zeus hung the little carved piece of cherry wood in his quarters. It wasn't the kind of thing that would normally have appealed to him. But he was drawn to the woodland scene it depicted, the rushing river and the ever-changing clouds. He was drawn to the piece as a true collector; he kept it in his quarters because he didn't want anyone else to look at it.

It had been Elton's idea to hire the belly dancers for Friday nights. The troupe consisted of Adara, whose specialty was balancing swords on her head; Calida, whose specialty was her intricate work with the finger cymbals known as zills; Enigma, whose specialty was her ability to keep her enormous tits from escaping their golden restraining cups when she shimmied across the Big Room floor, and Larry, who played an inspired percussion on the *doumbek*.

The devotees sat, slightly reclining, in comfortable orange-canvas sling chairs featured in MoMA's gift store catalogue. Each man held a crystal snifter of Remy Martin. Each wore an ivory-colored tunic and buckskin sandals, the official uniform of the retreat.

Zeus had positioned himself between the new fellow—a man named Alexander—and one of his business partners, Elton the executive. He barely tolerated Elton, but found himself drawn to the big Greek with the mournful eyes and rich baritone voice. Alexander was an honest man, obviously scornful of the mores of neo-Western Civilization.

The way Alexander looked askance at Zeus—while he was preaching, or leading them on a search for wild mushrooms in the woods—let him know that Alexander saw right through him, saw through his words and actions to his frailties and faults. Yet the man still managed to sniff out truffles of wisdom in the duff. Alexander could ignore the bullshit without forsaking the real. Few mortals possessed that ability. Zeus admired him for that.

"Women," Elton said with a conspiratorial grin. He leaned over toward Zeus to add, "They sure put the 'R' in *R and R*, now don't they?" He elbowed Zeus in the arm.

Zeus did his best to move his chair, managing to get about an inch away before giving up. Oh, well, he thought, and took another swig of cognac. He would have preferred something more extravagant for himself, but that might have looked bad. These Americans had been conditioned to believe in sharing.

Mr. Tom, the chef, was saving the *real thing* for the Saturday banquets: a seven-star Metaxa, a Greek brandy that Mr. Tom insisted was rather difficult to come by in the States. It was certainly less effete than cognac. Perhaps it was better this way, to deny himself in order to increase his appreciation for the future.

Oddly enough, the more he drank, the better the cognac started to taste. The better the dancers looked, too. He decided he liked Enigma and her talents, both of them, best of all.

But alas, Adara, the brunette, was up again first. She twirled around counterclockwise, giving each man ample time to leer at her vibrating abdomen. An emerald decorated her belly button and her harem pants were pulled below her hipbone. Her left foot never left the ground; she thrust out her right hip and tapped that foot against the floor to propel her turn.

Zeus could not imagine how the girls managed to stand, let alone dance. "Enigma," he called. His words were slurred and made him sound like he was asking for an enema.

Larry tossed Adara two silver swords that she caught by the hilt. She brandished them before her audience, before balancing them, in a cross, upon her head.

The other women whooped it up, a high-pitched faux Middle Eastern chant of "La la la la la la la la la la la!"

Adara bent backwards, as if doing the limbo, but held her head straight. Her belly moved in rollicking waves and her arms rose gracefully above her head. All the time, she kept the two swords balanced. The scent of sandalwood and jasmine filled the air.

At some point (by then Zeus had lost track of the details), Adara tossed her head back and the swords flew off and punctured the floor with a *ploing*. Larry's drumming began to pick up speed. He rolled his eyes back and slapped his palms furiously against the head of his doumbek while Adara worked the room, thrusting her supple hip close enough to each man's chair to collect a dollar, or five, in tips.

Except for Alexander, who seemed somewhat embarrassed by the whole display. When she saw he wasn't about to tip her, Adara shimmied and shook her chest as close as she could get to Alexander's face without knocking him senseless. Alexander looked to be the only man there who found the experience humiliating.

What a waste. "Enigma," Zeus whimpered. Where was she when he needed her?

The nervous little man, wearing a blue serge suit, white shirt, white socks and black shoes, and an oversized white badge on his lapel that said SECURITY, tiptoed over to whisper to Zeus that he thought their situation was precarious and might lead to trouble. "Union," he whispered. "Sexual harassment. It all scares me to death."

"You need a tunic, man," Zeus said, and the nervous little man said, "I suppose I do."

Sadly, Zeus realized that despite the entertainment value of the belly dancers, they did tend to make the men forget their stated loftier goals. He snapped his fingers as he tried to formulate another plan.

He called Barney the towel boy, to help him rise from his chair. Barney filled in his tunic better than any man there, with the exception of Zeus, and maybe the big Greek. "Looking good," said Zeus, clapping him on the back.

Despite his many regrets, Zeus dismissed the troupe before Enigma could take the stage with her promised reprise. Naturally, a few of the men acted out their displeasure. Harsh words were exchanged, drinks spilled, a fistfight or two ensued. All in all, an enjoyable night.

Yet it was vital he maintain a semblance of order. A rush of adrenaline permitted him to pour on added charisma. "Men!" Zeus shouted. He leaped atop the hearth to address the group. "You must not allow women to control you with their skilled manipulations of your hormones! 'Only he who is *man* enough will release the *woman* in woman,'" he said, quoting Nietzsche.

The room grew quiet.

"For if you don't seize control, you will forever be a slave to a woman's will, and never a master to your own."

"Hear, hear!" said Don the developer.

Zeus was making up the script as he went along. He breathed a sigh of relief that it seemed to be working.

Larry, the doumbek player, asked if he could stay.

A group of about eight men clapped their hands. "A toast to Larry!" offered one drunk. He attempted to stamp his feet, but fell over in his chair and had to be rescued by Barney.

This gave Zeus an idea. He jumped down to grab Elton's nearly full snifter and threw it into the fireplace. "If we allow ourselves to become servants to the grape," he cried, "then how can we call ourselves free men?"

A collective murmuring arose from the floor, but when someone lobbed a glass his way, Zeus decided to change his tactic. Outside, a full moon lit the night. "Howling circle," he announced. He motioned to Barney and told him to take three-dozen towels to the sauna and wait for them there.

"Follow me!" Zeus cried. He stripped off his tunic and urged the others to do the same. He rushed out to the front deck and grabbed hold of the wooden rail. He leaned back and lifted his face skyward to howl at the moon.

At first this felt utterly ridiculous, but in a matter of seconds his feelings changed to joy, release, excitement. The stars shone above him like a thousand fireflies. The air felt refreshing against his cheek, fresh and cool as peppermint.

He looked out to the garden, and the moving statue. Water trickled lazily into the fountain; a frog croaked. He stood there for some time and imagined that for once he saw the statue move before his eyes. "Isn't this great?" Zeus yelled. He sucked in a breath and howled again. He was god and man and beast, an integral extension of the natural world.

Elton the executive joined him on the deck. He mimicked Zeus's actions and shouted, "Yes! I can feel it!"

Zeus called back to the others, saying, "Get out here! All of you! We are not 'howling with the wolves'! We *are* the wolves!" He barred his teeth and urged them all to set their inner wolves free. "Close your eyes," he said, and when it looked like all had obeyed, he focused his magic and turned them all into wolfmen. They stood on their hind legs and bared their fangs and howled into the night. They sniffed at the air and hungered after raw meat. A fetid scent like a fresh kill hovered in the air and the men's eyes shone like opals. The atmosphere was charged with hormones and power. There was a squeaky noise, a howling Chihuahua sound, coming from the statue. Zeus smiled. The heart of a man beat even in stone.

Maybe Remy Martin wasn't the best hung cognac in the world, Zeus thought, but it evidently had enough balls to get the job done. In a matter of minutes a score of men stood naked on the deck, holding onto the railing to lean back and howl like crazed animals. Even stodgy old Alexander was there, towering over the others like a brick wall. In Alexander's plaintive howling, Zeus heard the makings of a ballad. The guy was good. Reminded him a little of one of his sons, Hermes.

He pushed away the thought. It hurt, sometimes, remembering all the children he had lost. One couldn't be both a god and a good father. There just wasn't time.

He howled and listened to the cacophony around him. "That's it!" Zeus cried. "Let it out!" He wanted to encourage his devotees. He really needn't have bothered. The men took to howling naturally, like infants (or even grown men for that matter) took to the breast. The howling crescendoed until it rattled the windows and echoed off the eaves and worried the kitchen staff into coming out to see about the ruckus. The cooks tossed aside their tunics and howled with the best of them.

The nervous little man howled too. Unlike the rest of them, the nervous little man kept on his socks and shoes, and gripped his badge of security.

꧁

It wasn't that Alexander disliked belly dancing as much as he disliked *the show*, but he felt the same about *all* artists who sold their integrity for money. Belly dancing was so beautiful, so sexy when performed as it had been intended: for women by women. He remembered one of the most erotic nights of his life. His soon-to-be-ex-girlfriend had asked him to drive her to a "re-creation" ceremony.

Ten women, nine of them belly dancers, one about to give

birth.

The women had allowed him to sit against the wall as a spectator, but not a participant. How timid he had felt, the lone man among a troupe of women.

"No need to feel you are controlling things," his girlfriend had said. Only later, long after the breakup, did he recognize the anger in her voice.

The woman in labor sat on large pillows in the center of the room beside her midwife. Her friends formed a close circle around her. As she suffered through her contractions they danced, pelvises rocking back and forth in the motion called the camel. They helped her stand in order to join them in dance. The movement seemed to ease her pain. The dancers warbled, high, loud trills that made the room vibrate with the music of life. They rubbed her belly with a sweet-scented oil that made her moan with thanks.

As her contractions increased in strength and duration, so did the dancers' undulating movements. Her language was lost for the moment, replaced by primal grunts, panting and screams. Her friends supported her by her shoulders and urged her to continue dancing.

Belly rolls. Fluttering.

Controlled movements that grew faster and more furious by the moment.

So involved were the women in ushering in creation that they soon forgot he was there observing.

He watched the women, in awe of their natural beauty and grace. For the first time in his life he thought he saw the true face of woman, of woman unfettered by her need to be seen by man.

When the baby was born, he had wept. For this show of sensitivity he had been rewarded with another two weeks in his soon-to-be-ex-girlfriend's bed. After that, things quickly returned to how they had always been. His need to control, her inability to resist.

Fighting.

Anger.

The end of love.

He was glad when Zeus put a stop to the dancing. He respected Zeus for that. It was shameful and inelegant for women to turn sexuality and sensuality, beauty and grace, into entertainment. It was shameful and inelegant for men to slobber over and desire what was only an illusion.

And Zeus had helped them all find true vision.

They had gone outside to face the night and had found light in the shadow of the mountain.

"Let it out!" Zeus had cried, as if they needed the encouragement.

True, at first, it had not come easily, but in a matter of minutes howling became a second language to Alexander. Power, strength, and happiness coursed through Alexander's veins. He howled at the moon and the stars and the mountain and the all-encompassing wilderness. For as long as he could remember, maybe for the first time in his life, Alexander was at peace. He never wanted to leave this place; he howled, announcing his intention to the world.

He howled because he knew at last how it felt to be a man who ushered in the birth of life. He howled because his vision cleared and he saw his place as part of an eternal cosmos.

He howled because howling was the language of creation, the language of life, and as he howled, he saw that it was also the language of death. His howling changed from a cry of strength to one of sorrow.

His daughter had been taken from him, and the pain was still so great that words did not exist that could adequately describe his feelings. And then, another loss, this one still fresh and burning: his love for the doomed boy, Igor.

There were no words to explain these astonishing revelations. An animal did not rely upon the falsities of language to express grief, but was content with the authenticity of his voice. Alexander howled, thinking he might never speak again.

CHAPTER SIXTEEN

M r. Tom had taught Zeus *exactly* how to slaughter the lamb to
minimize trauma and keep the meat from bruising. From there
the meadow ceremony sprang entirely from Zeus's imagination. He
was really quite proud of the way he had woven together ancient and
New Age traditions.

The guests had traded in their tunics for loincloths so they could
get more even tan lines. They looked exhausted, having slept little
and being on the verge of dehydration from so much time in the
sauna. Not to mention the hangovers. In this frame of mind, Zeus
found them more open to suggestion.

As Larry pounded his doumbek, Zeus told the men to streak
their bare chests and faces with warm mud and the juice of wild
blueberries they had gathered after breakfast. He led them to the
meadow, a sunny flat area at the edge of the property. Zeus slipped
off his sandals. He made wildflowers sprout before him; the grass
carpet felt luxurious. The wildflowers, he thought, were an especially
nice touch. At least the customers seemed to like them.

Zeus led them in a dance around the altar, a raised stone platform
that would double as a barbecue pit. The altar was surrounded by
white sand. A lamb bleated from a small shed about a hundred feet
from the altar.

"This is a solemn celebration," Zeus proclaimed, "of your manhood."

"I feel it!" cried Elton.

Most of the other men nodded in agreement. Alexander looked
as if he were too overcome to speak. Larry led them in frenzied
movement with his doumbek. They danced until each man grew so
exhausted he could no longer use words, only grunt and growl to
communicate.

Barney led the lamb into the circle and up the steps to the altar.
He carried a bucket-sized hammered copper goblet strapped to his
back.

Zeus placed his hands around the lamb's face and uttered an
incantation that put the lamb into a deep trance. He signaled Larry
to increase the tempo of his drumming.

The men chanted something incomprehensible in Swahili,
some macho fertility ditty Don the developer had taught them in

last night's midnight mineral bath. Zeus didn't understand a word, but it was oddly powerful.

Zeus lifted up the lamb's head with his left hand and waited while Barney placed the bowie knife in his right. He said nothing, trusting that the symbolism of the moment needed no further explanation.

Larry's drumming grew more furious and loud.

"Close your eyes!" Zeus shouted. "Can you feel it?"

There was a wave of shouting and grunting and Zeus turned them all into wolves for a few seconds and let them howl and sniff at the air. The sound was deafening and a musty smell, like dirty fur and piss, wafted about. Maybe next time he'd let them kill the lamb with their teeth, but for today he had planned something more civilized. He changed them back to human form.

The crowd went wild and continued to howl.

In a quick and painless move he slit the lamb's neck while Barney held out the goblet to catch the blood. With so many devotees focusing their energy upon him, Zeus felt his power surge. He turned the lamb's blood into wine and took a hearty gulp.

The men cheered.

Barney carried the goblet and offered it to each man in the circle. After all had taken from the goblet, Zeus changed the wine back into blood, and poured it over the sand to create stick figures representing Man and Woman. "We do not take life," he screamed, "But we bestow it! Let this blood give us strength and renew our vitality!"

By now, even the nervous little man had lost control and was dancing with abandon.

Mr. Tom came out now to see to the barbecue. His staff took over the preparation of the lamb. They cleaned and skinned it and tied it to a spit while waiting for the fire to be hot enough that the charcoals glowed red at their centers. Two men were assigned to turn the spit and baste the lamb with a fine olive oil and spices and drippings. As the day wore on and fat dripped into the flames, the air filled with the aromas of garlic and rosemary and roasting meat.

Large canopies were set up in the pasture to provide shade. The men wandered through the forests to rejuvenate their bodies in the mineral springs. Larry drummed throughout the day, as if in a trance.

Near dinnertime, Mr. Tom brought out whole eggplants, sweet onions, and red peppers. He sliced the vegetables and marinated the slices in garlic oil and wine. He set up a grill, and when the coals were white-hot, roasted the vegetables. Meanwhile, his staff brought out folding tables and blankets and chairs, along with platters of goat cheese, wild strawberries and blueberries, and honeyed dried fruits. They poured a coarse red wine called "Boutari" for the guests from bottomless carafes.

The guests consumed their feasts until they grew sated. They sang praises to the god who had given them back not only their manhood but also their lives.

After thousands of years, Zeus had reclaimed his crown. Soon, he thought, it would be time to reclaim his queen. He remembered the glorious redhead from a time long ago and far away. He wanted her, and when a god chose one specific woman, no one else would do. It had always been thus, and to muck around with tradition was to invite disaster.

The Fates intervened once again, when Mr. Bringle, that sneaky little shit, popped in to tell Zeus exactly where to find his bride. "I have something for you," he said, and pulled out a shiny golden chain. "A trinket really, but it screams your name. I've been meaning to give this to you," he said, a little reluctant to hand it over.

"I know that charm," Zeus said, holding out his hand until Mr. Bringle dropped the necklace into Zeus's palm. "Where did you find it?"

"In a bush. At the home of the young artist you so admire," said Mr. Bringle.

"Did you happen to see a cherry-haired beauty while you were there?"

"There was a woman," said Mr. Bringle, "but she wasn't my type. I don't really remember much about her."

"Not your type?" Zeus said. He was not surprised. "Good thing she's my type." Soon, Zeus thought, he would go to the cabin where she lived and claim her hand. Maybe even a bit more of her than that.

Later in the evening, after the men had time to recover from their feast, they went for another dip in the mineral baths. Exhausted, they gathered in the lodge, where Mr. Tom and his staff served chunks of bittersweet chocolate so smooth and rich that they melted on the tongue like a passionate kiss. The men sat before the fire, savoring snifters of the most magnificent brandy imaginable: Metaxa, a drink suitable for a god. Exhausted by a day unlike any other, they contemplated the joys of being men.

The nervous little man sidled up to Zeus and whimpered, "Do the wolf thing again. Please?"

When Zeus didn't immediately answer, the nervous little man began a chant, "Wolf. Wolf. Wolf. Wolf. Wolf."

It wasn't long before the others had taken up chanting. Even Barney longed to go animal.

The men were all keyed up and needed release. Zeus felt his power surge. He imagined a high fence and enclosed the woods. Then he cast a spell over every man and watched them make the change. Ears lengthened, followed by snouts, and tails. They sprouted fangs. Their fingers shrunk into paws; they bent down to touch the ground on all fours.

"*Ahwooo!*" Elton began. The howling grew thick as the stars.

"Run!" Zeus commanded, and the pack took off running through the trees. He watched them run through the night before changing them back. They looked exhausted, yet invigorated. He left them to find their way back to the lodge or fall asleep on the grass.

The boy was almost as tall as she was (which today meant he stood about five-foot six), and old enough to learn the truth about his father. Needless to say, Hera told him something else entirely. "Your father," she said, "is a very busy man. Nevertheless, I'm convinced that he loves you as much as if you'd sprung from his own head."

The three—Hera, Igor, and François—were sitting on the couch, staring at the small box where a large-screen television would have been, had they been back in civilization, where everyone had cable, instead of here.

Igor twisted up his face like he didn't know whether to laugh or cry. He rustled his wings, just one of his many increasingly annoying habits. He'd recently started dressing all in black and parting his hair back to show the vestigial bumps of his antennae. Maybe that had been cute when he was younger, but now it just looked trendy. And he wore this creepy leather jacket that he'd slashed at the back to make room for his wings.

Oh, he was tough, but she knew from searching his pockets that he kept that damned little terry cloth Horsie folded up in there like a tissue. Horsie had lost his last bean days ago. His fabric was damaged beyond repair and she imagined she could smell his musty stink from ten feet away but Igor refused to part with the piece of garbage. Funny how, no matter how you loved them, kids got on your nerves.

"What do you mean about springing from his father's head?"

François asked. "I don't understand." He exercised continuously to maintain his physique, and was at the moment alternating butt lifts with shoulder crunches.

"Didn't they teach you *anything* in your backward country?" she said. Honestly, the French. She had let her hair go to its natural black and had adopted a sinewy look, without all that excess baggage up front. A lean, mean, moody machine. It was time, Hera thought, maybe even past time, to take her place at the table.

"If your father could only see you one more time," Hera told her son, "he'd want you to come live with him forever." Me too, she added silently. If she were a mortal she'd have uttered a prayer about now, and begged the mortal's god to give her back her husband. Things being the way they were, there seemed no point.

"Where is my father?" Igor asked.

"Remember your big Uncle Alexander?" said Hera. She thought about him wistfully.

But Igor shook his head. "I don't have an Uncle Alexander," he said. "Only *Uncle* François."

"Gadzooks!" she said. "It's only been a couple weeks. You've got a worse attention span than a fruit fly."

The boy looked so crushed she almost recanted. She held her tongue. If his own mother didn't toughen him up, who would?

"Hera, please!" said François. "Don't tease the boy so."

"That's about enough out of you. Now, shut up," Hera said. So, she had finally gotten even with Zeus only to be shacked up with this ingrate. Somehow, she had expected that getting even would bring her more pleasure. She was getting a migraine, and slipped off the couch to lie on the carpet. "Get down here and rub some almond oil onto my back," she ordered François.

When he didn't immediately join her, she zapped him with an extra-strong dose of devotion tinged with desire.

He straddled her hips and began to massage her shoulders.

She felt his penis stir. The nice thing about these young lovers was how they could maintain an erection harder than a marble cast of Zeus's prick. She couldn't wait till the next time she faced Zeus, when she could rub in, as it were, that little fact of physiology. Maybe that would do the trick. Maybe equality didn't work so well without your oppressor knowing all about how you'd trumped him. She closed her eyes and unintentionally moaned. She looked up to see if Igor had noticed and saw him staring, alarmed.

Dang. He'd probably want her to explain.

The kid was always hanging around now that she was nice to

him, even when she didn't want him near her. "Why don't you get yourself some milk and cookies, go out to play in the sandbox, or whatever it is you like to do these days," she said, breathless. "Me and your Uncle François need a little private time."

※

Possum was afraid to leave Penelope's side. Her moodiness, and that business with the river changing course, not to mention Mr. Bringle's unexplained visit, kept him awake nights. Penelope's vague fears about the future spread to him. He loved her beyond his comprehension. After they made love, he stayed awake to stare at her and memorize the contours of her body. He fretted she would disappear, turn back into wood.

His anxiety got on her nerves.

Penelope was chopping onions at the kitchen table. It was her turn to make dinner.

He hovered over her shoulder, knowing that he was pestering her but unable to move away from her side. The onions made his eyes burn and tears streamed down his cheeks. "Can I get you anything?" he asked.

She put down the knife and drummed her fingers on the table. Onions did not make her cry. Despite her apparent anger, she spoke kindly. "Isn't there something you can do outside?" she asked.

He had done all the chores early, before she awoke. "You want some garlic?" he asked.

"That does it," she screamed, and, with the precision of a circus performer, threw the knife across the room. "Leave me alone!" she said. "I don't need you watching my every move! I've lived without you for thousands of years and I could live without you now, if I had to."

"I'm sorry," Possum said. "I'll go outside and work in the garden. Could she really live without him? Perhaps that was true. The tears that fell could no longer be blamed on the onions. Possum did not want to live without her. The time for being alone had passed.

❧

Hera treated Igor like a child, when it suited her, and like an adult when she wanted more from him. She paid him no attention otherwise.

Igor realized with increasing fury that she didn't even know he was angry with her. There was no point in telling her. She didn't understand him at all; he was starting to resent her as much as she resented him. There was something wrong with him; he was different from everyone else, that much was obvious. Nobody else grew wings or a hard shell on their feet the way Igor did. Nobody else changed so much from day to day. His life was passing quicker than a nature film done in time-lapse photography. There was something wrong, and it scared him.

His mother underestimated him. When she sent him out, he knew that she wanted to have sex, and it was all he could do not to scream at her that he knew all about it, and even why, because he'd had sex himself a day earlier. But there was no point in telling her anything. She never listened. She didn't care. She was the worst mother anyone could have.

He went into his room and flopped on the bed. He looked through a magazine, then sat up to play guitar. His instrument was puny, a toy. He wanted an electric guitar and a really loud amp. But this was all he had, so he made music with it. His guitar had the quality of sound of a human voice in sorrow. He plucked at some strings and made the instrument cry. He played a piece he had written, and for a moment lost himself in the music.

But then he heard his mother pound on the floor with a broom stick, yell, "Will you shut up! Stop playing that sad crap and play some dance music!" and he shook his head, packed his guitar in its soft case and threw a change of clothes into a backpack. He grabbed his leather jacket and sneaked into her room, where he found her purse and took two twenties from her wallet. And then he left, feeling even sadder because he knew that if he left her a note, she probably wouldn't read it.

❧

Eddie knew that it was impolite to stare at people, and even worse to follow them around. But when the dark one with wings came into the grocery store to buy cigarettes, Eddie couldn't stop himself from doing either. He'd seen the dark one a couple of times before, while making deliveries, though never quite this close.

He left his broom against the wall and wiped his hands on his apron. He shuffled forward to the front of the store and ignored the cashier's attempts to shoo him away. His dad was home sick today, so the cashier didn't really have authority. His dad was the one with authority, but he wasn't there, so Eddie didn't have to listen. He stood his ground. After all, his dad was the one who owned the store, not the cashier.

The dark one was wearing tight black leather pants and a black tee shirt with the sleeves torn off, and a hole torn in back where his wings poked through. The dark one had an orange and red tattoo of fire on one shoulder, and long crystals that made Eddie think of ice on the other. Stones like green diamonds pierced his mouth and nose and ears. His hair was shiny and black. He was probably about sixteen, but looked unlike any teenager Eddie had ever seen, even on television.

"What are you looking at, dickhead?" said the dark one in a grouchy voice.

"I am looking at you," said Eddie. He didn't know what a dickhead was, but he was pretty sure he wasn't one. He tried not to wiggle because whenever he wiggled people always asked him if he had to go to the bathroom, even when he didn't. He looked at the dark one's wings and wondered if it would be okay to touch them.

The dark one laughed. "Don't you know it's rude to stare?"

"Yes," Eddie said. "I know that."

This made the dark one laugh even harder. "What's your name?" he asked.

"My name is Eddie," said Eddie. It was rude to ask about the dark one's name, but it would be even worse to ask if he could touch the dark one's wings. Unless there was some way to change the words enough to make them not be rude.

"Do you have a name?" Eddie asked, and before the dark one could answer he added real quick, "Do you ever let strangers touch your wings?" There. He had said everything. Now, if he was going to get into trouble, at least he would get into all his trouble at once.

The dark one laughed another time. "Go ahead and touch them, Eddie," he said. He turned his back and made his wings unfold. They were longer than Eddie had imagined, and kind of clear, the way Pepsi looked after he put water in it so his dad wouldn't notice he had drunk so much of the bottle. "I'm called Igor," the dark one said. "I'm glad to meet you."

"Igor. I don't know anybody else with your name. I'm very glad to meet *you!*" he said. Sometimes when he got excited globs of spit fell from his mouth and dribbled down his chin. That happened now, but he didn't pause to wipe it with his hands, because it would be even ruder to touch the dark one—Igor's—wings with spit hands, and he was being rude enough without doing that, too.

He reached out one hand and closed his eyes and wondered

if the wings would be wet or cold or slimy. But they weren't any of those things. They were soft, but strong feeling like leather, and warm like a blanket. "Wow," Eddie said. "I wish I had wings."

"I wish you did, too, Eddie," Igor said. He opened his pack of Camels and tapped the top of the box against his knuckles. He took one out and stuck it in his mouth.

"You can't smoke in here, Mister," said the cashier with a familiar disgusted tone to her voice.

"Do I look like I'm smoking?" Igor asked. He nudged Eddie. "Tell her I ain't smoking," he said.

"He's not smoking," said Eddie. "He's just got a cigarette in his mouth. There's a difference, you know."

"Get outside, the both of you," said the cashier.

This time, Eddie decided to listen to her. He took off his apron and folded it and told Igor he'd be right back. He hurried to punch out and put away his apron, then went to look for Igor out in front of the store.

Igor was sitting on the bench Eddie's dad had built so that tourists could sit by the store and eat ice cream bars in summer. That would give more tourists the idea to get ice cream bars at the grocery instead of spending lots more money at the Food Emporium. "Got a match, Eddie?" Igor asked.

Eddie wasn't allowed to play with matches. He shook his head no. "My dad says smoking cigarettes will kill you and make you get cancer," Eddie said. "Maybe you should quit smoking right now before you die. I don't want you to die or get cancer," he said. "Maybe you could even get your money back, since you didn't even smoke it," he said. He started to wiggle because he didn't really know if the part about getting money back would be okay or not.

Igor's smile faded to a frown. He took the cigarette from his mouth and stared at it like he thought it was going to move. He kept staring at it even when it didn't move. His voice sounded kind of sad. "Tell you what," he said. "I won't let cigarettes be the thing to kill me."

Eddie wasn't sure exactly what Igor meant. He sat down on the bench, even though, technically, he wasn't a tourist eating an ice cream bar. He felt a guilty pleasure remembering that day Mr. Bringle had taken him to the Food Emporium for ice cream. He remembered the wonder of eating all that chocolate, with gobs of whipped cream and even chocolate sprinkles.

That was one of the happiest moments of Eddie's life. Something about Igor reminded him of malteds with whipped cream and sprinkles. Eddie was in the mood to do whatever he pleased.

Igor offered Eddie a cigarette. "You don't have to smoke it," he said.

Eddie put it in his mouth just like Igor, but after a while, his spit made the paper get too mushy and some tobacco leaves stuck to his lips and tongue. He took out the cigarette and gave it back to Igor. "I wish you could meet my dad," he said, after a while.

"I'd like that," Igor said. "I'd like for you to meet my father, too." He started laughing again. For someone dressed in black he sure did like to laugh.

"What's so funny?" Eddie asked. Now he was getting angry at Igor, because sometimes people laughed at him for being stupid. Maybe that's what Igor was doing. If Igor was laughing at him, Eddie was going to tell his dad on him, even though he already knew what his dad would say: "Ain't nothing I can do about it, son." His dad would tell him to ignore people when they were acting rude. Except that Eddie might have to admit *he* was the one who was acting rude, and then he'd be the one to get in trouble.

But as it turned out, Igor wasn't even laughing at Eddie. "It just seems funny," he said, "because I've never even met my dad."

Eddie thought now that maybe Igor was kidding. He smiled and pretended to get the joke. But Igor looked sadder and sadder and finally Eddie figured out that he wasn't kidding.

"Well, you should just go and meet him," Eddie said. "Everyone should know his dad." It all seemed so simple.

Igor smiled. "You're really great, you know that?" he said.

No one had ever called Eddie great. He started to wiggle, but sitting on the bench made it easier to remember to stop himself before anyone asked him if he needed to go to the bathroom. He made himself sit still, so still the muscles in his thighs began to tremble.

"Can you fly?" Eddie asked.

Igor's cheeks grew red and he answered, "No." He sat back against the bench and Eddie heard his wings make a crackling sound like the crunch of stiff leather.

He wondered if Igor would ever become his friend? He'd never really had a friend before. Well, he thought, I've already been so rude I can't stop yet. "I always thought everyone else was all the same as each other except for me," Eddie said. "I've never met anybody else who was different, like you, I mean. I wish we could be friends. Since we're both different, I mean." There. He'd said it!

"I wish that too," said Igor. He stood up and took a step forward, and gestured for Eddie to follow. "Come on!" he said. "Why don't you come with me to meet my dad." He looked off toward the Peak the way he had looked at his cigarette. "I could really use a friend to go with me," he said.

"Are you going to tell your mother where you're going?" Eddie asked.

Igor shook his head and laughed again and said, "I don't think so."

"How come you're not going to tell her?" Eddie asked.

"It's not really any of her business," said Igor.

At first, Eddie didn't want to go, but then he remembered what the old man had said about going on a journey. This had to be *that* journey. "Well, I should really tell my dad," said Eddie.

"What for?" Igor asked.

"Because I'm a good boy," said Eddie.

"A good boy? Christ, Eddie! You're a grown-up, not a kid! You're older than me, did you know that?"

"No," Eddie said. "Well, kind of."

Sometimes Eddie got tired of being a good boy. Sometimes he got tired of always asking permission and feeling guilty when he disobeyed. After he had told his dad about taking Mr. Bringle to Possum's house and about seeing the pretty lady with the long red hair in a wheelchair in the meadow, his dad had yelled and made him go to his room without enough supper.

The old man had told him to stand up for himself. So Eddie decided not to tell his dad about either the trip or about Igor. It really wasn't any of his dad's business, just like Igor said.

"Sure, I'll go with you, Igor. It will be okay," Eddie said, even though he didn't know if that was true.

❦

CHAPTER SEVENTEEN

Zeus would never understand the workings of magic. His powers were growing stronger, and he was imbued with more energy and magic than he had possessed in a thousand years. There were limits, still, but nothing like those sorry days in the city, where one small spell had wiped him out for an hour, or maybe two. This was great. How could he have forgotten how marvelous it was to be a god?

Now he could perform several feats at once. Exude charisma while creating a burst of fire in a dish of water. Charm a lamb to sleep *and* stop its blood from flowing until after he had made the cut (that sort of practical magic appealed to him because it served to keep his hands and clothing clean). He could cajole men to do his bidding and cause women to love and then forget him once he had grown tired of their presence.

But these acts were trifles, really, rungs on the ladder leading to all-powerfulness. He snapped his fingers, ready for a bigger challenge. It was time to take a bride, to experience the completeness that could only be experienced with the merging of masculine and feminine.

Zeus told Mr. Tom to give his staff a day off to recover from the weekend retreat. He gathered Mr. Bringle, Elton the executive, and the nervous little man together on the veranda.

Mr. Tom poured them tall glasses of iced tea.

How convenient that Mr. Bringle had located the would-be queen and given Zeus the trinket with the power to bind her to his will. If Bringle was correct, the nymph was at an isolated cabin about an hour away as the crow flies. Too bad Zeus hadn't thought to transform the men into crows. They would have to walk, well, actually, run. Zeus fingered the teardrop necklace in his hands. Whoever wore the necklace became enslaved by its charm. The time was right for him to return it to its designated owner. "I need you," Zeus announced, "to accompany me on a personal journey."

Not unexpectedly, Elton's cheeks puffed out and he stood as if so full of himself his Adirondack chair could not contain him. "Of course we'll be there for you," he said. "Am I right, boys?"

The others murmured their agreement.

This promise of loyalty was not enough to satisfy Zeus. He chanted incantations of gullibility and forgetfulness; when the magic had taken root, he transformed them all into wolves and the foursome set off toward Possum's remote cabin.

Running as an animal was pure ecstasy. He was close enough to the ground to smell the sourness of the grass and feel the thick pollen powder from the flowers cushion his footpads. The sun beat down upon his back, but his fur absorbed most of the heat, while allowing enough of the brisk air through to cool him down. He stretched out his forelegs and leaped nearly fifteen feet before landing gently in a soft patch of grass. His muscles contracted and expanded, always propelling him forward. This was heavenly. To show solidarity with the men, Zeus allowed himself to howl.

They could not help but join him and the four wolves rushed through the forest, frightening away deer and rabbits in their path. They understood the nuances of howling and communicated in this way, but there was little small talk.

When it was time for lunch, Zeus transformed them back into men. Fur turned back to clothing; clawed feet turned back to tennis shoes. Sure, they could have grabbed a quick lunch of raw squirrel, but Zeus didn't like the thought of getting anything stuck between his teeth just before a big date.

Mr. Tom had packed jugs of lemonade and water. They drank their fill, but nobody wanted to pee until they were once again wolves and could stand on three legs.

The nervous little man made them quiet down so he could check out the area with binoculars and heat-seeking devices. He was annoying, but useful. Sometimes, having an anal-retentive on the team was a good thing.

"Where are we going again?" shouted Mr. Bringle.

"To Possum's house, to fetch my bride."

"I wonder if we ought to bring in a woman for every man," shouted Elton. "You don't think there'll be any jealousy if you're the only one, do you?"

True, a spell might be needed to quell the weak ones, but the strong men, like Alexander, saw great virtue in not succumbing to base desires like jealousy, lust, or worse, love. Come to think of it, he was sorry he hadn't brought along the big Greek for moral support, though Zeus would have wasted a lot of magic to keep Alexander from questioning the morality of the planned kidnapping.

"You have so many good ideas, Elton," screamed Zeus. "I'll take this one under advisement." He filed it into the brain folder marked "Reasons to get rid of Elton."

"Ready?" Zeus asked, and Mr. Bringle led the way by shouting,

"Sure!"

At once they were transformed back to their wolf counterparts. When Mr. Bringle kicked up dirt into his nose, Zeus called upon a cloud to mist the trail. He had a little more trouble with the cloud than he expected. The aim was all wrong, and the cloud doused Zeus instead of the trail.

He hadn't quite gotten the hang of commanding water. He disliked having mud stuck to his fur. He did the next best thing and conjured up a bandana to tie around his face. At least this kept the flies from sneaking up his nose.

The summer sun beat down upon them and the men stuck out their snouts and bit at the air. Mortals worried too much about being exposed to the sun. The threat of skin cancer left many of them afraid to go outside without a coating of sunscreen. But transformed into wolves, they laughed at ultraviolet rays.

Now there was an idea, he thought, magical tanning booths. He could allow mortals to tan without exposure to harmful UV light. Charge them an extra couple thou and throw in a pain-free tummy tuck. He'd have to work on an incantation for group tanning and bodywork when they returned.

They stopped to eat and drink and rest before the final leg of the journey. Lunch was roast beef on peasant bread slathered with mayonnaise and a touch of horseradish, with crisp lettuce, and thin slices of vine-ripened tomato. The lemonade was still icy cold and not too sweet. This time, they were content to piss on trees before making ready to leave.

They ran for another hour and came as close to the property as the nervous little man would allow. The unpredictable and noisy river made Zeus a little nervous. Odd, the way it circled the property like a wedding ring.

Mr. Bringle growled and said in a wolf's voice, "There should be a shallow place right around here, where the water thins to a trickle. We can get across there without much trouble," or something to that effect.

The nervous little man proclaimed in his whiny growl, "That's the place to avoid then, because that's where they'll expect us!" He insisted on checking everywhere for traps. But in the end, they crossed at the shallow place without any trouble. The river was loud enough to hide their voices, allowing them a few minutes of unfettered howling. They hid their approach in the shadows of the forest and came to within a few hundred yards of the cabin.

As they drew closer, Zeus felt his powers surge to such strength he could barely contain them. "Stay here," he insisted to the others. He bounded so quickly to the cabin that his body must have looked like the blur of leaves rustled by wind. So fast did Zeus travel that the man he knocked out on the front porch never even saw what hit him. So fast did he travel that by the time the woman had the sense to scream with fear, he had already transformed back into a god, blindfolded her, tied her hands behind her back, and stuffed a gag in her mouth. She fainted when he half-transformed into an animal and held her in his hairy paws. Yes, Zeus thought. It was good to be reminded of times when women had been helpless to resist him.

A lexander considered his work on the amphitheater design his greatest architectural accomplishment. He was doing this for the benefit of all men, not just for himself. The structure was being built in the pasture where they held the animal sacrifices. He stood on the crest of the hill beside the site, wishing there was a way to air condition the outside during the hottest part of afternoon. He wore a lightweight linen tunic, sandals, and a straw hat that kept the sun from his eyes. He had almost forgotten the joy one felt in having a hand in creation.

A pungent scent permeated the air, released from trees that had been cut to make way for the heavy equipment.

A dump truck emptied its load and pulled away to let the bulldozer spread the gravel. Alexander was answering the contractor's questions about some altar specifications when he saw the boys approach on foot. Even from a distance, Igor's dark form and misshapen torso was recognizable. Alexander stopped speaking in midsentence.

Igor had brought along the small guitar.

"You were saying about the altar ... ," the builder prompted.

Alexander opened his mouth to answer, but no words came out; all he could manage was a weak howl. A few of the lambs bleated in response from the other side of their fenced pen.

As the two boys came closer, he placed the other one by his chubby build and shuffling gait. It was the grocer's son, Eddie. Alexander tightened his grip around his pencil. It snapped in half, startling him into nearly losing his balance.

"Mr. Alexander," said the builder, sounding annoyed. "I have a *lot* to do and not very much time to do it. Shall we continue this discussion another time?"

"*Ahh-ooh,*" said Alexander, softly, meaning "Yes." He walked away, toward the boys, then broke into a run until he had almost caught up to them.

"Igor!" he called. "Eddie! Welcome!"

"Hey, Uncle," said Igor. "What's up?" He was clad from neck to foot in shiny black leather that looked very hot and uncomfortable.

Igor let Alexander hug him, but did not hug back. His skin was flushed and wet with perspiration. The humps on his back distorted the line of his leather jacket, and Alexander saw that the zipper teeth were broken. The boy was still growing, even his wings. Alexander smoothed Igor's hair and kissed his cheek. "I am so glad to see you," he said.

Igor was either too old or too young for this display of affection. He stiffened and looked embarrassed before pulling away. "Uh, yeah. I mean, you, too. I was wondering if you were still gonna be here."

Alexander felt let down; Igor was not there to see *him*. Suddenly, the heat seemed to change from minor annoyance to a force that sucked vitality from his body and left him a desiccated shell. His eyes and nose and mouth went dry, and burned with pain until he shut his eyes and held his breath. When he coughed, the sides of his esophagus stuck together. He gasped, his breath catching in his dry throat like a kite on a tree branch.

"Something wrong, man?" Igor asked.

Eddie pounded Alexander on the back and offered him a drink of water from a plastic bottle.

The big Greek took a few sips. The water helped. Though still in pain, at last he could breathe and see again. "*Ahh-ooh,*" whispered Alexander, because howling seemed superior to words.

Igor looked extremely uncomfortable, and Alexander wanted to reassure him but, when he opened his mouth, he could only howl with emotion.

"Nice place," Igor said, ignoring Alexander's distress. "Guess I see why you'd want to stay."

Eddie spotted the lambs. "Is it okay if I go pet them?"

"*Ahh-ooh,*" said Alexander.

Eddie beamed and said, "Thanks."

Igor said, "Hera wants me to find him, you know." He was sweating and his cheeks were flushed from the heat. "My father. She says he loves me. She wants me to bring him back to her. So we can be a family again."

Alexander nodded. The moment was solemn. He doubted the boy was here because it was what his mother wanted.

Igor knew that too; he simply could not admit it.

Alexander put an arm around Igor's shoulders in a manly, pat-on-the-back sort of way, and this time, Igor let him lead the way. Alexander had been here long enough to know that Zeus never spoke of the boy.

The god was so charismatic you didn't realize you'd been caught under his spell. Regret was the cosmic punishment for selfishness. Alexander had been so contented living here that he had forgotten his mission to bring Zeus together with Igor. How quickly he had forgotten the importance of one child's dream.

Perhaps it was not too late to make amends for his many mistakes. Alexander looked at Igor, at his earnest face and deformed body, at the purity of his soul. The boy deserved a father, and Alexander vowed to do all within his power to give him that.

❧

It had happened as quickly as the unfolding of a dream. Penelope had been gazing in the mirror, her comb in one hand, a tortoise shell barrette in the other, when she smelled a fetid scent, felt hot fur brush against her cheek, felt herself being lifted off her chair and whisked away by some fierce animal. She must have fainted, because she remembered nothing of the journey away from Possum's cabin.

She had been brought to some compound and quietly rushed into a dark cell.

Penelope lay on the bed, blindfolded, ashamed of her powerlessness.

He had found her, just as she feared. Zeus had come to lock away her freedom. He must have known she had magic and that the magic was related to her tears. Her blindfold pressed down so tightly on her eyelids it prevented her from crying.

How easy it was to forget everything she'd learned and fall back into the darkness of his spells. The golden chain had wound itself around her neck like chokeweed and she could feel the teardrop charm burning against her throat, sapping her strength to fuel its fire.

Once again, Zeus had stolen her independence, her family, her home.

She slept for a time she could not measure, waking now and again to hear voices murmuring in the background.

When he came to her next, Zeus was so kind and caring that she wondered if she had misjudged him. He cupped his hand over her cheek and whispered, "Love. Passion. Devotion." She did not know if he was telling her his true feelings or trying to cast a spell upon her.

He instructed his personal assistant to bathe Penelope in rosewater and to rub her back with warmed salves. The slave fed her a paste made from almonds and berries, and dressed her in a long silk chemise; he lit incense that left her mind clouded. Her spirit grew weaker. Penelope slept.

🌿

The men gathered in the Big Room for a simple lunch, and though Igor wasn't hungry, he longed to be included in the group.

Zeus opened with a prayer. "Let me give you all a share of my strength and courage," he said. "Let me share with you a bit of my self-esteem." He sprinkled something in a wine goblet and passed the goblet around to all at the table.

Igor felt invigorated by one sip.

After lunch, Alexander brought him to the head of the table. Alexander still towered over him, though Igor had easily grown five inches in the last couple of days. He figured Igor was taller than his mother by now.

"Do you know who this child is?" Alexander asked, and Zeus looked at Igor and reached out to touch his wings.

Normally, Igor didn't allow that. He made an exception for his father.

The god took a sip from his wineglass. There wasn't a spark of recognition in his eyes. "Tell me your name, boy," he said.

Igor stood tall. It was time. He didn't understand his feelings, why he cared so much about a man who had abandoned him. He cleared his throat. "I am called Igor. My mother's name is Hera." He stole a look at his father to see the impact of his words.

Zeus choked on his wine but quickly regained his composure. "You need to shave, kid. Some people just can't grow a beard. How old are you, Igor?"

"Not so old as I look." Zeus's tough facade had faded just long enough for Igor to feel a twinge of hope.

"Just the opposite of me," Zeus said, and dismissed him.

The hard shell that protected Igor felt heavy, but oddly comforting. He peered into Zeus's eyes and shook his head. His wings itched; his eyes stung. He walked back to his place at the table.

Eddie leaned over and confided that he wanted to go out and pet the lambs. "Will you come with me?" he asked.

Igor said, "Sure." He ran upstairs to his room and picked up his guitar.

They took a fast-paced stroll to the meadow. The grass was a perfect oval of green, surrounded by orange poppies, blue delphinium, grass pinks, all in bloom. Beyond the meadow stood the forest, and beyond that, the mountain—Williams Peak.

Alexander had appointed Eddie "Master of the Lambs," and promised to arrange for a suitable plaque to be placed above the barn door. And Eddie *was* master of the lambs, Igor thought. A natural herder. They bleated when they heard his voice, and some of the younger ones trotted his way. Eddie fed them apple slices he had saved from lunch.

Eddie's pride over his new position made Igor smile. Eddie chased down a lamb that had found its way to the other side of the fence. "No, lambie, no!" he said, and herded the creature back to safety.

He was like a giant kid. Kind of like me, Igor thought. He looked over the meadow and wondered what it might be like to take flight and soar above it. He tried to make his wings flap, but could manage only an embarrassing flutter. Nothing about him worked properly, Igor thought. He was a mistake, a freak. It hurt to know that.

He sat on the grass, strumming his guitar. Zeus did not know him, which wasn't so unexpected. After all, Igor had changed so much in these past few weeks. But why had Zeus been afraid to admit Igor was the god's son?

He opened his mouth and sang too softly to be heard. "Nobody knows the troubles I've seen," he whispered. Not even the gods.

🦋

Days had passed, and still Zeus's reluctant queen continued to refuse his advances and hospitality. He was impatient, but unworried. He didn't expect it would take long to change her mind. A lesser god might have tried to rush things. Not Zeus. One advantage of middle age, he supposed, was knowing when you could afford to take your time to get what you wanted. He passed through the main hall, through a dark corridor toward the back of the building. He punched in the code to unlock the door leading into the bridal vault, and stood for a moment, just looking at her. Recovering his senses, he closed the door behind him.

It had been a rush job, turning a back room into a wedding chamber. The room's cathedral ceilings were lined with clear cedar. The north wall opened onto a deck overlooking the woods; the French doors leading to the deck were shrouded by heavy drapes that left the room dark and gloomy. The only natural light was filtered through high stained-glass windows along the eastern wall. Zeus had elaborate plumbing installed, and a computerized entry system that locked from the outside. Mr. Bringle had suggested painting the walls peach to promote a sense of tranquility and lesson the dungeon feel.

Penelope rested on an elevated bed, on a mattress made from European goose down. She'd been bathed, her hair combed, and she had been dressed in a cloying silk chemise.

Zeus saw the glint of gold from her teardrop necklace, once again resting in its rightful place. Penelope was gagged and blindfolded, and tied up to keep her from escaping. On her, it looked good.

"Hello, my love," Zeus said. "I'm back." He wanted to sound Paul Newman smooth and not *Silence of the Lambs* creepy, but sometimes it was hard to tell the difference. What he needed was a pocket sycophant to help him out in situations like this, let him know if he was getting close. Something like a Palm Pilot, only not so spunky.

He sat beside Penelope on the bed and stroked her satiny hair. He bent close, brought a long red curl to his face to rub against his cheek. "You're so beautiful," he said. If there was one thing he had learned about women, it was that they all felt insecure about their looks and craved reassurance. Her natural scent was that of sweet summer fruit that made him want to nuzzle against her bosom and lick her to a state of bloom and ecstasy.

Never had he wanted to possess a woman as much as he wanted her. Well, maybe once or twice, but that was all. Okay, so maybe more than a few times, but if a god couldn't have everything he wanted, what was the point? Her skin was soft as raindrops. Her body delicate and graceful as lace. She was completely helpless and dependent upon him. A rather nice change from most women he had met since that women's lib thing had taken hold.

He whispered praises to her. "You're so beautiful," he said. "I can't live without you."

Zeus used his tongue liberally across her neck. Women loved that sort of thing. It was a fact. He brushed his lips across her ears and loosened her gag with his teeth. He brought her to a sitting position and tried to give her a sip of water, but she spat it out and immediately tried to bite his hand. She missed. Good thing she was blindfolded.

"Jerk," said Penelope.

That stung. He was unused to this kind of treatment. She was brave, he gave her that. It wasn't fair. The power women wielded over men. The power of affection or rejection. But she had fallen for him once and she would succumb again. At least he hoped so.

He could wait to kiss her on the lips. And kiss her he would, she could count on that. There wasn't a woman born who could resist him forever. And what in the world was wrong with that love charm she was wearing around her neck? It had easily worked the last time he used it on her. He redoubled his efforts to be kind.

But she wasn't warming to his natural charm (now in a constant state of magical enhancement) and grew increasingly withdrawn. He was thinking of inviting a world-renowned hostage expert, a professor of psychology from Princeton, to come out to the retreat and provide advice in exchange for reduced tuition. The shrink had studied women who fell in love with their captors, and had written three best-selling books on the subject. One of the best things about modern civilization was the long list of experts. Works for me, Zeus thought.

He craved unflinching love and devotion, not apathetic looseness. Zeus sighed. Penelope was to be his queen; it was important that she desire and adore her king, while understanding he was free to play around. What point was there in being an immortal if you had to take the same marriage vows as the yokels?

Possum opened his eyes and grew accustomed to the darkness. His head throbbed, his nose was stuffy, there was ringing in his ears and a metallic taste of blood in his mouth. He had no memory of what had happened or why he was lying face up on the porch. When he tried to sit the pain in his head grew so terrible he had to lie back down and close his eyes.

Night passed into daylight. Again he awoke. By now, the pain was tolerable enough to move. He brought himself up to his knees and grabbed the railing for support. "Penelope," he called. She did not answer. The day blurred like wet watercolors. His muscles and joints, even his jaw, ached.

It took several more attempts before he was able to stand, and another few minutes before he was able to propel himself into the cabin. "Penelope?" he called.

She was gone, and his first thought was that she had never been, that he had imagined her, that she was no more than a delusion. His hands trembled and his walk faltered. He dropped back to his knees and crawled forward.

Of course Penelope existed. To think otherwise was ridiculous. He picked up a few of her long hairs from the floor. The evidence of her being permeated his life. Her scent, her clothes, the bar above her bed, her chair, the memory of her sweet tongue and the warmth of her body pressed against his skin.

What had he done wrong to make her leave? Had he taken advantage of her innocence? Hardly. No more than she had taken advantage of his. The thought made him laugh. She had been the only woman he'd ever kissed, besides his mother. But where was she?

Had she left him because he hadn't tried hard enough to push through her dark moods? What have I done—how could I let her go?

His injury and exhaustion left him unable to think; he dragged himself to her bed, where he collapsed. He dreamed that his vision was marred by a blackened area at the center of his sight that kept him from seeing all of life. In his dream, he painted only buildings and landscapes—the things he could see peeking around the edges of the blackness.

❧

Igor loved being in the lodge at night, watching the fire burn in the great stone hearth. Every now and then a bit of pine pitch caught fire and sent out sparks like tiny comets. He was exhausted. He had tried to pace himself, but it was hard and everything hurt. Igor figured it was all from growing so fast—the muscles, the bones—a body just couldn't take the stress without pain.

His frailty embarrassed him. Zeus was so strong, and seemed to admire strength above all else. Zeus was the fastest runner, the most accurate archer, and to hear him tell, the greatest lover. How his father must have hated to see his son, the wimpy geek. Even with the fire, Igor was cold, and he wore his black leather jacket over his tunic to protect him from the chill. He reached into the side pocket to pet Horsie.

A group of ten men sat around the big table, drinking after-dinner brandy. They were all wearing belted cotton tunics and looked pretty silly, especially the ones with the hairiest arms. Igor hated brandy almost as much as Eddie did. Zeus had wrinkled up his nose, but had finally caved in and permitted Mr. Tom to bring Igor a beer and Eddie a Coke.

"She wanted it again, and I said, 'Aphrodite, ten times is my limit without pausing for refreshment,'" Zeus bragged. "I said, 'Don't I even get a fig or a swig of wine?' Then she said, 'Zeus, baby, no one else ever managed more than five. Take all the figs you can eat!'"

Everyone laughed, except Eddie, who leaned forward to ask, "Why did Aphrodite want Zeus to pump so much gas?"

Igor said, "Never mind." He rolled his eyes. Why couldn't he have normal parents, who didn't hit upon their sisters and didn't brag to their kids about their sex lives? His back ached, and when Mr. Tom refilled glasses, Igor asked if there was anything to be done about the pain.

Mr. Tom looked to Zeus, who rolled his eyes and waved him away.

"Sure thing, kid," said Mr. Tom. "Got what you need in the kitchen." He returned with a glass of water and two blue pills. "Medicine," he said with a menacing look toward Zeus. "Can't live without it."

Igor swallowed the pills, hoping they would work quickly.

The men finished their drinks.

"Ready?" Zeus asked. He leaped up and began a few warm-up exercises to loosen up before their last run of the day.

"Come on, boy," he called, and gestured for Igor to join him at the head of the table. Eddie helped Igor to his feet.

"Let's go," cried Zeus. "A strong man is a powerful man!" He jogged out the door.

The sun was setting behind the mountain and the cool night air was doing its best to cover up the evidence of a summer day. Still, it felt fire-hot during the run. Igor did his best to keep up. The heavy leather jacket and the weight of his wings overpowered his slight body.

"What's the matter with you, boy?" Zeus called when he lagged behind.

"Nothing, sir," said Igor, trying to keep up.

A few hundred yards into the run, Zeus surged ahead. The pack pulled away, leaving Igor and a few others far behind. Igor could barely keep pace with Eddie.

"Slackers!" Zeus yelled back to them.

"Give me a break," called the nervous little man from the back of the formation. He was panting heavily.

Alexander slowed down, no doubt to keep an eye on Igor.

"I'm okay," Igor yelled. "Go on ahead."

Alexander frowned, and ran on, though not as fast as the others.

"Aren't you going to take off your jacket?" Eddie asked. His tunic straps came loose and the fabric pooled around his waist; a rope belt kept the garment from falling off altogether. Eddie's pale belly jiggled as he ran. He was huffing and puffing and had broken into a red-faced sweat.

Sweat poured down Igor's face. He felt ill and overheated. He could pretend it didn't matter but it was all about keeping himself in the race. Zeus was still within sight. If he couldn't catch him, at least he could follow. "What the hell?" he said, and slid his arms from the jacket.

"I'll carry it for you," said Eddie. His goofy smile made Igor happy.

Eddie had the look of a winner; it was obvious he was proud to be trusted enough to hold Igor's jacket.

"Does this mean we're engaged?" Igor asked, but when Eddie looked puzzled, Igor said, "Never mind."

He stretched out his shoulders as his wings adjusted to the sting of cool air. He let them unfurl. They were stiff, heavy, slow-moving. He had always kept them tucked against his body, maybe a little ashamed to show them off. Unfurled, their weight pulled uncomfortably on his muscles until he grew used to their heft. His wings had grown, matured as he had. It had taken them a long while to develop but the tips now reached the backs of his thighs. He shook them out, stretched again. There was something liberating about letting out the wings that had always seemed like a deformity. His step increased and he felt a slight boost of vigor.

"Well," said Eddie, "aren't you going to fly?"

Igor laughed. "What the hell?" he said. Prior attempts had been pointless, but things were different now. The caterpillar had morphed into a butterfly. Pride was an unexpected, overwhelming feeling. It took all his strength to flap his wings as he propelled himself forward. This attempt slowed him down a bit until he found a wing rhythm that complemented his footsteps. Would it really work this time? Would he really be able to fly? He forced himself to stretch his wings to their fullest extension. It hurt, just a little, almost like a torn muscle, but he held them out and willed himself to move, to flap, to build power and speed.

Ohmygod, he thought, as he felt the faint rush of air beneath his feet. I'm doing it. I'm flying! His wings held him aloft, barely inches above the ground. The sensation of gliding without walking was unlike anything he had ever felt; it was exhilarating, a dance with the wind as his partner. Igor was in love. He taught himself to twirl, slowly at first, then picking up speed as the evening shadows blurred into black. He rose to the level of the maple tops and understood how it felt to be giddy with joy.

"Look!" Eddie said with glee. "He's flying!"

Igor looked down and saw that Alexander had stopped to watch him. His father had run far enough ahead he could no longer see him. "Tell Zeus to look up here," he cried. "Tell him I can fly."

Alexander nodded and ran off to find Zeus. Igor flew higher, anxious to catch up to his father.

A sharp pain made his breath catch and the muscles in his back stiffened. It hurt too much to control the graceful movement of flight; he flapped wildly until his wings gave out. He fell to the ground, gasping for air. He tasted the dirt but could not summon the strength to lift his head.

Eddie screamed, "Help him!"

Shaking with cold and exhaustion, he used his wings as a blanket to cover and warm himself. He hurt everywhere, in his toes and elbows and ears. He saw that he had ruptured some of the membranous tissue of his wings and they were bleeding. But none of that mattered, for he had tasted flight and that small taste would nourish him forever.

Eddie said, "Are you going to be all right?" and though Igor answered, "Yes," Eddie suspected, for the first time, just how sick his new best friend had become.

🦋

Penelope awakened to the feel of Zeus's arms wrapped around her back, his strong body desperately pressing against hers. He kissed her neck and his breath was hot and rapid.

"I love you," he whispered. "I've always loved you."

Despite her misgivings, his presence awakened something inside her. She moaned, and he undid the gag from her mouth and kissed her gently. She did not understand her feelings for this man who had caused nothing but pain. Was it all a charm? Or did her feelings for him come from her heart?

He was embracing her and though she fought it, her body

cleaved against him. He untied her hands and they grasped his shoulders and pulled him close.

Her confusion was so great that she wanted to cry, but the blindfold left no outlet for her tears. "Let me see you," she said, and he removed the blindfold as she had asked. He gazed at her with cold animal eyes and the spell was lifted for an instant. The room was dark and cold; a wall of curtains shut out the world beyond, and only a sliver of light peeked through. She stared at her fingertips and saw the whirls and markings that reminded her of a tree's rings.

That's it, she thought. I'll become a tree again to keep safe from him. She made her thoughts hard, so dense the awareness of his nearness diminished. She felt strong, impenetrable. Her consciousness grew so hard the softness of her body could not contain it. She pulled away from her body. What was left behind was just a shell, but Zeus did not at first notice the difference. Her spirit floated upward and when she gazed down, she saw herself as she really was: held captive and chained, her affection for him forged by the golden fire around her neck. That bastard, she thought, determined to resist him. Brute force is not the only source of strength. She abandoned her physical self to him and floated higher, watching as her body went slack.

"Wake up!" he said, sounding like a spoiled child. "It was going so good!"

In a few minutes, he left her alone. She heard him bolt the door from the other side. She looked around the dark room, searching for an escape route. In her spirit state, she could not break through the window, but she spied a magical way out: a small wood carving hanging on the wall. She heard the whisper of her river and her woods and her clouds. As she stared into the carving, she saw the place where she had once lived in innocence. Her spirit floated closer and she fell into the carving and became a part of the moving picture. Zeus could not touch her here. She was safe.

She would hide from Zeus and his deceitful ways, biding her time until her strength returned and she could plot her revenge.

❧

Hera bathed in a tubful of warm clotted cream scented with vanilla pods. She had a good view of François working out in the bedroom on his Nautilus. Nice pecs. Nice abs. Nice ass. Boring. She yawned. Even perfection got old after a while.

The bathroom smelled heavenly; her skin absorbed the scent

while softening like butter. She had expected Alexander to spy on Zeus for the weekend, then report back early Monday morning. When he failed to return, she knew he had deserted her.

Just like Igor. Oh, the shame.

She opened the drain and rinsed off her skin. She stood with one leg elegantly raised on the lip of the bathtub to pat her foot dry. François would clean up the mess.

She was in a bit of a mood today, and decided to dress for battle in a tamper-proof sports bra beneath a rubber wet suit. François interrupted his butt crunches to watch her pull the zipper closed. She gave him a practiced smile as she slipped on thick wool socks, and laced her steel-toed Doc Martens.

"Get dressed," she called to her boy toy. "We're going out." She mumbled an incantation, a double-dose loyalty spell.

"I'll never leave you," François said unexpectedly.

"Damn right," said Hera.

CHAPTER EIGHTEEN

They had carried Igor back to his room, where Alexander had slept in a chair by the door, just in case Igor needed help through the night. By morning, Igor felt strong enough to trudge downstairs and join the others for breakfast. Eddie, of course, was already at the table, and from the look of his plate, was working on seconds. Even if the aroma of garlic homefries did little to whet Igor's appetite, he appreciated the gusto of someone who loved to eat.

"Over here," Eddie said, pointing to the chair he'd saved for his buddy. Igor nodded and picked up a tray at the buffet table. He decided on a bowl of oatmeal and a couple of strips of bacon; he carried the heavy tray back to his seat.

Zeus strode over to greet Igor. "Glad to have you back, son," he said in a most convivial voice. "Heard you managed to fly. Good work. Take off that leather and stay a while."

It meant a lot to Igor that his father had noticed him. He knew his smile looked goofy, but Igor didn't care. "If you don't mind, sir, I'll keep my jacket," he said, because the jacket worked like a sling to hold in his heavy wings.

"No problem. Coming hunting with us this morning?" Zeus said. He pulled up a chair to sit beside Igor.

"I don't know if that's such a good idea," Eddie said with brotherly concern. "He's not feeling all better."

"Of course it's a good idea," Zeus said. "Nothing like fresh air and exercise to make a man feel like a man. Well, maybe a few things."

"It's okay. I'm coming," said Igor. He hid the fact that he barely had the strength to hold up his spoon. The pain could wait until later; his father was asking for his company now. He pushed his plate of bacon toward Eddie, and asked, "Do you want that?" to distract his friend, who was sometimes overbearing in his role as protector. Igor's muscles were sore and weak and his head felt light; maybe he'd lost some blood in the crash. I have no idea, he thought, a little afraid, how I'll hold up the bow.

It was only 10:00 A.M., but already the temperature soared into the high nineties. The air was muggy and overcast, with a sour scent, like an old carved pumpkin. Alexander sensed that a summer storm was making its final descent and would soon land. Electricity coursed through the simmering breeze. Crows gathered in the maples and cawed en masse. It felt like something was about happen.

Zeus directed the men to follow a path, as they hunted for wild pigs, bringing home the bacon, as it were. "Eddie," Zeus called. "Come here, I've got something for you." He winked at Igor as he handed Eddie a slingshot, showed him how to shoot a pebble. "Now, I want you to gather up a pocket of small pebbles, and when you have enough, you can take out all the squirrels you see. Only one bit of advice: you are not to aim this anywhere but up in the trees, and if you hit anyone with a pebble, I'm taking it away. One more thing," Zeus said. "Remember our cardinal rule: anything you kill you have to eat!"

Eddie nodded with great solemnity, but grew distracted, looking for pebbles.

Alexander carried no weapon; for him killing was not sport. Igor hoisted a tall wooden recurve bow that dragged him off-balance. The stubborn boy refused all offers of help and an hour into the hunt, he stumbled and hit the ground.

Alexander rushed to his aid. "Are you okay?" Alexander asked. He uncapped his water bottle and gave Igor a drink. Startled, he noticed the boy was losing hair on top of his head. "Why don't we stop and rest for a while."

"No way. I'm just drunk," Igor said, no doubt trying to save face. It was tough to fall, tougher to ask for help standing up.

Alexander placed his large hand on the boy's back for support. Igor sat. His eyes were shiny and he licked his lips. He was probably dehydrated. The boy would not take off that damned jacket even when it was giving him heat stroke. "Have some more water," Alexander said, gratified that even if the boy did not accept his help, he accepted the water. "Would you like me to call the doctor?" Alexander asked in his most gentle voice. "You're not looking your best."

Igor shook his head. He picked himself up and stood shakily. "No doctors," he said. "I'm okay."

The poor kid tried so hard to fit in that he wouldn't acknowledge anything was wrong. Alexander understood this. But was Igor old enough to make his own mistakes, or should Alexander push harder to make him seek medical treatment? The answer wasn't clear. He tried not to give in to his worries that nothing could be done to help the boy. In any case, it would not be easy to convince Igor that a doctor could be trustworthy. He picked up Igor's bow and waited patiently as Igor worked to sling it over his shoulder.

The boy winced.

"How are your wings?" Alexander asked.

"Kinda sore," said Igor. "Guess I need to break them in kind of slow."

Alexander nodded. "Let's ice them when we get back."

"Good idea," Igor said. He took a few tentative steps forward.

"Okay," Alexander said. "Let's go."

They walked, a slower pace than before.

Eddie was just up ahead; he stooped to pick up a stone.

"Wait up," Igor said.

Eddie turned around and smiled with recognition. "I found some pebbles," Eddie said. "For my slingshot. Wanna see?"

"Sure," Igor said. "Show me."

Eddie explained where he had found each stone, with Igor feigning interest.

Alexander smiled. Until a few months ago he had lived a life where everything out of the ordinary could be rationalized using ordinary explanations. How his world had changed. Now there were magic spells to fight against, boys with wings and men who howled, and things that made no sense and had no logical explanation.

Igor's condition—his wings and his rapid aging—those weren't symptoms that doctors could cure. But the doctors would feel they had to do something. The way Sanders had felt. It wasn't that he was an evil man, Alexander thought, more that he was trained not to give up. That was how mortals were—tenacious, anxious to try things even when there was no hope. Maybe it was better not to think about a cure, knowing you had a sickness without a treatment.

Igor stopped walking. "Shhh," he whispered.

Eddie said, "What?" and Igor gestured for him to be quiet.

Alexander heard a rustle in the bushes. He watched Eddie fiddle with his slingshot; Igor prepared an arrow before lifting his bow.

A snout appeared, followed by a grizzled gray face as the animal rooted through the dirt.

"Look," Eddie said, taking aim. "A piggie. How come it isn't pink?" His shot was wide, so he lobbed a pebble at the beast. Despite his clumsy throw, the pebble glanced the head.

An arrow flew and hit the pig in the neck. It shrieked and fell.

Igor said, "I got it!"

"Me, too," Eddie added.

It was a mature hog, weighing several hundred pounds. Lucky shot, Alexander thought. Igor had severed the carotid. "Zeus!" Alexander called. "Looks like you have dinner. Come take a look."

Eddie tried to high-five his friend, but Igor turned away and stooped over, using his bow for support. His skin had lost its luster, turning a mottled gray, like an oyster shell left in the sun. His hair was white.

"I did it," Igor said, then crumpled to the ground.

"Zeus!" screamed Alexander. "Hurry!"

Elton was the first to jog back and scope out the problem. "What's wrong?" cried Elton.

Eddie knelt and took Igor's hand in his. "Igor's sick," Eddie said. "He needs a doctor." He stared up at Elton's leg. "I can see your underwear," he said, and giggled.

Elton removed his pager from his belt and tapped in a message before tugging down the hem of his tunic. He gave Eddie a nasty look. "Let's get the boy back to the lodge," he said.

"Zeus," Igor groaned. "I want to show you something."

"We killed a pig," Eddie said. "For dinner. Mostly Igor killed it but I stunned it."

"I see," said Elton. "Good work."

When Zeus appeared he seemed shaken to see Igor's skin was old-man loose and wrinkled. "This can't be good," he said.

The boy looked seriously ill.

Alexander tended to him, lifting his head to pour a few drops of water into his mouth. Alexander then touched the back of his hand to the boy's forehead. Igor was feverish, his breathing labored.

There came a point where you couldn't deny what was happening, Alexander thought. "He's dying," he announced, matter-of-factly.

Elton smiled genially. "Let's not alarm the other guests," he whispered. "They see one fellow get sick and then another one and pretty soon you've got a whole copycat epidemic to deal with."

"He's got a point," said Zeus. He noticed the dead hog slumped just off the path. "What's this?" he asked. "Who found this beauty?"

Igor's smile was weak. "We did," he said. "Me and Eddie." He coughed.

"Excellent work, boys," Zeus told him. He turned his attention to Elton. "Have someone from the kitchen gut this thing and get it in the BBQ pit."

"Yes, sir," said Elton.

Alexander noticed the look of satisfaction on Igor's face. Despite his discomfort, Igor was proud of himself. "You did good," Alexander said.

Igor smiled faintly.

"He needs a doctor," Eddie said.

"No doctors," Igor told him. "Just take me back to the lodge."

"That's the spirit," said Zeus. "You rest up before dinner and we'll make a toast to your superior hunting skills. How's that sound?" He cast a spell of healing, confident it would work.

"Great," Igor said. "It sounds great."

"I'm sure you'll feel better by evening," Zeus said.

"I feel a little better now," said Igor.

Zeus nodded.

Alexander hoisted Igor up to his shoulders. "I'll take him back," he said.

Zeus gestured at Igor, "I should return to my other guests. Think you can handle this situation by yourselves?"

"I don't think we need to trouble you, sir," said Elton, and Zeus looked relieved.

"Are you in any pain?" Alexander asked.

"It doesn't hurt," Igor said. He sighed and Alexander patted him on the back. "I killed a pig," Igor said, and then went limp.

Igor was sick in his bed, so in the afternoon, Eddie went out by himself to feed the lambs. Mr. Zeus had called Eddie's dad and convinced him to let Eddie stay for as long as he liked. Eddie liked it here. He liked it a lot. He liked it so much he wanted to invite his dad out for a weekend sometime. Eddie liked petting the lambs and going swimming in the mineral pools without having people ask him if he'd remembered to go potty before getting in the water. He didn't really know how to swim, and that was okay, because the pools were only deep enough to stand up in. He knew how to get almost all of himself—except his head—under the water, and paddle with his hands to make it look like he was swimming across. There were mostly fun things to do here and hardly any chores, except for feeding the lambs, which didn't seem like a chore at all.

He trod across the meadow, toward the barn where they kept the sacks of maize and barley for the lambs. Eddie was strong from carrying boxes at work, so strong that he could lift two bags by himself, and carry them to the feeding trough. He pulled open the sacks.

The lambs stopped munching on grass and one of them trotted over to meet him. It was black with white spots. He patted its soft muzzle and let it eat corn from his hand. The rest of the flock ambled over as he spread a thick line of feed into the trough. "Not so fast, lambies," he said, "there's enough for everyone." He watched them eat for a while, then checked to make sure they had water.

"Bye, lambies," Eddie said. "See you later." He waved, though he knew they were too busy eating to see him.

It would be another couple of hours before he could eat dinner. In the afternoon, Mr. Tom, the chef, set out snacks in the Big Room, so Eddie walked back toward the lodge to see what there was to eat. They had lots of good food here, the kind he hardly ever got to eat at home. Chocolate chip cookies. Cheese and crackers. Red meats cooked rare with plenty of salt and garlic (that his dad didn't let him eat because his dad said it would give him gas), and the good vegetables—like buttered corn on the cob and salads with as much dressing as he wanted—and none of the bad ones like *bristle* sprouts or green beans. And they got dessert with both lunch and dinner.

Mr. Tom sometimes let him help out in the kitchen and never yelled when Eddie dropped or spilled something. Mr. Tom let him wash pots and pans and wear a white apron like the one he had at work, only nicer, and a special white hat. Maybe he'd try to get a job as a chef.

Plus, his best friend, Igor, never got upset when Eddie asked him stupid questions. When he first met Igor, Eddie had liked him a whole lot, but he liked him even more the longer he knew him. In fact, he loved Igor, almost as much as his dad. Except that Igor kept changing, getting bigger and older all the time. That sometimes made things a little confusing. Because no matter how much Igor changed he always treated Eddie just as nicely. Eddie tried not to worry that Igor was sick, but he wished his dad were there. His dad always knew what to do when somebody got sick.

Eddie wasn't the only one who loved Igor. The big man, Alexander, loved him like a son. Eddie could see it in his eyes.

But the one Igor loved most, the one who was the boss of this place, didn't love Igor at all and that was sad. Eddie was thinking he should have a talk with Zeus and tell him all about love and why he should try to do it sometime. He needed to talk to Zeus alone.

Eddie tramped around the Big Room, grazing on snacks, while most everybody else was in the bar drinking stuff that smelled like toilet cleaner. It was happy hour, and Eddie felt happy because he could eat as much as he wanted. Maybe now was a good time to talk to Zeus about Igor.

Eddie sneaked over to Zeus's room and tried the door. It was bolted shut, and not only that, but there was a little gray box that looked like a time clock. Eddie looked for a punch card, only there wasn't one. At the grocery store, the time clock spat out the right numbers when he put his card in its mouth. That was how his dad knew how much to pay him, even though he didn't really get paid. Well, not like everybody else. His dad told him he got paid on paper.

He stared at the box until a solution came to him.

This must be a different kind of time clock, one where Eddie would have to feed it numbers instead of the other way around. It was the kind of time clock without a mind of its own. Eddie liked that kind of time clock because it made him feel smart to know something the clock didn't know.

He concentrated and thought real hard until he could see a bunch of numbers in his mind. He punched them in without making a single mistake. After each number a little green light went on and a teeny beep sounded. When he had punched in all the numbers the door swung open and he entered Zeus's room. Zeus wasn't there, but Eddie decided that since he'd gotten this far, he might as well have a look around.

"Wow!" Eddie said. It was like a television palace inside. The carpet was softer and thicker than lambs' fleece. The room was bigger than his bedroom, with a big, round bed in the center that reminded him of a trampoline. There were stained-glass windows on one wall that looked like red and green diamonds, which sparkled and turned the sunlight into rainbows. The rest of the wall was covered by dark drapes. Eddie looked around, and found the bathroom, and that was an even better dream.

The bathroom had one wall made out of rocks. A real waterfall ran down those rocks and into the urinal. Eddie started to giggle. It was a silly idea, but he wanted to pee in it and see what would happen. Even though he knew he shouldn't, he unzipped his pants and made a river with his pee. The waterfall took it away, just like that. He didn't even have to flush. He gulped a big drink of water from the sink so he could work up some more pee before he left.

He wondered if his dad would like to pee rivers into a waterfall. Not that he could ever ask his dad about that; his dad didn't like it when Eddie talked about pee or poop. Still, he wondered. Eddie washed his hands in a shiny gold sink and dried them on towels that felt like longhaired velvet.

He took off his shoes, thinking he might jump up and down on the bed. But then he noticed that the pretty lady he had met at Possum's was sound asleep, so he tiptoed away from the bed to look at all the pictures on the wall. There was a poster with a photograph of Zeus holding a lightning bolt that said, "I'm your God! Who the fuck are you?" and Eddie knew that was a joke, because his dad had told him that a man could not be God. Besides, if Zeus was really God, then he wouldn't have needed to yell as much as he did, so that proved it.

There were lots more pictures on the wall to look at, but Eddie thought he heard one of them say something to him. "Eddie," it said. "Come here." This was the first time a picture had ever talked to him and the first time a picture had ever known his name. This sure was a day for first times.

He walked to where the voice had come from and saw it was a picture carved into wood of a river and clouds and a mountain. At the front of the picture stood the pretty lady. She wore a long white gown that trailed behind her when she walked. Now that was really weird.

"Hi," Eddie said. He scratched his head, confused. The pretty lady in the picture was alive, like he was watching her on television.

"Eddie," she said, "I need your help."

There was something very wrong. On television, the people never talked to him. He looked back to the bed and watched the pretty lady's chest rise and fall in sleep. He felt nervous and started to wiggle, but stopped himself before she asked him if he had to go to the bathroom. "How can you be here and there?" he asked, pointing from the carved picture to the bed.

"It's a magic trick. But now I'm trapped here. Will you help me get out?" asked the pretty-lady-in-the-picture. "*Please.*"

"Why do you need help?" he asked. "You have everything here," he gestured around, thinking of the waterfall bathroom and the good food.

She smiled and looked down at her legs. She took another step forward. "I must talk with Possum. Will you bring him here?"

"Why don't you go get him?"

"I can't leave here," she said. "I need your help. *Please.* Find him and bring him here."

He understood that magic had trapped her in the picture and she needed Eddie's help to get out. He liked magic tricks, and hardly anyone ever asked him for help. Usually, people just told him to do something, and even when they said PLEASE it was usually just a telling PLEASE and not an asking PLEASE.

"Thank you for asking," he said to the pretty lady. He squinted to see if he could see her lips move when she talked. "I'll help you.

What should I do?" he said.

The pretty lady gave him a smile that made him feel warm and happy inside. "Do you remember where Possum lives," and when he nodded, she said, "Go and tell him I'm here. I need to talk to him. Before he forgets about me. Can you leave right now?" She didn't say anything else, but he knew from the frightened look in her eyes and from all his years of watching television that she wanted him to hurry.

"He won't forget you. Nobody could forget you," said Eddie, but the pretty lady shook her head sadly and said, "He won't mean to, but he will. It's the only way he can survive." She told him to be careful. "Don't tell anyone but Possum that you saw me," she said, and Eddie nodded.

"Be right back," Eddie said. He didn't really know how long it would take, but he always said, "Be right back," when he went somewhere no matter how long it took, and no one had ever seemed to care before, so that was how come he said it.

❧

Relief washed through her now that Eddie had found her. She watched him stumble back into the room where Zeus held her captive, and saw him leave. Penelope turned around, away from the room and into the carving, and was immersed in a world of beauty and calm. The river sung melodically in the background and the mountain cast its shadow over the meadow, providing just the right amount of shade to compensate for the heat of the sun. It was a paradise, much like Possum's meadow, but unlike that world, here she could walk on her own.

She stretched her arms to twirl barefoot in the grass until she grew dizzy and fell to the ground, giggling furiously. She practiced stretching out her toes, amazed that they so easily followed her command. It was possible to grasp thin blades of grass between her toes and pluck them from their roots. Letting them go posed a more difficult problem.

She felt safer here than she could remember. The carving was a womb made from wood, created to protect her from harm. "Thank you," she said with a solemn nod to her river.

She stood and looked out toward the horizon, then ran toward it as fast as she could. It was as close a sensation to flying as she could imagine. Her gown clung to her as her strong legs carried her over grass and sand; though she felt each landing, it seemed more of a pat on the back than a thud. The run invigorated her. Wind whipped through her hair and dried her skin before she could work up a sweat. She reached the rocks and stopped to clamber up to a vantage point.

She faced out, in the direction of the world, to watch the goings on in the dark room where Zeus had held her captive. Her body was crumpled on the bed, a shell with no will except to obey its master. Her hand went to her neck, but in this world, the teardrop necklace was cold. It held no power over her here. That was the real world, and this one an illusion. How easy it was to forget and escape into a dream.

If she went back out into the world, she would be paralyzed again. The solution seemed simple—stay here. If Possum joined her, everything would be perfect.

Her legs wobbled. She stared at the body on the bed, wondering how a part of her could exist in each world. The teardrop necklace glowed; even here, she felt the sting of Zeus's power. She tried, but could not pull it free.

She turned her back to that world and the burning feeling subsided. The ground was warm and smooth as melted chocolate. Honeysuckle scented the air and warm breezes blew through the trees. The mountain was a leap and a hop away. It felt wonderfully odd, having the ability to walk again. She could move simply by thinking about moving and her legs obeyed her whim as if by magic. Grass crunched beneath her feet, sand tickled her toes.

Life was a miracle that you didn't appreciate until it was taken away.

It was almost perfect here. Ever warm and comforting. She could walk and leap and run and even swim. This was paradise, and she need never leave and return to slavery. It would have been perfect, except that she was alone.

Possum awakened to the dawn. A shadowy figure moved slowly toward him. "Who is it?" he cried, fearing some punishing angel had returned to finish the job it had started.

"It's me!" said the visage. "Eddie!"

The grocer's son. Possum had never been so happy to see him.

The boy spoke so rapidly Possum had trouble following him.

"My dad ... Igor ... ice cream ... Zeus ... picture ... red-haired lady ... clocks-that-can't-tell-time ... lambs ... waterfall ... help!"

But in the end, he understood that Eddie had come to take him to Penelope, that she still existed, and that she remembered him, and that was really all that mattered.

🐎

It was Hera's fault for sending a man to do a woman's work. By Wednesday, Alexander had still not returned. This upset her more than she could say because she had truly believed Alexander cared for her, that his attentiveness was not entirely the result of her magic.

Hera was a washed-up goddess. No husband. No willing subjects. No plan. She had fallen as low as she could fall, unless she succumbed to ennui and crumbled to dust, like Artemis and Aphrodite and the others, who had given up the struggle to stay at the top of a changing world.

She didn't want to think about it.

She decided to pay a call on dear sweet Zeus and convince him that he needed her. This could be one of her more important meetings with the old codger, and Hera dressed accordingly. She stared at her body to see if she needed a quick tummy tuck, but in the end decided she'd be perfect in a Wonderbra. She zapped her hair blonde and set it into a cascade of soft ringlets that practically bounced with every breath. Her hoop earrings were the size of oranges. Her lips were Christmas-stocking red. She wore a black leather miniskirt and a deep V-neck jacket. Her sandals were made from spun gold. She ordered François to rub oil into her calves until they shone.

François began to cry. "You are beautiful, my queen," he said.

She ordered him to file her toenails.

Before he could finish preparing her, he grabbed his chest and passed out.

She checked her image one last time in the mirror. That ought to do it.

She was psyched, so full of energy it took nothing to create a chariot from an empty tuna can, and a flying horse from a cockroach. She picked up François and slung him over Pegasus.

"Let's go," she said, clicking her heels just for the fun of it.

Pegasus took one look at Hera's determined face and headed off toward the retreat.

Was Zeus *ever* going to be sorry he had abandoned her for some cheap floozy. Not that she was sorry she had done the same. Zeus need never find out about her little fling. That way, she could apply a tourniquet of guilt and squeeze buckets of unearned loyalty from him.

This whole trip was just like television, well, maybe even better, because Eddie had the feeling that on this trip, *he* would play the hero. It was his job to rescue the pretty lady. Maybe she would let him kiss her for a reward. That would be nice. He'd never kissed a girl before.

The only problem was, he was so exhausted after his journey to Possum's place that it was a struggle to hike all the way back to New Olympus. His knees buckled and his feet were blistered. He would have stopped to rest except that Eddie knew that on television, the hero never stopped for naptime. If he stopped for naptime, then someone else would get to be the hero, and Eddie might never have another chance besides this one. He couldn't bear to disappoint the pretty lady, and kept going.

So every time Possum said, "Should we stop for a while?" Eddie shook his head and made them walk on.

Every once in a while, Possum turned around to walk backwards. "Makes it easier to think," he said.

Eddie didn't understand why, and tried that, too. Possum was right. "Makes it easier to walk," Eddie said, "especially when you're going uphill."

Possum laughed. "It's all uphill, isn't it?" he asked. "That's a metaphor for our lives."

"What's a metaphor?" Eddie asked, and Possum grew so flustered trying to explain that Eddie knew he'd said a dirty word.

"Anyway, it's not *all* uphill," said Eddie. "Because if it was then there would have to be a top of the world and also a bottom of the world. And when it rained the bottom of the world would get flooded and the people at the top of the world might slip in the mud and roll downhill and then everyone would be dead."

"Good point," Possum said.

Hardly anyone told Eddie that he had made a good point. He was really happy. He liked being the hero already—it was fun. And the best thing was, he didn't even know what day it was, and since he always knew what day it was, that just proved how special this whole trip was. Eddie was so happy he could feel himself smiling.

Then it got too dark to walk backwards and they had to slow down to keep from stumbling and getting lost. There were crickets chirping and the black sound of wind in the trees and owls' faraway screeches, but Eddie wasn't scared at all. "Don't be scared," he said to Possum.

Possum said, "I'm okay," and Eddie said, "Good."

This was the first time he had ever stayed up all night and he couldn't wait to tell his dad about it. And if his dad got angry, Eddie would just tell him that he had to stay up all night because he was the hero and his dad would understand, and maybe, for once, be so proud of his son that when he said "I'm proud of you," it would even show in his face.

It took all night to get back to the retreat. The parking lot lights turned off just as they arrived. The rising sun turned the meadow golden and left a clear coat of gloss on the grass. By now Eddie was hungry and tired. They sneaked around to the backside of the lodge to crouch in the tall grasses and have a look in the window.

"Too bad," said Eddie. "Looks like the coast isn't clear." There were men in the dining room eating breakfast. Eddie's stomach growled like television thunder; it was all he could do not to run inside and grab a plate of pancakes and bacon and blueberry muffins, and a whole pitcher of orange juice, he was that thirsty. Except that heroes always waited to eat until after they had saved somebody. He didn't know if he could last that long, but he'd have to try. Eddie grabbed Possum by the collar, and the two of them hid in a cluster of cottonwood trees.

❧

Penelope asked the river how to reunite her picture side with her real life side and make her whole again. It frightened her, knowing that when she turned to face the real world she would face a shadow figure of herself.

She knew exactly how Possum felt, as if he had never felt whole because his personality was split along planes like faceted crystal. She remembered his pleasure in seeing those facets smooth as his love for her had grown. She thought of him now, of his intricate paintings and the deliberation of every move. Even if her picture side were reunited with her real life side, she suspected she might still need Possum to be complete.

"Make yourself solid," said the spirit of the water. "Like a tree."

Of course. Being resolute was the key to her magic. She forced her thoughts inward and let her mind grow hard until she was unmovable. She pictured herself as a thick tree with roots so deep it could never be uprooted.

"He will not win," she said. "He is not my sovereign. I am not his to enslave." The necklace sparked and caught fire; a strand of her hair sizzled in flame. She screamed and slapped at her head until she was certain the fire had gone out. There was a putrid smell of burnt sugar. This magnified her determination to outwit Zeus.

The light from her teardrop necklace sparked once more, then went out. Penelope touched a finger to her neck and said, "Aha. Now you will do my will." And when she next looked out into the room, she saw nothing, not even a shadow against the wall. The body on the bed had disappeared.

Eddie and Igor lay flat on their bellies, hidden by a flowering lilac. They watched the men file out from the lodge, carrying shiny wooden recurve bows and quivers filled with arrows. The bows were massive, carved dark wood, dipped in gold. Eddie sighed and scratched at his leg where the dried grass made it itch. Maybe sometime Zeus would let him play with bows and arrows. It wasn't fair. Grownups sure knew how to tease you and never give you everything you wanted. He imagined himself holding a bow and shooting arrows into the sky, maybe shooting a pigeon or something he could put back up in the sky after he was finished hunting. At least he'd gotten to shoot a slingshot.

Eddie wondered what day it was. Could it already be Saturday? Should he wash the laundry when he got home, or just wait for it to be Saturday again next week? He had never had to worry about skipping a day before. Only his dad could tell him what to do and he started to wiggle, thinking he should really call his dad. He wondered what the heroes on television did about their laundry. There were a lot of things that television shows didn't talk about, and laundry was one of them. Unless you counted commercials. "What day is it?" he asked.

Possum met his glance and motioned with a finger to his lip for them to be quiet. Eddie nodded. Sometimes it was hard to pay attention to the important stuff.

The men lined up in the driveway in front of the lodge and Zeus gave them more instructions. "Let's bag us a few pheasants," Zeus shouted. "We'll make headdresses with the feathers and have Mr. Tom serve us the birds under glass."

Eddie felt impatient. He could hardly wait until Zeus had led the men into the forest before the two of them sneaked inside. Eddie led the way to the locked room with its waterfall toilet. He was so excited about the waterfall that he forgot to tell Possum about the pretty lady on the bed or the magic carved picture until after he peed and watched his pee splash down the wall. A real hero would have waited to pee. Eddie felt guilty. This proved he wasn't a real hero yet. He pulled Possum to the bed, but the lady was gone, so he pulled him back to the wall and showed him the carved wooden picture.

Possum looked into the picture, and when he saw the pretty lady, he just about cried. He grabbed the picture and hugged it like he was hugging a baby. He talked to it and said, "I thought I'd never see you again," and the pretty lady spoke from the picture and said, "Not much chance of that, was there?" and Possum laughed and practically danced around the room with the picture as his partner.

Zeus had barely begun his lesson on the art of the hunt, when Alexander came running from the lodge. He was waving like a lunatic.

"Come quick," Alexander cried. "It's Igor."

"Excuse me for a bit," said Zeus to his followers. He asked the nervous little man to take charge of the hunt.

The little man twitched and stuttered, but managed to move the group into the woods.

"What's with the kid?" Zeus asked.

"He's much worse," said Alexander. "Barely conscious. Should we send for an ambulance?"

"No," said Zeus, casting a spell of deference. "Bring him to my quarters. Let me have a look at him before we do anything."

"Right away," said Alexander, who turned and rushed back to the lodge.

Evidently, his healing spell hadn't been strong enough. Zeus would have to work harder this time to come up with something strong enough to get the kid back on his feet.

Eddie heard running footsteps that meant someone was coming. He looked at Possum, who didn't seem to notice. Eddie remembered then that *he* was the hero. It was *his* job to do things and tell other people to do them too. He could only think of one thing to do.

"We have to hide," he said to Possum. "Quick, follow me." He didn't know exactly where to hide, just not in the waterfall bathroom. That was the first place he would have looked if he were seeking. Maybe under the bed ... Come to think of it, the second place to look would be under the bed.

Possum whispered, "Okay." He was still holding the wooden picture and wasn't really paying much attention.

"No," said Eddie. He put his hand on Possum's arm. "You have to put it back or else *he'll* know."

Possum looked like he'd been hit in the stomach with a four-square ball. "Put it back?" he said. "I can't leave her."

"Hurry," said Eddie. "We have to hide. He's almost here!"

From the way that Possum was staring up at the window made from red and green diamonds, Eddie thought he was thinking of trying to get away by jumping through it.

"No way," said Eddie. "We'd hurt ourselves and besides, we couldn't jump that high."

"Where will we hide?" Possum asked.

Eddie scratched his head. He had been hoping something would come to him.

The footsteps halted. The time clock that didn't tell time made little beeping sounds that meant somebody else was telling it what to think. It was too late to get out. They were going to be found.

No. The hero was the one who figured things out, like how to keep the bad guys from winning. They had to do something and he already figured out that something wasn't hiding under the bed or jumping out the window or hiding in the waterfall bathroom.

There was only one other thing to do. Eddie grabbed the picture away from Possum and hung it back on the wall. He would have to try the thing he'd seen done on television lots of times. He took Possum's hand and looked into the picture and whispered, "Okay, pretty lady, here we come." He jumped, pulling Possum with him, and the strangest thing happened. He was practically flying—his jump carried him through the room and into another world. It was a magic jump, better than anything he'd ever seen on television, even in cartoons.

And the next thing he knew, there they were, in a green grass meadow that smelled like wet straw with a noisy river behind them. They were standing in the shadow of a cloud and it was so dark right there that he could barely see Possum. Inside the carving, when Possum took a step away he practically disappeared. "Don't let go of me," Eddie said, but he could tell from the way Possum's fingers dug into his skin that his friend was just as scared as he was.

⚘

Then, there was an earthquake and Penelope's world began to quiver. She lost her footing, and when she recovered, looked out to see a black and white landscape of wavy lines, like a television at the end of daily programming. She blinked hard and opened her eyes. The world of the carving had almost returned to normal, but a little slower. The river no longer rushed—it trickled—and the clouds moved like snails across the sky. A fissure appeared in the mountain.

In a few seconds she understood why. She heard someone call her name from somewhere far behind her. She recognized Eddie's voice.

"Look who I brought you!" Eddie said with much pride.

⚘

Eddie looked around. The pretty lady was standing closer to the front of the carving, at least a hundred steps away, and beyond that, everything was fuzzy. Maybe his glasses needed cleaning or maybe the world just looked like soapy water when you were standing this far back in a picture.

"Too bad we jumped so far," Eddie said. He had always been a good jumper but this time, he wished he had jumped less. "I don't understand how come we're all the way at the back of the picture," Eddie said. "Why is everything so fuzzy from far away?"

"Perspective," Possum said. "Art is all about perspective."

"Don't worry," said Eddie. "We can still find her. He knew better than to ask Possum what perspective meant.

Possum's teeth were chattering, but probably not from cold because it was warm in the meadow, even beneath the shadow. Eddie remembered that Possum didn't have a television. Maybe he had never heard of jumping into pictures. Maybe he was scared. "I'll take care of you." He patted Possum's back the way his dad always did for him and that seemed to make Possum feel much better.

He sure liked being a hero.

Eddie heard voices coming from the other side of the carved picture. "Get down on the ground," Eddie said. He didn't want the bad guys to look into the picture and see them; in army movies they always got down on the ground to spy on the enemy while keeping the enemy from spying on them. The grass was warm but soft, like ink that had yet to dry. It smelled like ladybugs in summer—kind of sour and dusty at the same time. Eddie and Possum crawled forward on their bellies, as close to the edge of the meadow as he dared.

"I think this is far enough," Eddie said. The pretty lady was practically right in front of them now; she didn't turn around to look, and he was close enough to understand why.

When he squinted and looked really hard, he saw past where the meadow ended and into the room with the windows of green and red diamonds. Zeus and the big man from town was there, carrying Igor. Igor didn't look so good. His color had gone from shiny dark to nearly black. And not a pretty black like Don the developer's skin, but a dull black with too much gray, like something that got burned and might fall apart if accidentally stepped on.

Zeus stared at the empty bed. "Where is she, that little minx? There's something odd going on here," Zeus said.

Igor coughed and seemed to have trouble breathing.

"He's been really sick," said Eddie to Possum. Now he was starting to feel scared. Sometimes when people got really sick they died, and even though his dad promised Eddie that his mom was happy living with God, Eddie still missed her.

"I hope he doesn't die," Eddie said, feeling guilty.

Possum squeezed his hand and said, "I know," he said. "He's lucky he's had you for a friend."

Zeus told Alexander to set Igor on the bed. He frowned as he considered the possibilities. Something like this could be the kiss of death for this resort. He pictured the headline: "Kid Dies of Denihilism. God Blamed, Again." Great, he thought. Just when things were starting to look up.

Alexander felt frantic; for a moment, the uneven beating of his heart made him worry he was having a heart attack. He slipped off Igor's sandals and went into the bathroom to search for a wet cloth for the boy's head. It was too soon for Igor to leave them; no matter how old he appeared, he was just a kid. Alexander sponged his brow.

Igor coughed and cried out in pain.

"Maybe we ought to call the doctor," said Alexander, because he didn't know what else to do.

"Not a good plan," Zeus said. That was the last thing he needed now. "No doctors." Professionals would feel obliged to make reports, contact authorities. The best way to keep secrets was to never have to explain a thing to anyone. "I've studied medicine. I'll take care of it." He laid his hands on Igor's chest and tried to picture a healthy child, a child with vigor and a zest for life. But all he could think about was how every one of his children had died. He had outlasted them all. It shouldn't be this way.

He cleared his throat. They were both looking at him with expectation. He couldn't afford to let them down and fail with Igor. If a man was judged by his name, his deeds, or his children, could any less be expected from a god? Zeus had been father to thousands yet had nothing to show for it. His faith in himself faltered, not for long, but long enough for a nagging feeling to set in that he was past his prime and on the slow slide downhill. He stared at the empty bed. Where in Hades was Penelope? Magic was afoot, but it had nothing to do with him.

Igor was so weak he could barely talk. Something unsaid lingered on his tongue. "Zeus," he began, but could not continue. He lapsed in and out of consciousness. He awoke, the press of time more urgent than ever. It had all gone by too quickly. He was dying; this was no surprise and he had been expecting it to come quickly. Oddly, he had few regrets, few things he wished he'd accomplished. But before he left the world he wanted to hear his father say something to him, acknowledge their relationship. Igor didn't expect an apology from Zeus for abandoning him, but he wanted something from his father, something he could not articulate.

"Father," Igor said, reaching for Zeus. His throat was so dry it hurt to speak.

"He must mean you," said Zeus, pointing to Alexander. The boy had said his mother's name was Hera, but he couldn't have meant Zeus's Hera. Face it kid, he thought. Superficially, you might resemble her but you don't look anything like me. His Hera had plenty of flaws, but she was loyal to him, always had been. No matter how much the world changed, he could count on that. This boy, Igor, possessed the dark and brooding intensity of the big Greek. "I don't know who your mother is," Zeus said, "But I think you need only turn your head to see your father." He pointed to Alexander. "He's the one you ought to be talking to."

"Please," Igor said, and Zeus assumed the boy was asking for help rather than affection. Zeus placed his hands on Igor's head and cast the strongest healing spell he knew. He tried not to let his anxiety show even though something was terribly wrong. The boy was not responding to his ministrations. At the very least, his struggle should lighten, but if anything, the boy was getting worse. Death was imminent, and Zeus had never been especially skilled at bringing mortals back to life, even in the old days.

Zeus struggled to keep his composure. What kind of a god had no control over life and death? He winced.

Alexander knew he needed to fight against his emotion, or it would take over and leave him helpless. He had allowed that to happen once before and been ruined because of it. He watched Igor's pitiful face and saw the possibility of salvation for both of them. He could not allow his feelings to get in the way if that meant denying the boy's last chance at dignity.

Alexander grabbed Zeus by the shoulders until Zeus turned his head. "Igor is not speaking to me. I am not his father," Alexander said. He looked to Igor for guidance, and saw the boy shake his head. "Tell him," Alexander urged the boy. "We're running out of time."

Igor's breathing was rapid and gurgling sounds rattled in his chest. There was a blinding pain at the base of his neck. "I came here to meet you, Father," he said, looking deeply into Zeus's eyes. "I wanted to tell you that I love you."

"I don't think so," Zeus said. He didn't mean to sound cruel, but the kid did not take after him in any imaginable way. "I am not your father," said Zeus. "While I have fond feelings for you, as I do for all of my guests here at the resort, I do not love you as a son."

From inside the picture, Penelope watched her captor with increasing disbelief. Had he no decency at all? She gripped her gown in her hands, feeling so furious she feared she might rip the fabric. This god was more selfish and impotent than any man. His power was the only thing that marked him as a god, and what was the good in power without a sense of justice? "I renounce you," she said.

I love you like my own flesh and blood, Alexander thought. You shall be my chosen son. He replaced Igor's washcloth with a fresh one. He knelt beside the bed and gently rubbed the boy's feet.

"You have to be my father," said Igor to Zeus. He stopped himself from crying. "Who else could it be? Why won't you admit it?"

Possum was unsure if he was dreaming, yet he was terrified that he might be awake. Because if he was awake, it meant he had slipped over, gone insane. One minute he was standing in a dark room and the next he was standing in a verdant meadow staring back into the dark room. He heard a woman calling. It was Penelope, standing off in the distance. He started toward her. He felt lightheaded the way he always felt when he saw her. I don't want to wake up, he thought. I don't want to lose you again. He closed his eyes as if that could fix the dream and make it solid.

Alexander wanted to pick the boy up and hold him against his chest. Love was the only treatment you could give the dying.

This whole thing was getting more and more annoying, Zeus thought. "Sorry, kid," Zeus said, "but you've got me confused with someone else." His children were all dead, every one of them. Despite his bravado, it hurt to watch everyone and everything you've worked for wither and die over the years. Being a god took mettle. If you didn't have the stomach, stay away from the ambrosia.

Zeus didn't want the kid to die, but there were limits to magic, even for a god. It was easy for him to admit that. Only mortals had always denied it, tried to stretch the limits. Funny, how they failed to learn from their mistakes when their efforts didn't do them any good.

No sooner had Hera and her love slave arrived at the door to the lodge when the Pegasus/cockroach reverted to type and went scurrying off toward the kitchen. Hera's fatigue prevented her from stopping it.

François awoke and said, "Where am I?"

"We're here," Hera said, stepping inside. She had wanted a grand entrance and would now have to improvise. "Come here, Frenchie," she said. She slung the golden rope about François's waist and had him pull her chariot into the rustic main room. A few men puffed on their cigars and turned to watch, but she didn't appreciate their attentions. Her nostrils flared as she sniffed the air and caught the faintest scent of her husband's after-shave.

"Follow me," she said, fairly certain of which way to go. She could hear Zeus's voice coming from the back of the lodge.

Timing was everything. Always had been. Always would be. Hera had been hoping for a grand entrance and she got one. The only thing missing was the trumpets.

"Now," she cried, and François galloped into Zeus's quarters.

Alexander and Zeus were both there, but instead of looking at her, their attention was focused on Igor.

"Well, I'll be damned," Hera said as François collapsed. She unhooked him from his rope and strode over to the bed for a better look. It pleased her to see Zeus checking her out from the corner of his eye. She had obviously interrupted some intense conversation. Very well, she thought. She could wait another few minutes.

"You must be my father!" Igor whispered. "If you're not my father, who is?

"Sorry," said Zeus. "But I don't know."

Igor spotted Hera. "Mother," he said, "why won't he admit it?" His voice sounded so sincere and fragile she could no longer bear to deceive him.

Zeus stared at her accusingly. "This can't be! I'm not your father, boy," he said. "Now what in Hades is going on?" he asked Hera in a Ricky-paging-Lucy tone of voice.

The boy's lips trembled and his eyes narrowed to slits, as if he could not bear to gaze out at the world. His face was inhuman, but his voice was that of a frightened boy. "Who is my father?" he said quietly. "I have to know. If he's not my father, who is?

Hera considered telling Igor the truth, but what was the point? Gadzooks. The kid was going to die. Did she want his last thoughts to be about an invertebrate? She'd need to tell Zeus something later, but this seemed a fortuitous time to lie. At this moment, she owed more to her son than to her husband.

Igor moaned, obviously in pain. His eyelids fluttered.

A crushing feeling in Hera's chest made her stagger back. That poor child. Motherly love overcame her. She needed to do something for him. She cast a spell of comfort and saw him relax, just for a moment. She remembered her joy at first seeing the baby. She had borne enough children to fill a nation and every one of them was dead. No wonder her heart had turned to stone. A woman, even if she were a goddess, could not be asked to bear the pain of all history's generations. She wasn't strong enough to do what was expected of her. Beside her, Alexander, the big strong Greek, watched with stoic silence. "Can't you tell?" she wanted to say, but of course, he didn't know the whole story. She owed it to her son to tell him something.

She cleared her throat. "Zeus," she said, "you're the only one who could be his father."

Zeus was behaving himself and didn't make a scene in front of the boy. "There now, boy," he said. "You've got your answer. Does that help?"

"Do you love me?" Igor asked. He moaned again, either from discomfort or grief.

Hera kicked Zeus, but when he didn't respond, she thrust an elbow to his ribs.

"Sure," said Zeus, unconvincingly. "I love you. I love all my children."

Alexander lifted Igor from the bed to comfort him. "There, there," he said. "You're surrounded by love."

"Well," said Zeus, snapping his fingers. "Now that we've taken care of that, I think you and your mother ought to leave so I can get back to work."

"Zeus!" Hera said. "You can't be serious." What an insensitive lout. She was about to challenge him when she saw his eyes were twitching and moist, and recognized his impatience for what it really was: fear. It wasn't easy being a god, being the one in charge, the one blamed when things went wrong. Much easier to be a follower than a leader. No wonder all the others had given up long ago.

"I have a business to run," Zeus said. "And my paying customers are waiting for enlightenment. Now, if you'll all excuse me ..."

"Not so fast, buddy," called someone from the wall.

"I know that voice," said Alexander. He gazed around the room, puzzled, and when his glance lit on the wooden carving, he almost gasped.

From the inside of the carving, Eddie could be seen standing on a mountain ridge close to the front. Behind him stood tall trees, a mountain, and two human forms that seemed to be moving forward.

Eddie waved to Alexander. He could hardly believe what was going on. Igor was so sick and Zeus was still being mean to him. Eddie didn't like what he was seeing; it made him angry. His dad had always said that it was wrong to hit someone, but Eddie thought it might be okay, just this once, to slug Zeus.

"Be right back," Eddie called to Possum. He filled his lungs and held his breath, but just to make sure nothing got up his nose, he pinched shut the nostrils with his thumb and forefinger. He closed his eyes and forced himself to jump out from the picture, as far as he could, into the room. He landed with a thud, and fought to keep from falling backwards.

Zeus strode close, demanding to know what was going on and Eddie seized the moment to bust Zeus in the chops.

Zeus staggered back, a bit disoriented. The retarded boy had appeared from nowhere to give him a nosebleed. "Where in Hades did you come from?" he said to Eddie.

"From the picture," Eddie said. He pointed to the wooden carving on the wall. Then he waved to the two figures who moved from the background into the foreground of the picture.

"Okay," Zeus said. "Your little joke's over. Now get out." His skin was flushed. He reached to take down the carving.

"This isn't a joke," Penelope said, her voice tiny, yet clear.

Zeus looked into the carving, where he saw black clouds boiling across the sky. "Kopros," he said. "So that's where she went."

"Who?" Hera asked. "Where who went?"

"Penelope," said Zeus. "The nymph I used to go out with."

"That little strumpet! You told me you dumped her," Hera said.

"In a matter of speaking," Zeus said with a wry smile.

Penelope gazed at him, hardly believing what she was hearing. Her face was hot with anger, her gown torn and dirty. That scoundrel. She walked closer to the edge of the wood until she was sure that he could see her features clearly.

He blew her a kiss and she felt a cool breeze upon her cheek. The paralyzing feeling of being rooted to one spot returned, leaving Penelope numb, wooden. Zeus's behavior made her terribly sad, not for herself, nor for all the bad things Zeus had done to her. These wrongs paled in comparison to his cruelty to the dying boy. Son or not, Zeus bore some responsibility toward him, and to all of humanity. We never asked to worship you, she thought. It was the gods who had appeared and demanded followers. And how sad that Igor so worshipped Zeus, who took that sort of sentiment for granted. The gods expected mortals to bow before them, while offering nothing in return.

Hera had borne the child. How could she stand there, staring at her painted nails, ignoring the suffering of her child? They never changed, the gods. They toyed with mortals as if it were all a game.

Her sadness blustered into rage and she managed to shake off the numb feeling. Anger spilled from her fingertips and made the ground tremble. She felt her tears gathering, the fluid drawn from every pore. Blood rushed to her head and the throbbing did not subside until a river of tears flowed from her eyes. She gripped the ends of her teardrop necklace and pulled apart the chain. When she closed her fist around the charm, she barely felt its whisper of fire.

As if in response, Zeus looked up to stare at her. His expression changed from smug contempt to terror.

You *should* worry, she thought to herself.

What was the gods' purpose, if not to guard and protect the mortal world? Immortals had always depended on humanity to give them credibility more than humanity depended on them. Most people lived their lives without the slightest interference from the gods, and those who were unfortunate enough to cross paths with the immortals persevered despite the gods' interference.

Perhaps the gods existed to force mortals to discover their own strength. In that case, she ought to thank Zeus for permitting her this chance to rebel against his cruelty.

Poor Igor. Penelope felt compelled to do whatever she could to help him. But that meant that she needed to leave the safety of the carving, to return to the real world. She stared at Zeus, afraid but defiant. She had many things to look forward to: A life with Possum, children of her own, the joy of creating art and joy in the journey of life itself. The dying boy would know none of those things. The Fates had denied him a future. All he had was *now*.

She raised her fist and gave Zeus the finger.

He saw something shiny and golden dangling from her clenched hand. The necklace. She had managed to remove it. His hold on her was broken.

Zeus noticed with rising alarm that Penelope was weeping.

CHAPTER NINETEEN

The Oracle hitched a ride with a newlywed couple to a parking lot at the base of Williams Peak. They gave him a box of chocolate chip granola bars and a handful of smoked buffalo jerky strips and a cold bottle of home-brewed beer. The couple hiked with him part way up the path, but couldn't keep up with his pace.

"What's the rush?" asked the groom, panting.

"Don't have time to stop and smell the flowers," said the Oracle. "Got to get to my meeting."

The air smelled like the day before rain, and the Oracle warned the couple that a storm was headed their way and they could seek shelter in a cave, which they would find near a burned out white pine, just off the path.

"Oh, and congratulations on the baby," said the Oracle.

"What baby?" asked the bride.

"Just find the cave," said the Oracle, "and the baby will find you." He told them that their first child would be a scientist, and to name him after Albert Einstein. With that, he extended his stride and soon disappeared behind a puff of fine dust.

Penelope hated herself for her emotional outbreak. She wanted to be more like Eddie, to rush out and strike a blow against the god who had tortured her. Instead, she stood, crying. This seemed so unfair, that her tears released her magic. As she wept, her tears filled the creeks feeding the river.

In the world of the carving, the clouds thickened and grew heavy with rain. They covered the ground in shadow as they branched out to darken the meadow. A dank, muddy scent surrounded her.

Penelope had always been ruled by her anger. She opened her fist and stared at the teardrop necklace. The metal had dulled from fiery gold to scratched nickel. It softened and she smashed it as if it were limestone.

"No!" Zeus screamed. "Not that!" He ran toward her but stopped halfway and clutched at his chest. She had wounded him as no other woman had managed. The crushing feeling of shame and desire was so new an experience that he thought he was having a heart attack. He looked away, and found himself staring into Hera's angry face. He didn't need a charm to make her love him. He knew he looked utterly pathetic, which made his wife even happier.

The river crested and a wave of muddy water flowed over its banks. One breath later and the swelling waters reached Penelope and swept her along a meandering path. She rode the chill water downstream to an outcropping of granite rocks, and there, she managed to grab hold of a dangling tree limb and pull herself out of the river. The cold water had penetrated deep and it was an effort to make her legs move. A familiar feeling of fear took over, that she was once again paralyzed, but she refused to give into it and commanded her legs to carry her up the banks to safety. A cool wind pushed her forward. On the shore, she found Possum clinging to the thick trunk of an oak.

Her joy at seeing him there gave her the agility and strength of ten deer. She called his name and ran toward him.

"Hello," he said, and pressed his head against her bosom. She knew that he would have said more had he been able to speak. The river continued to rise to a level that was dangerously close in a matter of seconds. She called upon the spirit of the water to carry her to safety. A white cloud, like a flying carpet, appeared beside her. She stepped up to it and called for Possum to follow her lead. The cloud that held them aloft was soft and warm as smoke.

"This is weird," Possum said about the cloud. "Never mind. I take that back. It's all weird."

The cloud rose, carrying the two up above the carved landscape and into the dark heavens of the wooden carving. The cloud thickened as it rose, its density increasing to a spongelike platform. Penelope could see the flat top of the carving, heaven she supposed, and she held Possum tight, expecting to die. Instead, the cloud rose from the carving and floated several feet above the carpeting in Zeus's room.

Eddie had watched the pretty lady as she surfed down the river. It looked like fun, although she wasn't smiling. She ended up in a place close to Possum, and a cloud came, and the two of them began to float upward until they escaped right out of the wood carving. It was almost like watching television, maybe even like being inside a television.

Eddie laughed and clapped his hands to see a cloud inside a bedroom. What would his dad say about this? He reached out and when his hand passed through the spider web mist and met resistance in the center of the cloud, he squealed.

Penelope smiled. Eddie reminded her of what it meant to be a child. She tried to remember a time when magic had seemed miraculous to her, when it came, not from feelings of despair, but instead from feelings of joy. She remembered her mother plucking flowers from the meadow, then magically joining the petals into fragrant quilts to keep her daughters snug in bed and give them pleasant dreams. She remembered the spirit of the river transforming the sun into sparkling lights that warmed the wave tops. She remembered dipping her toes beneath the warm water to touch the cool river. How I long, she thought, for those happy times. But she'd possessed no magic then, and now that she did, her life was so troubled that only her tears were strong enough to drive her newfound powers.

Eddie shifted the weight of his body from one leg to the other. The edges of the cloud dipped close to the floor, and Eddie took advantage of its position to scurry aboard. It was like sitting on top of white cotton candy. He imagined he could detect a sweet vanilla scent. "Look, Igor! I'm flying," he said. "Just like you."

"Come on!" Penelope shouted to Alexander. She waved him forward. He looked worried, but obeyed her instructions and carried Igor close enough for the boy's legs to touch the edge of the cloud. Possum reached to pull them both into the cloud.

Alexander closed his eyes. It seemed inevitable that they would fall through the cloud, and he waited for the crash. Surprisingly, the cloud was actually strong enough to hold them all. And Igor's deformed body fit into the folds of the cloud and his expression changed to one of serene relaxation.

Outside, a summer storm pelted the building and the skies raged with lightning bursts.

"What about me?" Hera asked, and ran toward the cloud.

"I'm sorry," said Penelope. "I won't ride with you."

François used the moment of confusion to scurry out the door like a cockroach.

"Where do you think you're going?" Hera shouted. He turned and met her glance, then picked up his pace. "Cretin!" Hera said. Let down your guard for one minute and anyone who wasn't tied down tried to get away. She tried jumping up into the cloud without permission, but a gust of wind blew from the wood carving, followed by the startling crash of thunder. Hera lost her balance and landed on the floor.

This was humiliating. Alexander had forgotten her. François had deserted her. Igor was escaping with a bunch of strangers. She was wasting her time, trying to curry favor from all the wrong people. Was there anyone on Earth who would remain loyal without her magically forcing it from him?

Outside the lodge, the storm picked up more winds and rain. A pine tree, felled by winds, crackled as it split in two. The building shuddered as the crown of the tree struck and ripped apart the roof.

Rain pelted them through a gaping hole in the high ceiling.

"We need to get out of here," Zeus said.

"What about the kid? He needs me," Hera said, heading for the cloud again.

"He doesn't need you," said Zeus, "but I do." He held her back. The rain had soaked his toga and left it hanging over his skin like the wings of a drowning fly.

"Well, aren't you sweet?" Hera said, not that she trusted him. She was trying to save his ass, same as always. She had always been the practical one when confronted with his philandering. The Fates had determined that she could not abandon Zeus; it was up to her to make the best of the situation, not an easy task—fate or not.

The cloud had risen to the hole in the cathedral ceiling. Rain poured through the hole, releasing the aromatic scent of a forest in winter.

"Oh, great!" Hera said. "My hair."

"You ought to treat your wife a little better," Penelope called down. "Love is too precious a gift to squander."

Hera wound her arms around his shoulders and muttered, "There, there, you lying two-timing cur." It was disgusting, the way her husband had chased skirts throughout the ages. When the penis was erect, the mind was empty. That proverb still held true for the gods as well as for mortals. Hera had put up with Zeus's infidelities for as long as she could, then overreacted and blew millennia of virtue on some bugs and a sniveling man, none of whom liked her. Zeus was a terrible role model to look up to. No wonder mortals acted so reprehensibly!

Igor lifted his head from the cloud and watched his mother and father. Neither paid him any attention. He didn't understand them. When you were dying, you were forced to leave behind everything you thought was important, yet how easily the gods went on, oblivious to all things from the past. Was that what you had to do, if you knew you were going to live forever? Because, once you knew that death was imminent, the past seemed more significant than any possible future.

Without meaning to he caught Hera's glance and she muttered something, perhaps an incantation to make him feel better. Oddly enough, he did, but not in a way he could have predicted. Hera had passed on some of her strength, some of her ability to let go of the past. He no longer craved their approval. He looked at Eddie, who smiled and waved and said, "Isn't this fun?" Alexander cradled him in a loving embrace. His body relaxed, and his mind opened with awareness that there was no point in holding out for things that could never be. It was bad enough that his illness was killing his body. Now, Igor understood that he could prevent his illness from killing his spirit.

The warmth of the cloud wasn't enough to fight the chill slowly seeping through him, and he thrust his hands into his pocket. He grasped something then—the little Horsie Alexander had given him when he was a baby. Its stuffing had fallen out like grains of sand dropping through the neck of an hourglass. The fabric was a threadbare memory of a dear friend. He looked down, at Zeus and Hera. Soaking wet, they looked smaller than he remembered them.

The carpeting was soaked and Hera felt water rushing beneath the flooring. This was no ordinary rain, and not just because it originated from the lodge ceiling. The redhead had conjured up an inland hurricane or tsunami; if they didn't get out soon, they would be caught in the storm. "You can't just leave us here!" Hera demanded. Her bra was filling up with water and her breasts bobbed like vintage Japanese floats. She checked to see if Alexander had noticed her cleavage from his vantage point above, but his face remained impenetrable as marble. That man wasn't human. Zeus, on the other hand, grinned, impressed.

"There's no room. Find your own way out," said Penelope, breathless.

It looked bigger than a five-person cloud to Hera, but she watched it rise, carrying Penelope, Possum, Alexander, Igor, and Eddie closer to the ceiling.

Penelope said, "Hera! Zeus! Go on and save the others."

"Oh, swell," said Hera. "The others. Sorry, but I'm not the type." Maybe six thousand years ago, but not now. She needed to think, to save her ass first, then figure out what to do for any stragglers.

"Stop being such a bitch," said Penelope. Rainwater ran down her face and dripped from the shelf of her lips to her chemise. Her clothes grew heavy enough that it weighed down her legs. "Hera," she called down. "You're the queen of the gods! Act like it!"

And just what, Hera thought, should the queen of the gods act like? This was the problem; she hadn't the slightest idea. It was easier in the old days when she'd had a following because mortals had much lower expectations.

A crash boomed and a new hole tore through the wall. The roof peeled away like an orange rind and was carried away by wind. Outside, sheets of water blackened the skies. Alexander held Igor with the strength of Atlas. Penelope grasped Possum and Eddie, fearful one of them might be swept away. As the cloud took them out of the lodge it gained height and rose above the level of rain. Penelope looked down and watched the floodwaters crest above the river. She was no longer angry, just frightened. Lightning flashed so close it left a shadow picture of trees burned in her vision. "What have I done?" Penelope asked, not knowing how to stop her tears. They were heading toward Williams Peak and were halfway to the summit.

Igor lifted his head. "Where are we going?" he asked.

"To the mountaintop," said Alexander, unsure of how he knew that.

Igor dropped the fabric horse. "I'm very weak," he said. He did not sound discouraged, just tired. "I don't have much longer."

Horsie fell into the cloud and Alexander bent to pluck it from the folds.

"Will you bury me on the mountaintop, with Horsie?" Igor said.

Alexander found it difficult to answer. The boy had asked a favor. But you didn't bury the dead because you owed them a kindness. You buried the dead because of a profound respect for those who were still alive, for those whose lives had been touched by the passing. Alexander nodded. "Of course," he said.

Eddie was shivering. He felt cold and miserable and a little sad to see his friend so pale and sickly. Eddie had never been this wet and he knew his dad would want him to come inside and dry off. He held his hands over his ears, too late to stop the clash of thunder that had made them ring with machine noise. "I wish the rains would stop," he said.

Zeus led Hera through the lodge and onto the patio where they stood and watched the rain fall in sheets too fast to be absorbed by the dry ground. The Calypso River had overflowed its banks and was filling the valley. In a matter of minutes, it would destroy the lodge. There was no need to fake it; Zeus was worried. His newly rebuilt empire would soon float away. Could he keep his followers together long enough to find another hangout? It would be a test, but he'd survived worse. On the other hand, maybe this was a sign that he had taken a wrong turn, but if it was a sign, from whom? The property resembled a stuffed-up commode, with water spilling over into the low-lying lands. Part of a shed washed by and a lamb appeared to surf over the water. They had half an hour, he guessed, before the water rose to the level of the lodge.

Hera gazed down at her feet, dazed. "My sandals," she said. "They're ruined. This is all your fault."

She had always blamed him for everything that went wrong, even when it wasn't his fault. He sighed. "Not my fault," he said. "It was Fate."

Hera, obviously, did not believe a word. "You always blame the Fates," she said, "but did you forget you had a hand in this little predicament?"

"Maybe a little," he said. One thing about being a god was that you took your lumps when things didn't turn out as you planned. Gods couldn't declare bankruptcy when they lost it all; they didn't qualify for handouts or unemployment checks. History judged your name by your failures. It was the difference between being a programmer or just doing customer tech. But at least he still had Hera. He squeezed her hand and felt the burden lift when she squeezed back. He could bear losing everything, as long as she stood beside him.

Hera could not shake the image of Igor's miserable face. Though it hurt to acknowledge it, she loved the little mutant. How could she have let him go on alone?

It would have been easy to turn her back on this fiasco, to run away and start over. Except that there were mortals in need of divine intervention. "Zeus," she said, and linked her arm through his. "Snap out of it. We've got to rescue the men."

She walked with him into the Big Room, where everyone had had the common sense to gather and discuss a plan of action.

Zeus saw that Elton had taken out a white board and was pointing to the men and writing down their suggestions for escape. The nervous little man was pacing.

"You've all got to evacuate," Hera said. "Get to higher ground."

"We don't want to leave. Just make the rains stop," suggested Barney the towel boy to Zeus. "We have faith that you can do it."

The other men clamored in agreement.

"I'm not omnipotent," Zeus began, and immediately regretted the confession. Admitting your weakness was as good as telling the lynch mob to take two giant steps forward.

"Make it stop!" cried Elton. He looked outside just as the veranda collapsed under the water's weight. "My investment. I'm ruined!"

"We're all ruined," said Don the developer, shouting to be heard above the downpour.

Mr. Bringle scrunched up his face like a pitted prune. "My artwork," he said, "or did you forget you only have it on loan?"

Everyone looked to Zeus for guidance. Zeus couldn't do anything about the rain, but he tried to cover up the trouble with a spell of contentment. That did little good. In fact, the only one who smiled was Barney.

"It's not working," said Don.

"We're talking forty days and forty nights here," Zeus admitted with a shrug. "Takes time to stop these sorts of things." He closed his eyes and stood arms akimbo and chanted something that he made up on the spot, hoping it would look like he was taking action. What to do? What to do? Where was that damned Oracle when he needed him? A bit of advice sounded good about now.

It was impossible to stop what Penelope had wrought. This was the result of female out-of-control emotions; the logical mind of a god could not fix that. He felt vastly superior, yet helpless. He looked outside just as a flash of lightning hit the sauna building, which burst into flames. A flock of blue herons flew overhead, squawking angrily. One bird dropped a fish from its bill. The river, Zeus thought, panicking, had become an ocean. He was ashamed to admit, even to Hera, that he had no power over Penelope's spell. Women, he thought. They have more power than they'll admit. "The storm is too powerful," he said. "We've got to evacuate! Now!"

"You can't do anything, can you? What kind of leader are you, anyway?" screamed Mr. Tom. He threw a stainless steel crepe pan at Zeus, but missed and beaned François.

Zeus looked from his angry devotees to Hera. Gods helped those who helped themselves, but these guys did not want to be rescued; they just wanted to whine about how terrible their lives had become and who was at fault. Losers.

Hera met his glance and nodded. "Can't say we didn't warn 'em."

"Save me," he begged. Throughout the ages, she had been the only one both willing and able to do that.

Hera smiled. She waited for the perfect time to mouth her message so that only he could see. "Run!" she said, and the two of them made a mad dash for the door.

A wareness shocked Pee Wee into wakefulness. He tried to shudder, but shuddering in stone proved impossible and a crack formed at his belly and rose to his neck. "It's my time," he said, and knew that it was up to him to find order in the pandemonium. This made him very happy; he hadn't realized he had any part in Destiny.

He assessed the situation. Flooding was imminent. There could be landslides. Many here could die. The ground was turning into mud jelly. Their sensible course of action was to evacuate the premises, yet he watched from the fountain as men stood unmoving, like they were the ones made from stone.

Oh, but the rain polished a cool balm upon his brow. The rhythmic dripping lulled him back to sleep and he started to sink into inertia.

Only the screaming of the nervous little man brought him out of it. Pee Wee could not rest, not yet. The same strong force that had led him to the retreat now gave his stony ass another hard nudge. Not even a creature made from pixie dust could stay placid when there was work to be done. The men who had howled would die if he did nothing to save them. He felt a lament coming on and did his best to purse his lips and wail. A few grains of sand loosened and slid into the water fountain. He howled again, and this time, heard himself groan. Once you had become the howling wolf you couldn't go back to a life of silence. He knew he must save them all. The bond between them mattered, even if no one else felt it.

He forced one heavy leg to lift out from the water and cross up and over the edge of the fountain, followed by the other leg. His body emitted the noise of an earthquake. This small bit of exercise made it awfully damn hot inside his cement suit, and he could feel sweat building up from deep within.

Thankfully, the storm dumped buckets of rain over him, cooling him off. All around him, customers and staff stood complaining to Elton, demanding refunds or paychecks. At the sound of Pee Wee's belligerent quake, a few turned around in puzzled wonder. The intelligent ones screamed in panic. Only Mr. Tom possessed the right rain gear and the sense to herd the animals to safety in the higher grounds. Ye gods. Not another one of these mortals seemed capable of developing a plan of action to deal with the approaching floodwaters.

PeeWee moved forward, one thundering slow step at a time.

"What the heck is going on?" cried Elton. "The stone man is walking away. You can't just abandon us," he said.

The earth rumbled as underground springs began to fill with runoff and overflow. There was a booming clap as a fir tree toppled over in a mudslide. PeeWee exerted himself to the point of tears and managed to lift one heavy arm and point toward safety and the mountain. A chasm in his stone mouth appeared. "Go," he said in as commanding a voice as he could muster. "Up!" The canyon walls amplified his words, his warning was heard by all.

The nervous little man rolled his eyes and fainted.

"He talks!" said Elton. "The stone man talks."

"It's a sign," said Don. "I say we heed it."

"Heed away," said someone else.

Don ran for the hills. It didn't take long before the others followed.

Not bad, PeeWee thought, for a fellow who never really existed. It was nice, in a way, this making-a-difference thing. Too bad the mythology canon was long ago closed and no one else would ever know about his role. Ahh well. Those were the rules of destiny.

He felt thickheaded and heavy. The world looked gray and still. The ground beneath his blocky feet was turning to slush. He no longer wanted to move or go anywhere, and let himself sink slowly into the muck. How cool and comforting it felt as it enrobed him like a chocolate coating. His work here, he decided, was finished. The rain beat down around him. He thought for one moment about protesting his predicament and escaping with the men, but there really wasn't anything else he felt he wanted to accomplish. He had earned his freedom and redeemed himself to the world.

He sank deeper and deeper; along with the engulfing mud came a state of calm. "Good-bye cruel world," PeeWee said, with an existential yawn. He no longer found his jokes all that funny, a phenomenon he now equated with enlightenment. Mud slapped at his waist and he sank further. It reached his chin and he opened his mouth to see if he could taste the earth. It had no flavor, save the taste of his own tongue upon the roof of his mouth. Mud covered his eyes, his forehead, and then the essence that had made him alive was extinguished, and he was home.

The Oracle saw storm clouds gathering, but felt so weary that he stopped to rest from his climb. Instead of pressing onward, he considered turning around. Was it worth the effort and struggle when you knew that the outcome had already been decided? At times like this, he thought not. What would happen, he wondered, if he abandoned his role and let things happen without him? His head thudded; his heart pounded to the point of bursting; his breath caught like a blackberry thorn scratching his lungs. His suffering threatened to overwhelm his sense of mission.

It was miserably cold and he was soaking wet. He took a step, and lost his footing in the mud. The Oracle wrenched his ankle, but managed to avoid falling. All his joints and bones ached and his shoes were filled with mud; it took effort to walk without losing them.

What difference would it make if he gave up now, disavowed his destiny? What would really happen if he took the easy way out, the way everyone else did, and abandoned the journey?

It did not take an oracle to foretell the answer.

If the Oracle did not persevere, neither would mankind. When the leaders of the world—the oracles, the politicians, the clerics, even the gods—failed to live up to the highest standards, how could ordinary mortals hope to transcend mediocrity? "Oh my," he muttered, resigned to his fate. Pity so few others took their duties seriously.

All of his life had brought him to this moment of despair and he knew that he must choose the ordained path. He forced himself to climb onward to the summit.

His feet were blistered and his nose was running and sore; he used his sleeve to wipe away the moisture. When he looked up, he saw a cloud holding five passengers descend through the skies until it touched the ground. The Oracle noticed Alexander. Eddie was there, too, along with a lovely naiad, and a young man who clearly adored her. The big Greek was holding up the insect boy.

That's right, the Oracle thought. That child is about to travel on into the great mystery. He had almost forgotten about this little wrinkle, yet it was as important to these mortals as his own next breath. One man, one death. Just a speck in the scheme of things but wasn't that the beauty of mankind? They cared about the death of one, even when it was destined.

"I'm sorry I forgot you, boy," whispered the Oracle, chuckling at his fallibility. There was so much to keep track of when no one else paid attention. No wonder the gods had found it easier to survive by ignoring the world.

For generations, the Oracle had wavered on the threshold dividing mortality and divinity. He now remembered he was a human, and thanked the dying boy for reminding him of this, before it was too late. Eddie would have to wait a few more minutes before the Oracle could pass on the yoke of prescience to him. The more pressing duty was to help the big Greek help the boy.

"Hello!" the Oracle called out to the big Greek. "It's your old friend come to help you."

⚜

Hera and Zeus ran like Hermes and she was feeling quite clever at their fast escape. Until a wall of water swept them away and they rode it through the valley. A tree limb scratched Hera's ass and an uppity trout whapped her in the face. Her cheek smarted. They were deposited rather rudely in a muddy flat just below the town. There was an uncomfortable pinching feeling in her chest. Her hair was wet and plastered to her head. She'd lost her sandals and her gown was filthy. She knew she looked bedraggled as a sewer rat having a bad hair day.

She peered up at the mountain and felt sadness, knowing she would not see her son again before his death. The pounding rains made it impossible to concentrate on the future.

The future. Another hour of rain and it wouldn't be a rosy one. Hera gazed around her and marveled at the destructive power of Penelope's pain. Honestly, she thought. There were some folks you just didn't mess with. Hera was one of them. Evidently, Penelope was another. She had to give the nymph credit for that.

Their whitewater ride had made Zeus regress several thousand years and now he clung onto her like a frightened child. "I'm cold," he said.

She smoothed his hair. Given the right circumstances, comforting the man you loved when he thought he was about to die could be an aphrodisiac. "It will be okay," she said. "Mama's here." But she was not the passive type. There had to be something she could do. Suddenly it hit her. "I know," she said to Zeus, "how to make the rains stop. I know a spell more powerful than revenge."

"What could be more powerful than revenge?" Zeus asked, like he really wanted to know.

"Love," she said without cracking a smile. "Hokey, but it works." She closed her eyes to remember all her children and the friends she had loved, only to lose them over the millennia. Her heart beat with renewed passion and the strong pulse pushed a knot in her throat.

Ye gods, she thought, but it hurt to have survived them all. Yet you couldn't know love without knowing hurt. It made forgetting more attractive. She had made so many mistakes throughout her long life. Was it too late to redeem herself?

From the heavens, she heard the voice of the Oracle say, "It's never too late." Though Hera had never been the type to listen to what others said, this time she believed him.

She looked up at the mountain and felt so hopeful for the future that she would have done anything within her power to make it a better one. She blew a kiss so heavy with tenderness and love it possessed the magic to switch off a flood into a trickle. "Penelope!" she called. "Igor!" It hurt so much to speak his name that she needed a moment to recover before she could continue. "Rest easy, son."

She held Zeus to her bosom to comfort him and be comforted by his presence. For the moment, she found it impossible to work up any cynicism. It couldn't last. Thank the gods. She choked back her emotions. "Please forgive me," she said at last, and winced as she waited for an answer.

The clouds broke and sunshine streamed through like a beaded curtain. The rains slowed, then stopped. A rainbow appeared.

"Nice touch," she said about the rainbow. "You do that?" she asked Zeus.

"Maybe," he said.

It wasn't easy finding magic at a time like this, but she called on all her powers to fix her hair and take away the dirt and provide her with a strapless black velvet gown that practically screamed, "I can get sex anytime I want it!"

Zeus whistled appreciatively.

Everything Hera had done, she'd done out of enduring love for her husband. Not that he deserved her devotion. She was too good for a two-timing drum-beating globe-trotting midlife crisis has-been god.

For the first time in a thousand years, Hera started to question whether things were twisted around. Zeus was a terrible leader. Who put him in charge, anyway? Come to think of it, the answer was Zeus. Well, maybe her husband ought to take his turn and follow her around for a change, instead of vice versa.

Screw the Fates, Hera thought. They had certainly screwed with her. She thrust out her chest and stood arms akimbo. "Out of all the men in the world, here I am again, stuck with you," Hera said.

Zeus sat down on a rock and stared at the now calm river. He looked amused and gave Hera a wry grin, as if considering how to answer. "I suppose I could say the same thing about you," he said, but he patted the rock and motioned for her to join him. "Come here, old gal," he said.

She felt a dull ache that started in her belly, in the hollow place once filled by her womb, and spread down to her thighs and across her back. She winced, but managed to shake away the pain by ignoring it. You didn't live forever by wallowing in pain. You got over it. You moved on.

"Who are you calling old?" Hera countered. She floated to the rock to sit beside her self-declared long-suffering husband. "I'm going to need a little help on my next project," she said.

"Anything you want, my queen," he answered. He looked tired and uncharacteristically obedient.

"I'm thinking that a matriarchy would be topical." Hera patted his hand.

"Whatever you say, my sweet," said Zeus. He sounded exhausted.

It meant a lot to have him support her plans. "Things will be okay," she said. "I'll protect you." Together, they watched another sunset, never once mentioning their thoughts or worries for the morrow.

🌺

It hurt to breathe the thin air and the high elevation left Alexander dizzy and weak. The rains ended suddenly, leaving them wet and chilled. He held Igor tight and wished he could do more to keep the boy warm.

The boy's eyes were glazed; his mouth was dry, the lips cracked, the tongue caked with white. His breathing was irregular and shallow. If there was any peace to be found in death, surely there was none to be found in the act of dying. Why did the gods allow such misery to pass?

Their cloud had come to rest in a patch of warm grass and dissipated into mist. Alexander smoothed Igor's hair, loosened the straps of Igor's tunic to keep it from pulling on his neck.

Igor struggled to catch his breath.

Penelope collapsed on the slippery ground, and Possum bent to help her. "My legs," she said. "I can't walk."

Alexander heard a voice calling, "Hello! It's your old friend come to help you."

The Oracle.

Alexander felt a great burden lift, knowing the wise man was near. It was hard always being the one whom others depended on. Sometimes you just needed someone stronger before you could let down your guard enough to hope.

A few moments later, the Oracle stood beside him.

"Hello, old man," said Alexander.

"Don't mind me," the Oracle said to Igor. "I've come to ease the burden of passing to the other side." He closed his eyes and lifted his palms toward the heavens. Sunlight streamed down over him, and rainbows flowed to the ground from the tips of his fingers.

Igor stopped shivering.

The Oracle brought out a pottery cask from his pack and gave Igor a sip of water. He trickled water over Igor's forehead and said, "The water is cool and smooth and strong and can carry you over," he said. "There is no need to fear."

Igor opened his eyes. "I'm not afraid," he said.

Eddie felt Superman strong; he lifted Penelope to carry her to the trunk of an old red maple tree. The ground was dry, sheltered by the tree's thick canopy.

Alexander brought Igor there as well. He wrung a few drops of rainwater from his own tunic onto his fingers. He used that to wet Igor's lips. With moistened palms he washed Igor's face and dried his skin with the fabric horse. He leaned close to kiss the boy's cheek and cradle his head in the crook of his arm. He set Horsie on Igor's chest and smiled as the boy held tight.

Alexander felt the boy relax completely in his arms. He stroked Igor's fingers with his free hand. "I love you, son," he said, close to tears. He had been remiss not to admit this before now; maybe it was not too late. Had he told his daughter that he loved her before her death? Sadly, he could not remember.

"It's not too late," said the Oracle. "It is never too late to offer love. Say it now. Soon the boy can deliver your message to your daughter."

Igor squeezed his hand so lightly that for an instant, Alexander thought it a reflex. "It's not too late," the boy said in a whisper.

First one tear rolled down his cheek, then another and another. He rocked Igor, knowing that the motion soothed himself as much as the boy.

"Don't cry," Igor said. "It isn't so bad." He looked to the Oracle. "Tell him," he pleaded. "Tell him it isn't so bad to die when you aren't afraid."

The Oracle nodded solemnly. "He knows," he said. "I have been to the other side, and can tell you that you will find rest there."

"Father," Igor said.

Alexander realized the boy was speaking to him.

"Son," he answered. "My dear boy."

Igor closed his eyes; his chest no longer moved as his final breath left his body to rise up into the clouds. His expression, though not smiling, looked at peace. His fingers let go of Horsie and the paper-light fabric floated to the ground.

"I love you," Alexander said. With his brow pulled into such a terse frown it hurt his eyes. His body felt too small to hold so much pain.

He set Igor's body on the ground. The warmth of the sun smothered the underlying wind. Alexander stared at what was left of the little horse, and reached to pick it up. He thought about keeping it, but that felt somehow wrong, like stealing a precious relic.

Sweat beaded on his brow as he worked to dig a shallow grave with a chipped rock. The mud gave way easily, and Alexander looked to the Oracle to thank him. The Oracle tried to help with the digging, but the old man seemed so frail that Alexander bade him to rest.

"I'll help," said Eddie. "I'm good at digging." And he was.

At last the grave was deep enough. They lay Igor into the earth and stood over him long enough to say good-bye. He wanted to say something, offer some memorial, but to whom? He gazed upward, toward the heavens. How could he pray without faith, even in mankind?

"It's not too late," the Oracle said. "It's never too late. That's the only lesson worth learning. If we thought it was too late, we'd never accomplish a thing. Because it would always be too late, don't you see? If even gods can make mistakes, what makes you think you're any better?"

Alexander took a deep breath. He hardly knew where to start.

"Just start here," said the Oracle.

"Forgive me," Alexander said to no one in particular. He folded Horsie, solemnly, like one might fold a flag, and tucked the square beneath Igor's hand, hoping it might bring Igor comfort in his journey to the next world. They covered the body with earth and leaves and cuttings and handfuls of smooth pebbles.

Alexander no longer feared facing the rest of life alone because he did not feel alone anymore. He finished his prayer. Whether anyone had heard him he did not know, but that didn't matter. The

Oracle was right. It was never too late to seek comfort in faith. Especially when that comfort could not be found anywhere else.

The Oracle patted him on the back and said, "You're a good man. And I know you'll find happiness soon. Maybe even love." And then he laughed and added, "But why take my word for it? Go on. Find your way! The time for feeling lost has ended."

The rains were an ancient memory and his skin now warmed like a rock in sun. A calm feeling coursed through him. Alexander nodded to the Oracle and turned to slowly start down the mountain, not knowing in which direction he would face once he reached the bottom.

🦇

The river had retreated, the rains stopped, the darkness replaced by dappled light. Rainbows glistened on the fallen leaves. Penelope sat beneath the maple tree and thought about Zeus. She no longer wanted to get back at him. Her first impulse was to cry, but she fought against this. After all, she had gotten back at Zeus, in a roundabout way, by making him become a better husband. Sneaky, but by doing this, she had gotten back at Hera, too. Those two deserved one another.

And now what would happen? She looked at her useless legs and felt the moisture well up in her eyes. Again, she was helpless. Maybe all one could do when confronted by such stupidity was to cry. Crying was, no matter how wimpy it appeared to others, one method for people to use when resisting evil. She felt grateful to the rains, but now the world needed time to air out. Which meant she needed to work to make a better future, instead of dwelling on her lost past. The urge to cry dissipated like a cloud.

Eddie said, "We have to get out of these wet clothes or we'll catch our death of colds."

The old man smiled and said, "That's not how colds are spread, Eddie."

Eddie said, "Well, my dad says so," and the old man shrugged his shoulders. "So be it," he said. "I know better than to disagree with your father, but we will not become ill, I can tell you that much."

"How are you feeling, boy?" the Oracle asked Eddie.

"I feel good," Eddie said.

"The young lady will need some help getting down the mountain," said the Oracle.

"I can carry her," said Possum.

"No! Let me!" said Eddie. "I'm much stronger."

"He's right, you know," said the Oracle, and Possum smiled.

"Piggyback ride," said Eddie.

Possum led them down.

By concentrating, Penelope found she could wiggle her toes. This useless skill made her laugh, and when Possum turned to look back, she waved him off because she could not explain why she felt deliriously happy.

It was hard carrying somebody down a hill, and Eddie was glad when the Oracle asked to stop and rest. He set Penelope down on a flat rock.

"I rescued you, didn't I?" Eddie said, and Penelope looked at Possum with a smile, then looked back at Eddie and said, "Yes, you did. Thank you."

"Good job, young man," said the Oracle.

Eddie beamed. He leaned down, puckered up his lips, and waited for Penelope to give him a kiss like on TV.

"Come closer," she said, so he did.

Her mouth was soft and her lips dry and not at all slimy as he had feared. She smelled nice, almost like syrup; a loose strand of hair tickled his nose and made him want to laugh. He would have offered to love her and marry her, but she already had Possum and it didn't seem very nice to ask her to choose between them. Besides, it made him happy knowing that his friend had found love. Maybe he would find love pretty soon, now that he knew what it was.

"Don't worry," said the Oracle. "Love is just around the corner."

Eddie looked upward toward the place they had just come from on the mountain. He already missed Igor a lot. Maybe it was for the better, as his dad was always saying. Maybe now Igor could finally be happy. Igor had not discovered his father on earth, but in heaven, maybe his father would be able to find Igor.

"I'm a good friend," Eddie said.

"That's important," said the Oracle. "You're a brave man."

Eddie felt very pleased with himself. He was a hero.

The Oracle said, "It's men like you who hold the world together." He took Eddie's hand and held it in his.

Eddie felt a rush of power, like a strong electrical current, pass through him. He stood up straight, and could have sworn he'd grown taller since that morning.

"I give you my blessing," said the Oracle. "It's time for me to pass the torch to you."

Eddie only had a dim sense of what this meant. There was no torch. The Oracle was going to retire and he was giving his job to Eddie. "How much will I get paid?" Eddie asked.

"You'll get what you need," said the Oracle. "No one could ask for any more than that."

"Okay," said Eddie. "I guess that's good enough." He hoped his dad would still let him sweep the floors, even with this new job. He remembered that the Oracle had given him an old coin, and he fished it from his pocket and held it up to show he had remembered.

"That's the first payment," said the Oracle. "You'll always have what you need."

Probably, the men with flash cameras were going to come into his grocery store and take his picture for the newspaper. Maybe even the news lady with the white hair like a Barbie doll would put him on the television to ask him questions.

Eddie was smiling so wide he could feel it all the way around his head. And then he had a vision that he recognized as truth. Boy oh boy, was his dad ever going to be proud of Eddie and the way he had been a hero and saved the day.

WITHDRAWN

WITHDRAWN